L.......

In the year of the Common Era, 2008

J.A. McNulty

This book is a reimaging of some events which took place in Manchester. It is, though, a work of fiction and the characters are entirely fictitious and do not depict real people either living or dead.

I should like to thank all those people who helped me write this book for their advice, comments and encouragement; JG, PB, KM, ES, MD, DK, JH, CP, PW, RB, HM, MB, LW and especially DH.

This book is dedicated to my hero, Don Brown.

Contact: mcnultyja62@gmail.com

Dramatis Personae

Chief Constables of GMP 2008

Roger Mason. January 2003-February 2008

Paul Kenyon (PK). January 2002-January 2003, Her Majesty's Inspector of Constabulary 2003-8, Temporary Chief Constable February 2008-September 2008

Gabriel Hooker. Deputy Chief Constable April 2005- September 2008, Temporary Chief Constable September 2008 onwards

CID

Kenny Poole- Detective Superintendent

Sharon Bentley- Detective Chief Inspector

North Manchester Division

Clara Henderson-Superintendent, Uniform Operations

Brian Ashton-Chief Inspector, Uniform Operations

Brody Jones-Patrol Inspector, B relief

Charlotte Purvis-Probationary Constable, B relief

Chris Hayes-Custody Sergeant, C Relief

Robert **(Bob)** Brazier-Custody PC, C Relief

Gina Pendleton-Civilian Custody Clerk, C Relief

Matt Donnelly- Community Beat Sergeant, Moston/Harpurhey,

Julian Rose-Community Beat Constable, City Centre

Other

David Henderson-Property Developer

Michael Henderson-Security Consultant

Jenny Aaronovitch-Crime Reporter

Martha Maitland-Registrar

Paul Smith–Local Businessman

Mairead Keane- Paralegal

CHORUS

There is such a thing as the truth. And the truth is the thing you are not going to find out. Not in this book.

Do you know why? Because people like me control the truth, from people like you. So what you are reading is fiction, remember that. Not the truth.

The only thing new under the sun is the history that has not been written, and this history is not going to be written.

I have got away with it and I want you to know it.

Do you know how good that feels? No? It feels fantastic. Magnificent. Star-bitingly good.

Have you got in so far deep, but then you got away with it? Of course you have not. You probably, almost certainly, are not important or ballsy enough. You just read about people who are.

People like me, the Chief Constable of Manchester, sorry Greater Manchester. Self- important shithole of the North.

This is, indeed, my point. I am the Chief Constable of Greater Manchester. Who the fuck are you?

PART ONE

DAVID

I love my wife with all my heart. It hurts how much I love her.

I still hope we might have children when we resolve this police thing, I really do.

She was in such a state when we met, but we are never to talk of this. Suffice to say I was very much the person who saved her. She will never say that, but we both know it.

On our wedding night we got back to the hotel suite. We agreed we not try to make love but would sleep together. She lay on top of bed with her clothes on. I was next to her, holding her. She started to cry.

I told her I was sorry. She said, "No David. I am just so happy. I am not sure I deserve you or such happiness."

That's my Clara.

I love her and she loves me and I was fucking determined Chief Constable Roger Mason was not going to take her away from me.

MAIREAD

Imagine.

You are eleven years old, the only girl, third of four children. Your dad is a drug dealer. You live on the Monsall estate. Your dad was sentenced to eighteen months for dealing when you were seven. Your eldest twin brothers fight. I don't mean squabble, I mean spill blood wherever they go. I mean Kray twins.

Your younger brother lips do not move when he tries to read, because he just can't read. It's not the school's fault, he is that thick.

Your mum just about copes but she is not a strong woman.

You move, aged eleven, to your own house in Moston. You get your own room. However, this means your dad starts to come into your bed at night putting his fingers in you. Your mum's solution is to have you wear two pairs of knickers and a sanitary towel and tell your dad you have started your periods early.

You can hear your parents arguing. One argument is about whether you can go to the Bluecoats school in Oldham as the Head Teacher has recommended. Your dad is against it. He breaks your mother's nose when she won't back down.

When everyone is out of the house you can hear your mum on the phone talking to the police. She doesn't care that you can hear she is informing on her husband's drug dealing.

Imagine all that.

Imagine what I would have imagined my future could be.

Imagine, then, that it has all turned out exactly as I did imagine, as I planned.

Now, imagine what that feels like.

PAUL

Millions saw it on TV but I was actually there when it happened. I was there, and the minute it happened I knew.

The challenge wasn't even 50/50. It was always the keeper's ball. Afterwards, when replayed on *Match of the Day*, you can just see his eyes lift up as the keeper approached. He knew exactly what he was doing, it was deliberate. He left his studs up, straight into the keeper's face.

But that's not how I knew the lad wasn't wired right. No, it was what happened after. Players frantically screaming for the medics, pushing and shoving each other like puffs, one with his head in his hands running away in shock, the linesmen on the pitch, the crowd (well, the away fans) screaming for him to be sent off.

But him? Well it was like it had never happened. He wasn't arguing or protesting his innocence or trying to go to the keeper to see how he was. Not anything. He just looked on at the keeper, his face a bloody mess, as if it was all unremarkable.

And then dead-eyed in front of the referee, not a word, not anything. I reckon the whole thing unnerved the ref so much that he gave a yellow and not the red card it deserved.

Now I've seen all that before with Johnny, when he would glass someone in a pub for looking at him the wrong way. He was even like that when he offed Billy Gatland. It would always be like nothing of any significance had happened.

So when I saw Milan Dacic was the calmest man on the pitch, in the stadium, at the Manchester derby, I could see Johnny.

A true psychopath.

JENNY

Old Trafford doesn't look right. It is lopsided. You can't really say something so misshapen is iconic, can you? They need to build the other stand up to make it look right.

Tim tells me they can't because of a railway line behind. They would have to build over it and it would cost a fortune. Still, it will be a different view from the Command floor in a couple of years when the police move HQ to North Manchester. You will be able to see the Etihad then, symmetrical like a proper stadium.

Tim calls it 'The Council House' which he thinks is funny. Apparently City rent it from the council but surely the new Arab owners will be able to buy it outright? Boys on the sports desk have heard they plan to start developing all around Beswick. Tim says City will never match United's history. Why do I care?

I am here in the dark on the eleventh floor of GMP's HQ, Chester House, in Trafford. They have plonked me in a meeting room which I am sure was someone's office only a few months ago. I am not going to switch the lights on to make a point when Hooker gets free and sees me in the gloom.

Being made to wait comes with the job of being a reporter, but it does though, frankly, piss me off as it was him who has actually invited me here. Now he is keeping me waiting at 7p.m. on a Friday night. Not that Tim and I would be out on the town, those days are over, but it is still an irritation.

Hooker is on phone in his office. It is just chit chat. I can tell by his laughing now and then. Grrrr.

Check my phone idly, nothing else to do. One message. Tim. Photograph of a limp looking curry.

Microwave meal for one on a Friday night. Boo hoo

Shall I reply 'grow up'? No, can't raise the energy.

I am here to interview Gabriel Hooker who, it has been announced, is to take over as the Temporary Chief Constable in Manchester for a year. There had been a six month period where he had been the deputy to Paul Kenyon (PK), who had been Chief Constable of GMP for a year in 2002, and returned as Chief Constable in 2008 from Her Majesty's Inspectorate to stabilise the Force after the incumbent, Roger Mason, had gone missing.

Interest in Mason's disappearance is now fading, but only after a very long time. I have not enjoyed this last six months. Mason went missing when I was in Tenerife and I actually came back to cover it. I was not bothered, weather wasn't great and I was plain bored. I remember expecting him to be found whilst I was at the airport or in the air coming back. I need not have been so concerned. I feel everything I have done since then has been pointless.

Facts are Mason had booked a return flight to Ireland for three days. He told his PA he was going walking. Whilst it seems odd to want to go walking in Ireland in February there was nothing out of the ordinary about this for him. He did fancy himself as an outdoorsy type who went hiking on his own. He did not go on holidays with his current wife or any of his children by his three wives.

He had got on the plane. He left Dublin Airport on foot. He was not seen again. That is it. The rest is conversation, endless conversation. He has not been found. He isn't going to be.

Of course no news means endless speculation for the nationals at least who can disguise their speculation as exclusive news. We just cannot compete with this. This enrages my editor, Sarah Parker, who is an effing cow. Tim reckons she just blames me for not going missing with him and filing updates. That's the funniest he gets.

Why had he gone missing? Don't know and, to be honest, don't really care enough. If Neil was still doing the job he would have ruptured a vessel by now trying to be the one who finds out why, but it would have been wasted effort. I know this, no-one knows. Not really.

I would bore myself going through all the different theories people and the papers have. I did think at one point I had got a break on the story. I had heard a rumour that the enquiry team into his disappearance could not find a pen-drive which had details of some counter-terrorism job.

Don't know why I rung GMP's press office. They never knew what the enquiry team was up to and the enquiry team itself was a brick wall. Anyway few days later a detective in the Counter Terrorism Unit rang me about another matter. We got talking. He reckoned he knew something about this pen-drive, but made me go out on a date with him for the story.

It was a big let-down. All he did was confirm there was a pen-drive which Mason had lost before he went missing. The information on it was not a threat to national security and the pen-drive would have been encrypted anyway. There had been a real rumpus about this pen-drive going missing not because of what was on it, which was of no real importance, but it because it caused a debate about how far even Chief Constables could be trusted.

Date was nice, a meal out, could not really tell if he was interested. He said we should do it again sometime but he never did call. Did not tell Tim obviously.

"Well fuck a doodle do!"

Sarah was unimpressed, of course.

"Your exclusive is that you got a story about a pen-drive going missing but it's not a story. Brilliant. Keep them coming, Jenny. The new Eddie Dunford."

I had never heard of Eddie Dunford, had to Google him. Transpires he does not even exist, sort of defeats her point doesn't it?

Where is Hooker? He is dialling another number.

You previously would not be able to see Old Trafford from Command reception but PK ordered a complete rearrangement. Mason had had two large offices and en suite with all the secretaries crammed into cubby holes.

PK had changed all that and had taken a small office and turned the large offices into meeting spaces. He wanted to create 'an open culture of communication'. His own office was small, no memorabilia, not a photo, not a certificate. Mason's had hats of armies and police forces, empty grenades, framed newspaper articles and letters from the famous, photos of children. No photos of wives though.

He was now onto his third wife. Mrs Mason No. 1 lived in London with an adult daughter, neither would not talk to the press.

No. 2 was an ex-Met officer who sold her story. She had two teenage boys and she had had to give up work because of behavioural issues with her youngest son; it meant Mason was paying out a fortune in alimony. He spent one weekend a month in London in hotels seeing this family and was paying for a special school for his son.

No. 3 and current, who had been his mistress in the Met, had moved with him to Avon and Somerset where she is now a chief inspector on part time hours with junior school kids. She stayed in Bristol when he got the Manchester job.

Papers managed a bitch fight between No 2 and 3.

Met wife, no. 2, claimed he said he still loved her and spoke about how much he loved the kids, she hinted they were still having sex. Bristol wife, no. 3, spoke about how unhappy he was with Met wife spending money and generally being a lousy wife. It was clear she did not know he was funding the special school though. All horrible to read really.

The next week they then broke the story of Judy Evans, a Command team staff officer, and current mistress. She was not talking to the press but she had 'confided' to a group of Command secretaries on a drunken night out and someone rang a national. Not that Judy was much of a secret.

To be honest that whole business left me ashamed to be a reporter. I mean what is the point in publishing all of this? It just causes misery for everyone.

I must be where her office actually was. He was supposedly to have had sex with her here on the floor and the desk.

The floor and the desk? Honestly. How do you do that on a desk, physically, and still keep your balance? Seems very impractical on all kinds of levels. And a carpet? Really uncomfortable, I mean you would get burn marks, and it's unhygienic. Would this be the carpet here? God, hope they have shampooed it.

I received a text from Mason one day about hoping I was wearing suspenders for a meeting the next day. I had been in court with my phone switched off and had not picked it up straight away. It was followed by another text an hour later.

Oops wrong number! Trying to do two things at once. Please don't print this. LOL. Roger x

We had not been due to meet at all. Wondered a few times about that. I am Jenny, she is Judy Evans so both begin with a J and I do appear first in many people's phonebooks, my surname beginning with a double A. Was it a mistake?

Hooker's door bursts open, with a flourish.

"Jenny, sat alone in the dark. Come in."

No apology.

Noted.

Rude.

CHRIS

This is the best part of my job. It is probably the best part of my life.

All prisoners asleep or, at least, not hurling themselves against the walls of the cells. Most of the boyband cops who gate-crash my custody office with their prisoners have now been successfully fucked off to other parts of the station to write up their arrests in their sub eleven-plus English.

It's now like the party is over and you and friends are helping clear up. Often enjoy this bit of parties best. As if I go to parties anyway now Sheila has gone. As if I have friends. She took them all.

They say you know you are getting old when police officers seem young. Well you know you are getting on as a custody sergeant when the young cops get on your nerves more than the prisoners do. Tonight being no exception.

They have just brought in four juveniles at 3 a.m. for 'going equipped'. They won't prove anything. Four of them stood near a bag containing some screwdrivers and a crowbar. Waste of time. Takes ages to book in juveniles and I made the cops bring them in one at a time as Bob was on his refs. Should see their childish, sullen, pulled faces, the cops that is. Do they think that makes me go quicker?

One of the juveniles started to cry and asked for his Nana to be informed of his arrest. Of course this caused hilarity amongst the boybanders.

"He wants his Nana."

Anyway gave me the excuse to blast the arrogant fuckers out of the office soon as I had finished. And, let's be honest, in my time we would have definitely have sworn blind one of them had hold of the bag and got somewhere with the job. What a waste of time and effort.

People complain about Bob all the time, but he treats the prisoners alright. Well, he does not look down on them anyway.

Ashton had me in the office last month to rebuke me. He wanted his staff to be making arrests so that dangerous people were taken off the streets. I am discouraging them from doing so by my 'negative attitude'. I also needed to get a grip of Bob who is perceived as being idle and obstructive. Bob actually works harder than he would care to admit, and there is more to custody than booking people in quickly. But, well, what's the point of arguing?

Getting a bollocking still rankles though. It's just that I cannot imagine when I was a PC that any chief inspector would not wholeheartedly back his sergeant against the staff. Or do I just see the world differently now?

Tonight was busy for a Monday which is normally deathly dull. Booked in nine prisoners and managed, early on in the shift, to get some paranoid drug addict admitted to hospital. Sort of result, for once.

I had had one prisoner recently who was actually barking like a dog on all fours in the cell. On all fours like a dog. The doctor declared him to be fit to be detained, "oriented in time and space," he claimed. Doctors just don't want to know about prisoners with mental problems. We often play ping pong with A & E. We send them there, they send them back. Pisses me off, pisses everyone off I am sure.

Bob, of course, has to be contrary.

"Doctors are right Chris. When I have my inevitable cardiac arrest, hopefully on the vinegar strokes on top of Thelma in Comms, I do not want to be behind some knob-end junkie in the queue for treatment."

Not a bad point when you think about it. After all most prisoners now have mental health problems because they take drugs or should that sentence be the other way round? Too tired to think that through properly. Anyway, getting one admitted for once was a result.

I will stay now at the front counter printing off charges and filling out the risk assessment forms to hand over to the escorts tomorrow to take the prisoners to court. I won't go in the back office to be seen to be listening to Bob's routine, which has started already. It is funny, I suppose, but have heard a lot of it before. Might get a brush out, everyone else seems happy to leave this place a tip. I have let Gina go home. She says her husband has to be up early for work driving lorries and she needs some sleep before looking after young grandkids. So Bob has an uncritical floor.

He should not really be in custody now as it has all been civilianised on the other shifts. Yet he remains. I do not quite know how he manages to defeat the repeated enquiries from HR to redeploy, but he does. His fabled bad back, of which I have seen zero evidence, manages to keep him from being booted outside. It's like he has a magic shield round him.

Take his uniform. In defiance of the order from Chief Constable Mason that all would wear the black polo shirts in custody (as 'we are all crime fighters') he wears the traditional white shirt, yellow at the armpits, no tie with the bottom button missing to expose his beer belly. Socks, if they matched, would be white. Ashton, who is fanatical about uniform, never says anything to Bob. Don't know why really. Probably because he never comes in here, on second thoughts.

Bobs trademark, though, is the glasses. Thick steel rimmed spectacles, inevitably misshapen and never cleaned unless Gina takes them off him. Don't recall them ever being clean or straight. No other custody sergeant would put up with Bob but, together with Gina, and in very different ways (I do not fantasise about Bob), they keep my spirits up.

Couple of kid PCs in the back office make up Bob's audience for tonight's performance. Charlotte, pleasant, confident, well spoken (for once) probationer PC doing a tour of the various departments, in custody for a week before she goes out on independent patrol. Plus another gelled hair, boybander PC returning the paperwork for his drink-drive prisoner who has lingered to sniff round Charlotte. She is way out of his league. I hope. He should not be there but wouldn't be enough of an audience for Bob, so, let things lie.

Cannot see Bob, but would be sat back in the corner in his special chair designed for his 'back problem'. He has just done his 'David Bowie is a fraud, Mick Ronson is a genius' routine. Now onto U2. Heard it before.

"Luckiest man in the world? Without a shadow of a doubt, Adam Clayton from U2.

Larry the drummer formed the band so you can't argue with that.

The Edge, pathetic name for a grown man and overrated guitarist who just puts it on echo all the time. But he does get the riffs and writes the songs so again deserves his share. No real argument.

And then the gobshite Mr Paul Hewson. Wants you all to know we should write off third world debt, which means us taxpayers have to pay for it. Does he want to put his hand in his pocket and pay his fair share? No, does he fuck. Fucks off to France to avoid the Irish taxman thank you very much. But he can sing and he does writes the songs.....so again...

.... but Adam Clayton? Seriously, Adam Clayton? He could be playing bass in a pub band, instead he is in the socialist collective of U2. So instead of getting £50 a night, which is what he is worth, he lives in a mansion in the South of France, all the cocaine and booze he wants, yachts, the works. "

"He gets to shag Naomi Campbell too."

Boybander's predictable contribution. Charlotte is way out of his league, please God surely?

"Yes, but no, no could not be doing with her. No way. Moody stroppy bitch. No way."

"That's a crying shame Bob because I am sure she would be all over you if she met you."

Could hear Charlotte laughing as she spoke. Good for her.

I can't resist. I shout through.

"I am not sure the draw of your semi in New Moston would be enough for her Bob."

Buzzer goes off next to Bob.

"What?"

"Got a cup of tea, Hong Kong."

"Sorry kitchen's shut"

Inaudible.

"No I AM BUSY"

Now that Gina has gone the visits to prisoners will not get done properly, if at all, with Bob. What is her name again.........?

"Charlotte? Can you drag yourself away from Stuart Maconie for a minute and do the visits. Remember those with a red star on the board have to be woken and spoken to because they are drunk."

She is a nice girl; 4.35 a.m. but still full of life. She bounces past me smiling with list in her hand, grabs the keys and sets off down the corridor. Did she wink at me? Did she? I better listen out for her, she should not be doing these visits on her own as she is not signed off for independent work.

Bob continues with Boyband. So which football team did he support?

"United."

"Oh well I suppose if you are proud to support a team founded on the selling of condemned meat to school children and now owned by …….."

Can just about hear Charlotte. She's actually talking to the prisoners. Best Bob would manage would be to kick the door and see if they grunted or moved.

Bob was in full flow.

"….not actually in Manchester so really should be called Trafford United. Ever read any Gibbon?"

Bob was clearly not waiting for an answer.

"One thing is for sure empires rise and empires fall and those who think that Manchester United will reign forever have short memories and haven't read their history, or even current affairs. Manchester City is now owned by medieval misogynists with a shit load of pocket money to convince the world they are actually nice guys. Whilst you, you, my friend are paying off the grubby debts of a trailer park racketeer……………"

Charlotte has gone quiet.

I better go and check, see if she is alright.

BRODY

This is going to be good, so good. Better than sex.

8.30 briefing is with Superintendent Henderson, her Ma'amness. She will have only just got into the office as she still thinks 8.30 is the crack of dawn, so she will not be prepared. Ashton is stuck in traffic, set off late today because of some problem with his kid.

You have to thank God for such tender mercies it's her and not him today.

Knock then walk in without being asked.

"Morning Ma'am Inspector Jones your 8.30 briefing."

She does not look as worried as she should be. Excellent.

She always looks the part, have to admit. Tracy, my custody sergeant, reckons those blouses she has have been specially altered. I can't see how, but she is sure. Women see these things. She always has a slip underneath her blouse too.

"Morning Brody and please call me Clara."

"Sorry Ma'am it's a habit. I was brought up to respect rank. Old school."

"Well what have we got?"

"Target crimes Ma'am seven burglaries, two robberies one personal and one at a shop, the cars parked on Ancoats avoiding parking charges have been raped again, thirteen in one day. We are way above target. I have spoken to the volume crime time and they are going to do some more obs at Ancoats today see if we catch the misunderstoods."

She nods to move on, she would though. Ashton would have me on this forever asking asinine questions. She knows zip about volume crime and does not seem to really care about such stuff. She leaves it all to Ashton who has a hard-on for it all.

Normally would try to worry her a bit about it but no need today.

"Well just the one outstanding high risk missing. Carly Mackenzie 14 years, 13th time missing. A care home girl she is just shagging around and will be back when she feels like it or is hungry."

Oh, she has gone all sniffy. Sat back, crossed her arms. Sport. It's on.

Does she object to the word 'shagging'?

"13th time, have we worked out where she goes? Where does she go, boyfriend?"

"Boyfriend? So to speak Ma'am she is just one of these care girls who has been groomed by our Commonwealth brethren".

'Commonwealth brethren'! Surprised myself there, but a nice touch. Have I pushed it too far? No she is pretending not to have noticed. God, she is useless, bothered about the very item on my briefing that does not matter.

"But don't we know where she goes and can't we just, well, rescue her… get her?"

She corrects herself but too late.

"Rescue her Ma'am? She doesn't see herself as being in need of rescuing. She is having the time of her to-date-miserable-untermensch life.

Always got to remember Ma'am she has already had such a shit life that she was put into care. Now someone actually takes some interest in her. Some new jeans, trainers, perhaps some drugs, drives her around. Someone is doing nice things for her. She probably thinks she is in love. She probably thinks her buck-toothed Asian boyfriend is Omar Sharif.

She is not going to thank you for rescuing her, as you put it, ruining her fun. Reality is there is very little to be done, she is not coming to any real actual harm."

She is not speaking. Ram home my advantage.

"We have had a go at this before. Girls like Carly will not co-operate. They will talk to you but I am sure they make half of it up mainly because they know that's what the Make-up Squ...."

Steady. Steady boy.

".....Sexual Exploitation Unit want to hear."

I know I get carried away. I don't always talk like this but there is something so prissy perfect about her she brings it out in me.

Anyway she is deep in thought.

"There must be something more, I keep hearing that nothing can be done."

"Well you could try putting the divisional surveillance team on this but that means pulling them off a volume crime target and not sure what you can really do. You can hardly wait until they are getting fu ...engaged in sexual activity before you ....."

"Is there anything else?"

"Well we could ask for Force assistance via bidding to the central Hub for more resources as a serious issue we cannot solve."

"Could we?"

"Yes but we would not be clearing up volume crimes and improving the figures, just finding missings....."

Why am I talking her out of this? It would have been hilarious. She would have got nowhere and made a fool of herself with Force Command.

"The missing aspect is not the important issue obviously it's the …."

Then she just suddenly gives up.

"Anyway thank you for raising this Brody. You have jogged my memory about this matter. Thank you."

I did not expected to be thanked by her. I don't want to be thanked by her. I don't want to help her.

I mean it's debatable what Ashton has ever done to get promoted. Not sorry that's not true, he bored everyone into submission with his roundhead mentality. However he did do the hard yards like the rest of us I suppose. But to promote her in directly at superintendent from being a PR executive? I liked Mason but there can only be one reason she is here. The oldest of sins, for sure.

"No it is just that we never seem to make any progress in this area…"

She trails away clueless. And clueless is where I will leave her because I have bigger fish.

Here goes, held back long enough.

"Anyway Ma'am the main issue is the detainee in intensive care. Hospital have put him into an induced coma."

She stares blankly. Get in there. She hasn't a clue. It's on. Superb. Take your time.

"Have you informed Internal Affairs yet, Ma'am? Obviously not my place to do so."

They have already rung me to say they are coming and want the cell taped off.

"I don't know, has anyone done anything wrong? We would need evidence that somebody has neglected their duty wouldn't we? What happened?"

"Well Ma'am to answer those questions sequentially. No there needs to be an investigation regardless of whether we think we have done anything wrong to determine this. If he doesn't pull through then it's a mandatory investigation by the IPCC and a full Article Two Human Rights Coroner's Inquest. IPCC get really arsy if we don't notify them and this has to be by Internal Affairs. He may well die so we have to start an investigation.

What has happened? From what I can gather a prisoner was found in his cell this morning about 4.40 a.m.. He had stopped breathing or at least he had stopped when the ambulance arrived. It's not clear why he wasn't breathing but a bottle was found which could indicate he had drunk a whole bottle of vodka in that cell. He was also drunk when he was brought in."

"We search prisoners when they come in?"

"Obviously, Ma'am, obviously, so that will be a line of inquiry. Don't think I am jumping the gun in telling you the records indicate that he had not been visited in his cell for over two hours when he was on a regime of half hourly visits, so whatever was wrong with him could have been spotted earlier. In fact records reveal no-one was visited in those two hours. Now the records could be wrong and they were visited and they were just not recorded."

….with Bob Brazier as custody clerk, I know what my money is on.

"Is custody my responsibility?"

Oh hors de prix. Don't smirk, don't smirk. Only problem is if that gem gets out it can only have come from me. I will make sure it does get out though.

"Yes Ma'am. There's a team at HQ that does policy but you are responsible for standards, staffing, the whole shooting match. This could be a real problem, we have let the night shift go home in which case we may have lost evidence from arresting officers. I have had the cell sealed off and the CCTV seized. Chris Hayes not too good I hear sat down in the exercise yard afterwards. Head in hands."

Chris indeed had kept going on over a fuck up getting the ambulance. Keep that to myself, no point getting Chris in any further trouble. Also it was the Internal Affairs that moaned about the night shift going home but it was actually my shift that arrested him tea time yesterday, not the night shift. Not telling her that also.

OK, the cheap shot. Now. Aim. Fire.

"Do you know his ethnicity, Ma'am?"

I know it.

"No I know nothing about this, it's not on anything."

She turned to her computer to look through her emails.

"Yes here it is Jesse Brooks, 22 years old from Miles Platting. Doesn't say."

Oh yes, Jesse Brooks, the black sheep of a black family.

"Well I will check Ma'am for you. Think you better sacrifice a goat to the Gods of policing that he both lives and isn't BME or you will be lost in a world of shit."

Bit dramatic I know but, as I said, she makes you like this. Three 'yous' anyway. She got the message? Not sure. She is staring at me. What is she going to say? She is debating to have the discussion about whether it matters if he is BME? Bring it on if she does. That said, better leave before I start to help her.

"Ma'am must go, need to prepare for Mr Ashton's Star Chamber at 10.30."

"How are the officers involved?"

I've heard, but am heading for the door and not for turning.

Victory.

BRIAN

You know something, nobody ever asks how I am? Never.

Everybody is concerned about everybody else these days. Even the Tories want to hug a hoodie. Yes it's all 'welfare' and 'emotional intelligence', whatever that means. Mr Hooker is at it now. He wants us to be kinder to each other. But it all never quite extends as far as Brian Ashton does it?

No-one is going to ask me how my day is going.

Here goes anyway. So I was late for work today which I hate. It actually turns my stomach a bit, get a bit panicky when it happens. Well I wasn't actually officially late, Mrs H says as long as I do my hours I can come in when I like. It just doesn't work like that, she will find out.

Danny had thrown a tantrum about going to a new school and argued with Claudia. I had to turn around just as I was arriving at work, go all the way back to Timperley and take him to school. So I only got into work about 9.45 because I had to fight through traffic.

Then I find Pete, an old cop who acts as a sort of PA to me, has gone sick. I mean I did him a favour in letting him have a day job and he did know today was supposed to be important, the big performance meeting. So I had to run the slides off myself and get the projector set up in the main meeting room.

Mrs H didn't ask me about Danny or comment about being late. She had got herself in a tiz because Brody Jones had wound her up about some incident in custody. Transpired no one was dead and these people always pull through. She will learn that. You cannot afford to worry about things that may happen, in the police there is enough actually going on.

Then she wanted to know about a missing. For a minute I was worried. Then I find out she was talking about Carly McKenzie. Same point again, we only look for missings to check they are not dead or coming to harm. For me she should not even be classed as missing.

So I had barely prepared for this meeting and was on the last minute as I walked back into the room.

Now this was supposed to be the big meeting when we start to pull things round and get crime rates going down again. I made it clear that I expected all the relevant sergeants and inspectors to attend even though it was their rest days. What do I get? Just over half full. You know the drill, apologies, child care, blah, blah. Can't they find a baby sitter for a few hours? This is important.

Tony Learmonth never attends and sends a PC in his place, Julian Rose. Do you know what Rose was doing when I walked into the room? Reading *The Times.* Rose thinks he is untouchable since he did those raids on massage parlours and got some Eastern Europeans charged with sex trafficking. But he does precious little to reduce crime on his beat, the crimes that matter to local people. Next to him was Brody Jones, sat there bold as brass, pen behind his ear but no paperwork in front of him. He never misses a meeting. He comes to life at meetings in fact, but in the wrong way.

So I had set out quite clearly I wanted to see, some positivity, some ideas to improve performance. I was naïve thinking perhaps I might actually get something. What do I get instead? Excuses.

I will just give you some examples.

Why is there a spike in theft from cars on Harpurhey market? People are buying satnavs which are getting stolen. Even when they put them in the car front pocket the thieves can see the sucker marks on the windows.

Ok, why is our rate of fingerprinting the cars that are broken into so low? People don't want to wait for fingerprint people to turn up. They also do not have the time to take them into surgeries during the day (my idea) because they are busy. They will get paid out on insurance anyway.

Ok, why, when we do catch someone, are we not charging them with the offence that day? CPS want a victim's statement before a charge and we can't find the victim who has parked his car and gone into town, so we have to bail the criminal.

Ok, when they do confess to the crime why don't they confess to them all and have them as TICs to boost detections? Solicitors all tell their clients not to have them because they get longer sentences at court.

Ok, why, when we do charge, are these people still being bailed out of police stations instead of remanded in custody as I had instructed? Good question, no-one from custody even at the meeting.

Brody Jones decided to contribute.

"Sir, I think it is the small matter of the Police and Criminal Evidence Act 1984 and the Bail Act of 1976. The relevant provisions must apply….."

No and nothing to do with the custody staff being too damn idle to look after the prisoners. Just want them out from under their feet.

"……Home Office circular clearly states we should only remand in custody as a last resort. Anyway Sir I was discussing les événements of last night with Ma'am earlier. You were unavoidably detained I hear this morning. It transpired she did not even know she was in charge of custody here."

Mrs H walked in right at that point and takes over.

"Well yes Brody thank you and I have just been down to custody to speak to Tracy. They do feel very alienated down there. A bit unloved."

Here we go. Of course everyone suddenly had something to contribute now it was a free for all about custody and not a discussion about performance. And then it degenerated into a discussion about whether we should be having a discussion about performance at all.

I think Julian Rose started it off saying that the emphasis should be measuring ourselves on 'harm reduction'. And of course, instead of Mrs H telling him that is all well and good but it is not what we are actually measured on, she invites him to a meeting she wants to set up to discuss missing girls.

Then Matt Donnelly got onto his favourite subject, which he tried to relate to harm reduction in some way, gangs and drug dealing and the interminable feud between the Bruens and the Keanes. Apparently there had been a punch up over in a pub who had put money down on the pool table and Pat Keane was outgunned by the Bruens because his twin brothers were now in prison and had got a slap.

I had had enough of all this. I put my hand out like a traffic officer's no 1 stop sign. I have learnt this trick from a self-help book. It's a powerful signal to stop people talking.

"Yes very good, Sergeant Donnelly, very good. You have slipped a bit of gang business into this meeting on performance. The soap opera that is these two families is all very interesting and we could chase our tails all day on this while crime stats go through the roof. That two lowlife gang families do not get on is hardly breaking *Sky News*.

It is just not a priority for us, we just need to tackle the crimes that matter to people locally, burglary, vehicle crime, drug dealing if it's on the street and affecting people's quality of life. Pass your intelligence to the Force Intelligence Bureau re the drugs issue and tell the landlord that order in his pub is quite firmly his responsibility. Licensing can visit him to give some advice. You really need to concentrate your efforts on getting more detections and getting crime down. Is that clear?"

There was silence in the room, Donnelly sulking, people nervous looking at their papers, Brody Jones trying, not hard enough, to suppress a smile.

"Clear Sergeant?"

"Sir, yes."

So now I am the bad guy.

PAUL

The story goes that the club had bought Dacic to make sure the other side of the city didn't get him, £35 million for a seventeen year old Serbian with one cap.

Papers had criticised them because, it transpired, they had not scouted him in person. All they had seen were videos of the hat trick on his international debut. Manager threw a tantrum at a press conference, when pressed on the issue, claiming anyone who knew anything about football could see he was world class.

Of course, he was right, it's just everyone was asking the wrong question. The question everyone should have been asking is why were Belgrade so eager to sell a world class player? You could see the reason that day. He was loco.

The FA could not take action against him for the challenge because he had already received a card. So instead of keeping his head down what does he do? He gives an interview to a paper without telling the club. Says he feels God is talking to him when he is playing but that the Devil can also appear in flashes. Which is, of course, admitting he maimed the keeper deliberately.

He also claimed that it was growing up in the Yugoslavian Civil War that shaped him. The next day there were articles everywhere trying to get him suspended given his apparent admission and, of course, ridiculing the fact he had been born when the war was over. He grew up in a comfortable suburb of Belgrade.

Three weeks later he comes off the bench to score a brace in front of the Kop from one nil down. He puts the other team's keeper out for the season and turns over the old enemy in Liverpool. A legend.

Fans sang 'War Baby...He is our War Baby' for minutes on end, every time he played. Better than Kinkladze, Benarbia, Giggs,

Kanchelskis. This lad was as good as Best and Bell. Speed, balance composure and he never missed, clinical.

He scored 31 goals that season aged 18 years.

More to the point though that season he also buggered the wife of the reserve goal keeper against her will, the buggery that is, she was up for everything else; put his cigarette out in the face of a paparazzi (paid off handsomely) and celebrated the end of season by taking two academy players to Paris on a private plane, taking a suite at a top hotel and hiring seven hookers for 48 hours. They left the room with barely concealed cocaine over the table, a turd on the floor and £2000 for the cleaning staff. That was the final straw. Club had had enough of him and were touting him to Madrid for a loan next season.

Now I know all this because it was related to me by his PR agent, the top guy in London. You will know him. He had rung me out of the blue. I thought it was a piss take when I first answered. After a bit of ringing each other back to check each other out he tells me the story.

He works for Dacic's agent and had been taken on to massage couple of those stories by selling a couple of 'B' listers on his books down the river. The keeper's wife story had not seen the light of day but the father of keeper's wife however did not see the funny side of the whole thing though. He had hired a security firm who had got some stuff on Dacic and they were now trying to shake him down.

Did I want the work?

"What does he want me to do?"

"There's a meet at the Lowry in two days."

"And that's it?"

"Yes, that's it. Had the father on phone at length yesterday. He's a wealthy guy, Tony Chappell, owns a factory in Stockport that makes plastic bags, turns over £7 million a year. In his eyes this makes him a Master of the Universe. Kept telling me of all the people he knows that I have never heard of.

You can quickly tell he's the type of guy who has to be in control of everything. So when his precious daughter gets taken up the council gritter by a dirty Serb he has to do something, be the big guy. So he hires a security firm, BWI. Heard of them?"

Nope.

"Well, anyway, from what Chappell says they have been on Dacic for a while so he will have spent a fortune on this."

"What's he got?"

"He won't say. I know Dacic's agent is worried. Could be anything with that crazy dude, drugs, another player's wife, under-age girls. Who knows? When I volunteered to come to the meet he said that Dacic would not need me but a miracle worker."

"What does he want?"

"Fuck knows."

"The club?"

"They know nothing. Don't even know I work for Dacic, well, his agent."

"It's a set up?"

"Can't see it myself. Too much notice. Too planned."

"Why me?"

"Well you are Manchester's Gangster No. 1 aren't you?"

Oh yes the famous *MEN* article.

"Look, his agent is on holiday and Dacic has seen this article and now wants you. I promised I would contact you. I know it's weird but he was insistent.....look........that Chappell is full of shit, telling me I would need a miracle worker. I've seen this type of thing before. Big time Charlie Potatoes hiring surveillance thinking they are movers and shakers, then suddenly realising they have no idea what to do with their stuff and they are out of their league.

I guess he doesn't want to go to the press in case that finishes up with his daughter being dragged into it. And he either does not have any evidence of crime to go to the police or he just does not want to go down that road for some reason. Bottom line is he's out of his depth but can't admit to himself he has spunked his money up against the wall. So this meeting gives him the chance to act as the big guy.

Look that's my take for what it's worth. I guess it's not something you would not be interested in although I honestly don't see much downside to it. If it helps the fee is £50k though. Seriously, I have the money in my account on retainer. If nothing comes of this you get £50k. Only stipulation is you can't sub- contract. Dacic wants you there. Do you want to think about it?"

Obviously.

Contact in the industry told me BWI were less than a year old. Ex- police superintendent called Warnock had put his pension money in to set up the firm. He had not shaken any trees in his career. He reckoned it all fitted with the PR guy's view. Reckoned Chappell would know this Warnock through the Masons or the like. Warnock would be new to the game and have just seen the pound signs. No proper security firm would have touched work like this.

So Warnock and Chappell had talked each other up with a lot of big time talk. A lot of money would have been spent. Just now needed me to read them their fortune. £50k for a couple of hours work.

Chappell and the no mark ex- cop didn't bother me, but I should have been bothered by the lad. I did not know him and I have always said you should never dance with a stranger.

But he wasn't really a total stranger. I already knew he was a psychopath.

DAVID

If I did not have money I don't think I would have Clara. That's why I like having money.

You can make money if you have money. It's a crowded island with not enough houses. Owning houses and making people pay to live in them is, well, easy. Not proud of what I do, I am not making the world a happier place, but I am not ashamed of what I do either. It has to be done.

Owning and building flats in Manchester almost can't go wrong. The population of Manchester City Centre was under a thousand some thirty years ago, just some Chinese living above their restaurants. Now it's thirty thousand and growing.

Cities are growing all over the world. London cannot keep expanding. Big countries are going to need big cities other than their capitals like USA has Chicago, Los Angeles, San Francisco, Seattle. Manchester is in pole position. If you connect up Liverpool, Manchester, Leeds, Sheffield that's about eight million people. That's an economic powerhouse with Manchester at the centre. You can forget about a fast rail link to London.

And Manchester is ahead of the game already. Harvey at the Town Hall is streets ahead of the other city Chief Executives. Smart move after smart move. Got the politicians dancing to his tune. They can play at being left-wing and he gets on with the real business.

If we hadn't got the Commonwealth Games we wouldn't have the ready-built stadium for the Arabs to buy City. Spinningfields is going to be a success. You watch, he will get the buses out of Piccadilly Gardens eventually so it can be properly developed. I would love to do something with the old Fire Station on London Road one day, premium hotel perhaps. It will come. It will all come.

So it's all good news for me. Right place, right time.

All sorts of problems come with having money though. Lot of people don't realise this. For a start, you can only really mix with other people who have money. If you have money you make other people who don't have money feel uncomfortable. You make them feel their lives are a failure, which, of course, they are not, usually. They really don't want to be around you. That applies to old friends too. It's quite sad.

People who have money are ok to mix with. They are no different to anyone else. Not smarter, nicer, do not work any harder on balance, have all the same problems as others. They even have money worries. In fact, they usually have money worries.

One key difference with having millions is your relationship with the law. At this level of wealth you cannot rely on law enforcement to protect you and your money. You have to hide away from other people within gated communities or protect yourself with CCTV and monitored alarms. It becomes a constant worry.

Rich people are also preyed on by people for easy money. In my business expensive equipment gets stolen from the building site, security are threatened, squatters move in, people don't pay. Here's one I bet you have not heard of; gangsters move lowlifes into expensive flats they have bought so people like me, who want to keep some places quite exclusive, have to buy them back at a premium price. Seriously, there is nothing these people haven't thought of.

Now all this can be handled, but at a price. You have to find the man who can stop all this happening. You don't want the man who claims he can stop it, but the man who really can. I really don't want to be trying to work out who is who and be dealing with such people. So I have Michael who does all this for me. Michael, my brother, ex-Special Boat Services.

Now Michael wears a uniform of corduroy trousers, checked shirts, pullovers and a cravat and talks with a cut glass accent.

He looks like a retired judge, nothing like me, thin, tall, eagle-like features, makes him look older than he is, but let me tell you a story about Michael. Michael was expelled from public school two terms before going up to University. He beat up the school bully, lad called Walsh, who had been hassling me. Michael would be then, say, nine stone wet through and don't think he had been in a fight in his life. He calls it his David and Goliath moment.

Michael had planned to go to University and then join the Marines but was forced to join instead at eighteen with lousy 'A' levels from the local comprehensive. So he spent the Spring of 1982 marching across the Falklands, getting trench foot and having bullets whistling past his ears on Two Sisters, instead of being out on the piss, playing the field and sleeping in until eleven at University. All because of me.

Still he is doing ok now, has a lovely family and his own private premium operation. All ex-military, mainly Special Forces, Marines and guys from 14th intelligence, couple ex-Box. Michael tells me he does not employ Paras as they are just too gung-ho.

Michael deals with Hamas and Hezbollah so Manchester lowlifes are no problem for him. He knows the people who know the people who make these things go away. £70k diggers are suddenly returned, flats are vacated, people who threaten my security never return again. I can tell you he employs seriously, seriously impressive guys.

I have had to ask Michael to do me a couple of jobs since Clara joined the police. First one was when an ex of mine decided it was time to cash in and sold his story to the press, just after it had been announced that Clara had been recruited to the police about a year ago.

Call from the journalist on the Thursday, they were going to publish on Sunday did I have any comment? Did Clara know I was gay etc.? Rang Michael instantaneously, did not know if this was something he could help with.

It was odd to see him spring into action. I knew he was impressive but never seen him in real time.

"Name of journalist? Phone number is on your mobile? Ok. Name of ex-partner? Do you have any contact details for him? No. Do you know what he does for a living? Lives London somewhere probably Balham area or that's where he last was. Ok do you know if GMP's press office know? Ok. Leave it with me. I will ring you once we have news. I am sure I can make this disappear. You have to tell Clara not to answer the phone unless she knows who it is from."

Anyway it was, say, about 3 o'clock Thursday when the paper phoned. It was about 9.30 Friday morning when Michael phoned.

"Problem solved entirely David."

"You're kidding? You sure? How did you do it?"

"Well nothing illegal David but I think I will let you decide how much you want to know."

"How much do I owe you?"

"David, David, he's not heavy."

"But you must have had expenses."

"Well some but you know, wouldn't want the money. Four guys were involved in different ways. But they see the matter the way I do. This was personal, not business. They won't take any more money. I usually take them out for beer and curry to thank them for stuff like this. "

"Michael done, bring them to my birthday party. It's sort of beer and a curry anyway."

"Didn't know you were having one. When is it?"

"Guess."

I had hired out Shimlas in town on a Saturday night, not cheap to do that. I fancied a curry rather than use one of the places I have an interest in. I decided to up the ante on the party and booked a great soul band, the best the agency could offer. Told Michael his guys could bring their friends and family. Champagne, lager and the best curry in Manchester. Whole thing cost far more than Michael would have charged commercially, I am sure.

Got a bit nervous before the party. You know you worry if people will turn up and, at the same time, worry whether everyone will fit in if they all do. I think Michael was bringing nearly twenty in all, which was quite a number and the band were now taking up a load of space. Plus I had not explicitly stated to Michael they couldn't talk about how they had come to be invited.

I should not have worried. They all turned up. Nice guys, polite but not deferential. It was like they were all in uniform too, jacket, shirt no tie. None of them had dolly bird wives or girlfriends just normal, middle aged women. Teenage and adult children beautifully behaved. Joined in, did not sit there sulking.

Turned out, after a few drinks, they made the party. A sensational night though, fantastic, everyone danced, waiters included, until 1a.m.. Watching Clara (best looking women in the room by a mile) dance with Elaine, Michael's wife, I was the happiest, pissed obviously, relieved everything had gone well. I asked him how he did it?

"OK rang the journalist to see if he had rung GMP, which he had not. I asked him not to do so until noon the next day. It may save him a lot of money. I got Peter sat over there to find out where matey boy was. He had his mobile phone number in 30 minutes, triangulated to Baker Street, London within another 15 minutes. I got Martin, Gibbo and the Jimbo to scramble and with 90 minutes they were on a train to London with a file of the target on their phones.

Matey had moved from what seemed to be his work to a bar near Westminster. They found him there straightaway from a picture and persuaded him to move outside for a chat.

"Did they threaten the little bastard?"

"No need to, they just told him what they had done in their previous lives and to consider how they had found him so quickly. They worked out he had signed a contract for £5k and had had an upfront payment of £2k. They got him to promise to give half his money back to the paper and the other half to a veterans charity, their idea. All done by 9 o'clock that night. They stayed in London that night, just in case, at my club."

"You only rang me the next morning? I was up all night worrying."

"I had to check with the paper he had made contact and was retracting and handing the money back. Then the boys came back."

"You make it sound simple?"

"It was simple. It is simple. Most things in life are about who has the bigger army. It's all also about having the right people who will drop everything to do a job, not draw attention to themselves, and you must have complete confidence in their discretion. Complete.

Look at everyone, how many here have I brought? Twenty people? I will tell you now only the four involved, you and me know the story. These guys here don't have to bull themselves up by telling their story to others. We also haven't had to sit down and discuss a cover for the reason for the party. The wives will just know it's a favour we did but no more. The families have learned not to ask what their dads do for a living.

You noticed they all are with long term wives and girlfriends David? It's about trust. They cannot afford to be in relationships where there isn't trust."

I looked at Clara and Elaine dancing, the others all happy, unembarrassed, all comfortable with each other and realised, more than ever, that this is what I was missing. This is what I wanted. To be a man of the world like Michael. To have friends who you trusted, to have a family you cared for and who cared for and trusted you. This was the proper adult world. Having money and being gay get in the way of this. Yes it's nice to throw a party like this but then you feel just a bit vulgar, ashamed like you are showing off, buying friendship.

But don't think I married Clara for respectability or to be normal. It was not a lavender marriage of convenience. In many respects it has raised more eyebrows. No we married because we were in love. I was certainly, still am. But, I have to admit, I have always still just wanted what we all want, the normal things, wife, children, not the Elton and David thing.

Clara was worth fighting for.

"Michael, I have a bigger problem I need to discuss with you."

KENNY

I should have remembered PK is actually capable of being ruthless. After all, he brought me all the way to Manchester from Lincoln, broke up my marriage and then left me high and dry, but I had forgotten all that.

I remember his coup the day after Roger went missing six months ago. He was sat in Roger's office, in Roger's recliner, like he belonged there, like it was his office. Sat back away from the desk like a patient at the dentist, legs flopping over the end.

Long gangly bloke, Brummy drawl, but spoke a bit like a vicar too. Wore a tunic in all weathers, don't know anyone else who does. Sharon pointed something out once; he wears long sleeve shirts underneath and has his wrist watch on the outside of the cuffs of his shirt. Odd.

I had been summonsed in by my PA, HMI wanted to see me in Chief's office. I was the Temporary ACC Crime for GMP trying to fight fires with the press about a missing Chief Constable and the last thing I needed was to brief some dusty, tired HMI.

And a pretty ineffectual HMI let me tell you. Being questioned about him when he was inspecting crime was like being mauled by a dead sheep. He would start off with a question which just finished up as a speech by him about how great he is, or was. Sometimes you did not even have to answer. He just answered himself. Very much just another of these self-important non entities who cannot let go. So the way I saw it he should be letting me get on with it all on a day like this of all days.

Hooker was already stood in Roger's office, coffee in hand, liked he belonged there, both using Roger's set of cups and saucers. They had clearly been talking for some time. Roger never let Hooker stay in the office a moment longer than he had too.

PK started talking the second I walked in, no preamble. There was not to be a Manchester CID investigation into Roger's disappearance. PK would take personal charge and use experts from National Policing Improvement Association (now there's a contradiction in terms) led by a guy called Bill Callaghan and a few handpicked staff who would liaise with the Garda. He had dragged the chair forward to the desk now but his head was down all the time he spoke. He could not look at me.

I had barely slept since I had the call last night. I had got six hours at most. Been working on getting a team set up. I had Sharon Bentley on first flight out to Dublin this morning. In fact I had just been briefed by her on the phone as I had thought HMI would wanted a briefing from me.

Obviously not. Quite the opposite. I was not asked anything.

"Sir, with all due respect, isn't that a decision for Mr Hooker as the effective Chief?"

"Des Lyons is going to announce that I am to take over as Chief with immediate effect. Sort of a recall from Colombey-les-Deux Églises so to speak, would be unfair on Gabriel to take over in such circumstances."

Bloody hell, that was quick. Never occurred to me to ask why it would be unfair? Never heard of anything like this. But then again Chief Constables don't often go missing, I suppose.

"Well I just think, thought, finding Roger would be the priority. We need the best people."

 Brummy drawl. More Brummy than C of E today, that's for sure.

"Well I think that assumes that appointing Manchester CID means we have the best people. These NPIA people are national experts, Kenny."

Superior smirk on his face. Hard to tell whether he was having a pop. Not sure he is capable of it.

"Anyway, it's the Garda's show really. This side of the enquiry will finish up more about his personal circumstances and his decision-making won't it?"

Will it? PK stopped and looked at me, as if there was a clear implication I would be aware of. I was slow on the uptake today, tired, kids had woken early. I would have loved to have said it was not even clear he had got on flight to Dublin but this had just been confirmed by Sharon. He had also been seen leaving airport Arrivals on foot on CCTV.

"And we cannot have any suggestion of nepotism, cover ups, you know. Mason was somebody who did not play by the rules. We can't have his beneficiaries, well what may be perceived as his beneficiaries, investigating this."

Who are the beneficiaries of his nepotism? Me? I was never Roger's mate, not my style. Not in anyone's club. In fact I think Roger gave me this job because I was not anyone's mate. Was PK having a go at me? Too tired to taken aback, to be properly personally offended.

PK drained the last of his coffee with a flourish and stood up to his full height.

"Roger Mason eh? Always has to be the rock star."

He was looking at Hooker as if there was an in-joke.

I thought there would be a conversation about what Sharon had established and then hand over to PK's team. He glanced at the clock on the wall, obviously not. It was time for me to leave, so I left.

Two days later he demoted me.

Two ranks.

CHRIS

Gina has put on more make-up than usual. After all this is a big night for her. Gina likes being involved in other people's problems, the mother figure for the boybanders and their problems. She goes to funerals of ex-officers who she never even knew, out of 'respect'.

So this is Christmas for the trauma junkie. She has asked me five times in fifty minutes if I am alright. She keeps rubbing my back or arm in support. This is the third cup of tea.

"Come on Chris. Look, try smiling even if you don't feel like doing so."

"Gina the only thing about all this that makes me smile is that if I get sacked then Sheila will miss out on my pension."

And now she has gone off in a huff.

The IPCC should have been here at 7p.m. i.e. when I was supposed to parade on but are late, no explanation. I have been in the station anyway since 4.30 at Ashton's request/order to see him. People do not disturb you off nights early for fear of waking you up so only got my first call at from Fred from Federation at 3, but I had not slept at all. Ashton had wanted to see us both. Bob, of course, was not answering the phone.

Fred's a nice enough guy, standard advice, do not talk too much and 'try not to worry'. 'Try not to worry', is there a more redundant piece of advice ever given?

Ashton had erected a poster behind his desk with words I TOLD YOU SO, or he might as well have done. He was in a foul mood. Didn't seem to occur to him that others may be having a bad day. He absolutely revelled in painting a dismal picture. Took great joy in going through all the mistakes, booking in, risk assessment, visits, the bottle in the cell, the defibrillator, the ambulance.

You know all I could think of as he was sat there was that in 1940's Germany he would definitely have been a Nazi. Not a keep- your- head- down- try- to- get- through- the- war type but an enthusiastic Eichmann type character, keeping weekly graphs of how many people his camp had gassed this week. Like those graphs he has next to his desk of burglary and robbery rates.

"A kinder GMP, apparently," Fred muttered as we left.

So it is now 8 p.m. Ashton has made Tracy stay on just to cover while IPCC speak to us but she's now flouncing out, pissed off with the world as ever. IPCC pass her as she disappears. They have a sergeant from Internal Affairs with them, tall, dapper, tanned, relaxed, handkerchief top pocket. Seen him around and about.

Dapper does the introductions in a cramped side office with me and Bob. Two IPCC staff Zoe something and Phil Hattersley. Zoe, mid 30s pleasant, crinkly ginger hair, anxiously smiling. Phil, an insouciant 17 years old. He had a satchel slung across his shoulder, v- necked jumper and jeans, drippy, floppy hair, Geography 'A' level student. Did I hear right? He was the lead investigator?

Zoe is, at least, pleasant. All kinds of the formalities of 'determining the mode of investigation', 'criminal or misconduct', ' supervised or full independent investigation', 'fact finding stage' .

Bob was sitting arms crossed, doing his 'unimpressed' pose.

She asked how we are?

"Fine, haemorrhoids are a bastard. Itchier when on nights but hey ho. How are you? You must be tired after such an emotional and draining day. I am taken aback by your thoughtfulness visiting at this late hour."

Zoe looks flummoxed. Bob is going to be a proper dick. Why have I used the future tense?

"Well we are obviously concerned I have seen these things go on for a long time and….."

I try and get things back on track.

Zoe makes a hum of concern. She knows GMP is very good at supporting officers in difficult circumstances etc.. Phil takes charge, impatient to get to the point.

"Think it would be fair to let you know where we are in this. We've not seen the family yet, had difficulty contacting them so I don't want to say too much."

He did not need to, Ashton had pretty much told me all I needed to know. Bob makes to get up.

"Well in that case mate, we will wait until you have got your shit together."

Phil's head is down looking at his notes, not acknowledging Bob has stood.

"Couple of issues. The empty bottle found in the cell seems to be missing. PC Purvis tells us she left it in an evidence bag on Inspector Jones' desk. It certainly is not there now."

Bob plonked himself down, arms crossed, outrage.

"What you trying to say?"

He looks at me, how-dare-they-suggest, defiant.

"Just whether there is an explanation for such a mix up. We could have run some forensics on the bottle. Also we have the tape of the CCTV office and we cannot hear on the tape what is going on in the back office but there seems some confusion and raised voices. Constable Brazier, you seem to have had a text message you refer to about the ambulance. Do you have your mobile phone with you?"

"No."

Bob still arms crossed, passive but mainly aggressive. The phone is actually glowing in his pocket of his white shirt as he speaks. He looks like a Tellytubby.

Phil's turn to be taken aback. Dapper intervenes.

"It seems to be in your top pocket Constable Brazier."

Bob stares ahead at Phil never looking down.

"Is it? My error thought I had left it in the back office."

No movement from anyone. Horrible silence. Eventually, Phil nervously.

"Well we will have to seize it as evidence."

Silence. Bob still impassive, arms crossed, stares at Phil, then takes his glasses off to wipe them on his shirt.

"This requires a response? Oh well, my response is good luck with doing that. You will need to know your powers of seizure won't you? Which, of course, you will have no idea about.

Look it goes like this, and I am sure I can speak for Sergeant Hayes here. It clearly would be better for us if you could have been be arsed to turn up on time because we now have a custody office to run and prisoners we have to prevent from dying.

We have left Mrs Pendleton on her own for more than five minutes now. So there could be a queue of five prisoners out there to book in. Mrs Pendleton though will have done little else but wipe down the counter with bleach and texted her daughter to ask what she had for tea. You know the important stuff. So why it might, in other circumstances, be delightful to talk, now is not the time.

I will want representation obviously before I do speak after being so clumsily accused of destroying evidence."

Bob lumbers out to embarrassed silence, having to squeeze past Zoe and Phil. Did he fart or was that a friction noise from getting up off the chair? The fart/chair noise conundrum makes my mind up for me. I cannot, under any circumstances, stay in a room with them pretending not to notice a Bob Brazier fart up my nostrils and I am not waiting to find out.

I get up too to walk out and leave them there. Not sure if that was wise but, too late, I have done it anyway.

Gina has, as Bob predicted, not booked in any prisoners. Her union has told her it is not in her job description. Only one prisoner waiting anyway Darren Hall, hopeless junkie. He shambles from the holding area to the charge desk more forlorn than ever. He is in handcuffs but surrounded by four of the volume crime team. The designer posing dickheads have Darren in handcuffs.

I suddenly feel enormously tired, sad. Dapper and the IPCC are emerging from the room. Fart it was then.

"Constable, sorry can't remember your name?"

"Adam Fletcher, Sarge, 3786."

"Why is this man in handcuffs in my custody office? Does he pose a risk of violence or flight?"

"Both Sarge. We brought him in in the car, not a van, and have not searched him properly and we obviously want to prevent his escape as there is a magistrate's warrant for him."

IPCC are now watching. Two of these four from the crime team had been part of a three part series on Sky (*Policing the Naked City*) and think they are film stars. I love pretending not to know their names.

"Obviously indeed. Well constable, you can take the cuffs off Mr Hall. We will take the risk that Darren will not attempt to escape now, will you Darren?"

"What Sarge?"

"Not use your extensive secret service training Darren to overpower these four officers, then take one of us hostage and force your way out of this cell block to escape the warrant for non-appearance on the charge of theft of a can of coke or whatever you have done now."

"No way Sergeant Hayes promise, not if its double chicken curry tonight with some bread and marge. Is Hong Kong working?"

Where is Bob? Can't hear him. He is not in the back.

"He's gone out," Gina mouths to me on her way to do the visits, puzzled hunch of the shoulders.

The IPCC are now stood in the booking in area liked bemused tourists, making desultory conversation with Dapper. Not sure what they are doing there. Ah yes waiting for one of us to buzz them out. I could do that but decide to book Darren in instead and go as slowly as I can just to piss everyone off.

I can see out of corner of my eye Bob coming down the corridor with a tray of drinks and heading for the IPCC team. He making a performance of it, huffing and puffing, the sheer exertion of carrying a tray thirty yards. I am behind the counter, cannot head him off. I know precisely what he is going to do. He's done this gag before.

The tray has two drinks with cups and saucers and an orange squash with a straw.

"Sorry about earlier, strain of it all. Zoe, Sergeant made you tea hope that's right. Help yourself to milk and sugar. Dig in."

He places the tray on the charge office counter with a flourish.

"Darren, my man, chicken curry tonight is it?"

"Yep, Hong Kong, alarm call at about eight with the *Daily Mirror*."

"Really Darren? Had you down as a *Star* man. You going posh on me?"

Bob turns to Phil. Here we go.

"Philip I found you some orange squash and some Jammy Dodgers as a treat. Been a long day for you."

He holds out the glass with a straw for Phil. No one can speak or move. There is nothing I can do to rescue this. Phil is clearly trying to think of something to say but can't get it out.

"You don't want them? Do you want this squash Dazzer then?"

"Ah cheers Hong Kong, ta very much, can I have those
        jammies? They are my favourite."

"I think so. Someone seems to have unplugged our IPCC
        friends here from the mains electricity."

We all watch Darren stuff Jammy Dodgers into his face whilst gurgling down the orange juice.

He uses the straw provided.

JENNY

"Useless reporter.....soppy life."

Sarah Parker called me that. She is a total fat floppy tits grimy teeth bitch of an editor. Don't think I can even tell you now about the argument I have had with that B-I-T-C-H. I am so angry.

All started with the Hooker article and the editorial, which I have never done before, an editorial that is.

I suppose it will help me calm if I go through that night I saw Hooker rather than what has just gone on with Sarah. Yes that seems sensible, sets what has happened in context. Ok. I will do that.

Now I had seen him (Hooker) before at Police Authority meetings before but not spoken to him in person. Well, there is only one word to describe him, weird. Everyone says that. Weirdo.

He doesn't look like a Chief Constable more a children's TV presenter. He's definitely not tall, gelled spiky black hair and John Lennon tinted glasses. Early 40s at most, doesn't speak properly also, has a kind of speech defect, pronounces 'things' as 'fings'.

I must have been stood there for ten minutes while he fidgeted, moved papers and tried to dress himself. He could have just asked me to sit down while he did all this. If he had told me he wanted his radio harness, for example, I could have told him it was on the chair in front of him, it would have saved a lot of time. All the time too he was going on about PK, about how he had started to turn the tanker around that was GMP, moved it away from the 'cultural hegemony of performance'. I didn't ask him what that meant. I sort of knew anyway and didn't want to give him the satisfaction.

He enquired if we were meeting the photographer in the city? I told him I would be taking pictures on my new IPhone. He looked curiously disappointed but then asked to look at my IPhone. He told me he would be getting one of these. Got the impression he had decided that when he saw mine.

"Right who am I today?"

Hooker had pulled open his double wardrobe and I could see it was packed with GMP uniform all neatly set out on hangers. Fluorescent jackets, tunics, combat trousers, anoraks, white shirts, black T-shirts and those blue shirts the firearms officers wear, boots, flat caps, handcuffs and police baseball cap. Inside the door was a mirror with pocket for a clothes brush. Has his own mug, I see, on a shelf; it says 'LABOUR: MORE POLICE'.

"I reckon the black bomber jacket, look operational, but white shirt and tie to offset it, you know contrast. Will not put on the body armour, though, jacket does not hang right if you do."

He looked at me for approval. I just shrugged, not sure what he expected me to say. He will still look ridiculous.

We set off in the lift to the underground car park. He kept banging on about how special PK was, that he saw qualities in people that often others had neglected. Indeed he had first come across PK when he was inspector in West Midlands and PK was a Chief Superintendent. He was being disciplined by him because he 'had been drinking too much and had messed up'. PK took an interest in him and his life 'turned round from that day onwards'.

"Perhaps he should be beatified?"

I could not help myself. A bad habit, lack of confidence I suppose. To be fair it was better than 'get a room', which I had been thinking of saying.

He did that blink that he does. I honestly thought he was going to carry on that perhaps PK had some special spiritual status, or that what I had said was blasphemous. Perhaps he did not know what 'beatified' meant. Not a Catholic like me then. He had stopped talking. Was he was sulking or thinking of something?

We walked to his car in silence. It was a Yaris, a three door Yaris. He could see I was a bit taken aback.

"Yes this is my car. Trying to set an example to all the rest of the Command team. I mean you just can't justify the freebies Mason was handing out to them. Cars with police lights fitted as a tax dodge, big gas guzzling X5s, just obscene really."

We got in.

"What's it to be Killers or The Artic Monkeys?"

He held up two CD cases. I was dying to say 'The Killers or Arctic Monkeys' but thought better of it after the 'beatified' comment. Anyway I never got to answer. Arctic Monkeys had already been chosen. So we set off on the short drive into town with Hooker singing the words to *I Bet You Look Good on the Dance Floor,* not at full pelt but loud enough to stop conversation, I just looked straight ahead. I can tell you I was relieved he did not know the words to the following tracks on the album. I reckon he hadn't actually ever listened to any of the other tracks on the album.

He drove to the Town Hall and down a little cobbled street which was barriered off but he had a pass for it. He parked his tiny car next to the Mayor's limousine. It was strange because I was expecting him to park at Bootle Street Police Station. I thought he would be on patrol with some PC from the North Manchester division, that's what Mason would have done. It would also have been some attractive photogenic policewoman with Mason too, no doubt. Yes it was no surprise when Mason announced his first Recruit of the Year was an exlingerie model from Altrincham and not a plumber from Wigan.

No, Hooker was going to do this on his own. No sooner had he got out of the car he immediately started talking to any passer-by he could find, I mean anyone. I thought this approach would cause all sorts of problems but it is strange how politely people reacted, deferential to his confident manner. He was telling them about how stability at the top mattered in GMP after turbulent times and that people must be relieved that this had now been achieved. They all strangely agreed, as if they understood and cared. I could see it was to get shut of him and continue on their night out. I would have placed money on someone doing the 'called the police last week and no-one turned up speech' but no, no-one actually did.

I was a touch mesmerised by all this and just looked on. When he had finished with a couple he turned to me.

"Thought you were supposed to be getting shots of me meeting the public, we are losing light. If you stand there the next one will have the big wheel in the background. Iconic."

I sensed some irritation with me not doing quite what he wanted. He accosted a couple of people in Exchange Square but he seemed to be losing some of his bounce. We moved down into Deansgate and he decided upon two young girls, barely eighteen, getting out of a taxi obviously on the start of a night out.

Now this definitely had to be a bad move. He hardly got to speak to them before they took over. They just wanted to pose with him with his hat on and the other holding his handcuffs. He had little choice as they weren't for taking no for an answer and the crowd outside the Moon under the Water were getting some spectator sport. The confidence visibly drained from him but he had little choice but to take part. This is precisely why he should have had a PC sidekick.

Photos taken the girls departed into the pub to a burst of applause from those outside. One girl calling out over her shoulder.

"Them's funny blue specs. Are you a bitter Bertie?"

I had to explain to him that meant a City fan. Tim would love that story. I would tell him when I got home.

Hooker had immediately had enough and set off back for the car without speaking to anyone else or me. All this was done in less than 40 minutes. I had expected a night of traipsing round town, perhaps for a moralising piece on late night drinking culture. I actually felt a bit disappointed that we did not do more.

Hooker suddenly got quite business like again when we got into the car to go back to HQ. He started going on about the article as if he was writing it himself. What I could put in what I could not. He was beginning to really annoy me now. I was the reporter after all. He kept on about this collage of pictures. I had not got as many pictures as he would have liked for the collage he had envisioned. He would send me some. I tried to explain I did not deal with this kind of thing, that the news desk people put the paper together, I just did the words. Not sure he was listening.

"I don't know if you should mention my alcoholism. I will get back to you on that, and obviously you can't use that picture of me with the young ladies."

'Obviously'? 'Young ladies'? Really?

I don't even recall him telling me he was an alcoholic or that he could decide what was off the record. He seemed to have this divine sense of being in charge.

"I think the tone as such should be, 'steady as she goes'. New Chief Constable, some stability at the top. You see I want to make GMP more compassionate, less Manichean in outlook, but that can come later."

Manichean? No me neither. Still not sure what he meant even after I looked it up.

Anyway, the good news should have been that I would be home earlier but felt a sudden wave of apathy come over me. What would I be going home to after all? Felt bad about this apathy, not like me. Remembering what Mason had texted me about suspenders, I decided to text Tim. After all he claimed I was never spontaneous.

`I will be home soon. Lucky you. I will put my gear on`

I don't often do this. That's a lie. I had never sent a sex text before, unless in response to Tim.

Rarely put suspenders on actually, just hard work doing all that, and you have to take them off again five minutes later. But thought perhaps I should make the effort, as I said Tim had been complaining recently. He should talk though, his idea of dressing up for sex is to put his Wayne Rooney No. 10 shirt on.

Anyway, got home and there he was slouched on the on couch, hands down his jogging pants scratching his balls watching Spanish football. He never mentioned the text, couldn't be bothered to ask whether he had received it.

I put my pyjamas on, got a book and went to bed.

MICHAEL

David always feels badly that I missed out on University after beating up Walsh. Truth is I had already decided I was not going to go and was going to join the Marines instead. I beat up Walsh in the spirit of freedom that making this decision had given me.

Walsh was an uncouth vicious bastard with no redeeming features. He looked like a nasty bastard, curly black hair and terrible acne. He was pure malevolence. Parents had sent him to many schools but he was always getting expelled. He had only been at the school for a term but he walked around with a couple of hangers-on like Sykes from *Oliver Twist*. Lord, he was feared. He handed out ferocious beatings. I wasn't there when he beat up David but was told he had kicked him round the floor of the corridor like a rag doll calling him a 'fucking faggot'.

On reflection Walsh must have had some animal cunning about when and where to dish out his beatings to have even lasted a term at our school. He probably realised David would not report anything for fear of talking about his sexuality, but I had decided Walsh was not going to get away with it this time. He was going to get a taste of his own medicine. I was sure to get expelled but a silver lining was that it should save endless arguments with my parents about joining the Marines and not going to University.

Now I knew Walsh would, of habit, go for a smoke in the toilets the minute it was lights out. So I waited for him that night. I had seen this trick in a film *Scum* where you wrap two snooker balls in a sock. I was even lighter than the ten stones I am now and Walsh could have beaten me to a pulp in a fair fight, so this felt like David's sling.

Anyway it worked a treat, the moment Walsh came into the toilets 30 seconds after lights out I caught him a beauty straight on the cheekbone, just as he was lighting up. I am sure I heard it crack or was it the snooker balls banging together?

He didn't fall though. He just stood there dazed holding his cheek, bent over in pain and shock. He peered up at me.

"Henderson?" he said, puzzled, stunned. Then I changed my plan.

I had only intended to hit him the once to teach him a lesson. But whilst he was dazed and still standing I tried to hit him again, missing as he backed away. So I tightened the sock round my fist and swung a third time. He let out a kind of howl of pain as the balls hit his nose and cheek. You could definitely hear the cheekbone crack this time. He sank to the floor but only onto his knees.

I could see the bruise raising on his cheekbone, blood pouring out of his splattered nose. I kicked him straight in the face on the raised cheekbone and he curled into a ball. I then kicked him round the toilets until I had no breath left. I remember the other boys had got up to see what was going on but no-one attempted to pull me off him. Was there a round of applause after I had finished or is that memory playing a trick on me? I do remember hearing Walsh cry like a baby.

It was my last day at school, obviously, but I had no regrets. None at all.

You know why it didn't just hit him the once as planned? I hadn't lost my temper. I was not overcome with a feeling of fury to avenge my brother after landing the first blow. I wasn't frightened that Walsh may have fought back while still standing. It wasn't even deciding I needed to inflict more damage to ensure I got expelled, although that did cross my mind. No, it was none of that.

It was just seeing Walsh stood there, dazed, cheekbone probably fractured, I realised that one blow would not be right. It would be just a pose, a gesture and no more. Walsh was a mad dog who had inflicted severe beatings on many. He needing teaching a proper lesson and one blow wouldn't suffice.

Beating Walsh to a pulp was justice.

KENNY

Yes one of the very first things PK did when he became Chief Constable again. He demoted me two ranks. Not one, two.

Yes, technically, it was one rank because superintending is one rank but he put me down from ACC to superintendent not chief superintendent. I was a mere superintendent again. He could do this because these were temporary ranks that Roger had given me, but it still beggared belief. Truly to this day I still can't credit it.

I had four years to do to get my thirty years in for my full pension. Not sure PK would know, or care, how much money he has cost me. Varna cried for days.

We did the maths together last night. So all that time as a Temporary ACC Crime can't count towards the pension, which is best of last three years. So it works out at a probable loss of what could have been £305k in commuted lump sum (tax free) and an annual pension of £40k. Instead I will get a £215k in commuted lump sum and about 28K pension.

Would anyone take that lying down? I just wonder if I have left it too late to sue, it was six months ago.

PK isn't remotely bothered about the effect things like that have on ordinary people. It's people's lives and livelihoods we are talking about here. He doesn't think of regular guys like me with kids, struggling to make ends meet. He does this otherworldly 'I'm in another dimension' spiritual act but he, personally, will be minted, trust me on that one, a Chief's pension and HMI salary. And he is not a patch on Roger, he was a proper gent.

Been remembering back to 2005, three years ago, when Roger offered me the crime detective chief superintendent job. It had been a terrible time. I was superintendent at Salford and we had just taken Jamal Hussein to trial for conspiracy to murder. Finished up it was all about TICs not murder.

TICs, crimes that are 'Taken into Consideration'. When you are convicted at court you admit to other crimes that you have done which clears them up for us as detected and also means you cannot be prosecuted for them in the future. Win, win really, but few go for it now because solicitors reckon judges give them harder sentences.

Anyway, Salford division had the highest rate of getting them. Poor old Brian Burford, the DCI and his sidekick Inspector Tony Barnes thought they had really discovered the knack of persuading prisoners to accept TICs. They had posters everywhere in the station and even messages painted on the ceiling of the cells telling prisoners about TICs so they could see them when they were lying down on the benches.

His division were top of all their similar BCUs in many Forces for detections. It all went to poor Brian's head. He sent an email to all DCIs offering to host 'a masterclass' at HQ in getting detections. He had a very public row with some civil liberties people when they objected to messages in the cell. He went on BBC and described Liberty as 'lefty graduates who had never had a proper job and had no conception of the real world.'

Then Jamal Hussein decides to decapitate Billy Walker.

He did not personally decapitate him. He got someone else to do it. We got the henchman on DNA pretty quickly. But we reckoned also we could prove Hussein was behind it. It's a long story but it was all over drugs money. Always is.

We had a good case against him, mainly based on phone traffic on the night. We had people, Walker's 'friends', who were surprisingly willing to give evidence in court about an encounter when Walker had threatened Hussein two days before the murder.

I was in charge of the case as the Senior Investigating Officer (SIO) but anyone will tell you that, as an SIO, you are not really in effective charge. You may be in charge of a few cases at any time. Brian was the deputy dedicated to doing the day to day running. Brian had just not put two and two together and realised that the witnesses were all the same people who had had TICs for him in the past.

So it all went Pete Tong at court. Witnesses went bandit on day of the trial. They alleged they had been offered pizzas, cigarettes and even to have prostitutes allowed in the cells as inducements to have TICs. They then went on to state they had also been promised money to give the evidence at this trial and their evidence was made up.

I mean, prostitutes in the cells, just inconceivable, but people watch too many films and believe this kind of garbage.

Defence asked to look at these TICs which seemed just a bizarre move in a murder trial. It soon transpired many of the TICs just did not stack up. One burglary was later found out to be an insurance fraud and never happened, another occurred when the offender was on holiday in Ibiza and another when the offender had actually been on remand in prison. Defence were relentless on this. They had me, Brian and Tony in the dock for days about our dealings with TICs and how these witnesses were treated. The argument was if the TICs were bogus then the evidence about the murder could not be trusted.

Judge had no bottle whatsoever. He grew weary of it, too quickly, in my view. He concluded that not only could the witnesses not be trusted but also that behaviour of Brian and Tony called into question the whole investigation.

Judge was quite fair to me in that he said that it was 'clear I did not know what was going on'. Some people misinterpreted what he meant by that. Anyway, he had the prosecution in, told them what he thought and they offered no evidence.

It broke Brian completely. There was a long investigation into him and he had a breakdown. He got quite nasty about me. Complained that I spent my time dealing in shares when I should have been working. Just rubbish, I gave him a few (profitable) share tips and he turns against me. Sad that people end like that. I mean he wanted all the credit when things were going well and but blamed others when it went wrong. He got a medical pension in the end but remained a bitter man.

So you can imagine I was wondering what Roger had in stall for me when I got the personal call to see the Chief Constable. I had never seen him before but knew he was ripping up trees wherever he went. The acquittal had embarrassed him though.

I was certain it was a uniform posting or back to Strategic Change branch. I remember meeting had got off to a good start. I had on a Baumler three piece on, Varna had been forcing me to spend money on clothes, said I dressed like a hobo. Roger liked it, asked me where I had got it from (Slaters). Didn't tell him I had bought it especially for this meeting.

It was coffee and biscuits, Roger was sat on his couch, arms out. Large file, on me, in front of him.

"So Kenny Poole. It's been an annus horribilis."

"Well Sir, suppose so."

"Long way from home too Kenny. You came from Lincoln what three years ago? On the back of a paper you did on the Junior Command Course at Bramshill which PK got to see when he was tossing it off there doing some lecturing instead of running the Force."

"Well if you put it like that, yes, longer story but in a nutshell yes that's it."

"Read the paper last night, interesting. Flatten the policing hierarchies, do away with the divisional structure, small community teams lead by inspectors, less cops but large civilian specialist teams to handle volume crime via a call centre/internet model of operating, reduce custody capacity by 75% rely on voluntary attendance and summons. Save the Force about 40% in costs overall. Impressive."

Could see the way this was going, back to some strategic change job.

"Impressive but ignores the culture of the police, human nature and civic pride. Nothing straight is built on the crooked timber of humanity."

He tossed the paper on the desk.

"So let me get this right. You have to do this as part of your Junior Command Course project as a chief inspector at Bramshill. PK sees your paper and, on the basis of this alone, offers you a promotion in GMP?"

"Yes. He said the place was a sleeping monster after years and years of Cyril Richards and he needed fresh ideas"

"So he promised you superintendent rank and you up sticks from Grantham?"

"Yes I was going nowhere there. Dead men's shoes over there. Big Masonic thing."

Well it was the truth. Should not have said it though. Who knows if he was? He did not react.

"Family?"

"Pamela was all for it. Said she would come in due course but wanted the boys to finish GCSEs in Lincoln. She just had eyes on the bigger pension. Took up with my best mate back there. I say took up but recently found out it had been going on before I even left. Perhaps that's why she encouraged me to go."

Roger laughed. I did not mind for some reason.

"Well been there mate, been there. Yes all for the extra dosh, then refuse to up sticks at the last moment. Sorry for laughing. So just tell me, from your perspective, what happened when you got here? Career wise that is."

"Well got put to work at Sedgley Park with a team of about twenty. Did a huge analysis of the Force and basically mapped out a future with a ten year plan for the Force. Worked every hour being away from home. Massive piece of work, incredible really. I remember we could not bind the document it was so big. Had to come in two parts. Handed it to PK and then, well, then nothing.

He said it would be a great basis and provide him with a road map. In the meantime I needed to get some experience as he had plans for me and sent me as detective superintendent to Salford....."

"....to take on Jamal Hussein."

It was not what I was going to say but I let it go.

"Do you know he showed the paper to Des Lyons at the Police Authority who just said 'no'?"

"Why?"

"Why? Well he is a trade unionist at heart so saying 'no' is the default setting. Do you know what he did before he became a full time councillor and head of the Authority? He was a gardener for the council. He cut the grass in the parks. Herbaceous borders are his limit. All too hard to do for him.

Sorry Kenny lets rewind. What's your educational background, qualifications, all that stuff? Anything special?"

"Me standard stuff. Geography degree from Hull, 2.2 all bog standard. Always interested in how money works though I suppose. You can save money, police waste so much. Well, all the public services do. In the genes in Grantham, you know, thrift. Make a few quid in shares, currency dealings you know also. "

"Yeah, big money?"

"Probably six figures, in the last five years.

I was trying to be coy but it was a lie anyway. I had that as a profit at one point. I had lost a fair bit of that since coming to Manchester. Too much spare time meant I did trades when I was bored rather than when I had spotted something.

"I could save this Force a lot of money if you want me to do something like that."

He looked out the window for the longest time. At one point I nearly felt I had to remind him I was in the room. He jolted into life.

"Ok Kenny. How do you fancy being Head of CID?"

Could he do that?

"Can you do that?"

"I am the Chief Constable, I can do what I fucking want, despite what the Superintendents' Association think. Look to stop any argument we will just make it temporary for now."

"But what's happened to Kevin Kershaw?"

"Nothing yet. But I have got plans for Kevin. Look Kenny, I am going to improve performance in GMP big time. It needs an enormous boot up the arse after PK's year of navel gazing. But the truth is no boss loses their job because his burglary rate is up or his detection figures are down. They lose their job when they fail at the big stuff. Look at the Soham murder last year. I need to improve things round here but also I someone to keep me safe. I just need someone who I am sure is not part of Kershaw's crew. I still don't know GMP well enough to know who knows who. I just need someone who isn't part of that set-up. "

"But the trial....?"

"Well there is a lot that could be said about that. Look the man who never made a mistake never did anything. One thing is for sure Kenny, you won't forget the experience. Anyway it shows Jamal Hussein who really is the boss. He would expect me to throw you under the bus now. Well fuck him. Hear that intelligence shows he had actually been paying these lads to have TICs years before on the eventuality that such a moment might arise when he needed to have discredited witnesses."

He stopped as if he had reminded himself of something.

"And there will be far more to it than just that. No he ain't stupid for sure. Look you now know what we are up against. You won't be fooled again. You better not be."

It was certainly not the time to tell him I had not been fooled, it was Brian. Anyway, bottom line he wanted me for the job. If I said yes the job was mine.

He explained there was going to be a number of changes in CID. There was a Sharon Bentley who he was making Head of Murder Investigation Teams and a couple of others.

"I've got some good people round you. You will have everyone questioning the appointment, scheming against you. Just grind it out, walk the line, keep me safe. If you have a real problem come direct to me. Ok? Direct."

He seemed pleased with himself. Put his hand on my knee.

"Kenny, I won't leave you high and dry like PK. I can guess what you must have been feeling after the trial. In the flat in Manchester, microwave meal for one, miles from home, someone else sat on your sofa in Lincoln, feet on your coffee table, substitute dad to your kids. So today's your lucky day, big boy, come on give me a smile."

I was too taken aback by events to smile. Needed to say something though.

"Well, actually, things started turning for the better during the trial in a way. Met a girl, a policewoman who was dealing with the admin side, bit of a whirlwind romance. It's going well. She is well…………."

I hesitated, Roger looked at me expectantly, I had to go on.

"…..well bit of an Amazonian."

"Amazonian? Great word. How so?"

His face animated, leaning forward, eager. I was committed now, I had to tell him.

"She will give you a blow job without you actually asking for it."

He laughed out loud, uproariously, almost wiping the tears from his eyes. He put his hand on my knee again.

"You and me, Kenny, we are going to get along fine, just fine."

JULIAN

I am not wearing a constable's uniform today. I have on blue blazer and grey trousers. My Dad reckons it is classic, fits all occasions. Also got a white shirt and a red and blue striped tie with black brogue shoes. I polished them last night.

I use to like wearing this outfit last Friday of every month when I worked at the management consultants. I wore my blue three piece suit all the other days. When they fired me they quoted the fact that I wore the same suit every day for work as an example of why I was not fitting in. They had forgotten I wore the blazer outfit also once a month.

I have actually had three jobs since leaving University. I worked for a policy centre in London doing research. One day I was sent to deliver a talk after a colleague was ill and had to drop out. The issue had been a debate about the desirability of 'equality'. I did the standard stuff of the policy centre. Inequality was an inevitable part of a free society. Indeed Mrs Thatcher had saved this country by creating more inequality; the most creative and productive society in the world, USA, contains a great deal of inequality.

Then the debate moved onto talking about equality amongst humans. I pointed out that it was clear that humans are not equal in all kinds of abilities and faculties. Of course I went onto say that the whole discussion about which race may be more physically superior or capable or moral or intelligent is based upon a dubious humanist philosophy which has its roots in Christian theology which sees humans as some kind of teleological goal of evolution. Evolution, in its nature, is not teleological. No-one seemed to listen to that.

I was not fired. I just did not have my temporary contract renewed. It was related to complaints about what I had said. Apparently I had gone off script.

I did not last a year at the management consultants. The problem was a variation upon the same theme. Miss Clare, who fired me, told me that the best way to sum matters up was that the firm had to actively keep me away from clients because I often said things that they did not want to hear. Miss Clare also quoted a number of anecdotes about me which could only have come from colleagues. Petty things about tea funds, socialising after work and the blue suit. Had to have come from colleagues which is disappointing, considering how much I had helped them.

From my experience the police has been the most tolerant profession. I am allowed to get on with what I have to do, more or less. The community job is ideal as I can pretty much work on my own and do the things I want to do.

I seem to have been thrust into 'limelight', so to speak, after my successes with trafficking of women for massage parlours. Sergeant Learmonth has started sending me to management meetings which have been interesting.

Unfortunately I upset Mr Ashton at the first meeting I attended. Mr Ashton was ascribing a fall in burglaries to his plan of having PCSOs patrol within a hundred metres radius seven days after any burglary took place. I asked whether he had applied the statistical concept of 'regression to the mean'. I did not even hear what his reply was but it was something dismissive people laughed at. He certainly did not even ask me to explain what I meant.

Mrs Henderson invited me to her office later to explain it to her, which I did. In a nutshell if you do very well or badly in any endeavour in one iteration it is more likely you will revert back towards the average on the next attempt. She understood it and it is no more than common sense. It's not an abstruse concept. She apologised for how Mr Ashton had spoken to me. I also got an email from Inspector Jones thanking me for 'my contribution'.

Anyway Mr Ashton has now banned me from his meetings now.

I like Mrs Henderson. I know a lot of people do not, but based on what? That she has been directly promoted in? She was offered a job and she took it. A lot of people would have accepted. Indeed the people who seem to dislike her most don't want to be superintendents, so why are they so bothered? Baffling.

I would like to a superintendent in the future but it takes a significant leap to believe Mrs Henderson is standing in my way. I suppose it's not a significant leap, she is mathematically probably reducing the chances, but it is by some infinitesimally small amount. May try and do the maths on that tonight, quite a lot of factors. I suppose even if the statistics showed some real connection, the attachment of personal animus still is puzzling.

Mr Ashton tells me I have difficulties communicating with senior officers but, here's the thing, to use the modern demotic, I write to Mrs Henderson with ideas and thoughts and she always replies. Sometimes she tells me she does not understand but we always get to a point where she does, that is good communication isn't it? Mr Ashton never does. That is rude and poor communication on his part, surely?

Mrs Henderson wrote to me to ask me expressly to come to this meeting. She said in the email it is because of my 'expertise' in this field, my 'intelligence' and 'creative-thinking'. She is wrong about my expertise. She has confused trafficking of women with child sexual exploitation, they are only tangentially related issues. It is also odd to think I am viewed as being this 'Two Brains' character. I am not. I have had my IQ tested. I am 128. Better than average but hardly a genius.

I am also sure I am not creative, I just research other people's ideas. Just because you try to think things through, and read the documents upon which meetings are based, people think you are some kind of super-intelligent being. To me that's just about being logical and professional.

However Mrs Henderson has asked me personally, and I like her, so here I am on my day off. I am prepared. As it is my day off today I feel permitted to wear this outfit rather than uniform. I feel good in it. I hope people may see more than someone who is a constable. I think I have something useful to say.

Don't speak too soon, leave it to the end when people want the solutions, that's my father's advice.

It is written on the pad in front of me.

BRODY

Another day in GMP, another meeting.

Not many here though. Two Brains is looking sharp in his blazer, a bit tense perhaps? He has written something on the pad in front of him. Strange, strange lad.

The Make-Up squad are out in force, Sergeant Lesley Atkinson, Petra, Monica and Sheila. All sat together at the top of the table next to Ma'am. It is their big day after all, big smiles, outfits all round.

Why are they all in the Make-Up squad? Track record of commitment to child protection? Hand- picked for their detective abilities? Well, not quite, Lesley Atkinson is half-decent at her job but Petra and Monica were booted out of CID and into this because they are plain incompetent. Think Monica had a 'little local difficulty' when caught out taking sixty days annual leave last year. She was only not returned to uniform because transpired most of them in CID were also at it.

Sheila has been in the cops two minutes but has pissed, moaned, groaned and taken out grievances until she got a job not on shifts that suited her 'lifestyle'. I think the official version is that she required special adaptations because she is a single parent. Aren't they all, though, nowadays?

No, I reckon the overriding common denominator amongst those four is a desire to work Monday to Friday and go home at four, earlier on Friday.

Ma'am B is all smiles with them. Can't quite hear what Lesley and her are talking about? Is it 15% off Estée Lauder?

Anyway Ma'am suddenly opens up. Important meeting, serious issue, thank you just attending shows commitment, hope everybody to get to contribute, hope to get some product out of the meeting, blah blah blah, asking Lesley to give a summary of the situation as she sees it.

Well its gush to Ma'am for at last, Hallelujah Praise the Lord, taking this seriously. This was the meeting they had been waiting for, hoping for, praying for, for over a year. They knew there were fifteen girls in care being exploited by what they believed to be forty six men. The girls would talk to them, no-one else, but the girls do just not see themselves as being exploited so you cannot get them to understand they are being exploited. It was as simple as that.

People in the station did not care about the girls they just saw them as troublesome missings (everyone seems to look at me at that point), they were grateful for the support Ma'am gave them personally but ultimately they felt they needed more officers to form personal relationships with the girls to gain their trust. If they got their trust it would be more likely the girls would give evidence.

Petra has taken over speaking. Some anecdote about a girl she had spoken to who had been in a care home because her step-dad used to fiddle with her and now she spends her nights with five lads from the kebab shop taking turns.

"I asked Lucy, who is only fourteen years old mind, where did she see herself in five years' time? 'Don't know' she replied, 'probably dead'."

She seems the verge of tears. Petra love, your day job is not in jeopardy. Don't overdo it love.

Hmm, step-dads. Yes think I can liven things up by giving my speech on how you are thirty times more likely to be abused by a step parent than by a natural one. Always gets a reaction.

Sheila starts talking. This will be enlightening. Hold fire on step-dads.

"Look the elephant in the room is race. We all know that. It just needs saying. Part of the problem we are getting nowhere is these men are Asian and the girls are white. They would not treat their own women like this but they will with white girls. It's something to do with it being in the Koran that it is not a sin to mistreat an unbeliever. White people will not act or speak out because they feel they will be attacked as being racist. The Asian community shuts its eyes to this."

'Asian community'? Well, the unit has improved her, marginally.

Two Brains is off. Here we go, sport.

"Crimes can become normalised in all closed communities, but if we are to ascribe any failures in investigating to issues of race or culture we would have to be able to carefully articulate what precisely is blocking investigations. You could argue the case of normalisation and internal pressures blocked investigation in the Catholic Church where the victims have often been separated from the outside world, but that's just not the case here. The girls have access to the world outside. In fact you talk to the girls all the time. I think your theory, at least partially, fails at this point.

The germane issue is that this is a crime that defies traditional modes of investigations. Firstly, we do not have victims as is commonly understood. In all crimes, apart from murder quite obviously, the victim has to confirm the crime. Here the victims do not see themselves as victims and we don't treat them as victims."

This is more like it.

"But they are victims," more than one of them butt in. Lesley takes the lead, "I, we, take offence at that, the girls are absolutely treated as victims. It's outrageous to suggest…."

"….so how many crimes have you recorded? I know the answer, one, and that was when a girl fell pregnant and that did not result in a prosecution. What is going on is underage girls report crimes to us on a daily basis and we, well you, are just listening to them and not recording them as crimes. I would imagine if Mr Ashton knew he had had some three hundred odd undetected rapes then we would be doing a lot more than we actually are."

Two Brains has everyone's attention now. Imelda Marcos has not slapped him down yet. He is not remotely abashed, just carrying on oblivious. He looks and sounds like a barrister. He has missed his way in life.

"Of course the problem is recording crimes usually requires victim confirmation and we don't have this. Even if we did manage to get a girl to say she will testify she will be cross examined in court and more likely than not be discredited at some point.

So if this is a crime without a victim what do we do? Well, in the case of such crimes what we do is pro-actively chase the offenders. We are very good at this. Look at how adept we have become in tackling drugs supply. We surveil, we monitor phones and then we raid. But we cannot do that because, in this case, society would be squeamish about us watching girls being raped simply to produce evidence."

Sheila snorts in derision, common cow, that's about right for her. Lesley and the others are furiously writing notes to each other on a pad they are passing round.

"Yes the reality is that the emotional damage to the girls has already been done and surveillance would ultimately have results but there is some irrational logic that prevents us doing this."

"Julian you are saying this is insoluble?"

Ma'am has queried. What is she thinking? Clearly the girls have thought the fact that Ma'am joins them at 9.15 to touch up her make up meant undying support for their right to work days whilst achieving the square root of fuck all. Perhaps, perhaps not. Will she sell the Avon Ladies down the river?

This is true entertainment. Come on Two Brains.

"Yes by a direct approach. All our traditional means of tackling this will fail. Indeed they are failing. That is why we have heard the attempt to blame forces we cannot control. Blaming the Asian community is just pointless. Whilst Islamic communities particularly, and immigrant communities generally, do produce a greater internal coherence than the norm, the idea that somehow these people can be spat out by their communities is just wishful thinking and probably, in itself, racist. We hardly blame local councillors or priests in the white community for condoning white crime. Similarly the idea that officers are frightened to tackle issues that involves race is simply not borne out by the evidence. Indeed the evidence points in the opposite direction, that is to say we believe allegations against members of BME communities more readily."

Sheila mouth is wide open. All this is way over her head. Lesley looks to Ma'am who is not looking at her but at Two Brains. Lesley turns to Two Brains.

"So what do you advocate?" The 'smart arse' at the end is barely unsaid.

There's only one Two Brains. Son I could kiss you. You are definitely on some kind of spectrum but this is a bravura display, my little Asperger's friend. You have then rattled.

"Well we need to be lawfully audacious. We need to arrest everyone suspected of exploitation."

"But you need EVIDENCE."

Sheila, whose ill-disguised racist, albeit accurate, outburst had started this, puts her tongue into the bottom part of her mouth to emphasise the utter stupidity of what he's saying. She is shaking her head, drama queen. Look at me.

"Well no you don't not need evidence. This is a very common misconception and I am surprised that so many police officers make it. Indeed a detective superintendent at the Lawrence enquiry made the same mistake. So you are in good company."

Two Brains looks up to the ceiling musing.

"Well, perhaps not good company on second thoughts but I suppose you understand what I mean."

She doesn't, of course. She mouths to Lesley 'I'm walking out', but does not move. Shame, she should.

"No, in policing you only need reasonable suspicion on which to act. It is reasonable suspicion that allows you to seek further to then find evidence. It does not act the other way round. If you think about it, it must act this way.

Now you have not garnered any evidence in the last year regrettably, but you have amassed a load of intelligence, or so you say you have. What we need to do is act upon it, arrest the people we know, search their houses, seize their phones and computers and see if that gets us any evidence. At the very least this should have a very serious prophylactic effect. It should, though, get us some real evidence. People who engage in group coitus are more statistically more likely to have videoed it. There should be some evidence of telephone contact with the girls as well."

Normally would have said, 'hands up who knows what prophylactic means' but do not want to stop the lad's flow.

"We need also, together with partners, to make life just generally difficult for the people we suspect of offending on the associative enforcement principle. Look at the licenses for the kebab shops they run, the taxis they drive and so forth. There seems to be a close tie in between this abuse and drugs. Nearly all criminality has a soft underbelly which can be attacked and if we can't convict them of child sexual exploitation we can get them for something else.

It really should all be quite simple. These people have, because no one has done anything effective for the last few years, come to think they can easily escape prosecution and they will not have their guard up. It really should be quite simple with application and commitment."

The Make-Up Squad stunned, cross armed, faces chewing wasps, bulldogs, lemon, smacked arse all of them. This is so good I can't put the sentence together. Wish I had a camera. Why can't life be like this more often?

They look to their Spiritual Leader. She is looking at Two Brains, intently. What's the judgement?

"Julian, I really like the thought and energy you have given this. I really think this is something we have to act on. Could you draw up a proposal of what you have in mind?"

The oldest boss trick in the book of killing an idea. Yes 'send me that in writing. That will shut you up'. It does sound like she means it though this time.

Two Brains reaches down into a Lidl plastic bag he has to the left of him.

"Here is a draft business plan I drew up this weekend Mrs Henderson. We have not discussed issues of a cultural change plan so officers in the station see these crimes in a different light, the plan addresses that and there are some suggestions I have regarding lawfully audacious but legitimate surveillance of the girls when missing. I have put my personal mobile number at the bottom. You may ring me when I am off duty as indeed I am now in the sense that I am not getting paid but technically am on duty by contributing to this meeting. Anyway I would be happy to discuss."

It was heat bound in a plastic folder and marked 'Confidential'.

"Make me an acting sergeant and give me three new staff and I will operationalise this concept all within three months."

In summary, 'sack those useless bitches and give me the job'. He stands up, walks round the table and hands the document to Her Highness.

Give that man a round of applause.

Fuck it. I am going to.

JENNY

Calmer now so I can tell you what happened.

I wasn't in the best of moods today to begin with anyway I suppose. Never sleep well on Sunday nights. Tim had left the kitchen untidy after he had promised to wash up before he went to bed last night. PMT as well.

Opened my emails to find last two were from Hooker sent late on Sunday night. First had two photos attached. One a posed GMP picture of himself in Chief Constable's uniform and another at home in his study in checked shirt and jeans, framed certificates behind him.

The second asked to see the copy and layout before it goes out. It also says I can mention his alcoholism which PK saved him from and that he does attend AA. He goes on to say in six months, when all has settled down, we can do a piece about a compassionate culture. Perhaps in the meantime I could say he was less interested in the target culture Mason had created and viewed crime more 'holistically'.

Then I notice these emails are not even sent to me but to Sarah with me cc'd in. Charmed, I am sure.

On reflection I was under no time pressure to do the article and I should have done something else, something easier. However I have this thing about getting through my 'to do' list and not putting things off. I knew as I started writing I was not in the mood and should have stopped.

As I got into the article I did start to like Mason more though. Remember when I first met him he wanted to know what the people of Manchester would want to hear from a Chief and what my views were. Not sure I really had anything to suggest other than doing the 'copper's copper' or 'no-nonsense copper' approach but he agreed.

Mason was easy to write about in this respect. This I struggled with. As for doing an editorial, well, I have never done one before so I really had little idea. Anyway did it and sent it to the sub see what he thought and went out for a sandwich.

Sarah was standing by my desk when I got back. She did not even have to say 'my office'.

She started speaking the minute she re-entered her office still walking with her back to me. Rude. Sub-editor had sent her this because they wanted to check if this was the sort of thing she would want in the paper. She was appalled. Of course she was. Here we go.

Firstly, and most basically, no information about Hooker's home life, married, kids etc.? Yes, my bad, basic error, must check that.

Then it was obvious the intention of the article had been put in to ridicule Hooker. 'Only on Deansgate for thirty minutes', the episode with the girls and the reference to his alcoholism. What on earth was that all about?

"The alcoholism? He wanted it in. You got the email too. In fact it was sent to you. He specifically asked."

"I've not read it but, if so, he is a fucking idiot who needs saving from himself. I will tell him that myself. But please tell me you left your computer unlocked while someone else wrote this editorial piece as a piss take."

She read it out word by word.

GMP now has at its head a young Chief Constable who has got a top job earlier than he may have expected, but he is undaunted. His decision to talk about his alcoholism shows bravery and should be applauded.

He is unafraid to speak his mind. The clear, single purpose approach of crime fighting is going to be replaced by a more holistic approach. Many would say a more ambitious approach. It is not entirely clear what the future holds. One thing is for sure he believes he can do the job and not only restore some much needed confidence in GMP after some turbulent months but also improve the service it provides. We wish him well.

Please, where do I start? Yes at fucking 'holistic'. Yes a word we use a lot in the *MEN*."

"Well it's supportive."

I thought, perhaps, it is a word you might use on an editorial. I could see her point but I definitely did not intend to take the mickey the way she made out. She just twists everything.

"No it fucking is not. It reads we now have a naive fucking idiot in control who gets bullied at school could have his hat nicked off him at any moment. Further he is soft on crime and will get pissed when the going gets tough. In summary now you decide to royally take the piss out of GMP's Command to compensate for your failure to get any real stories about things that matter."

"Sarah, I was not trying to..... "

"Oh you were young lady, don't treat me as if I am stupid."

Off she went. The paper did have responsibilities to Manchester and that the paper wanted to build good relations after the damaging perceptions of Manchester that Mason's disappearance had left. Manchester is on the up and up and the paper was not here to drag it down. Been hearing more of this recently from her.

The whole thing needed a rewrite into something entirely bland, supportive and devoid of any meaning at all.

"Have you got that? Bland, supportive and devoid of meaning. Not a hint of piss take. Not one fucking wafer thin holistic hint of it. Clear?"

"So what is this? *Hello* magazine for GMP?"

I remember Neil using this phrase about the coverage of Mason. I just said it because it was a clever thing to say to annoy her. Well, I I had PMT.

She exploded, spit coming out of her mouth, which I have seen happen only once before. Ugh horrible.

"When I was a reporter for this paper…..."

Yes, everyone knows this story. You shagged the head of CID, Kevin Kershaw, for information. Indeed it had apparently developed into something of a love triangle with Kevin leaving his wife for a couple of nights before sulking back home with his unopened suitcases.

But Lord, look at you now, Sarah, spitting out of your manky mouth. Can't imagine you a sex siren even 15 years ago, overweight, oversized floppy boobs, grubby, needing a dental hygienist. Spend your life in the office by all accounts. No-one knows what you do on your days off. You are seriously blotching strawberry up your neck now though.

"……I would not be in the position of having to go along with everything GMP and the council wanted if I had reporters, like me fifteen years ago, and Neil, that gave me stories that would leave me in a stronger position, as an editor to be feared. To be feared. I cannot think of you ever getting anything useful. We don't have to print it but something we could hold over GMP to show we knew what was going on. Have you ever? Go on have you ever, ever got me a decent story? The Chief goes missing and you can't find one."

She actually pulled clippings from her bottom drawer in a folder marked 'Mason'.

"I keep this to remind myself of all those stories you never did. I had to read London papers to find out what was going on my own fucking doorstep."

We are going to do all this again are we? Apparently so. We did the lot.

Mason's money problems.

Sunday Telegraph. He owed a lot of money for someone on £200k so the nationals claimed and had missed two of his rent payments on his flat in Castlefield in the centre of Manchester. This produced articles on money problems potentially being the source of his problems, debt being so endemic in Britain that even men on £200k were not immune.

The story also mentioned an alternative theory, supposedly leaked from the enquiry, which suggested he may have been hiding his money and had now escaped with it. It was obvious there had not been a leak. It was no more than a detective had been unable to rule out a journalist's speculative questions. I tried to explain this to her.

"But it's a story you did not think of Missy."

Did the IRA kill Mason?

Daily Mail had discovered he had been a territorial soldier when younger and speculated on an IRA execution. The story started to speculate this may show a split in the IRA as the Provisionals would never have authorised such an assassination or even kidnap.

Common view was it did just not seem likely that this can have been so well organised by a splinter group as to seemingly not leave a clue. However the completeness of his disappearance suggested that whatever had occurred had been well planned and well executed. It is ridiculous to suggest this is something we would or could have run.

I did not even say anything to this, just shrugged my shoulders in insolence. She shrugged her shoulders back at me.

"Yes that is the best you can do isn't it? Just shrug your shoulders?"

Mason and the gangs.

Sunday Telegraph again. His disappearance may have been revenge for Mason's attack on organised crime in Manchester.

His much publicised (by me) Op Ocean multi agency attack on organised crime had certainly been deemed a success. Intervention at teenage level had almost ended random gun crime in South Manchester, the doorman industry in Manchester had been shown to have been heavily owned by organised crime, links between event car parking, door security, scrap metal dealing had all been exposed and convictions obtained. The main players, Hussein and Smith, had both been acquitted of murder charges but were seeing their profits dwindle.

Right I had had enough.

"I suggested doing a piece on this. You weren't sure. By the time I had got something innocuous together they had already run this piece."

"Don't recall that specifically but it does not take away from fact you were the local crime reporter when a major national story broke and you had nothing apart from that crappy pen-drive story."

She had a magazine on her desk.

"I read this last week. "

She showed it to me. It was an article comparing Richie Edwards to Roger Mason. It was entitled 'For Real'. It was about people who cared so much about what they did it drove them to the extremes and possibly to the brink of suicide.

"Yes it's a pile of utter shite but shows some fucking imagination. Something you know nothing about. Now you, you, when you do get a big piece to do you try to make Mason's successor look like a complete dick. If I did not know better I would think you were shagging Mason. I hope you were because that makes a kind of sense for your behaviour. If not well, if not it seems you are just really are what you seem to be........ a useless reporter with a soppy life."

Walked out before I cried in front of the bitch.

What was that all about though? She must know a regional paper just does not have the resources or financial muscle to compete with the nationals in standing up these speculative stories. She must surely know that?

More to the point, why does she hate me so much?

GINA

Just read on the BBC Manchester News on the internet.

Police are increasingly concerned for the safety of a Bob Brazier a PC who has gone missing

The picture of him must be a good ten years out of date. Still the same glasses, though, before they became wonky.

Oh Bob, what have you done?

He was later than usual for work today, which meant he was late. In Custody we change over about twenty minutes early. Most people keep to this which works well for everyone, apart from Bob. You see Bob has to be different, breeze in with only a few minutes to go. Of course it goes without saying that this did not stop him going early if he was relieved by others. That's Bob. Me, I have a hundred and one things to think about in my life and I am here twenty minutes early.

So my mobile number rings and it was not even 7 a.m., I felt my stomach drop. This early in the morning I felt there must be something wrong with Tammy, it had to be, the call you always dread, number withheld. It is never good news at such an hour. Steeled myself, please God.....

........it's Bob.

"Gina, Gina love. Just can't face work I just can't. Not today not, perhaps, ever. So I guess it's goodbye Gina. Yes goodbye Gina."

I found myself talking to a phone that had been already cut off. He never gave me time to talk. I have been repeatedly asked exactly what the words he said were. So I have written them down. Those were his exact words, I think.

And I have been asked how did he sound? Well how much can you tell from that? It was odd but there is not much more I can say. He was not laughing, he was not crying.

That tall good looking sergeant from Internal Affairs was supposed to be coming in today to tell Bob and Chris what restrictions they would have from working in the custody office. To be honest I had been tossing and turning at the thought of this. I have been doing this job for four years and been with those two all this time. Had a few jobs in GMP but none of them have seemed to work out. This sort of works because of Chris and Bob.

Do not know if I could cope with another team. I have worked with others on overtime and Bob and Chris are the best. I wouldn't want a woman as my boss, not that Tracy. Too strict. She has a little wind up alarm clocks that goes off every time you have to do the visits. Would definitely not get flyers off nights with her.

Anyway where was I? Oh yes I thought I better ring Bob back before I bothered Chris. After all it wasn't clear if he was taking a day off or going sick. I was a bit confused.

Straight to voicemail.

"Hi this is Bob. Don't bother leaving a message because I will not listen to it."

That was a new greeting. Can't remember what the old one said something about the bookies, the pub and the curry house. Bob playing silly buggers as usual.

Now it took me some time to work out why I didn't tell Chris straightaway what had happened. You see he was deep in conversation with the night custody sergeant handing over, so I did the visits. Then I got stuck on the phone with Cumbria police about a prisoner we had to pick up.

It was only when I could see Chris was trying to phone Bob I told him.

"Sorry Chris, Bob is not coming in today. He is sick."

"Bob? Sick? Today, of course. Bet he has thought of something stupid to say? Piles?"

So I told him what he had said and about the voicemail. Chris looked up to the ceiling. I could tell he was thinking this is Bob being Bob. We were busy and I could see Chris was pre-occupied so we didn't speak about it for a couple of hours until Chris made me repeat what Bob had said. He rang Bob's number a few times then just suddenly put on his civvie jacket. Told me was nipping round to Bob's.

I was all on my own, completely on my own. I just didn't know what to do. Uniform arrived with a prisoner about five minutes later. They had to stay with the prisoner in the holding area but I felt safer with someone around. I told them Chris had been called to see Mr Ashton suddenly.

Chris was back after 30 minutes. He booked the prisoner in quickly then called me into the back office. Bob's car was not on the drive. No answer at the door.

"What do you think Chris?"

"I think it's Bob being a dick, that's what I think."

"Don't you think we should tell someone, cover our backs."

Chris grimaced.

"Don't know Gina."

Then Mr Ashton appeared in the office. He was annoyed because he had had to buzz four times before he was let in. Had we heard from Bob? Apparently he had called round drunk at his girlfriend's a couple of hours ago (didn't know he had a girlfriend) and said he was off to his favourite place to end it all.

Well I can tell you when Mr Ashton found out what had been going on this morning he went berserk with Chris. All to the effect if Bob was found dead then questions would be asked and it all would be Chris's fault.

Within thirty minutes I was telling my story to D/S Keegan, a real gentleman, and Petey who has just gone into CID, who was taking notes. D/S Keegan was very thorough and precise. A real proper professional detective.

'Had Bob done anything like this before?'

'Could I write down precisely what he said?'

'When was the last time I listened to his voicemail message?'

'Why did I think Bob had rung me and not Chris?'

'What family does Bob have?'

'How was Bob when I last spoke to him?'

'What did I think was Bob's favourite place?'

The answer to the last was obvious, Mr Shabaz's and the White Horse. Oh and they asked me lots of other questions about things I would never have thought of.

Petey came back at about four o'clock to update us. Bob was not at home, or at least not answering the door. They could not pinpoint where his phone was as it had been switched off in the Preston area. His car had triggered a number plate camera thing in Kirby Lonsdale about an hour ago. Bob's next of kin were his mum and dad on holiday in Spain. The only thing they could say was that they used to holiday in Shap so they guessed Bob could be heading there. Sister had no idea where he was and his ex-wife said she had not seem him for six years.

Petey wanted to know whether he visited the Lake District? Was he a rambler?

"Bob gets a taxi to go to the pub not just come back from it," I told him. Chris laughed at that.

Petey took a call on his mobile. It was from the police at Bob's house, they had got a key from the neighbour. There were blister packets all over his kitchen table in disarray. They reckoned he had taken about hundred paracetamol.

JENNY

All I have ever wanted is to be comfortable. I don't just mean financially, I mean in life.

Isn't that what everybody normal wants, really?

It may sound strange but I could not understand my friends going to university living in dingy flats, getting drunk, and therefore hungover, having no money and eating beans on toast. I cannot see any fun in that. I wanted some money, my own bed and a regular life.

Took the job in the *Evening News* on secretarial. It suited, the tram trip into town from Altrincham, had my own room at my parents and some money to spend. I can honestly say I was at my happiest on Fridays watching TV with my parents in a warm house after a tiring week. I would have enough money to go out on Saturday, lie in on Sunday and save for a car.

An environment and local government reporter called Brian took an interest in me. Wondered what someone with my 'A' level grades was doing in secretarial. He got permission to take me out on some assignments and showed me how to do stories. Anyway his interest in me was not all it first seemed.

There was a horrible incident when he took me to an empty flat for a story on living in the City which I don't really want to talk about. Nothing happened, but only just. I mean I had to hit him to make it clear. So no big surprise to later find out he was not separated from his wife.

I felt so stupid that I felt I had to apply to be a reporter after all that had happened. It's strange, this showed a kind of lack of confidence but, in another way, it was the confidence I got from hitting him which encouraged me to apply.

Bottom line is that I went into reporting not sure if I would enjoy it, but I did. I had also by then saved up for a little Fiesta which the new job helped insure. I snogged Tim in a nightclub, went on dates, then holidays, then moved into a flat with him on Deansgate Locks.

I remember he told me I had 'an impossibly sexy body, but did not seem to know it'. I had forgotten that. Yes he did say things like that once.

I thought I liked comfort and routine but he is worse than me. Clerk in a solicitors, he watches Man United home and away including Europe, spends all his money on that. He otherwise lies on the couch watching Sky Sports with his hand down his trousers. I must be subsidising him, bet I am.

I was doing general reporting when Susan, deputy crime reporter, got pregnant. She had been having an affair with Brian who had left his wife. She seems happy. Makes you think though whether she knows about his methods, I mean how did they get together?

I had never wanted the crime job but felt flattered when offered it by Sarah. I was needed to provide some reporting balance, she told me, do some straightforward crime stories. Neil had become obsessed with the machinations of GMP and settling scores with senior officers and detectives who did not co-operate with him. He wasn't doing enough crime stories.

Then Neil is brought down by a crime story. I never quite understood what he had done but it was something along the lines of being in contact with a detective on a murder enquiry and using expenses to pay him for information, I think.

So all of a sudden I am full-time crime lead with a good pay rise. Sarah said that she wanted me to continue to be a proper crime reporter, stick to crime and less of police politics. She had chosen me as a sensible hard working choice who would be especially good with victims of crime and who could maintain good relations with all. I was to stay away from the politics.

Sarah now seems to forget she had been constantly praising me for my work and I had done some good features on tackling gun and gang crime and Manchester's night time economy. My stories were getting more hits on the website than Neil's had and were increasingly being used by the nationals.

Then Mason went missing.

Suppose it was deciding to come back off my holiday made me realise it had become a bit more than a job, more anyway than I had previously thought. I think I am good at it. The key, I have worked out, is not to take professional relationships seriously but to take those with the public seriously.

Have I explained that properly? I mean don't start getting worked up about the way the police treat you. Don't start getting off on gossiping about cops or inducing rabbit fear in senior officers about any story that places them in a bad light. Neil loved doing that. He also loathed the girls in GMP's press office too. He used to read out their press releases to the office, 'GMP is committed to' or 'GMP will not tolerate' or 'GMP is working tirelessly' in a stupid voice. They really upset him for some reason.

Conversely, though, you have to take the public seriously. I know Neil often would not knock on the door of the families of road accident victims. He would just report back no answer or that the family did not want to cooperate. Even as a general reporter I would get sent on crime stories, especially at weekends when staffing was thin. But I always knocked. It was part of the job and I tried to do it properly.

I remember going to one address and a young child had come to the door. I presumed it was the younger brother of the nineteen year old stabbed in a fight outside a chip shop and had asked whether his mummy or daddy was in.

"Daddy is in heaven," the child had replied, "but I will get Grandma."

By the time Grandma had come to the door I was in tears and had to be asked in and comforted by her. I got a really nice story. Hope you understand that was not my intention in crying.

I told the story to Neil later in the office.

"Well Jenny, as the old prostitute said 'when you start to come with the clients then you have to quit'," was his response. Put me off him for a very long time.

Perhaps it does indicate a problem I have. I don't have the killer instinct that Neil had. Then again he could not even knock on those doors.

I would not want to finish up like Sarah though if that's what it does to you. I have got by so far by solid reporting. Do not know why Sarah has taken against me so much, but that accusation of being a useless reporter, I don't know, it's made me realise I do want to be a proper reporter. I really do.

In fact I am going to show her. The fat bitch.

The fat, grimy teethed, floppy tits bitch.

CHARLOTTE

I have had a lovely life for twenty two years. Now I do not seem able to stop crying.

Being on attachment in custody that night was really bad luck, but things had been going wrong before then.

I keep thinking about that day just after my final exams at Durham, when Daddy had taken me to Manchester to Alan's flat.

Since I can remember Daddy has transported me uncomplaining, unfailingly, everywhere. Round Exeter to girlfriends, parties, clubs and then up to Durham. I would come home from Durham University after Christmas and Easter terms by train but when I needed to take everything home after each year he would turn up, after a night in a Travelodge, to take me and my gear home. I would watch downloaded films, headphones on in the passenger seat or just sleep, trusting while he drove.

This was the final journey though into full adulthood. Daddy to Durham, Travelodge, and then to Manchester with me to start my new life. It felt like he was giving me away. He had said he would be getting a smaller car from now onwards, the Saab he found 'too much'.

I had stayed in Alan's flat before but had always got to Manchester by train and not noticed how to get there by car. I had never needed to. I can recall Daddy actually woke me when we were close to the centre of Manchester and asked for directions. I had no idea where we were at all. I still don't. All I knew was Alan's flat was on Lever Street in the Northern Quarter, very close to town. I would recognise it when I saw it.

So as we headed into Manchester we had to ask for directions. No-one knew precisely other than the Northern Quarter was right in the centre of Manchester.

The Northern Quarter is a criss-cross of streets, some one way some not. Little back streets with lots of no entries, or no left or right turn. As we got increasingly disorientated it lost the bohemian feel I always felt it had. It suddenly seemed tatty, seedy. Saw things I had never seen or noticed before, sex shops, graffiti.

I kept thinking the next turn would show the street but we could not find it. Daddy was getting angry with me for not knowing where the flat was. It was so unlike him. I had just thought it being on a main road so close to town centre would make it easy for him to find. I remember at one point we were briefly on a tram line heading towards the Arndale with a tram behind us hooting. Daddy got really panicky.

When we did get on the right road I only recognised the flat at the last minute so we just could not stop and we had to drive past. We seemed to heading back towards the tramlines. Daddy suddenly swerved off without indicating or braking down a one way street against a no entry sign.

He stopped and exploded in anger.

"Charlotte you live your life in a dream world. How on earth did you think we were going to unload this stuff on a main road?"

He took off his glasses and put his head on the steering wheel which sounded the horn and made him jump up. He seemed to be on the verge of crying. A white van drove right up to us bumper to bumper. It seemed he expected Daddy to reverse back onto the main road. Daddy froze, literally, he did not speak or move.

The man got out to start an argument and went to Daddy's window. Daddy just stared ahead, did not acknowledge him at all. The man banged on the window.

"Fucking wanker."

This was accompanied, of course, by the hand gesture. It was horrible. He then got back into his van, reversed, and then inched past Daddy. As he went by he wound down his window.

"Get lost from Adair Street looking for somewhere for her to nosh you off? You dirty old wanker."

He felt compelled, again, to use the inevitable gesture. Daddy just looked straight ahead.

When the man had gone Daddy pulled the car forward onto the pavement a few yards further forward. I just knew he was not going to drive any further. So we got out with very little said and swapped places. I had never driven an automatic or an Estate before but after a 15 point turn I managed to turn the car round and back onto the main round. I drove some eighty yards back up the road and parked on the main road opposite the lights. Hazard warning lights on.

"If a warden comes we will just have to explain we are bumbling Devonians lost in the big city," I said, which was true.

Luckily Alan was in and came straight down. I felt stupid for not ringing him earlier. Daddy was happy to guard the car while Alan and I got everything into the foyer of the flats. Alan knew a car park where he could put it. Daddy had decided not to drive back that night after such a shock. Alan found a hotel for Daddy just round the corner. He said he would take us out for dinner.

It had been a hot day which I had not noticed because of the air-conditioning in the car. It was starting to cool, we sat out now in the creamy sunshine. Two glasses of white wine and chicken liver starter seem to have restored Daddy back to a sort of normality. He started to tell stories of his wedding night with Mummy; she had had some previous sexual experience but he had had none and he 'failed to come up to speed', as he put it. Alan nearly chocked on his food laughing. I was obviously shocked but I was just relieved he seemed back to a kind of normal.

I had thought there would be too much traffic and noise to sit outside the restaurant when we sat down but now traffic had calmed. People were walking past, there was (Alan's) laughter from our table, the noisy, seedy, urban tatty had turned back to bohemian. I suddenly had a sense of sublime happiness. Do they call it peak experience?

The days of being examined, subject to other people's judgement, were over. I was now a free adult. I was a country girl moving to the city like Eva Peron in Buenos Aires. The episode with my father seemed just one of those unfortunate events but no one was hurt. I actually felt me taking charge, driving the car, deciding to risk parking on double yellow lines when he would not have, further confirmed my move into adulthood.

Alan and I were to live together and I was to be a policewoman in Manchester. Not what Mummy and Daddy wanted but I was certain it was right for me. Everything I was doing seemed an affirmation of all I was, with the all freedom ahead of what I wanted to be.

And now?

And now you want to nip out to Tesco for some stuff you have to walk past dirty drunks and beggars. You don't get used to them. In fact they start to annoy, there is nothing really wrong with them, they are just professional beggars. They make me anxious though. It is hardly like going for a walk. Thought the neighbours would all be, I don't know "cool", but some look a bit what Daddy used to joke as 'lower deck'. They call the Northern Quarter 'shabby chic' but I am really unsure how that works. Shouldn't it just be 'shabby'?

I spoke to guy few weeks ago who was coming into the building same time as me. He lives on the floor below and invited me in for coffee. Ex-military in fifties, he runs some kind of mercenary security operation in Middle East, sounds exotic. He said not, it involved staying in his flat on the phone.

I have to tell you this, when I was in his flat he took a call. He said little, then said, "Charlie, you've just got to handle the situation. You are the man on the ground in Baghdad not me. Let me know if you think it can't be contained. Yeah just do it".

It was like in the films. 'Yeah just do it.' Fantastic.

Anyway he explained that he was the brother of the person who originally converted these flats. For some reason he sold the building on. The new landlord of this building sold most flats at a premium and then let the last few go to Housing Association. You sell at high prices and then deliberately run the place down so you could buy them back at a profit and then lease to Housing Associations for regular income.

"Is that the way it will all go?"

"Not sure maybe in some of the outer places but I don't think it will work in this block, there are ways of dealing with such things. My guess it will stay gentrified. You know what they say? In the future it may be how high you live which will determine your social status above the noise and in the clearer air."

"Like *Blade Runner*?"

"No idea what you are talking about, Charlotte."

He laughed.

I liked that he used my name. He was interesting to talk to. He was encouraging about me having a degree in Law and French from Durham University and joining the police but I could tell he had his doubts. Kept asking what my parents thought. Said seeing as though we both spent a lot of time on our hands during weekdays we should do lunch. Gave me his number and told me to knock on anytime see if he was free.

Alan just thinks it's creepy and should not go to any lunch. That stuff about the landlord anecdote is trying to sound worldly wise when it's just bullshit. He reckoned he had made up that Middle East phone call.

I would have gone, he isn't creepy, but Alan has now put me off. Don't want to cause any trouble.

The police has just been a disaster. The funny thing is the one night I spent with Sergeant Hayes, Bob and Gina was the happiest I have been. They were all really nice and gentle people. Loved Bob, could listen to him all day. Cleverer, in his own way, than nearly everyone at Durham.

'B' Group though is horrible. Everything is just so basic, reductive, whatever is the opposite of uplifting. Have you read that the police are taking more and more graduates? You would not think so. The talk is all of Big Brother, football, 'shagging', money and moaning. All the bosses are 'tossers', the public are 'shitheads' and women are either 'fit' or 'moose heads'.

Stupid repetitive phrases, 'wassup?' 'would you?' 'nice one' 'smashed it', they just moronically repeat to each other. There are so many in-jokes that I can barely understand them sometimes. They repeat the same thing to each other all the time, all the time. Usually the latest impression by Sergeant Parker. The latest two come from some lads who approached his car when he was in plain clothes; 'are yous C. I. Dees?' or the Asian kebab shop owners greeting, 'hallo mayt bin bizee?'

All the time, all the time the shift say it to each other. It just might be funny once but it can't be funny all the time. I just don't get it.

I was tutored by Darren. Nice enough lad but dull as dishwater. Think he is a bit on the fringes of the group and tries hard to fit in. He does not do the impressions. He would like to but cannot do the voices and is frightened of the ridicule.

I told him that Alan and I had been to see to Opera North's *Madama Butterfly* at the Lowry Theatre. Mistake.

"I hear Charlotte likes opera. Give us a song Charlotte," was the Sergeant Parker attempt at repartee when we were all in the van on overlap on Saturday night. He then tried to sing *Just One Cornetto*. Side splitting, apparently, by the reaction.

Next time we were on overlap they thought it would be hilarious to tie me to a chair on castors and drive round in the PSU van with me rolling around. Alan thinks I should have taken it further but everyone knows what happened and no-one seems to be bothered.

Been asked out twice now by Sergeant Parker who is married and plain creepy and also by Petey who has gone to CID. Both asked me out for a drink. No effort to find out whether I had a partner or to hide that they had partners also. Also how does asking me out twice work? I said no first time but now I would suddenly give in second time after he showed me pictures of his torso and muscles? As if that would suddenly swing it.

But do you know what the thing that sticks in mind most? It is not even the low animal amorality of it all. It's not that, it's the fact that it is for 'a drink', not a meal or a show or to go somewhere. A lousy, cheap drink.

Daddy has been diagnosed with some kind of dementia, of course, to do with the blood supply to his brain. I went down to see him last week and he has really deteriorated quickly. He could not really put a proper sentence together. He seemed to be blissfully unaware of what was really going on but then as I came to say good bye he started to cry. Wet tears on my cheek. Poor Mummy.

I just guess my vision of joining the police was romantic and I definitely don't want to stay in Manchester. It's just a bad luck place.

Alan? Don't know, it's not his fault all this did not work out but he seems to come with the bad luck. Be wrong to break up with him now when all this is going on. I may not be seeing straight.

I think I will go back to Devon for Christmas and I may just stay there, help Mummy and then see what I want to do with my life.

I have always been happy until I came to Manchester. Now I can cry at any moment.

JENNY

I was rather hoping, perhaps expecting, Jesse's mum would be deranged and angry with grief, firing off accusations. Should have learnt by now you never get what you expect when you knock on the door. Dolores Maitland was not like that at all. I loved her.

House was on a main road through a council estate in Miles Platting. Dark and small inside, it was old fashioned with antimacassars on the chairs, the ticking of a grandfather clock. Pictures of family everywhere on the walls, no clutter other than books stacked on the floor next to her chair.

Tea served on a tray with cups and saucers with homemade cake, orange and polenta. She had a faint old school Jamaican accent. She spoke slowly, but moved quicker and was dressed younger than her years in jeans and high T-shirt and slippers. Her hair was unusually short and perfectly grey/white. Dignified, is the word.

She was actually Jesse's grandmother but had brought him up as her own son as the effective youngest of six. She showed me pictures of graduations of her children, and then her grandchildren and their achievements at school.

Jesse's mum? Had become a heroin addict in her teenage years when she had had Jesse, having met a 'rascal' called Brooks. She had tried to do everything for her including chaining her to the radiator for three weeks once, but the drugs had got its grip. She now did not even know whether she was alive or dead. There were no adult pictures of her on the walls.

"The thing is lovey, Jesse's death, he won't live, is all my fault. All my fault. I took him as a baby but just never felt the same about him as I did my own. He'd cry all the time and vomit up his milk and I got tired of it. I had already had five children. I took him because it was the Christian thing to do and felt I should. Not sure I had a real choice, but this heart was not in it and I just did not bond with him. I knew as a baby it was a mistake. I think he was damaged anyway by his mum being an alcoholic 'fetal…. something syndrome'. I know it its 'fetal…'"

She just stopped, shook her head.

"Old age lovey. I could have told you this six months ago. Anyway I just did not love him like the other children. There is no more to be said lovey, no more to be said."

I thought that was going to be the end of what she said. She just sat in silence. I was trying to think of something. She suddenly started up again.

"I knew he wouldn't be as clever as my children even though his mother was sharp. He just did not achieve or try as much as his other brothers and sisters. I did not push him or encourage him or love him though. His other brother and sisters were that much older than him that they did not see the differences in the way they were treated. My husband had died. The only person who knew was Jesse, he knew I was giving up.

And my, he always wanted me to love him. He did try at school at very first but he just was not as bright as his brothers and sisters. In a different family he may have been ok or perhaps if I had encouraged him a bit more….but he went the way of Julia bit by bit. I did not chain him up like her and to be honest I was happy to see him go.

It is just that when he was drunk or sometimes on drugs he would come back to the flat. I never changed the locks and I always left out twenty pounds which I would put next to the phone to make sure he did not take something valuable. We understood each other but he changed in the last few months. He would come back and would want to sleep in the spare room. He would ask if he could stay here. He said he would give up the drugs and the booze and get a job as a chef. He said I could chain him up if that's what it took.

He used to say he would look after me in my old age which would be more than his brothers and sisters were doing who had moved away…. but it was talk, I suppose, he was full of talk. Talk, talk, talk.

The night the police took him away he had come back roaring drunk, roaring. It was only 5.30. We hardly spoke and he just sat there blankly looking at the TV. The thing was he smelt badly and for some reason I just wanted rid of him, you see I've not been well recently. He kept going on about why I had never chained him to the radiator like I had done to his mum.

I could have left him and he may have fallen asleep. I had called the police before when he was being difficult. They were always good to me and took him away. So I called, I said he was being difficult and was bothering me, when he wasn't really, and I had four police at the house within minutes.

I recognised two of them who had been here before. The sergeant, nice man I think, said as he was leaving, 'don't worry Mrs Maitland we will sort him out', that's what he said. They just picked him up off the sofa you are sitting on and tried to walk him out of the house. He started dragging his legs and then they picked him up one with an arm and a leg each. There was no trouble or anything like that………….

…..God forgive me. The people have asked me if I had any alcohol in the house but I don't. I just don't know where he got that bottle from of vodka from. Wasn't here."

She was impassive. If she felt anything she was holding it back, sat ramrod straight in the chair.

Usually people are trying to manipulate me for their story. Sometimes they are too frightened to tell me anything because I am a reporter. This was very different. Mrs Maitland had not said what she did or did not want publishing but wasn't the time to ask yet. There was a long silence. I gazed on the religious artefacts on the wall. She saw me looking.

"Do you believe lovey?"

She didn't wait for an answer.

"Not sure I do, not anymore, if I ever did. I keep thinking about how Jesus only came recently and what happens to the souls who lived before him. What happens to Chinese people who've never read the Bible? I have lived this long life sort of believing but I don't know......look lovey just do a nice story about Jesse, please. A nice story. I am sure you will, but don't do the grieving mother because it would not be right. It's my fault he is in that hospital."

She sat there staring outside into the autumnal gloom. The interview was over but she did not get up.

Loud children, just out of school, passed the window but her eyes did not move to follow them.

MARTHA

Jesse was in hospital for three days and no one told us. I found out when a friend texted me asking me if I was alright. She had read about Jesse in the *Manchester Evening News*.

Rang my mum. She said the police had put a note through her door couple of days ago, whilst she was at the doctors, asking her to contact them. It had got caught up in the junk mail she gets.

They had left a message on her voicemail to ring them but no number. She rang the switchboard who put her through to custody but the person there simply said they weren't holding anyone of that name. She thought Jesse had simply asked her to be notified of his arrest, he would now have been released and hadn't thought any more of it.

My mum found out when a couple from the IPCC came round. They thought the police had told her about Jesse. I am not sure she grasped the seriousness of the matter. Not ringing me was bizarre though, I am usually the first port of call.

I drove up from Coventry the minute I had spoken to mum on the phone. She had not even seen Jesse in hospital. It was Saturday morning before we saw him, a body connected to tubes. My mum did not even touch him, just stared speechless.

Doctor was a Nigerian guy, his English was execrable, not convinced of his medical abilities. As usual I got the full run down from a nurse. Of course, it being the weekend, the IPCC were closed and the police no better.

Mum was so different, robotic, diffident, passive. Nothing like the woman who brought us up. She didn't even really seem pleased to see me. She didn't ask about the children. What had she been to see the doctor for? No real answer, her knee. When I asked to see it she decided it wasn't about her knee.

She didn't volunteer any information about what had happened to Jesse either. It came in dribs and drabs. It was her who had called the police to take Jesse away because he had come round drunk to take money off her. The police had put him in a cell and early that next morning they had found him unresponsive. That's all she knew. A reporter from the *Evening News* was coming round to see her on Monday afternoon to do a fuller story.

Did she want me to take her to see Jesse again on Sunday? No thanks, she had church that day and that would be enough. I did not want to go but could tell she did not want me to stay. So back onto the motorway to face Sebastian, the kids and the havoc caused by me being away for one whole day.

Monday morning when everyone was back at work was no better. No one was available to talk. I had to leave messages while I did my rounds. Got a voicemail from a Zoe at the IPCC, she had seen my mum and told her all she could. I was welcome to be with Mum next time they saw her. Well, thanks for that.

I was driving home when I got a call from a Manchester number at last. It was a Jenny from the *Evening News*. She had just seen Mum now.

"How was she?"

"Well fine I think, considering. I am used to visiting distressed relatives. I wouldn't…….."

"No I know that Jenny it's just she seemed different when I saw her this weekend."

"She didn't say you had been up. You live down South?"

"Coventry, south of Birmingham anyway. Look sorry to mither Jenny but as someone who had not met her before how would you describe her?

"Er, I really don't know what to say. A bit stop start. There were very long periods of quiet with her."

"Lucid then confusion then lucid."

"Yes I suppose."

"Jenny, no-one is telling me anything about Jesse. What do you know?"

She told me that she knew Jesse had been taken away at Mum's request and been placed in a cell to sleep off the drink. She had heard from a police source that they hadn't visited him in the cell for a couple of hours but he seemed to be alright because he was snoring loudly.

"You are joking. That's a sign the airways are constricted. Don't they know anything?"

"That's useful to know."

"They did not know that? They told you that as a good thing? Seriously, as a good thing? What do they teach them? You know this happens all the time don't you Jenny?"

I had been doing my research on Sunday night.

"All the time, Jesse is hardly exceptional. The police are being called to people, mainly black by the way, in some form of distress usually some acute mental episode and needing help. The police only deal with these things in one kind of way with is control and restraint, control and restraint. That's all they know. It's all they are taught. So they finish up killing these people.

Trust me that is what is happening. It's been going on since Colin Roach and Mikey Powell and it has never changed. You would have thought it would have but it really has not. It really has not. People are being held face down on the floor outside and in vans.

If Jesse was as drunk as the police say then being held down for even a very short period of time can be very dangerous and stop his breathing. The police aren't daft. This does not happen in custody offices on camera but occurs in vans where there aren't cameras. You hope it is not racism but you can't help but wonder.

Sorry I have ranted. I have a load of stuff I can send you at home when I get back. Did Mum say anything about the way the police treated Jesse?"

"Yes she said they were nice. Nothing more. Look sure you are right about some of what you've said. Have been doing some research myself but, at the end of the day, your mum says not."

"Ok just wondering if Mum was playing it down because she feels guilty about calling them. Look Jenny got to go, think I have got the police trying to get through, been waiting all day to speak to them. Ring you later.......Hello Martha Maitland."

"Hello this is Chief Inspector Brian Ashton from North Manchester Division. Is that Martha Brooks, sister of Jesse? "

"No its Martha Maitland, sister of Jesse Brooks."

"Yes I am so sorry I just assumed. You are married now."

"No I am not married."

I am, but not going to explain further to him. Long pause, I am not going to help.

"Ok well what can I do for you?"

Not much it transpires, and no real apology for taking three days to tell my mum her son was in intensive care. Refused to divulge any 'operational detail'. Then he wanted to know how I knew what I did know, apparently I wasn't supposed to know. It quickly got into a ping pong argument of why he thought I should not know what had happened to my own brother. I would not budge and decided I would stay and argue for as long as it took.

I was actually parked on the driveway of the childminder for ages. I knew she would be irritated and want me to just get the kids but I was not for conceding anything to an idiot like him. Nanny emerged from her house with them in their anoraks just as Chief Inspector Ashton tried to wind up.

"Look Miss Maitland let's just hope he pulls through. In my experience people like this often do."

"Well Chief Inspector Ashton if by 'people like this' you mean people with decompensated liver disease with a low GCS reading before ventilation then I have to say in my experience 'people like this' do not pull through."

"What are you, a Doctor?"

JENNY

My idea that of a police brutality splash story had fallen at the very first hurdle i.e. the facts.

You always want that bigger story but somehow the reality of what you find out never comes up to the mark. Pervy Brian told me that. It was trying to sex up the story that got you ultimately into trouble, probably what did for Neil.

I have a picture of Jesse some seven years ago on a school trip. I will do a feature on him as a liked pupil at school who had wanted a career as a DJ. I think people see through these pieces though; career as a DJ= unemployed, old picture = now an emaciated addict.

GMP press won't say anything at all as the matter is entirely with the IPCC. They won't even confirm or deny the two hour missed visits and the snoring. IPCC press even more difficult than GMP's as they always say nothing. I decided to try the investigator directly, Phil Hattersley, have his number from a fatal road traffic pursuit he attended some months ago. He looks like Dec from Ant and Dec that is when Dec was 15 years old. That would make him PJ or Duncan? Don't know which one is which.

Missed call but he rings back within five minutes but from a withheld number, which is always promising. Surprisingly he wants to talk, it's clear he doesn't like the officers. Story he reckons is a runner. Brooks had been carried into the cells as he had not been able to stand up when he came in. The problem was that anyone so drunk that they cannot stand up should have been taken to hospital.

He was on half hour visits and, I was right, the visits seem to have stopped at about 2 a.m. and he was only discovered to be struggling at 4.30 a.m.. Police do not seem to have visited him at all in that period although they claim they walked past the cells and could hear him snoring. They had also made an almighty balls up of getting the ambulance. They were trying to piece together from the taped calls and the CCTV log what did actually happen.

It looks as if he has suffered brain damage and that earlier intervention could have helped. They found an empty bottle in the cell. Brooks, it appears, had not been searched properly. Could I not mention the bottle until they had done more work?

There was a sergeant and two PCs under investigation and they had been restricted in their duties so they could not work in custody.

Well that was more than any IPCC investigator has ever told me. Shame he ended it with the weaselly repeat of 'do not ascribe to me and in future go through the press office so there is no suspicion on me' as he was beginning to impress me.

Hattersley was clearly thinking he was some kind of Deep Throat when all he was doing was setting out what were the facts of the case. The only area where perhaps could be accused of straying into speculation was that if Jesse had received treatment earlier he could have been saved from what appeared to be brain damage. Seen enough of Coroners' enquiries to know that this kind of claim is always contentious, also seen enough to know no-one could also say this was wrong.

I wonder what had provoked this limited outbreak of openness? Beginnings of a story though.

I know what Neil would do now. Why not? This will spook Hattersley. Text to his mobile.

`Thanks for that info, really useful. Anytime you want to do lunch bell me Jennyxx`

Neil's theory is that people in bureaucracies are spooked by even a basic recorded acknowledgement of a relationship from a journalist they worry about what you may do next. So they continue talking to you to take or regain control.

GMP won't, of course, give out the names of the restricted officers. Back to Hattersley on his mobile. He answered straight away now. Did he have the names of the restricted officers?

"Sergeant Christopher Hayes, PC Robert Brazier, PW Charlotte Purvis."

He would never have answered or given me those names if I had not sent that text. After all he had not given me them in the first place, had he?

The subtlest of blackmail. Yes, think I have makings of a good story here. Yet I know I am missing something bigger.

CHRIS

There's hardly an international manhunt for Bob.

He has switched off his phone, his car is not registering on ANPR and he is not using his bank cards. No way of easily locating him but, after the flurry of the first day, everyone has lost interest. As Tony Keegan said he is either dead or ok. He clearly isn't overly concerned which one it is.

He's not on his own. Bob's parents didn't see fit to cancel their holiday in Spain. His girlfriend couldn't care less. She has gone to London and they are struggling to find her. The station is hardly in mourning either. No one cares.

I've been thinking if you kill someone insignificant, and can make it look like they have just gone missing, you will get away with it. No-one gives a shit after a while.

Gina, of course, has talked about it non-stop and got a bit emotional yesterday in the custody office. The effect was ruined somewhat when she started to speculate on who would replace Bob (if he was dead). A whole list of characters she did not want to work with, Tracy being top of the list.

In general though the whole thing has perked up Gina. Other people's problems are her speciality alright. She has started turning up earlier for work I am sure because she is so excited and does not want to miss out on anything. Sure she has been sprucing herself for Tony Keegan last couple of days too. Personal numbers exchanged so he can 'update' her on her days off.

Do I even care about Bob? Not sure I do much. I have spent most of the time trying to work out how his disappearance affects the Brooks case. Well how it affects my position to be precise.

Do I think of what might have happened to him when I go to bed? No, I think of Gina. She will be lying in bed now next to Peter Sutcliffe, probably thinking of Tony Keegan.

PAUL

I have always thought of my life as a graph. Am I going up or down?

For a very long time it was trending up. Up, since I failed every exam at school, got sacked from my only paid job, got Janice pregnant at seventeen, teamed up with Johnny, got into the drugs trade, then another unwanted pregnancy and even when I was charged with the Gatland murder (acquitted), up. It was always trending up.

Then came the *MEN* article. Front page.

Gangster No 1

Picture of me flat-capped, putting the grandkids into my Vectra outside a school in Chadderton. Since then it has been going slowly down. Surely, slowly, down.

I left school as soon as I could. Did not want a trade, did not want to work for someone in an office, a wage slave, I just always wanted to do my own thing. I bought and sold clothing, seconds from Barney at the mill in Newton Heath and sold them on Harpurhey market. Soon as I parked up in the morning I would be surrounded by Pakis, mainly women. Would have most of the stock sold in half an hour. It was good money, easy money.

But it was glasses that really got me started. Barney put me onto a bloke that had a garage full of glasses; pints, halves, wine glasses. A garage full. I could not tell you if they were nicked or it was a bankruptcy thing but I got them for under a grand, which was all I had then.

As soon as I got them I realised why they were so cheap. You have to sell them on. No-one is going to buy a garage full of glasses from you. So I realised I had to sell them box by box, glass by glass. I went into every pub, set up market stalls all around Manchester and sold and sold. I reckon it was four months of hard selling, day in day out that summer. Finished up with fifteen thousand. I kept the last pint pot and have it on display in my lounge.

That is what made me. Pint pots, not drugs.

Few months later I still had £15k in the bank, a pregnant fiancée, was pissed off freezing to death on the market and worn out by Pakis trying to knock you down on price.

I met Pete Keane with Johnny in the Wellington one night. They needed finance to buy some gear from a guy in Oldham who was branching out on his own. Pete was a stand-up guy, as thick wannabe drug dealing shitheads go, and I couldn't believe anyone would dare to try to rip off Johnny, so why not?

And that's it. I soon packed in the market. We built the business. Good money was made by all. A pecking order developed and the rest was inevitable. Pete was not bright enough to stay out of prison, Johnny did a bit of time for assaults but got away with most of what he did. I had some real money.

Very soon, though, you get to a point where the game is no longer advancement but to protect your position and that was, and is, the beauty of Johnny. He was good at protecting our position. He was very good at it. I can honestly say we never went after anyone or sought any trouble, but common sense simply dictated on occasions some pre-emptive action was needed. Johnny liked pre-emptive action.

And if you want some longevity in this game you also cannot stray too far from home too. You have to be with people and in places you know and trust. In fact, you have to stick to what you know in everything. So I didn't stray. I bought a four bedroomed detached in Chadderton, I stayed married to Janice, I rarely ventured out of North Manchester.

I learnt to have a life nicely contained, neatly separated. Yes that is something I learnt I could do, keep matters compartmentalised. I still have a whole other life Janice just does not know about. A different me. For years I felt I played it just right, made enough money but did not overstretch. I had everything nicely in order.

Then came Roger fucking Mason, his war on gangs and then the Gatland murder charge. They never had any real evidence against me but I would be lost if Johnny got sent down. I got some help from Jamal which helped secure the acquittal of both of us though.

And I had got away with it. You know the saying, well I have actually done it. I have got away with murder. With one bound Jack was free. I walked out of the dock into the courtroom. I didn't even go back to the cells to be documented and released. I was a free man after all. I could do what I wanted.

Few people can have any idea how that feels. To be involved in killing someone and then be cleared, absolved. It's like you have broken through the clouds above everything. Sometimes I felt dizzy with the exhilaration. The rules didn't apply to me. The rules applied to everyone else, but not me.

It was the highest point on the graph, almost off the scale, but it didn't last long.

The *MEN* article, front page, headline.

GANGSTER No.1

It was worst for Janice. She had visited me in prison before the trial. I had insisted that it was a mistake getting caught up with Johnny but I was an innocent man.

"Do I look like a gangster Janice? Do I behave like one? Would I let you down?"

"I don't know Johnny there's no smoke without fire."

I got the benefit of the doubt from her after the acquittal. She ignored the smoke. But then the article came. It was never quite the same after that between us. She resented most the loss of friends and the distancing of her family.

Of course, I also had debts from the trial. I had paid £100k up front to the solicitors and barrister for the pleasure of them looking down their noses at me. I also owed far more to Jamal for his 'consultancy services' in securing my acquittal.

If I made a mistake though it was not taking the advice of my most trusted advisor. She reckoned I should get Johnny to slice the reporter, Jenny Aaronovitch. I thought it made no sense and just drew attention to myself. Plus if any word got back to Janice I was finished. I hadn't fully realised the days of staying under the radar were over though.

Mine wasn't the only article that week too. There was one on Jamal too. It was clear Mason had authorised information to go the *MEN*. The collapse of the two trials had embarrassed him and it was his way of getting back at us.

But, unlike me, Jamal fought back. He did what Jamal does. He sued the paper. Won. Then went on *Granada Reports* to demand the Chief Constable be sacked. Now he wants to stand as MP for Salford.

People wonder why he does all this, but looking back on it he's right. Once you are out there, you can't take anything lying down. If you do you are finished. I should have made an example of that Aaronovitch, got some respect back.

Since that article my margins have been cut. Bruens and the Keanes are paying me less for the stuff. Jamal keeps inventing extra charges for his services. Six months ago someone threw a petrol bomb against my front door. Fairly sure it was Jamal's boys, he's annoyed he isn't seen as Gangster No 1. Since then Janice has made me feel not entirely welcome in my own home.

Then the call re Dacic. Perhaps the graph line could turn up again?

£50k would help keep Jamal off my back. It also seemed a like a bit of excitement, glamour. I was breaking my own rules, stepping outside of what I knew, but I couldn't see much downside to it. Quite the opposite, perhaps it was the time to strike out, be a bit more like Jamal. I know Janice actually became worried when I suggested we go shopping, have a meal and then stay in a suite at the Lowry. She would have preferred a takeaway, film and our own bed.

"What's come over you?" she asked. Should have listened to her.

Shopping in Manchester I picked out a navy Paul Smith (well yes) suit for the meeting and some Loakes. Janice loved the suite at the Lowry and she did that thing where you fall backwards on the bed with your shopping. She had a bath for over an hour and we went out to eat at the new high rise Hilton. I would have been happy to stay in the Lowry but Janice wanted to step out.

You know I enjoyed it all and started to think I should do more of this. I have worked for it after all. Perhaps this is also what Janice wants as well.

I had packed some blue pills Johnny had got snide from China and popped one whilst Janice was getting ready for bed. Shouldn't have bothered. She put on her new blue M and S pyjamas she had bought, got into bed, thanked me for a wonderful day and was asleep immediately.

Up but nowhere to go. Had a thinker on my barrister friend Sheila. Then what? Janice's snoring was driving me mad. I have a spare room I can bail out to back at home but I was stuck here. I couldn't sleep in a strange bed and it was well past three before I slept. You should stick to what you know.

Of course I woke up totally bunged up from the pill. Steaming hot shower didn't entirely clear it. Packed Janice off after breakfast, not before she tells me not to wear a tie with the suit, it's the latest fashion. Where did she get that from? She was right though.

The meeting was set for a room in the Lowry. Just Dacic, me and the Charlies. I told Dacic's agent we would meet for fifteen minutes before and that they were to leave all the talking to me. Kept stressing that, leave all the talking to me.

I felt good in the suit, tan shoes, white shirt. Sat in the reception of the Lowry, coffee and pastry, I felt like I was a proper player. I was experiencing a bit of the high life gangsters are supposed to enjoy. Looked forward to controlling that meeting and a successful outcome. Forgot all about what time I had got to sleep, and the dull ache in the sinuses.

So I thought I better check out at reception where the meeting was. Anyway the meeting rooms, it transpired, were booked up. I rang the agent but he had a foreign ringtone and wasn't answering. PR guy who set it up was unavailable too. I didn't have Dacic's number.

Christ, was I being set up? Surely this is the last place Jamal would make a move? Was it? Why would he go to such lengths? No there must be a mistake somewhere. I went back to reception, perhaps one of the booked rooms was really ours and booked in a different name for some reason. Supercilious puff behind reception was certain, all were already in use and had been all day.

I was just about to walk out sensing something was up. It then occurred to me perhaps they had booked a hotel room instead. Wasn't going to make a cunt of myself a third time and ask him to check, so just sat down. Someone had taken the pastry and coffee away.

"Mr Smith, Mr Smith."

The guy at reception beckoned me back excitedly phone in hand.

"It just occurred to me and voilà I was right. Your meeting is at the Lowry Theatre, not here. People get confused all the time usually mistaking the theatre for us, so I just thought perhaps, could be the other way round and yes I was right. Aren't I the brightest button in the box today?"

He clapped his hands together in front of his face.

"Sooo... I guess you need a taxi?"

I had no other option. I had five minutes to go to get there on time, to hurry things up I waited outside. I had been there only a minute when I noticed reception guy was now stood right next to me. He spoke out of the side of his mouth.

"The label is still hanging from the bottom of your jacket."

He had a pair of scissors in his hand. He raised the scissors up as if for permission and cut the label off.

 He winked at me.

"Good luck with your meeting Paul, love the shoes."

CHRIS

Bob was actually down in the cells visiting prisoners when I came in. So it was only about 7.30 when I realised he was actually back at work. Gina said he had been there when she got into work. Of course she did not think to tell me.

I wanted to feign indifference but couldn't raise the energy to do so. I set off into the cell complex to find him. He was deep in conversation with a prisoner in a cell, some mid-thirties woman. She had her knees up eating breakfast. Breakfast that Bob had been bothered to make, well microwave. Perhaps he is unwell after all.

"Well good morning Christopher. Do you know Maria? Brought in by the night crew for a fail to appear warrant. Miserable bastards, she had told them she would come in this morning but they wouldn't let her off. Maria, Chris."

I nod to Maria. Yes seen her before, long time ago though. Bob gets up.

"Can't stay here all day. Work to be done."

I bundle Bob into the side room where we had met the IPCC.

"Well, what's going on?"

"Turned over a new leaf, Christopher, and I am from henceforth going to be a model caring custody clerk. You know Maria, good shoplifter and credit card merchant? Says she does it to support her kid but has a very nice flat in Prestwich actually thank you very much. Seems to have gone all the way of the world, got on the smack and was found on Adair Street last night loitering for the purposes of. Has not turned up at court, which is unlike her, so there's a warrant for her arrest.

Haven't seen her for the longest time. She was telling me that she had begged them to let her hand herself in this morning because she had her kid at home with a paid babysitter. They had to ring her mum to collect the kid. She was just asking me whether she would get sent down today and could I get her a message to her mum if she was? She had never failed to appear before today so she should be alright. Women don't get sent to prison.

She should be on the way to court shortly so she won't see the drugs workers. I told her I would get her some leaflets so she can refer herself on for treatment."

"Marvellous. I am so interested in Maria I can't shit Bob. I am so glad you took the time to tell me all that, and in such detail too. I look forward to working with the new caring and diligent Bob. I think they run night classes in counselling at Abraham Moss Tec. Anything else, Bob?"

Bob does the bemused look. Not a hint of a smile.

"Nice break Bob?"

"Yes just needed to clear my head for a few days. Had some bracing walks on the West Coast etc. Some nice pubs selling that speckled mothers shag type of thing to Steeleye Span lovers. All around my hat, you know, too loo ray eh."

"Bracing walks, of course Bob. Do you know people were looking for you?"

"Yes just saw some note on my kitchen table when I got in this morning something about ringing Tony Keegan. He will be in about 8.30. I will bell him then. Problem?"

"Yes problem. People were looking for you? Where did you stay?"

"Camping in a farmer's field. You know me Christopher, eternal Boy Scout. Then got a caravan in Shap, bit too cold in the field."

"Camping?"

"Yes loved it all so much stayed until very late last night and have just only got back for a shower at mine and then came straight here. Bit early I am so invigorated."

"Camping? I am thinking of camping this year. Would you lend me your gear?"

"Most welcome Christopher. Just give me the word. It's old, mind you, fucking hard to put up but sturdier than the newer pop-up shitty ones."

"Course, Bob. Is it still in your car? You could hand it over now?"

"No put it in the garage soon as I got back."

"Shame, I'll pick it up on the way home sometime. And your girlfriend, never knew about her, what's her name?"

Bob more uncomfortable, now moving from foot to foot.

"Wouldn't say she is a girlfriend, more of an economic arrangement you know Chris. Man cannot live by bread alone."

God, he is uneasy. This is new.

"Why? What did she say? What? What do you know?"

"Said you were off to kill yourself"

"Oh bollocks the stupid cow. I told her clearly I was off to Shap for a few days to clear my head. I think she was upset at not getting invited. You know missing out on the old Brazier steam hammer love magic."

"All those paracetamol tablets?"

"Well had a banging head so was looking through an old medication tin to find some. All I could find was loads of discarded packets that I have put back in the tin, must have left them on kitchen table. Wasn't expecting my house to be broken into after all. Have to say I feel a bit violated. They didn't bother my parents did they? They are elderly you know."

"Bob, you are a dick."

"Sergeant, I know you missed me. We all need a little time, a little space. Come on give me a smile."

Gina's head appears at the door. Escorts are ready to take the prisoners to court but they need the sign off from the sergeant.

Two G4S staff are slumped over the counter. Its 7.45 and they already look exhausted. It's old Ron with some scruffy kid I haven't seen before seen before. G4S always had new staff.

"Morning Sarge only three today, one female is that right?"

Ron, in thick flat Scouse accent.

"Yes, Bob and Gina just getting them now."

Bob reappears stuffing some drugs information leaflets, I presume, into an envelope for that Maria. I thought he was joking when he said he was going to do that. He grins to see it is Ron. Here we go.

"Aha Ronald my little Heysel-denying friend. What's not your fault this week?"

Ron isn't for biting today. He does not turn to Bob but stares ahead at me over the counter. Dull weary tone.

"He's going to get you in trouble one day Sergeant, mark my words."

JENNY

How does memory works? I knew there was something more to the Jesse Brooks story. Then returning back to bed last night after getting up for a pee, woken by Tim's complacent snoring, I remembered it. Robert Brazier is Bob Brazier, the guy who was missing in the Lakes.

After the usual pain of speaking to the press office I found that he had returned today. They say it had been a misunderstanding, that he had been on holiday and that he had turned up for work in custody today.

Bit of a let-down, thought there may be another angle there. I wrote a bland piece about Jesse but just couldn't get an angle on the main story. I decided it would be best to do a straight factual story and not use the IPCC stuff yet. Will create more of a splash on a follow up piece. Truth is I still felt I was missing something.

So I rang Martha, Jesse's sister, who had left a message with the news desk to ring her. She was still stuck on the police brutality thing which was a non-starter. Anyway during the conversation it transpired she did not know about the bottle in the cell. She went quiet the minute I told her.

"Martha, shouldn't have told you this, well I mean can you not mention it yet that you know?"

"Yes I understand but you will publish won't you? I cannot keep quiet for long. I just cannot understand why the IPCC haven't told me."

I should have remembered she was her mother's daughter, that unexpected reasonableness and intelligence.

No sooner had I put the phone down I realised the memory itch had not gone away. Something I am still missing. I have been sat here for fifteen minutes now. Must be the conversation I have just had with Martha. Was he assaulted before he came into custody? Snoring? IPCC not telling Martha? The bottle?

Perhaps my mind is still playing tricks with me. Perhaps this is just an echo of what I had missed previously. Anyway I am wasting time. I will write a straight story for now and then follow it up with more details in a follow up article.

Half way through the article it comes to me. Glance at the clock, 2.30 p.m., he should still be there. Pick up the phone and ask to be put through to North Manchester Custody.

"Custody, PC Robert Brazier, how can I help you this fine afternoon?"

Robert Brazier.

'Back of the net,' as Tim would say.

CLARA

The thing about the police is that everyone has known everyone else for a very long time. You are told a story demonstrating someone's abilities or, usually, shortcomings. Then you find out this happened twenty years ago. It's all very unhealthy but it's the stream you have to swim in.

It's obviously alienating for newcomers too, as you are never quite sure who knows who. No-one helped me when I joined, really helped me understand who I was dealing with. Sharon Bentley called me and said she would fill me in on the 'bedwetting boys' club that was GMP' but we never got diaries to match. I had been hoping that my mentor would be able to start piecing things together for me. So who did I get as a mentor? Gabriel Hooker. Roger's sense of humour I suppose or perhaps quiet revenge?

First time I was to meet him for a mentoring session I knew that gossip wouldn't be high on his agenda but I still had a host of things I wanted to talk about, practical stuff. So he took me to a tiny lounge area off the 11th floor and put a 'Do not Disturb' sign on the door.

I think I can just about remember his opening gambit.

"Well Clara, we are all put on this planet with brains packed with genetic material that makes us what we are. But in another way it absolutely does not. Imagine you had been born into a background of crime, poverty, abuse. Would you be the person you are today? No of course you would not. No you would be someone else. You, like us all, are just a version of the person you could be and I hope to help transform you now into the person you want to be.

You are going through a huge transformation in your life. Clearly by taking this job you have opened yourself up to the possibility of transformation and my job is to open you up more."

No, that is what he said. I wanted to say, 'oh you are awful', but desisted. Only just.

He went on and on in similar fashion. Then he asked me to just close my eyes, lose my thoughts, just breathe and concentrate on my breathing.

Whoa, back that bus up. Oh no, no.

"Now then Gabriel. My mum warned me about boys like you. Hope I am not going to suddenly find myself back in the room after an hour with no memory of what has happened and an itchy front bottom."

All said with a smile on my face but he got the message. Not playing.

He carried on talking about creating a culture of compassion, valuing people and difference, accepting we are all flawed people trying to do our best. I mean I am sure this has a value but it was all absolutely no use to me right here right now. For all that, for all that, there was no real curiosity about actual real people. It was all abstract. Did I have an upbringing of crime, poverty and abuse? It never occurred to him I actually might have had. He never asked.

He was no wiser to who I was after the meeting, not that I really was much wiser to who he was too. One thing is for sure, for someone so people-centred he did not seem to care about people. Which is all a long winded way of saying I didn't like him. I don't like him.

He cancelled the next two meetings, to my relief, but there was one in the diary today.

Today of all days.

So he had had the newspaper laid out on his coffee table in his empty office which Sonia, his secretary, had shown me into saying he would only be a minute as he was finishing a meeting with the staff associations. He was forty. Presumably the paper was for my benefit, as was the delay.

I could hear him coming down the corridor engaged in fake bonhomie with the Federation contingent. He stood at the door, calling after them as they passed.

"Ok we will call it a two all draw today. I get the uniform changes and the new divisional pilot structure. You get the underground car park passes for the Fed reps at HQ and the increase in mileage allowances."

"That means we win Sir. Away goals count double."

Laughter all round.

Face darkened the minute he saw me. No apology for being late. No hello, coffee or kiss my arse. He just looked at the *MEN* on the table.

"Well?"

MICHAEL

Every time Elaine and I are out with them we have the same conversation in the car on the way back.

I reckon David is such good company, funny, knowledgeable, lively and very generous. Clara does not have much to say for herself once you get to know her but she compensates for it by being interested in you. I think, her I- am- applying- all- my – attention- to- you routine a bit manufactured.

Elaine says David is a show off who married Clara for reflected glory. Clara is good natured and lovely and always tries to fit in and cares for David. I forget how intimidating ex-public school boys can be socially and Clara just finds a way of dealing with it by showing an interest in others rather than talking about herself.

'He is lucky', Elaine will say. 'No, she is' I counter. A routine of our marriage.

We have given up speculating about their sex lives, but perhaps that Monday morning meeting with David was always going to come. It was only a fortnight after his birthday party. I met David in my flat. I should have asked him to come later. Monday mornings can be hectic and I had a load of stuff to do.

"Michael, why don't you get a proper office and a PA?"

"It's finding someone who is good enough and I can trust David."

"You have been saying that for two years now. Look at your desk, amazed you can find anything."

"Funny thing met the new neighbour yesterday. Lovely girl down from Durham University. Just joined the police but I can't see it in the long term. She has a degree in French and Law. She just had that something about her. I would have offered her a job there and then if it weren't for the police but, we shall see. Next time I speak to her I will mention it."

"Aha subject matter- 'women who should not have joined the police'. Well that's an easy introduction to what I need to speak about."

He explained. Clara had been getting itchy feet after eight, nine years with him, running the PR agency and being Mrs Henderson was becoming boring for her. She had been talking about having a baby as her biological clock was running out. Then she runs into Roger Mason at some fundraiser. He asks her to apply to be a superintendent.

He sees a sudden change in her. She starts exercising to be fit enough to pass the police fitness test. She starts reading the *Independent* newspaper, she had previously read the *Express* when she could be bothered. She buys books on policing and the law. She hires someone to tutor her on interview skills.

David kept hoping it would all blow over and she would lose interest or fail, but she passes the interview for the job. He knows this must have been fixed, she did not have the proper experience or educational qualifications. I counter but suspected he was right.

The night she was due to go out for a meal with Mason and others to celebrate was the turning point. They had had a bit of an argument about the dinner in the first place.

"Can't imagine he takes all his promoted superintendents for dinner?"

"David, this isn't like you at all. It's just dinner. Don't worry I can handle a man like Roger Mason."

He had reflected that perhaps she was right and, well, it was just not his style to get jealous. However he saw her before she went out, she had a revealing black dress on and looked just fantastic. He felt he had already shot his bolt and could say no more but he told me that was the moment he knew it was for real. There was either something going on or there was going to be.

She came in that night late and just went straight to her room. David said she would have been able to see his light was still on, he had left it on deliberately, and would normally have stopped to talk, but she did not. Something had obviously happened. She did not even really try to pretend it had not.

Same in the morning. She was up far earlier than normal and went straight to the gym which was out of her routine. She had been so out of sorts she had left her phone on the kitchen top. He had found a text on her phone.

Dreadful night. He had a camcorder in his bedroom! OMG do not know what to tell David!!!!!

The text had been composed but she had not selected a recipient, just left there on her phone. He panicked and suddenly felt wrong looking at her phone. He wished he had not. He had put it back on the kitchen table and had never tried to look again. He did not want to confront her about it all because he should not have looked at her phone. Typical David.

He had sort of guessed this moment was always going to come but he had not really wanted to think about it. After all he had his rugby friend which she did know about, but this was more than an affair with some random. This man was a man of power showing interest in her, giving her a job; he felt threatened.

"David, you are rushing to conclusions, getting way ahead of yourself."

"Am I?"

No. Probably not.

He started crying.

"Michael, you can't make it go away like you did last time? Or like you did with Walsh?"

"David, Christ. He is a Chief Constable of a big city. How did he ever get a job like this? Christ, so open to compromise, blackmail. I mean just the terrorist angle. He is doing that investigation into what police intelligence there was on the 7/7 bombings, isn't he? You can't have people like that..."

"I knew you would go on that track, big brother, a *Daily Telegraph* editorial. Bollocks to all that, he has fucked my wife.

On film."

CLARA

"Well?"

Well? Well it started with the *MEN* leading today with the headline.

STILL WORKING

Underneath pictures of Sergeant Chris Hayes and PC Bob Brazier, the custody staff who had been on duty on the night Jesse Brooks had gone to hospital. IPCC had put out a statement that they had given quite clear instructions to GMP that they should be removed from custody duty but it just had not happened.

They had been due to be restricted on the day Brazier went missing but that got cancelled. So instead our Internal Affairs sent an email to Brian who had been on annual leave for a week. He had left an out of office message but no-one in Internal Affairs seemed to have noticed this. I was cc'd in and had just presumed Brian would deal with it. He is so efficient I just assumed everything would be dealt with. I had not really thought it through that there would be a gap while he was on leave. I should have done something. Stupid really.

Anyway had got a call from our press office last night. I told them simply to say it was an error that would be rectified. I did not think that much of it. Press office seemed happy with my response. They did not seem overly worried. Never imagined something as ordinary as this could headline.

Hardly the end of the world you would think. Apparently it is.

"Well?"

Well? To which the answer should have been, 'well good morning to you too, Gabriel' or 'no bean bags and joss sticks today then?' or even 'new hair cut suits you, by the way', which it did.

As soon as I started to explain to Hooker, he interrupted me. The superintendent and chief inspector were a team and should step in for each other. Had I not noticed that they were still working in custody in my own station? Eyes to the ceiling, mock horror, big drama queen, a touch of camp that I had not picked up on before.

Well I was not going to tell him that I rarely go down into the custody area. I have to say I find it a deeply unpleasant place. When you walk in the staff don't look at you, just keep their heads down as if so busy they cannot look up for one second. It's oppressive, no light, constant banging on doors.

And why didn't I alert him to this? Told him I had informed the press office. Apparently I had not stressed the seriousness of it, therefore my fault it seems. I had been planning to give him a full apology but he could go whistle now. If he wasn't interested in listening to me then there was no point speaking. Of course not speaking looked like insolence, which it was. I was actually just staring him down.

He reached for a file on his desk and pulled out the business plan drawn up by Julian Rose re the missing girls. I had forwarded it to him by email when I read his blog about more compassion in the police. I had linked the two issues. Again, my error it seemed.

Long, man of the world sigh.

I needed to understand what the priorities are. Staff can always distract you with pet projects and alarm you to all kinds of issues. If you took them up personally they will just come at you with more.

Firstly, to deal with the suggestion that the BCU was under recording rape crimes that were taking place. This was an interesting suggestion and one that had implications across the Force. He had sent it to the crime registrar to have a look at but on no account, repeat on no account, should I be creating a load of undetected crimes on my BCU now more than ever.

He shuffled his papers.

"However, the suggestion that we should arrest a load of men, Asian men, based on no evidence is naïve and alarming and, to be honest Clara, plain racist. What would happen is that they would all go 'no comment' and we would get no charges authorised. The episode would be condemned, quite rightly, as a fishing expedition. You would really damage relationships with some of the councillors in an ethnically challenging area. You need their help, not alienate them.

You cannot just arrest people on reasonable suspicion and then see what turns up? Even if it is a lawful approach, even if it is, we would be asked why have we just chosen Asian people to be treated like this? I cannot stress how much more thought and preparation needs to go into something like this before you can take any action."

"You have no idea what these girls..."

...tried to gobble the words back but too late.

A longer sigh. He closed his eyes, looked to the ceiling, then stared directly at me.

I was going to get the bottom line speech.

He and PK had thought the appointment of direct entry superintendents was a terrible idea and that PK had privately got some legal advice at terminating their contracts. However he had decided to carry on and support them in their roles. I should be grateful because the advice was delicately poised and could have gone either way. If it had been down to Hooker he would have terminated their employment immediately.

And I was unlike others in that....

"………they had track records or qualifications for senior management whereas I think we both know you should not really be doing this job."

I could feel my eyes watering, with anger. He would think I was upset. I am not going to cry.

I see. Compassion, kindness and understanding has its limits. That limit is mistresses of Chief Constables.

I am not going to tell him that I don't need this job, or to be frank, even want to do it. I would love to have resigned there and then but it would be victory for him. So another staring contest beckoned.

Fortunately a knock at the door. Saved by the bell. One knock and straight in actually. Instant access, interesting. It was scrawny, peacock faced Carol, Head of Press and Publicity. I am sure she did not know I was in the office when she burst in. There had been a kind of double take on seeing me, don't think she entirely registered.

"You both need to see this."

She had a tablet in her hand which she held out to Hooker. I could see it had the on-line edition of the *Evening News* at the front.

"Don't know if they knew this when they ran the article this morning and have decided to turn the screw. Sarah Parker is not answering my calls but I will give her a piece of my mind about this. We never even had a chance of reply. I think we are going to see more of this as they target those promoted in by Roger."

Well don't mind me, darling.

"Is this true?"

Hooker handed me the tablet. I could feel the looks between them as I was reading.

AM I IN CHARGE?

Evening News reveals that local Commander,
Clara Henderson, did not even know Custody
was her responsibility at time of Jesse
Brooks detention

PAUL

My watch showed me just ten minutes late when I got into reception at the theatre.

Yes they could confirm that Mr Chappell and his associate had booked a meeting room and had arrived early. They did not know if anyone else had arrived or was expected. I would also have to wait here to be shown to the meeting room as it wasn't easy to find.

I kept thinking 'meeting at the Lowry', is it an easy mistake to make? Who would think it would be at the theatre not the hotel? Should I offer my apologies and admit to the mistake or just stroll in as if keeping them waiting twenty minutes was the plan?

It just occurred to me I wasn't now completely sure Dacic was attending the meeting in person; perhaps I was just there to represent him? Couldn't decide whether I should continue to wait for him after my escort arrives. Fortunately he, just then, strolled through the double doors, large Parka-type coat on, hood up. He was taller and thinner than you would imagine, slight, sallow, pale, looked unhealthy, panda eyes. You would never imagine this was a world class athlete.

"Milan, Paul Smith. They are in a room somewhere waiting for us."

He looked at me blankly. Of course, he can hardly speak English.

"Listen just let me do all the talking in there. In there. I talk."

He shrugged a bare assent.

Lanyard wearing chirpy young girl took us up some stairs, then ramps, through double doors and more doors to the room. Dacic walked behind us, his Parka hood still up like a remedial.

We entered the meeting room. It was bare, a small table, bowl of fruit, tea and coffee on sideboard. Two guys sat behind a table. Chappell, fat and sweaty in a purple striped blazer, grey flannels, white shirt, some old school tie. Warnock, denim, shirt and jeans, small, insignificant.

PR guy was right. Chappell was obviously a major league cock. Public school accent, big smile on his sweaty face, obviously nervous, he tried to take control.

"Mr Dacic, twenty five minutes late I see," he checked his watch for effect, "please be seated. I am sorry I do not know who you are?"

"I do," says Warnock. I could see the defeat already on his face. Looked like this was going to be a piece of piss.

"Well Mr Dacic, this is going to be your lucky day because Mr Dacic I am a man of reason, now then…."

Dacic had sat for a mere second with his hood still up then pulled it down. He jumped up away from the table, grabbed Chappell's tie and a piece of shirt and produced a handgun from the front of his jeans. He reached across and held the gun to Chappell's head. He then let go off the shirt pushing Chappell's head down side onto the table. The gun slipped off Chappell's sweaty head and hit the table. For a second I thought the bang was the gun going off.

And he said nothing. Absolutely nothing. Chappell was machine gun whispering with his head against the table, eyes closed.

"Don't kill me, don't kill me, please don't kill me, please don't kill me."

Dacic clicked his fingers as he pulled the gun off his head and pointed at me.

"Now you listen to mister good."

And that was it. He started to leave, gun in hand. I stood to prevent him passing me.

"Milan, the firearm please? The replica, firearm please?"

I held my hand out. He stared at me. I did not want a stand-off but if that crazy bastard got caught with the gun I would be in a world of shit. He looked at me with that deadpan look.

"Yes, you kill. Gangster No 1."

No idea whether that was a joke, a description of my profession or an order. No idea. He put the gun in my hand and left. Done. Over.

Christ had I done the right thing? Now I had the gun. Why didn't I let him leave with the gun? What would Johnny have done? I should have taken Johnny with me. Why hadn't I taken Johnny with me?

I didn't know if the gun was real or not. Janice had taken all the bags so I had nothing to put it in. It would not have fitted into pockets of my suit which were still stitched together anyway so I had absolutely no where to put it. I put the gun on the chair that was next to mine and sat down.

"Gentlemen, please be seated. My friend is a touch dramatic but I think you can see he is upset. Please be assured I do know about guns and this is a replica."

Chappell had a phone to his ear, his hairy chest and fat belly showing all as his buttons had come off.

"Police please...."

I picked up the gun, pointed it at Chappell. I had never pointed a gun at anyone before.

"Tell him to put the phone down."

Warnock slowly took the phone from Chappell.

"Now Mr Chappell."

"It's pronounced Shap-elle, Shap-elle."

I knew that. PR guy had told me.

"Now you don't know who I am but your friend does."

"No I haven't a Scooby, who the fuck are you?"

I could just see a patch of damp against his grey trousers.

"Well I will let Mr Warnock fill you in. I can see you urgently need a change of clothes so it's quite simple. I will leave you now. Mr Dacic will never hear from you again and the police will not hear of this. If not, I will be displeased."

I couldn't think of anything more to say so I walked out of the room, gun down the back of my trousers.

Could start to feel my heart thumping. I had tried the reasonable approach sounds menacing routine you see in films and TV programmes, but perhaps that only works in films or it comes from a genuine psycho like Johnny. Felt lame when I said it. Had I made everything clear to them? Would they be now be calming ringing the police?

This was all going to be a problem, and I was trying to madly calculate what to do but failing, which I suppose means I was panicking. Right the first fucking problem was getting out of the place. Turned left and came against some double doors but they wouldn't open, in fact they had a keypad next to them, so turned round and headed the other way. Same. Fuck. How did they expect us to get out of here? Stupid bitch had not given us the code.

It took me a while to realise there was a green stopper button underneath the keypad which released the doors. This took me into offices, couple of people looked up vacantly from their computers, then went back to their work. About face the other way back to where I came from, that door also had a green stopper. Through that and where was I? On a circular balcony but I couldn't see any stairs down, just a lift in front of me and some inset double doors immediately on my left. Not going in the lift with others with a gun so went through the doors, then more doors. I was in the upper circle of the theatre, cleaner there hoovering under the seats. Again, fuck.

Back on the balcony I could see that the stairs were practically in front of me, how had I missed them? I suddenly felt hot, at this rate I could get caught in here with a gun. I didn't want to be walking down the stairs on full view of everyone else in foyer below with gun in back of trousers, so pressed for lift. Opened immediately. No-one in. Excellent.

It stopped on the first floor to open for, who else? Dacic. He had his retarded hood back up. No point asking what he was doing there, clearly lost like me. He got in with no acknowledgement, not even a grunt. Not a word was said but we were bound together now.

On ground floor we headed for the double door exit. No real thought yet of how I was going to get out of here. He went to a large truck- like vehicle parked, more abandoned, on the mini roundabout that was next to the Lowry. I got in, it seemed the best way of getting some quick distance from here.

We juddered off straight over the mini roundabout and onto the opposing carriageway taking us out of Salford Quays. I thought he was just overtaking a couple of cars but he stayed in this lane. I had no idea what he thought he was doing, whether he had temporarily forgotten he was in England or driving in the wrong lane was just part and parcel of being a psycho.

It's a long straight road out of the Quays and I could see a cop car some distance off coming towards us. So Chappell hadn't been remotely intimidated by me and had called the cops who were already en route. No, perhaps not, the cops hadn't got their sirens on.

Dacic though crashed down the gears and accelerated up to 60 mph towards the cops pulling over into the correct lane too close to them for my comfort. We sped past them and I could see them in the mirror carrying on. So they were going definitely to the Lowry. Fuck, he had reported it. No they were tuning round. Fuck, they were going to try to stop us. They put their blue lights on.

Dacic pulled his hood down, he had a smirk on his face. He put his foot down to seventy but had to brake immediately to take a right at a mini–roundabout. He skidded into it and only just about managed to stop the car from tipping over. The lad clearly couldn't drive for shit. We were going to get caught. I was going to get caught. We headed up a short incline to the junction with a dual carriageway. Junction lights were red and one-way traffic on the main road ahead was blocking us in any case, he had to slow.

I could see he was going to force his way to turn left into the line of traffic against the red light but this was my only chance. I opened the car door and jumped out. Well, fell out, I went sprawling. The gun skidded along the road under the truck. I decided to leave it there. No, it would still have my prints on it. The wheels ran over the gun but it didn't seem to damage it at all. Would it have taken the prints off? No idea. I could hear the cops coming through the mini roundabout behind us, less than a hundred yards away. I scrambled to my feet, grabbed the gun and set off running across the junction.

I looked back and could see that no cop was chasing me on foot. I could just make out across the line of traffic in the carriageway that Dacic had either stopped or crashed and the cops were behind his car with their blue lights flashing. I needed to get out of sight. I took the first road off the carriageway I could but I was already out of breath and had to stop. I was on some estate, no idea where really, no idea what to do. Less than an hour ago I was having a coffee and a pastry in a top hotel like a player, now I was on some shitty estate in Salford in broad daylight with a gun in my hand.

Had to keep walking. Put the gun in my trousers and decided to try to navigate what would be back towards town but using the back streets of this estate. This didn't work as I kept turning down dead ends. I could not think of any other option, just needed to keep going through the estate towards town until I saw some place I recognised. Should I phone Johnny and tell him to start heading over? Not sure where I was really so little point, no stick to the plan, head towards town.

As I emerged from a ginnel I saw to my right a large metallic blue/black Range Rover on the main road that ran beside the estate. It was stationary across the entrance to the road I was on, its engine was running and occupants, couple of heavies, seemed to be looking at me. I carried on down the ginnel I was on then took a left. Dead end, turn round. Car was still parked across the junction of the road ahead, sure I could see the heavies laughing and talking to someone presumably in the rear, couldn't tell who as rear windows were blacked out.

I went back up the ginnel and then turned right down a road and then left onto a crescent shaped avenue. The same vehicle then pulled into view in front of me about sixty yards away. It stopped then flashed its lights.

My phone went off. Unknown number.

"Now you should know who this is, so don't say my name because you never know who is listening."

I knew who it was.

"Now I was just settling down to an egg and bacon balm when I get a call that some complete cunt in a wedding suit and holding a gun is running onto the Ordsall estate, my estate. Now this I had to see for myself. And who is it? Manchester's plastic gangster.

No fucking idea what you are doing, but then again it's clear neither have you. I would love to know what you are up to but now's not the time. I can hear cop cars wailing on Regent Road and the Quays, and think over in the distance I can see GMP's helicopter heading over. So here's the thing. I can put the wheel on for you right now for, say….let me think…. 75k. Yes or no?"

"Yes."

"Ok. Turn round and go down that back entry again turn right and about five doors on your left you should see a house with a green gate. Never know the number but it's a green gate. Friend of mine called Monica lives there, Monica, she is in. You can lie low there. Fuck her if you want, she will expect you to. In fact thinking of it, I absolutely insist you do, part of the deal. You got all that? Down the back entry, right, about five doors left, green gate, Monica, fuck her, wait.

Now switch your phone off so you can't be tracked and think of where you want to be taken to tonight. You obviously can't go home. I will send a driver round later. Now I am going to back to my breakfast and will then make some enquiries as to what the fuck you were doing. Then I am going to lie down in a very dark room and try to work out how a useless cunt like you ever got anywhere in this game.

Oh and be careful with that gun, if you pull the trigger it goes bang you know."

The car flashed its headlights at me again. I turned. I had no other choice. I was certain this was a set-up but just could not work out how.

It took days to fully realise it wasn't. I worried for longer how I would explain it all to Janice when the coppers raided my house, but, you know, they never turned up.

Sorry I lie. They did. Just one. The Chief Constable.

Roger fucking Mason.

MATT

I have caught an everlasting cold, a shivery dry cold. Always think I get one early Autumn and it goes sometime in April.

That's being a married man with kids and working shifts. I thought it might get better when I left Brody's shift last year and started to be a community sergeant. It has not.

I am looking at Ma'am in her office. I cannot imagine her with a cold or looking anything other than fantastic. Here for a one-to one, she wants to see all supervisors personally in her first six months. I thought she might cancel after she made the news today but no. She seems a bit preoccupied though, hassled. Oh but you so definitely would. Would not know where to start breaking it down though. It's like there is a reinforced wall round her. You couldn't just ask her out for a drink.

What am I talking about anyway? Married man, never been with anyone else but Mags. I would not really; unless, of course, I knew it was definitely on and I could get definitely away with it.

She's keeping me waiting sat opposite her but has already apologised she wants to finish something. Ashton does that as a matter of course when you go into his office. It's a power trip for him.

Nothing about her on the desk though, no photos, nothing, no kids. 'Mrs' Henderson, must be a hubbie. He will be loaded.

"Sorry Matt just needed to send that email. Not been a good day today."

"I know Ma'am I have read the papers."

"Before I forget help me with this. What's a BCU?"

"It's a Basic Command Unit. Bosses use it now instead of calling them divisions. Would not worry about papers Ma'am.

Comes with the job. You must have known that when you joined in the circumstances you would be an easy target. Would not let it bother you, sure you don't really. I know you were at the Palace of Dreams this afternoon. Would not that lot bother you as well."

She is not sure of me, whether I am being supportive or taking the piss. I'll carry on.

"When I look at that top floor Ma'am they all remind me of the kids who got bullied in school. Getting their revenge back on the world now. Don't let them get you down. Mr Mason was an exception to that though, a proper copper"

Why had I mentioned Mason? Like I was telling her we all knew he was sorting you out. Kudos to him, nevertheless.

"I really did not know him well enough Matt to be truthful. You don't seem quite the same as other police officers. A bit more independent? Don't run with the crowd. Is that fair to say?"

"Er don't know Ma'am, just try to do my best."

I know what she means but let's see which way this all goes.

"Last week you seemed to be really concerned about this family gang dispute which Brian was less concerned about?"

"Well yes Ma'am. The problem with these type of things is that some people think they seem to be an irritation from real policing. After all it is just shitbag gangster on shitbag gangster so why should we bother? We should concentrate on protecting the innocent, decent public. Thing is it then escalates and we have to intervene, react to intelligence of threats, investigate shootings. This takes up loads of energy and resources and then we don't have the resources to fight the volume crime Mr Ashton gets so excited about."

"Sort of like preventative medicine. If you don't do something, one day you may get a serious illness?"

"Precisely Ma'am."

"Matt, it's the thing I am really struggling with in the police, just don't get it. Everything you are saying to me now makes perfect sense. I get it. Brian, though, sees it a completely different way; he loves his volume crime figures. May seem silly but I thought you would all agree on what was important. Something else occurred to me about this. Do you mind if I share with you confidentially what I was thinking?"

"Stays in this room Ma'am."

"It's just this crime is up or crime is down or whatever. Based on what from what? It cannot go down forever can it? Every time I hear whether crime is up or down I want to ask on last week? Last month? Last year? If we get crime down here won't it go up again? Those who had high levels get it down and they are praised and we are criticised if it goes up from a low level. It seems like snakes and ladders. I haven't expressed this well."

"I am afraid you have expressed it very well."

"Matt I am sorry. I know this meeting was supposed to be about you but I have to ask you about something else then. These girls who go missing to have sex with men. Why does nobody do anything about it? I suppose it's a sort of naivety on my part but shouldn't we be protecting people who can't protect themselves? I really don't get it. Do you know Julian Rose?

"Two Brains."

"Well yes. He was talking about the matter last week at a meeting. It suddenly seemed to make sense to me. Funny thing was, he does not care. No shouldn't say that. You know what I mean? Oh God what a day I am having."

"I know what you mean"

She looked at me. I must have looked blank. I was struggling to respond.

"Sorry Matt It's been a very, very bad day. I know, in the police, superintendents should not speak to sergeants like this. Sorry. I've embarrassed you. Anyway this was a one to one where we were supposed to talk about you. Sorry."

"No Ma'am I am happy to help anytime."

I really did like her, wanted to help.

"Ma'am all I can say is that you have just got to trust yourself. I cannot help you really I have been in this for so long it makes a sense to me but I can see how it seems from the outside......."

Not sure where the next bit came from.

".....Ma'am bit of advice if I may?"

She indicated to go on.

"Well I know Brian Ashton well, joined with him. Tell you something though one thing he certainly was not, and that was a crime fighter. Quite the opposite. He quite liked doing missings, sudden deaths, outside enquiries for other forces. He liked being out of the way doing such stuff so he did not have to deal with the shitheads I reckon. Remember there were some rumblings about how few arrests he made. Our inspector used to defend him saying that every shift needs an Ashton, a water carrier, lets everyone else do real police work. He used to do actually volunteer to do sudden deaths.

You know Claudia his wife?"

Claudia, heffer divorcee with the biggest outsized arse you have ever seen; not if you paid me a thousand pounds.

"Well she was the Coroner's Liaison Officer. He got together with her because he spent so much time doing sudden deaths he was always in her office."

"Perhaps he volunteered for deaths as an opportunity to meet Claudia? Oh that's quite sweet."

"Perhaps Ma'am, perhaps."

No I was not going to leave it there. Started, so finish.

"Look Ma'am, if we are doing confidential, take this any way you want but trust me this is friend advice. Ashton, at heart, is an idiot. Don't think you have some safe pair of hands, because you don't, he will get you in trouble.

Look, I know this seems a strange example but do you read those emails of encouragement he sends out to the whole division every week? With lines from Churchill or American cop films? See the latest? It's in response to Mr Hooker's blog saying we should not have individual arrest targets….."

I am looking at my Blackberry.

"…..well you will know Ashton was all for them under Mr Mason but now he is completely backtracking and saying he agrees with Mr Hooker. Anyway……where is the email?…..yes he says here, 'Targets were limiting because it established a culture of the lowest common denominator. Always bear in mind the saying, 'You should not be comparing yourself to others, if you do so you are insulting yourself.' ' Do you know that is a quote Ma'am?"

She didn't. I did not, at first. Brody had pointed it out to me.

"…..a quote from Hitler. That is precisely how clever Brian Ashton is, Ma'am. The man quotes Hitler."

She just stared at me. Of course there is nothing she can say to that. She has taken me into her confidence and I have abused it and put her in a difficult position. I have come across as vindictive, mean spirited and with a grudge against Ashton.

I was also going to advise her to not start pissing about trying to investigate what happens to missing girls with Asians but it was too late. I had crossed a line and anyway that piece of advice is something she would not want to hear.

She ignored the Ashton thing, proving me right. I had gone too far.

"Yes well Matt. Could you do me a favour please? I am not quickest on uptake and need to think things through so could you send me a summary of what you were saying about gangs and the Keane/Bruen thing. Just help me fully understand."

So she has wrapped it all up by changing the subject and now making me submit a report. The oldest trick in the book of bosses who want to get rid of you, 'put this in writing please'. I need to retrieve my newly acquired dickhead status, that report better be good.

"Yes will do, first thing. Look as far as the one to one thing is all you need to know about me is that I always give you 100%. I won't let you down."

Well that improved my standing with her. Brilliant, confirmation I am a dickhead. There is just something about her has this effect on me.

"Thanks I am sure you won't Matt. Look Matt you have helped more than you realise. Just nice to hear something that makes sense. Perhaps you were agreeing with me to be nice. Anyway it was welcome today of all days. But we will do this again to talk more about your career, there is a difference about you I like."

She got up from her desk and came round and kissed me, on the cheek. It was well surprising, lush, she smelt lovely.

Not lovely, sexy, got a bit of a semi to be honest. Now I still felt like a dickhead, but more like a dorky one being seduced by teacher.

You know what I mean.

SHARON

It was Hooker, who was a DCC back then, who rang to tell me I was going back to chief inspector. He said I was collateral damage, a pawn in a bigger game. PK was determined to reduce Kenny back to the rank he was before and, as I had risen with him, so I fell with him.

Well that was honest if nothing else.

He understood how difficult it would be now, being junior to people I had been in charge of. Also talked about GMP needing strong women and that, once the dust had settled, he was sure he could do something for me. Perhaps we should meet to discuss my personal development?

No thank you.

I have to admit though he was, well, ok about it all when I was a bit of a bitch with him. Typical of me. But my career path linked to Kenny Poole's? I will have to think long and hard about that.

Kenny texted me to offer to buy me to lunch to thank me for all I had done for him. Do you know I did actually think he meant lunch out at a restaurant? Lord knows he owes me. Accepted with kisses and hearts just to wind Varna up. She reads his texts. I am safe with Kenny though. I know he thinks I am a raving lesbian. I mean I have shaved hair, swear a lot and am single. I must be.

Well it was Chester House canteen. I was surprised that I was surprised that he meant lunch at work. Of course he did. Friday, so fish and chips or steak pudding.

And of course he didn't want to thank me. He wanted to talk about Kenny's favourite subject, Kenny.

"PK rang to tell me."

"How was Varna about it?"

"Well you can guess."

I could, that's why I asked. Kenny is ploughing forlornly into his pudding and chips. He now has gravy on his waistcoat.

"Come on Kenny no-one has died. We had a good run."

He looks up.

"Do you know what gets me Sharon? When I pointed out to PK that none of my acting will now count towards my pension do you know what he said? Do you know what he said? 'Well Kenny never really thought about that but we never joined for the money did we? This is a vocation, after all. And you are hardly struggling on a Superintending rank's pay?'

Can you believe that? Can you actually really truly believe that?"

He went on and on. Brings him over form Lincolnshire, causes his divorce, then drops him, now this. Acts like an impoverished vicar but he is loaded.

"He's not a Christian anyway he is a Baha'i."

"A Ba what?"

"PK is a Baha'i. It's some mystical Persian religion, believes all the religions of the world are the same, we all believe in the same God or have same imaginary friend. Don Regan told me recently he told everyone back in 2002 when he attended the first Superintendents' Association meeting as the new Chief Constable."

"Yes all things to all men. Typical."

"Yes that reminds me Don told me something else, you will like this. He said Kevin Kershaw asked him at the meeting what type of Chief Constable he would characterise himself as. You know the kind of tossy question people ask at Association meetings? The sort of thing you would ask actually Kenny. Do you know what the Brummy wanker replied? 'I would like to be thought of as a kind of Philosopher King'.

That's why he is called PK. Nothing to do with Paul Kenyon. Philosopher King."

Kenny chewed on his steak pudding in contemplation.

"Yes I did all that for A Level, Plato's Republic. Yes that all fits too. Socrates walking round the agora interrupting busy people to ask them about justice and the nature of reality. He just got up everyone's noses in the end and they poisoned him for being such a smart arse."

Which all made me realise I prefer Kenny when he is down, it brings out the best in him.

BRIAN

7.05 a.m., five minutes ahead of schedule, A56 White City Roundabout, Trafford on way into work at North Manchester division. My boss, Mrs H, will still be asleep, no doubt.

Time for my inspirational mix CD. Bit of Mr Esposito. Come on baby.

YOURE THE BEST, AROUND

Mr Hooker has just called me on my mobile. I heard he does that as he is driving into work from Whaley Bridge. Told me he knew I would be the sort who is up early and driving to work also. I never expected he would call a chief inspector.

I knew him briefly when I worked in the old Chief's office but did not have much dealings with him at all. Mr Mason did not have much time for him to be honest. Now he rings me out of the blue, friendly as anything, remembers my wife's name. I know, I know, it's cheesy but he did still make the effort. I should do more of that. Think I could be back in the running. Claudia will be delighted. I will tell her tonight.

"Guess who phoned me today?...only the Chief Constable"

Better say his name. Claudia may be freaked and think it was Mr. Mason. Ha, ha.

Claudia always says Mr Mason let me down. She doesn't mean by sending me to North Manchester and then reverting me back to chief inspector, after all I had done to get volume crime down. No, Claudia thinks he let me down by going missing just before the promotion centres which PK cancelled. She gets really angry if I try to point out that he may have other things on his mind before he disappeared.

She thinks I am too soft and easily used. Then again my mum thinks the same of me for marrying Claudia and taking on Danny. Don't think I will point out it is the only thing they agree on.

Do you know I have just realised that was the last time I spoke to Mr Mason was when he rang me after I had learnt I was being reverted to chief inspector. He called me latish to say how sorry he was. He had asked the head of HR to sort out placing his direct entry recruits and he had not realised what had happened until the email had gone out. He told me he had played merry hell with HR but that he would now have to live with it and could not intervene. Promised me that I would be there or thereabouts in the next batch of promotions. Just keep my head down and plough on.

No, he was right. You have just got to plug away, that's what I have learnt. It usually comes good in the end. Straight course. Head down. Do your job. Stick at it. I know there are people cleverer than me out there. So I have to get up earlier than them, stay the course. Try to educate myself anyway, read books to improve myself. I throw quotes into my emails from books and articles I have read, keeps morale up.

I have always tried to do my job properly. It's got me where I am today. It's a sad truth that many people don't do their job though. It's beyond me why they do not. Life is so much simpler if you just do your job.

I have got to get crime down. Don't make friends doing that, pointing out where people could do better, but that's what I get paid for. I always say it's not a popularity contest. People bring personal feelings into all this stuff though. Just do your job. Look, if you are in custody that means you have to visit a person in the cell every thirty minutes if they are drunk. You have to rouse them and check they are ok. That's what you have to do. Simple. Do your job. If you do your job you are covered and also it is less likely anyone will come to harm. It's not hard, it's not rocket science, but people don't it.

Here's the thing though. It sort of mystifies me when people don't do as they should but what I just can't accept is this; when they are caught out do they say 'fair cop my responsibility?' Oh no, God no. Oh no. They bleat about being understaffed, or too busy, or hadn't been trained or claim they did the visit but forgot to record it. There is always, always, an excuse.

Now the custody staff are saying I should have been checking on them. I got a call from some woman in Internal Affairs about what 'processes' we have in place to make sure staff are doing what they should be doing? So it's my fault they were not doing their job? Unbelievable.

They are also saying they were tired from working twelve hour shifts. Everyone on 'E' group in custody had gone on the sick over the dispute I had with them taking their refreshment break so putting the others on 7/7s was the solution. I don't recall them complaining at the overtime they were getting.

I mentioned all this to Mr Hooker today when he rang. Oh yes I got that one in, I'm not so green as cabbage looking. He seemed to know about it. 'Trapped rats' is what he called them but told me not to worry. It was just something Internal Affairs had to do. He agreed everyone should do their job properly.

He said he had called just to say I was on his radar. He said everyone appreciated what I had done at North Manchester but crime needed to come down after Mrs H had let it creep up. Now this bit is interesting. His exact words were 'things may turn round quicker for you than you think'. He said North Manchester was as tough a place as they come and he felt that perhaps the previous Chief had made a mistake putting her there.

Hmmm, Mrs H may be on her way? I think so. She has had a hard time of it. I think he may be taking her out of the firing line. I think it showed Mr Mason was feeling the strain thinking he just could promote civvies straight in.

Mr Hooker asked to be kept informed. I know what that means. I will comply. You have to be loyal to your Chief Constable. If I am perhaps I could step up a rank if she goes?

Anyway I got in that I had read his blog on kindness and how much I liked it. Well, you have to do these things don't you?

I feel better than I have for a while .Think I will ring Claudia rather than wait until I get home, ask her to do a couple of steaks, its Friday night after all. Bottle of wine. Got a box set of *Spooks* that needs watching.

Tell her I might put on my Spiderman outfit later. Hope Danny behaves himself.

7.17a.m. three minutes ahead of schedule. Pulling in now, last song. Oh yes, Survivor.

IT'S THE EYE OF THE TIGER

Bloody hell, that's Sergeant Parker's car parked in my dedicated spot, again.

I will get Brody Jones to get him to move it and, whilst he is at it, to remind him, again, to cover up the tattoos on his arm.

MATT

Having the kids on my days off does my fruit. Mags has to do ten days a year in the tax office to keep her hand in while on extended career break which she does when I am on rest days. But kids are hard work. Two hours and I have had enough, exhausted with them already. Off to grandmas they go. I am off to work, I have enough to do.

Some people get offended when they see me at work on a day off. Federation Fred tried to give a lecture about hard fought rights which I was giving back. He was actually serious, which is rare for Fred. Fed don't know they are born sometimes. The hours my parents had to work to keep the bakery going. Killed my dad in the end.

By my reckoning makes sense to come into work on your day off anyway. Just for an hour or so. You don't get mithered as much. You can get some paperwork done and clear the decks generally. Just makes for an easier time when you next parade on for duty. Compensates when you have to take a flyer. Also means you don't have to look after the kids on your own.

Surprised to find a pretty young girl in uniform, clearly a probationer, in the office. I know 'pretty young girl' sounds a bit wanky, but that's what she is. Charlotte, posh voice. Hmm, no suppose I wouldn't. I like them more milfy.

She was sat there doing nothing and with nothing to do. For a crazy moment I thought all my PCSOs had actually gone out on patrol by 10.15 in the rain which would have been a double first. It transpires they had gone to one of Ma'am's monthly drop in sessions where staff could ask her questions about any issue. They had not the manners or grace to ask Charlotte along, just left her there.

"They told me I should answer the phone and take any messages while they were gone."

I bet they did.

It was odd seeing her there as I had not expected the next probationer attachment to the office for a couple of months. She explained she had recently been working in custody when that Brooks guy went into a coma. She was under investigation and had to be 'restricted' and not come into public contact while she was being investigated. Mr Ashton did not feel it would take long.

"Well I would not bet on that."

Regretted that the minute I said it, could see the look on her face. So then had to then ask her about the whole story. I think the first words out of her mouth were Chris Hayes and Bob Brazier. Well that was an accident which had been waiting to happen for a very long time. I always tell my staff not to make arrests when they are on.

"Do you know why they call him Hong Kong Bob?"

"He said it was all the Chinese food he eats."

Not quite, I decided against enlightening her further, it would only make her feel worse. She was marginally relieved when I explained to her that at some point the IPCC could rule she was no longer under investigation because she had done little wrong, but the investigation would continue.

"Problem is you will then be a witness against your colleagues, which brings problems of its own."

Why did I say that and alarm her more? How can I make her feel better now?

I told her everyone gets in deep shit at some point in their career. Some it happens to early and some late. The earlier the better because it gives you a better perspective on the job. Made me sound worldly wise. I had actually been told this by one of my old inspectors.

"Do you know Sergeant, everything you have said is really useful. I just get 'don't worry, you've done nothing wrong' from most people.... anyway, Mr Ashton said you needed help as you had a number of crime hotspots and I could help in some way."

I had to give her something to do but was determined not to invent some job to do with Ashton's precious figures. I had planned to do that report for Ma'am, in fact that was the main reason I was in, so I gave her the Bruen/Keane file which I had been trying to keep but it was in a mess. I asked her to search the local systems against any of the names or addresses in the file to see if anything had happened recently. If so print off and put in the file.

She seemed happy enough with this. All quite useful as it allowed me to complete that report for Ma'am at the same time. I told her not to answer the phone. The way I reckoned it neither of us should really be in the office so we were within our rights not to answer.

It is incredible how much you can do if you just apply yourself without distraction. We worked in quiet for about two and half hours and it was soon lunchtime, well past lunchtime. Charlotte had not disturbed me at all. She showed me what she had done so far, smile on her face. Everything re-ordered, divided, each divider with a picture of the person followed by record, followed by intelligence, followed by miscellaneous.

"That is superb."

"Yes perhaps some kind of personal assistant job would suit me."

Normally I would have saved the email to Ma'am to re-read for another day, but I wanted to get it sent off straight away to impress her. In her inbox less than 24 hours after she had asked for it.

I asked Charlotte to give it the once over. She started to read it over my shoulder and suggest changes. I was soon out of the chair and her in it. She worked at speed commentating as she went, 'don't start sentences with 'but' or 'and' ', 'Keane Family' is only one capital', 'its 'you are' not 'your', 'turn the sentence round and make it direct'.

"Told you I should be a PA, Matt."

I have to say it was a lot better. Send, gone, bosh, great bit of work. That's why you should come in on your days off.

The PCSOs were coming back into the office, having had lunch, of course. Could see the plan, bit of admin, phone calls to complainants and suddenly it would not be necessary to go out at all that day. Yes, thanks that will be £22k a year please, all for a job where you never have to arrest anyone.

I think I would normally have ordered them all on patrol but today just could not be arsed with the inevitable arguments, sullen faces. It was my day off. Charlotte had been there since I presume 8 a.m., we needed to get out of the situation.

"Come on, I will buy you lunch. Just put a jacket on over your uniform. We will go round the corner."

Taking a girl out to lunch, hey? I've changed my mind. I would give her one, if she asked me nicely, and talked posh whilst I fucked her.

CHARLOTTE

Tracy had warned me that Matt Donnelly was a bit pervy but I am not getting that vibe. Well I sort of get it, but I think it more in the way he presents himself rather than him actually being a perv. I feel safe with him.

I know he is in on his rest day but he has jogging bottoms and a T-shirt with last night's tea and today's breakfast on it. He should not really be in work dressed like that. I have to say also if you do have adult acne then you should really try to make the best of yourself. His wife should tell him.

This car is a mess too. I suppose if you have triplets you have other things to worry about, like money. Kept going on that the fish chips and peas at this cafe was £3.49 and sometimes the manager gave it to him for free, but he wouldn't accept that all the time though, that would not be right.

He kept trying to persuade me to have the fish and chips, happy with salad though. He was nice enough to listen to me wittering on about my problems, and I did witter on. Got onto the subject of 'B' group.

"Well you were just unlucky there. I used to be on that group. Mr Jones was a good boss but as soon as Parker arrived on it he took over. It all just got out of hand and he could not control Parker. It's why I came on the area. Brody, Mr Jones, now gets his kicks now winding up the bosses at meetings and Parker is in effective charge.

Look Charlotte, you are too good for all this. Hard to explain but you will miss your way if you stay here. There are just too many piss taking sly fuckers in this job, like Parker, who would want to bring someone like you down. Look at the way the PCSOs treated you this morning. Trust me on this, you can miss a turn in life and next minute it is all you are. That's what happened to me."

"There is a Philip Larkin poem about that, sand clouds looming behind you things suddenly hardening into all you have got. Forget its name it will come to me. Yes I have a big decision to make I suppose, 'there's a tide in the affairs of man.'"

"Yes that's Larkin too? Thought it was an old cliché?"

"Shakespeare, the last bit, I think."

"You should meet our kid Phil. He likes all that shit. Went to Cambridge to study English. Now lectures at Nottingham University. Published a book, reckons one of Shakespeare's plays may have been written by Marlowe or the other way round. Something really fucking useful like that."

"I'm impressed, Matt. Did you miss a turning you said?"

"Yes well the youngest is the most loved and all that. Phil was always the golden bollocks. I left school at sixteen, no bit later during 'A' levels. My dad had just keeled over from a stroke and my mum could not cope. Tried for a year or so to keep the business but if I was honest I did not properly pull my weight. So I messed up my education and lost the family business. I did all kinds of daft jobs before I found this one."

"That's terrible. You happy now?"

"No love the job, Charlotte, love it, but I would be a lot wealthier now if I had applied myself at the bakery after Dad died and not let Mum drift. Spilt milk, though."

I just couldn't tell how he felt about all that. He seemed phlegmatic.

"You know I went to school with a lot of them round here. My dad grafted his bollocks off in that bakery and people used to think we were posh because we had a few quid. We worked hard for our money. Christ knows what time Dad got up. Sure that's what killed him. These lazy bastards wouldn't do anything that meant getting up early or breaking a sweat."

"Do you mean your staff or the public, Matt?"

MATT

"Do you mean your staff or the public, Matt?"

She is a seriously smart girl. She was laughing but a good point nevertheless. I suddenly realised I had been talking too much.

"Look while you clog up your arteries I am just going to nip over to Asda across the road get some things if that is alright?"

"OK I'll finish up and drive the car round I will find a spot near the front door."

Finished, paid and headed for the car. Regretted the fish and chips, too dry, leaves an aftertaste. Tried to work out if I could squeeze in the gym and pick up the kids before Mags comes back. Parked in space close to the doors, Charlotte could not miss me.

I decided to ring the office to warn them no one better be still in the office when I come back, even though I wasn't coming back. Mobile to my ear was ringing out when I saw Pat Keane in the wing mirror striding towards the car. Yes thought it was him I had driven past earlier. He was on a mission, you could tell that.

Pat Keane, IQ of an amoeba, but ok as gangsters go. He would at least talk to you. Not a nasty bastard like his brothers, just dense. But there was something about him today. He was up to something. Wound down the window as he passed me.

"Hey Pat what's got into you? Wrong side of bed?"

He could not have not heard me but he did not even turn towards the car. Now Pat Keane did not strike me as being the type who popped into Asda for a sandwich or a pint of milk. No, he did not look like he was going to do the shopping at all. He looked purposeful, determined, angry. I got out of the car, driver's door open. Pat was already some twenty yards away from me.

I could see the sliding doors of the supermarket open to reveal Pop Bruen, sheepskin, flat cap and his wife in bag lady chic. One huge trolley of shopping, the other stacked with boxes of beers and lagers, standard Bruen fare, two grandchildren hanging on either side of the trolleys. Pat stopped, as if surprised.

He then reached into the back of his trousers to produce a handgun. I instinctively ran forward then stopped. Truth was I had no idea what I was thinking of doing.

Keane took a couple of running steps to within ten feet of the Bruens and aimed at Ma Bruen who ducked down as if avoiding a cricket bouncer. Pat simply lowered his gun and then fired. Pop Bruen seemed to lunge forward towards Ma as if to protect her and Pat fired again. He ran forward and fired two more shots.

I was now about ten feet from Pat, I reckon I had been unconsciously creeping forward towards him but had frozen while he was shooting. I decided I would now try to tackle him as I was directly behind him.

He swung round pointing the gun arms extended, as if he knew I was there. I could hear the screams and the scattering of people as Pat turned. The two grandchildren had run away in different directions and having run away started to continue to run erratically without actually going any further away. No one was near them.

People had gathered at the sliding doors and then had headed back inside. A security guard lay on the floor outside the door with his hands over his head. Pat was now pointing the gun straight at me, I took a few paces back, arms up.

Pat looked to his left unflustered. He then looked up straight ahead at me. The only upright person not hiding or running away.

Nobody moved. Pat looked left again and swung his gun round to the door of supermarket. It seemed almost silent, no screaming, eerie, just the two children running in circles, a prostrate guard on the floor, some customers' heads peering out of the doors. Pat turned round to point the gun at me. The doors opened and Charlotte came out. She had taken her jacket off to reveal uniform.

"CHARLOTTE. NO."

This alerted Pat who swivelled round. I had hoped by shouting she would head back inside. She did not. She had taken a few paces forward but had stopped as I shouted. She stood motionless, she put her arms out in a kind of surrender.

Pat held his gun straight at her, looked back at me but with the gun still trained on her. He grinned.

Without turning his head he fired twice.

CHARLOTTE

I am alive. He lifted the gun as he shot over my head without looking. It was a warning. I am alive.

It is strangely quiet, uneventful, you could say peaceful. The gypsy couple are on the floor. I think they are dead. This crazy guy is pointing a gun at me but he is staring back at Matt. There is an old security guard lying on the floor with his hands over his head.

Nothing is happening. I just don't know what happens next.

Matt and this guy are just staring at each other. Those poor kids are now just stood at the side watching, blank.

Have I done the right thing taking my jacket off identifying myself as a police officer? Should I have stayed inside, watched and tried to get a message back by phone? Is he going to run for it? Is Matt going to tackle him if he does? I will have to help if he does.

That nice guy I met on the landing with a cravat. He will be the one I will talk to when this is over. He will be able to explain it all to me, what I did, what I should have done. He will understand.

What should I do? Should I try to talk to the man with the gun? I should be in shock I nearly died but I feel ok. Is that normal? How many bullets does a gun hold? Think I have heard four, or five, six?

The guy is not moving. A taxi is pulling up but there is nothing to be done. He has got in quite casually. Rear seat. Try to remember his face. Yes might have to pick him out in a line up. Look at his face. The taxi is moving off at low speed as if taking a fare. Does he not realise he has a killer in his cab?

Run to the bodies with Matt. The lady is lying on her back, her skirt has ridden up, she is blowing bubbles out of her mouth but her eyes are fixed. She is going to die or perhaps is already dead.

I don't know.

The old man is lying with his head between her knees face down. He is alive. I lie down face flat to the ground to see if I can speak to him.

"Cunt cop," he hisses at me.

I follow his eyes which looked directly up the lady's skirt. I stare at her big red knickers inside her tights. He can see me looking with him.

"Cunt cop? Cunt cop? Hey it's you who will be dead in a minute Pop with any luck, you fucking piece of pikey shit, and those are your last words? Cunt cop? Sheer class to the end."

Matt is stood over him and me. I like Matt but that's not nice at this moment. Or perhaps this is the real world I joined to learn about?

Screech of tyres of a car behind me.

The noise of the getaway car.

No he had already gone.

Must be police.

No siren. No, there had not been a siren. There is not a siren.

I look up from the ground.

It's the taxi, being driven by the guy.

The guy who shot at me.

At speed.

It is not going to stop.

Matt bends over.

Grabs my arm….cunt cop….

…Daddy……… Mummy…………………………………….

…..red knickers………

Big red knickers.

PART TWO

CHORUS

I know how I came across last time.

Well I had been celebrating and got a bit carried away.
Drinking is not good for me.

I am one of those people who changes when I drink so I really
don't much now. Hardly ever.

They say it makes your true character come out but I am not
sure we have one true character do we? There are always a
number of versions of ourselves aren't there?

You just saw one version then. You weren't shocked. People
get into power so that they can look down on others, you
know that.

I hope you see though that, if nothing else, I can be an honest
person. I was prepared to share that side of me with you, and I
have been clear, you are not going to find out the truth.

That's why I am not going to tell you my story. You can't hear
from me. Then I would have to lie to you and I don't want to
do that.

But I do want you to know I got away with it.

MAIREAD

I took my GCSE's in a maternity smock. I found out I had got eight 'A' stars and one 'A' (chemistry) the day Oisin was born.

I stayed at home with Mum until he was eighteen months old when Dad got out of prison. Made my peace with him, moved out and got a job.

Mum was disappointed, of course, but I wasn't.

It was all as I had imagined.

As I had planned.

PAUL

Yes. Chief Constable Roger Mason, knocking at my front door, at my detached house in Chadderton. Roger fucking Mason.

If he was any smaller you would describe him as small. Black hair meticulously parted, red pullover, pressed jeans. He looked old fashioned, I was reminded of English cricketers from the sixties.

It was sometime after 6 p.m. on a miserable Sunday. He was dripping wet and had his jacket over his head to protect himself from the rain. He had parked his car round the corner so it wasn't seen outside my house.

My first instinct was to keep a copper outside my house, especially Mason. I didn't blame him for the murder charge, he was only doing his job, but I did for the newspaper articles. I knew they were his idea. This was the man who had fucked up my life, now he wants to walk into my house, but he was here for a reason and he had surrendered being a copper by turning up at my door. I needed to hear him.

Don't know if he done his homework because the last of the children and grandkids had just left. The derby had been at 1.30 p.m. so we had had Sunday lunch after that. Janice was clearing up. Of course she offered him some of the leftovers and, yes, he accepted some. And he accepted the towel she brought for his hair. He even let her dry it for him, he was not daft. I could predict he would find her leftovers 'delicious'. He did.

So there he was in my lounge tucking into a stack of roast beef, Aunt Bessie's Yorkshires and roast potatoes on his knee. I am sure *Songs of Praise* was on. Fuck it, I thought I would play along and went upstairs and got the slippers my daughters had got me for Christmas last year which I never wore, might as well complete the domestic scene.

To be honest I did not immediately think it would be about Dacic, that had been ages ago. Why would he visit me about this now? I was baffled. Was it the tension between the Bruens and the Keanes? Perhaps he was going to tell me my life was at risk? From who? Jamal? I knew that.

Suppose it did not take long to realise that a personal visit from the Chief Constable meant it was going to be about something I would not be able to predict. Let it happen.

We talked about the game. He had heard the result as he was driving up from seeing his kids, said he was a United fan.

"Of course you are. You are not from Manchester."

"Well yes this problem, it's about football, as you know."

So he told me the story. Chappell hadn't rung the police directly, he was a very good friend of someone on the Cheshire Police Authority and had got to speak to Mason personally that day. Outrage, no wonder it's called Gunchester etc. The ex-cop at the meeting was sure gun was real, a Walther .22.

Chappell wanted to complain? Well no, there were delicacies. Of course there were.

He got his ACC, Kenny Poole, to bury it. In a few days he had it all sorted, produced a nice report. Chappell and Warnock offered their accounts but not making a statement. Any approach to Dacic would put this in public domain for no result. In any case cops would look stupid, they had chased him and seen someone run off from his car but in the end all they had done was seize the car for not being insured and got a picture of themselves with Dacic.

Club, who did not know anything of this, had already decided to cut their losses on the psychopath anyway and loan him to Madrid next year. He wasn't coming back, so no point approaching them. It would be pointless confronting me. The gun would be gone and I have never answered a question in the police station in my life. Why would I volunteer any information now?

Nice job all round, everyone happy enough. Ok, now beginning to realise it was must be him in trouble, I can relax and try to act like a gangster.

"So why are you in my lounge, in my house, Chief Constable?"

Mason became sheepish. The report had also mentioned that my behaviour in the whole affair was uncharacteristic. I had spent the night in the Lowry and not at home. I had always made a point of my ordinariness, living on an estate in Chadderton, driving a Vauxhall Vectra. This was an unexpected turn. It went on to speculate that perhaps this was one of the signs I was losing my grip. I also did not know the location of the meeting and had clearly panicked when trying to get out of the theatre. All hardly the actions of a top gangster

However, the report did remind him of the difficulties in pursuing a case against me i.e. the conspiracy to murder two years ago. Finding a barrister to take it on, for example. The one in the conspiracy trial had had a private detective find out about his affairs and his wife shown the pictures. The officer in that case had had his house burned to the ground in broad daylight, and the main witness disappeared from the witness protection scheme.

Yes and Jamal is charging me a fortune for all this, still, on top of the £75k.

Now he could only be telling me this because he had either lost, or someone had leaked, the report but still wasn't sure why he was here eating my wife's shop-bought Yorkshires. To say sorry for saying some disparaging things about me?

"And someone has leaked the report?"

"Not exactly. It's been stolen. We corresponded by email. When I wrote back NFA we both deleted the report from emails and I was supposed to put a pen-drive copy in my safe. Anyway it was a Friday I had to get down south to see the kids and had an appointment before I went. I left it in my jacket pocket which I think I emptied in my flat before I left. I am sure I left it in a drawer next to my bed.

Well the appointment, you see, was that I was banging this piece from the BBC in my flat. Anyway I was in a hurry to get back to see the kids in Bristol so I left her having a shower. She must have taken the pen-drive then. In fact she got so flustered taking it, she left her purse."

Do you know I expected a bit better from a Chief Constable? 'Banging this piece', can't he think of a better expression than that? And hardly a heart-warming story about wanting to see his kids either. Don't think I approve, reckless. How did he become a Chief Constable?

"Oh dear Chief Constable. Never dance with a stranger. A man like you should know that."

He had his Counter Terrorism Unit have this reporter in for hours on the pretext it was a national security issue. She had agreed to have her house and computers searched, but no trace. She denied everything.

"So you want me to kill her?"

"If you don't mind. I hear you are quite good at this kind of thing."

Suppose that was funny.

"Or perhaps, on second thoughts, just get the pen-drive back, with minimum fuss. It's going to appear somewhere and I will be finished."

"With minimum fuss? You think you are in a position to tell me how to do my business?"

"Sorry. You know I'm used to telling people what to do."

"And as they say, what have you done for me lately?"

"Well I would be grateful."

"Ah it's a deal then. Kiss my ring and just call me Godfather. Seriously what's in it for me?"

"I just thought some of that stuff embarrasses the both of us."

"How would it embarrass me?"

"Well, thing is we know everything that went on. Everything, you know lost in Ordsall....."

He lowered his voice, a raised eyebrow.

"Monica..."

So the rumours about Jamal were true. Ok front this out.

"Not entirely sure what you are talking about but doesn't embarrass me, mate. No-one would print a word. They would be too frightened that I would burn their houses down after you put it about that I do such kind of things. Remember Gangster No 1? I am beginning to think you are in the wrong place my friend."

He couldn't reply. I did not speak, let him dangle. He must have been desperate, had to calculate quickly. Could just throw him out now and get the pen-drive anyway, see where it got me. Decided against it, not sure why.

"OK. Be nice to have a grateful Chief Constable. Give me her name and address. Then please vacate the property, you know where the door is."

I did not move an inch, knew that would unnerve him. He had to get up, take his tray to the kitchen and retrieve his coat from Janice.

"He was a nice man," Janice said watching him through the lounge window scampering off through the rain to retrieve his car.

"Seemed a bit of a lost and lonely soul though.

Who was he?"

MICHAEL

Why did I do what I did?

It was only months later did I really start to understand why I risked so much.

I have had to look out for my brother all my life but this was more than that. A lot more. It had to be, I was risking prison after all, a long sentence.

Trust me when I spoke to my contact in Box, they wanted a security liability like Mason gone. They had had their concerns about him for a very long time. They had been warning the Home Office for years about him but there was little they could do. She said it was the big failing of the British police, the tie in to democratic localism. It meant men like Mason could not be removed, well not lawfully.

Now I believe in the British police, operationally independent under the law. It is the institution foreigners admire the most about us. I have been all round the world and I know how important the proper rule of law is. I have fought wars to make sure democracy and liberal values prevail. Friends of mine have died, lost limbs in this cause.

So what's the point of doing all this if you don't fight the enemy within? We saw it in the 70s with syndicalism, in the 80s with the left's attempt to take the Labour Party. Now it's an attack from within in our institutions themselves, eroding away at standards, at authority.

David thinks I am some kind of Colonel Blimp character when I talk like this. But think about it; do we want a society where the head of the second largest police force is a security risk and vulnerable? It matters. This all matters. I am absolutely certain of this, it matters. It's not some outdated romantic view of the world. It's very realistic. It's hard headed.

So I was right to do what I did. To be honest it was also about me as well. I was proud to be a soldier. I am proud of what I did as a soldier. I killed people in the past but I did not know them. That was just a very small part of something else so much bigger than myself. I don't feel part of that history. Had I never existed there would still have been peace in Ireland, the Falklands would have been freed. Now I just do things for money. I make a lot of money in Civvy Street with my consultancy, a lot of money. Occasionally I get a buzz when we extract someone from a difficult situation but most of the time I am just a mercenary, a military prostitute.

So doing this brought back the first buzz I got from dispensing justice to Walsh. Doing something personal that made a difference and this time, this time I felt a small part of history. Not just a soldier, a real player.

I did the state some service by getting rid of Chief Constable Roger Mason.

MATT

I feel no pain, just a humming in the room. Radio waves emitting from my head.

"Big red knickers. Charlotte. Big ones. You dirty bitch."

"Charlotte had big red knickers on?"

"Bruen, Ma Bruen. She had big red knickers on. That's what Charlotte said. Big ones."

"When? How?"

"Before the car. Big red knickers. Big ones. Bet you wear big ones."

"Look Matt, the Doctor said you would be ok to speak. I'm sorry, I will go."

"No I am sorry. Honestly, I am ok. I know what I am doing, just need a minute. Just pass me the water. No sorry about that."

I know where I am, what I am doing. I am in hospital. I think it's the morning after. I can't move much but it doesn't hurt. Woozy. And I am talking to that chief superintendent woman with the short hair.

"No I am ok. You are Chief Superintendent Sinead O'Connor. Yes you are. Hello my name's Matt. Nothing compares to you."

"Well I am a chief inspector now. Got demoted but yes, and it is Sharon Bentley not Sinead O'Connor, you are not the first."

"Do you want a statement?"

"No."

She laughed.

"I just thought I would see you on the way home."

"What time is it?"

"10.30."

"Why you going home so early."

"No its 10 at night."

"Thought that. Thought that I had been here longer too."

"You've been here over two days now Matt."

Two days. Fuck.

She held my hand. I felt tired again. If I closed my eyes I would fall asleep.

"Charlotte's dead?"

"Yes Matt. She is dead. You have been told."

"Yes, thought I had. Can I have a coffee with one sugar?"

I needed to wake up properly. She went out and returned with two paper cups of coffee. God it tasted good. Never taken drugs, but this was a rush.

"Yes. Just checking. She's still dead is she? My fault."

"Yes. And not your fault. You did your best. CCTV shows it all, you know that?"

"I killed her. I took her there."

"You knew what was going to happen?"

"Yes."

"What, that there was going to be a shooting? At Asda that day?"

"No but I took her there. I knew there would be a shooting. I told everyone. This had been coming."

Coming fully to my senses now. I feel some pain, tired, headache, head in a goldfish bowl. Another coffee required, two sugars this time.

"Sorry Matt. Did you know there was going to be a shooting at Asda that day? Had you heard something? Were you following Keane?"

"No neither. I just went for lunch with her, then I saw Keane, then it happened. But I knew it would happen."

"Sorry Matt, this is important. You had no intelligence or anything that Keane would be there, is that right?"

"Yes but it's my fault. I told everyone this would happen. There is a load of intelligence, big file on my desk."

"I had a look at your desk today when I went to see if Charlotte had left any personal effects, couldn't see it. Right, you mean that you could see something like this happening? The dispute had been brewing and you had warned people?"

"Yes. Mrs Henderson, sent her an email. I warned people, I tried to tell them and now Charlotte is dead. I knew this would happen. I killed her, the job killed her."

She held her hand up to stop me.

"Matt. Listen. It's late but I have come too early. Just lie back and listen to me then I will go. Stop this. Listen carefully.

It's no one's fault, this is what gangsters do. It's what makes them gangsters. It goes in circles. They have an understanding or a deal. Then one rips the other off, or slags another off, or shags his girlfriend or sister or daughter. Then there are threats, then a fight, then a door gets shot at, then sometimes there is an actual person on person shooting but these idiots can't shoot. Usually no one dies. At this point they have scared each other enough and there is a return to the status quo.

No one gives a flying fuck about this. Sometimes we get a conviction before someone gets killed and sometimes we don't. As I said no one really cares. I know I don't.

Now just sometimes, and only sometimes, it gets out of hand and someone is killed, but the Bruens are no loss. They are in this circle, gangsters threatening gangsters. We can't spend our time refereeing their disputes.

Bottom line is we had no warning at all an innocent cop could be killed.

That was just bad luck that you were there, at that time, in that place.

Never, ever, ever forget that, it was just bad luck."

My lullaby.

JENNY

People say I had a good shooting.

In the first two days of hectic reporting the *Evening News* had the advantage on other papers as it had the history of the Keanes and the Bruens. Gangster families go into aggressive hysteria after things like this and it can be dangerous for journalists or, at the least, frightening. Nationals did not go near them.

I knew Keane's sister Mairead. I met her when she was at her parents when there was attempt to firebomb their house about nine months ago. She was quite different from her family. She had some job in Manchester at a call centre I think and was, well, normal, bit like me. She seemed sensible, happy with her lot, a young kid just at primary school, job in Manchester. Got the impression she did not get out much at all. Reminded me of a saying of my grandmother's, 'she could make more of herself'.

It seemed odd to think of such a normal girl tied up in a gangster family. Not her fault I suppose, after all you don't choose your family and upbringing.

She answered my texts straightaway and was happy to send me pictures of Pat as a child for the pieces we ran on him. She rang me to tell me about his mental condition. She said he had always been a hypochondriac but this deteriorated after his brothers went to prison. He started talking about having a terminal illness, one week leukaemia, then a brain tumour. He wondered whether the Bruens had poisoned him. He had decided that he needed to settle things before he died. She had no idea that this meant killing anybody.

I have to say got a real buzz when I had that obnoxious DCI Sharon Bentley on the phone asking where I had got my story from because she did not know about this. I could not tell her of course, ha, ha.

The editor had held back the Hooker piece I had done, it had not been published before the shooting. So it was changed into a piece about the man thrown into the maelstrom. They had used my moody picture of him arms crossed with the Manchester Eye in the background.

IN THE EYE OF THE STORM

had been the piece with an editorial headed,

WE ARE ALL BEHIND YOU

The next day Hooker had a letter published in the paper. It was in response to criticism from a retired cop, Don Regan. He had been touting round news studios on how the police had been ignoring gang activity at the expense of volume crime targets. There had been a feud between these families for some time and questions should be being asked about whether they could have done more. Did this signal a return to Gunchester?

You will all be aware of recent speculation by certain sections of the press that the tragic shootings of last week were in some way avoidable and that this awful episode in some way indicates that gun crime is out of control in Manchester.

I do need to point out that last year we recorded the lowest number of firearms discharges in Manchester for eleven years. This has been due to assiduous and brave police work which has been matched by our partnership with other agencies disrupting gang crime at source and in particular diverting children away from such a lifestyle.

There is of course an investigation which has still to locate a suspect and of course we are looking at the circumstances of how PC Purvis came to be at Asda at the time. It would be wrong to say any more on this matter.

However I think I can speak on behalf of all police officers at the distaste for former colleagues engaging in such wild and hurtful speculation.

I am proud to lead this Force in this great city and am humbled by the messages of support I have received in the last weeks. GMP will continue to work tirelessly to make Manchester as safe as possible for you all. I look forward to your continuing support in this dark hour for Manchester.

And then I got the 'Dark Angel on the Moor' tip.

Even Sarah had to admit it was a great story.

KENNY

So guess who gets to investigate the Bruen and Purvis murders? Well no prizes. Superintendent Poole and C/I Bentley. I insisted on having Sharon as my deputy, loyalty is important.

I can do murder investigations stood on my head. I was a crime trainer in Lincolnshire for years so I know how incident rooms should be run. It's actually really quite simple.

Manhunts are different though, and this was a manhunt not a murder enquiry. You don't get many of them so I am not sure anyone can claim to know how to conduct them, especially not for someone as potentially volatile as Keane.

It took some exhausting days for the picture to fully emerge of what had occurred. I put some hours in I can tell you.

After the shooting Pat Keane had sent text messages to the Bruen family to say he knew they had been planning to attack his family so he had done this 'pre-emptive strike' as a warning to them. He had selected the oldest members of the Bruens so as not to 'ruin young lives', which is why he had not shot the two grandchildren.

Nice guy after all then and capable of typing 'pre-emptive'. Well he missed out the 'p' and the 'e'.

He was going on the run and would not be caught but he would be watching what happened. If anything happened to his family he would return to sort the matter out finally.

It seemed the Keane family were unaware of what he was about to do. His sister, who lived by herself, was a bit more onside and finally co-operated when we worked out she had been briefing the press. She told us he was having some mental episode and had convinced himself he had a terminal illness. From what she described to us psychologists disagreed on whether he was psychotic or neurotic or was experiencing the manic episode of bi-polar disorder.

Or just taking the p**s, as Sharon suggested.

There had, of course, been a lot of search activity on the Moors the day we found the car. When the *Manchester Evening News* managed to get hold of the story of Keane being a 'dark angel' on the Moors it went crazy. Press office made me go out onto the Moors to be interviewed. They told me it would 'reassure' people. Not sure how, I just got soaked through.

No other member of the family was co-operating. From mobile phone intercepts and a listening device in the Keane parents' home it appeared they genuinely had no idea of his whereabouts.

It transpired the taxi driver who had picked him up was an innocent. Records showed he had been ordered to collect the Bruens. He did spend eighteen hours in custody before this had been finally established. He had driven Pat to the bottom of the car park whereupon Pat had ordered him out at gunpoint and had driven back to the scene himself. The taxi was found at the just off the motorway in Saddleworth at the Yorkshire/Lancashire boundary later the next day.

The real 'getaway' driver was soon traced. His was the last mobile number that Pat had rung some five minutes before the shooting. He was a 21 year old local associated with the family. He described himself as his cousin but it was not a blood relationship. Called Keane's mum 'Auntie', something working class people in Manchester do, which is confusing. Anyway his car was captured on CCTV coming into the car park some five minutes after the shooting, turning round and driving away.

He explained he had been rung out of the blue by Pat Keane who had told him to pick him up now at Asda and to take him to Saddleworth. He had said no more and the call length was only 25 seconds. He had not time to explain he was not at home but had been staying at his girlfriend's in Salford so would take him longer than normal to get there.

For reasons he did not know Keane had taken to calling him to drive him about but Pat Keane was simply someone you could not refuse. The lad had recently bought a brand new Golf with an inheritance from his gran. He presumed Keane liked being associated with that. On balance Sharon and I believed him. The semi- disorganisation of Keane on the day matched his reported mental state. Everything made a kind of confused sense.

So three weeks in and no further on to catching Keane. We just have no idea.

We had a meeting scheduled for Friday afternoon with all staff involved to review where we were at. Sharon was going to take the meeting as Varna had been run ragged all week with the kids. She seemed happy enough with this, said people may offer more ideas and contribute more the less number of bosses are present. However Callaghan, the ACC promoted in to replace me, told me yesterday Hooker had wanted a fundamental review of progress so far and had asked Callaghan to come to the meeting. I needed to be there then.

It was going to be a long day so I took the morning off get the eldest to nursery and allow Varna a lie in for once at least. Finished up running a bit late after being given a shopping list, then there was an accident on the M60 so only landed at HQ bang on 2.

The meeting had been re-arranged from the incident room in North Manchester to the top floor meeting room at Chester House. Typical, twenty odd detectives had to traipse over there just to fit Callaghan's needs. So when I passed his office was surprised to see him there with Hooker and not at the meeting. I popped in. To be honest if I turned up late with the

ACC it would look as if the reason I was late was that ACC had detained me. I am not daft.

I could see there was a load of diagrams on the fixed whiteboard in Callaghan's office. Hooker explained they had been with consultants for the last three hours, exciting meeting apparently. They had clearly been at it for some time, trolley tray with discarded remnants of a working lunch. They were planning to completely reshape the Force and, in essence, abolish all divisional CID officers for a more holistic, integrated workforce. Yes, PK's wet dream, the very thing I had been brought here to do.

Well I can tell you, lightbulb moment or what? Roger had always been dead against this. I have to admit now I can see he was right. We would lose experience in CID where it really mattered. But yes it all made sense now. I was demoted because they knew I would be against this and would have some inside knowledge. Hooker needed a 'yes man', that's how Callaghan got the job. To be honest, I was angry.

"What do you think Kenny? It's not a million miles from the recommendations you made all those years ago."

Oh no, Mr Hooker, I am not playing your game.

"Well you will have to get it past Des Lyons in the Police Authority."

"He is all in favour of it."

Hmm. Does not compute.

"It's exciting though, isn't it?"

Is Hooker goading me? Not sure what to say. Callaghan interrupts before I say what I really think.

"Think Kenny has other things on his mind. If you don't mind Sir, Kenny and I will pop out and review how things are going with the enquiry."

"Yes, of course, no problem and good luck with all that Kenny. We are all rooting for you. Terrific work you are all doing on that I know."

Callaghan nodded at me.

"You go on ahead Kenny, I told Sharon to start without me. I have a couple of people coming with me also who have been caught in the same jam as you."

So by the time I get in Sharon was in the middle of summarising where we were with the team. We had all the evidence we needed from Matt Donnelly, from CCTV, from mobile phone triangulation and from the simple fact that he was now missing, to convict Pat Keane of the murder of Ma and Pop Bruen, PW Charlotte Purvis and the attempted murder of Sergeant Matt Donnelly.

The objective of this enquiry was now moving from evidence gathering to simply finding Keane. We had quietly surveilled the family, tracked their movements by phone, bugged the houses and phone and absolutely nothing. The family did not seem to be talking in code in the house. They genuinely seemed to have no idea where he was. Our friends at Box could not help. There were no leads of any use. The publicity was leading to many calls from public not one of which was providing any real intelligence and was just draining resources.

Callaghan had just come into the room but Sharon did not seem to see him as she summed up.

"So has anyone got any ideas how to catch this f**ker?"

Callaghan had a couple of young looking uniform sergeants with him, male and female. Did not recognise them but two staff officers seemed a bit steep. I was unhappy at them just coming into a confidential briefing. They sat next to me on chairs in the back of the room rather than at the full round table. It did not take long for Callaghan to start speaking though.

What was the threat from the Bruens?

My intelligence sergeant picked this up.

"The sons and Pop Bruen's younger brother are all capable of revenge. They are making a point of following their routines, drinking in the same pub but they do not seem to be active or planning anything. Their calculation seems to be to wait for this to die down. Would not anticipate anything in the short term."

Callaghan then stood up to address the room.

"Mr Hooker is aware of the good work all of you are doing and asked me here to thank you all on his behalf but the bottom line is we are spending some £25k a day in resourcing a hunt for someone who does not want to be found and for who there are no real leads. There is little point spending all this money on someone who clearly knows how to avoid capture.

Now I know some of you want to start to be more proactive in dealing with the family but this may provoke further violence from Keane. All the best advice is that we should wait for him……. "

"…to kill somebody else."

Old detective down the end of the table said this not quite quietly enough. Better to ignore but Callaghan did not.

"No. Wait for him to make a mistake. He will probably contact his family anyway. No the sensible move is to be vigilant and wait."

The detective was emboldened now.

"We should not be soft peddling with a shithouse family like the Keanes, just to save money."

Shows Callaghan's inexperience reacting to a comment like that. Happens a lot with these teams, you have to ignore and rise above.

Callaghan just stared at the constable. Not sure who is supposed to speak next. There is an air of real tension in the room. It's unclear who is in charge of this meeting. Callaghan has looked at me next to him but I am not chairing the meeting. Sharon, who is, seems to have given up. She is looking across at Callaghan. She has her tongue in the side of her mouth as if ruminating.

But I know what she is doing.

JENNY

My source for the 'Dark Angel' story? Well, I had to let everyone assume I had a source in the investigation team. In fact I got the information from the top.

The very top. His nibs, Gabriel Hooker.

Hooker rings me a lot, in truth. Always does it when he is driving to or from work. He adopts a manner that he is chewing over something I already know or is already common knowledge. If I show any surprise or ask him to repeat anything he will suddenly become coy or cautious and insist that he was speaking off the record. So I have learned to play along as if he is not revealing anything new or special. I have noticed his information is always something a number of people would have known about and would not be strictly confidential, but he is usually putting me ahead of the game.

It is odd way to go about things though. It is hardly as if anyone would be listening to his calls is it? The games some people play, but there you go. So in this case while talking about the shooting....

"....of course this typed note he has posted to his family saying he is camping out around Britain living wild but will watch over them and protect them like a dark angel is probably a load of baloney but the family do say there are a couple of references in it which can only have come from him......."

"By the family you mean the sister."

"Can't say Jenny."

...and so it goes.

He never asks afterwards whether he had been the source of any story. So not talking about the story once it is published becomes another rule of the game. He has just rung me now and mentioned the cost of the operation to catch Keane so I guess he wants me to do a story on that.

Now another rule of the game is I now have to ring the press office with the information provided by their own Chief Constable. I am asked where I got it from. I refuse to answer. I then ask for confirmation and will find in due course that the information would be confirmed one way or the other. It really is that simple, and stupid.

Do you know since that day Sarah said I was not a proper journalist things just seem to have come together? Stories seem to have dropped into my lap, from Phil in the IPCC, Mairead, Hooker. All I have needed to do is just slightly notch up the risks I would take. It's not been a big change, just a small one, but it's made a difference.

I have to say I do feel bit bad about my treatment of Clara Henderson and the custody story. I had not been entirely fair with her. I would normally have tried to get some context but published before the press office got back to me. I knew I had a good story and felt I was on a roll.

Hooker couldn't disown her quickly enough though. He had been on the phone that evening after I had broken the story driving home to Derbyshire hills. Important to understand Mrs Clara Henderson was neither PK's nor his appointment, she had to be of the same standard as other superintendents (implying she was not) and that IPCC would be considering whether to extend the case to her management oversight of custody. He reminded me that the ACC sitting on the panel would be strictly independent. He provided me with contacts in Black Mental Health UK who were taking an interest in the case. Yes I knew that already from Martha Maitland, but I did not let on.

I felt doubly worse after I saw her crying live on TV. It made me cry too. Charlotte's mum cried down the phone to me too when she told me how kind Clara had been to her, which made me feel like a right bitch.

The debate about whether police should cry on camera strengthened her position and detracted from the custody piece I had written about her earlier. She was also imperious and immaculate at hosting the daily press conferences for the next few days after the shooting. She was photogenic and papers loved running pictures of her. This contrasted with a shambling Kenny Poole who went on TV on the Moors in his grey three piece suit and no coat just as a heavy shower blew in. A member of the public actually sent in a coat for him.

Perhaps Clara and I could both be said to have had good shootings then. And do you know she actually sought me out after the latest news conference? She told me she had heard so much about me and the good work I had done and thanked her on behalf of 'the police family'. She handed me a business card with photo, not the standard GMP one. The old me started to say sorry about the custody story but she waved a hand as if to say let's not go there.

"We girls need to get to know each other better. Let's have a proper boozy lunch in town, my treat not a ten minute brew in my office. I have got something I want to run by you. Call me, you've got my card. Do it, Jenny. I mean it. Please."

That is so much better than those who would simply blank you or abuse you after running a story like that. She obviously has her motives but, hey, it certainly makes a pleasant change.

PAUL

Well that BBC reporter still swore she did not have the pen-drive after Johnny loaded a shotgun in front of her then put it up her clacker.

That's was good enough for me. She just did not have it.

It made me think whether the stupid cunt had simply mislaid it.

CHRIS

"No, no, no, no, no Julie, that's bollocks. The idea that Brian Wilson was a genius who ruined his brains with drugs and would have been pop's Mozart had he continued. Garbage."

Bob and I are now on restricted duties and have been moved out of the custody office. Bob is in the roll call office. It does not sound like his levels of industry have altered.

I am in the performance management office working directly to Ashton. I work with Pete who is also on restricted duties. Pete is slowly dying from stomach cancer in front of me but cannot get an ill health pension for some reason. Neither of us can work a computer properly nor really understands statistics but Ashton wants information on everything. Pete told me on day one the order of the day is 'can you break it down?' You give Ashton say, burglaries over the last month on the division, he would then want the rates breaking down to when it was raining, when there were school holidays, when 'B' group were on duty. Pete takes it all in his stride.

It did not take me long to realise how he did it. He made most of it up.

"Give him the figure with confidence and, most importantly, the figure he wants to hear."

"You'll get caught out Peter."

"Doubt it very much and anyway...."

Yes, you will probably be dead, but I digress.

Bob wants to meet and I have walked in on him at the end of the day treating Julie, the clerk, to one of his set routines, the Beach Boys one. Can't say she looks impressed or interested.

"Christopher, felicitations, come in Julie is just going. Oh yes you are talking bollocks Julie. Look at all pop groups, all of them, they all run out of inspiration within a few years. They all do. Yes some keep trucking on forever in stadiums and arenas but it's just their greatest hits plus new shit no-one wants to hear. No, you have it, then you lose it, Julie. Brian Wilson is no different, just can't admit it to himself. Anyway I am keeping you, it's double Corrie on later so it's a big night. Give my regards to Alex.

Take a seat Chris, I will make us a coffee and we can talk about how we are going to approach prison. I am thinking of going cissy. What about you, taker? Giver? Or going to fist fight your way every day? Think you need to rethink the comb over you have, people will take the piss. And, yes, saw you checking out Julie as she left the office. Your passion for Mrs Pendleton fading? Absence not making the heart grow fonder in this case? You could do worse than Julie, do you know her history?"

I did not but he was going to tell me.

"She will be up for it. She used to be a PW back in the day. Only in for a couple of years when she took up with Alex Foster. You would not know Alex Foster? Old school CID, bent obviously, like they all were, but otherwise a stand-up guy.

I was there when they met. There was a shift night out at Bernard Manning's Embassy club. Anyway he was on a separate CID do and did not know Julie. She had this leather jacket on and scarf when she walked in. Alex was opposite her when she sat down. She took off her scarf and jacket in front of him. She had just a low neck vest top to reveal the most mammoth tits you have ever seen, gargantuan, I am talking a dead heat in a Zeppelin race.

Alex could not speak at that moment of revelation. You see he was a fully paid up mammarist and must have thought he had died and gone to heaven when he saw them bangers. I am telling you it was the moment that changed his life and I was there Chris. I was there, actually there.

Well it was the old story. She was star struck with a proper detective ten years older being interested in her. He just could never get enough bouncy bouncy. Within months he had left his wife and young kids and moved in with her. She got pregnant almost straightaway. Alex was in dreamland, they would actually get bigger.

Anyway, she decided that after her first pregnancy her back would not be able to take her boobs getting any bigger ever again and she wanted more children. She had a reduction. It was unheard of in those days, must have cost a fortune.

Alex was devastated, I mean devastated. He would have left her but he could not afford two lots of payments for kids and live on his own. He had left his wife and kids for those tits and she took them away from him. She took them away from him. He never recovered from the betrayal.

They are still together but hate each other. He is a retired bum spends his days in Weatherspoons with other ex-job talking broken biscuits in Tesco jeans and white trainers. He drinks so much I think it's a good bet it will have been a long time since she had her tyres rotated so, in summary, Chris I can put in a good word if you are interested ……….."

"Bob I will pass on that but have to say you are a born story teller. It's the way you turn everyday tragedy into a thing of beauty, it's a real gift."

Bob looked lost in his own thoughts, wistful, not rising to it at all.

"Yes breast reductions are a sin against God's natural plan crying out to heaven for punishment. If I were Prime Minister I would outlaw them."

Bob eventually came out of his reverie.

"Fuck off then just trying to help you."

Coffees made, Julie gone, he became serious, as serious as Bob ever gets.

"OK big boy, thought we needed to compare notes. Firstly we both need to keep praying Jesse Dumbfuck stays alive for obvious reasons. We do not want a coroner's enquiry, drags the whole thing out. Coroners have integrity and independence and all that bollocks, would not be able to manipulate them. We are stuffed if he dies, the lad needs to stay a vegetable."

"I know I do think of him, if we had acted quicker."

"Don't waste your time on that shit, that'll fuck with your head. He was due to have his TV series cancelled shortly anyway. Probably will live longer on a ventilator. May be having beautiful dreams of being a DJ at Glastonbury on the Pyramid Stage. That's what it said in the paper he dreamt of wasn't it?

Anyway to what we can control. Bet your solicitor has told you to blame me for not doing the visits etc. and that you had trusted me to book Brooks in properly. That if you had booked him in you would have made him stand up and carry his own weight and would have determined he was in no fit state to be detained and have sent him to hospital. That you would never have just let them carry him to the cells but you were tied up with that mental health case. You would have overseen a search and the bottle on him would have been found. That you had every right to believe I was experienced clerk who knew what I was doing and you feel let down. You will have to concede it was your responsibility as a sergeant to ensure everything was done correctly but you just did not have the staff or more pertinently you had the colossal fuck up that was Hong Kong Bob."

In a nutshell, yes.

"Now before you say anything I am advised to say that I should not have been in the position of having to book him in and that was your responsibility. Also that I had not been trained to book people in and that you knew I was on restricted duties"

"What's that?"

"My back, special chair etc., doctor had recommended I could work in custody but only in a back office capacity and not have full contact with prisoners."

"Come on, really Bob? I thought it just prevented you from wearing body armour."

"You will find Christopher there is documentation which I have from the doctor which shows my restriction, no adversarial contact. It is five years old I grant you, but there is none rescinding it showing me fully fit. So I, out of the goodness of my soul, and my indefatigable commitment to GMP continued to work with a bad back. I could only do one-on-one visits without actual contact with the prisoner so I used to pull the cell hatch down or just kick the door. I thought you knew that."

"You are taking the piss?"

"Christopher, of course I am taking the piss. May I continue? And obviously that your, as yet, unrequited passion for Mrs Pendleton's doubtful charms caused you to let her go early exposing me to a dangerously low staffing level with an untrained probationer, sadly no longer with us."

He held up a hand to stop me intervening, I wasn't going to anyway.

"Look here's the plan. We have two hurdles to get over. One is to not be charged with criminal conduct i.e. misconduct in a public office. The threshold for this is high so we just need to convince the investigators we are common or garden fuck ups rather than people who have done something seriously wrong.

Don't think we will have much difficulty in that. I mean look at me on the verge of a mental breakdown lost in the Cumbrian wilds, Collyhurst's King Lear. You? Look at your comb over. Should be a piece of piss."

"Of course winding up the IPCC with the orange juice stunt has helped."

"All part of the plan Christopher. Confusing the enemy so they can't see straight."

"An alternative theory is that you just thought it was funny and could not help yourself."

"That has some validity I would agree. Look to return to the point at hand. We did not beat him up or anything like that. We are incompetents, not thugs, and that is our defence against a criminal charge. I am advised it is relatively easy to avoid criminal charges as long as we do not hang each other out to dry. The bigger hurdle is not getting sacked through discipline.

You will have seen the kind of stuff the PR department GMP has put out and the pressure that black bitch sister is putting on by mouthing off in the papers. Hooker clearly has visions of a headline where he tells everyone where he will not tolerate this kind of behaviour in his new GMP, sucking up to the black lobby. Don't get me wrong don't blame him, that's what I would do."

If they made you Chief Constable Bob.

"So he has decided we are getting sacked my friend. So all the pleadings in the world will get us nowhere. We will be sacked. This has got too political so we need to think of other plans. We have worked too hard and are too close to our pensions."

I will let 'we' in the 'we have too worked hard' pass.

"So you think that suing the Force for getting your picture in the papers twice in one week will help?"

"God no. Cannot see how that would affect the hearing though. No that is an insurance policy for later. They will pay me out when this is all over, trust me. They always do, they always do."

"So Johnny Cochrane how are you, we, going to do this?"

"Don't know precisely but multiple lines of attack. Firstly we play politics like they are doing. Most obvious one is that we are the real victims. We should have been managed properly. We were bullied to accept too many prisoners by Ashton. Management were not interested in prisoner welfare. I have dug out a load of stuff from HMI inspections about the ways they should be checking our work and they do none of it. Let's face it, and this actually is true, no one gives a shit about what goes on in custody until it goes wrong. Obviously we were exhausted from working 7/7s and Ashton had not provided staff to replace us on our refreshments."

That's the kind of advice I was getting too from my solicitors.

"The Henderson thing is harder to work out how to play it. What she said about not knowing she was in charge is gold. I've been hearing Hooker has it in for her and could be a feather in his cap if we could offer her up a management victim but not sure if this could fly?"

Bob looked so earnest as a political spin doctor weighing up his options. Fat, wonky bespectacled, white-socked Hong Kong Bob.

"Probably not. Anyway she had a good shooting all right. Never off the TV. Bursting into tears live in TV on the day was high risk but it paid off 'she was such a beautiful girl, such a beautiful person'. It was nicely done you have to accept that."

Seemed very human and touching to me. No point in trying to argue with Bob though.

"Bob not sure if this would work, thought you said anyway Hooker is determined to have us sacked."

"You need to build them a golden bridge to retreat across though, don't you read your Sun Tzu? Of course, the biggest asset we have is that these bosses think they have integrity."

"You'll have to expand on that one Bob."

"Look Chris when we joined all the bosses were bent, but then again we all knew they were. They did not pretend they weren't. We all were, that's how the system worked. It was necessary to do your job, no DNA and CCTV to get convictions then, we had to make it up, all of us. So we were all in the same boat, we all knew where we stood. Our job was to keep the shit out there at bay by any means.

This meant the top brass could be proper bosses, make proper decisions without fear of being challenged or exposed because everyone was in on it. If you blew the bosses out you blew everyone out. The bosses had networks to deal with those who tried to step out of line. Even I played the game then. It all worked. Police were respected then and the shitheads knew their place. We were the envy of the world, all that bollocks.

Now we have these graduate guys at the top who are just as bent but they don't think they are. They think they have integrity. They think they have cleaned up Dodge with their ethics and compassion so it entitles them to loot the public purse for cars, retainers, tax free contracts, conferences abroad and all other kind of bumfluffery. They are just as bent, more so because they don't give a fuck what happens out there.

So now it's a jungle. People like me take the piss constantly and they have no authority or means to get deadbeats like me in line. So they have to twist in the wind to make sure they survive......of this, no more Christopher. It is important though we don't hang ourselves on interview. Chris this is important.

That's why I asked you here today, and the pleasure of your company obviously."

"Look you just don't want to be dropped in it by me. I get that. Bob have you given any thought to what you would do if you are sacked?"

"You might as well ask me what I would do if I had no dick. No."

"Well Bob. I can't sleep. I can't eat. This is all I think of all the time. Not just getting sacked, we could go to prison."

I was having other thoughts too but wasn't going to tell Bob.

"OK Chris you need to get out more. Look if Julie doesn't do it for you give Gina a call, do it. Ask her to lunch, women never say no to food. Never. There's a £5.49 offer on at the Harvester if you order between two and five, two courses. She lives near there.

You can let her talk about her problems. Women love doing that, making themselves more unhappy talking about what makes them unhappy. You know living with Peter Sutcliffe, her daughter tapping her up for money, having now to work for a living with Tracey in custody who sets an alarm every half hour to make sure visits are done in time.

You don't have to listen to it all. Indeed you can just think of your problems and that face will make her think you are empathising. Anyway after she is done tell her you have wanted her to stroke your big boy for the longest time. Now what's there not to like about that plan?

Best scenario you have an afternoon of hot rumpy-pumpy in your bungalow at Royton, result. Worst scenario she gets all 'how very dare you?' which she won't. But if she did it will take your mind off your problems and it's all out there. A load off your mind."

"Bob, not just a story teller but an agony aunt."

"Fuck off then just trying to help. You can lead a horse to water.

No, we are not going to go to prison Chris. We are not even going to get sacked. In the immortal words of Sid Wadell, 'this is David v Goliath but this time David is going to win.'"

CLARA

Crying on live Sky TV was mortifying. I hate it when people see me cry.

I thought that this was the final straw that proved I could not hack it. I had already heard whisperings that Hooker was planning to move me. Brian was quiet in the office afterwards with me. He was nice but he clearly did not see it as anything other than totally unprofessional. Hooker sent me a message that night about all of us being human; always double edged with him.

Well the reaction the next few days in the papers was completely unexpected. I was a national treasure. It was double mortifying in that it felt this was all suddenly about me and not Charlotte. Jocelyn Purvis phoned me. She was just so lovely, she just understood exactly, her daughter was dead and there she was understanding what I would be going through, thanking me. Of course I blubbed again.

She emailed me some pictures of her baby Charlotte growing up in Devon. I printed one off, of her on top of a horse, she must be fifteen or sixteen. I have framed it and have it in the kitchen in the flat in Manchester. I know I did not really know her but every time I look at the picture I think of all that potential. I cannot help but think of where I was at that age. I have to have that picture there but I cry if I look at it for too long.

I keep thinking of what Matt Donnelly said when I spoke to him on the phone. I had wanted to see him but his wife was banning visitors.

"She should never have joined the police. She had taken a wrong turn. She should have been a doctor or a barrister in Devon."

He was right. Jocelyn told me that her husband had thought she could do better than joining the police but she had told him to stop cribbing at her, to let her forge her own life, that if it was not for her then she would find something else. She tells me this every time we speak. Guilt is awful. It's always the people who have the least to rebuke themselves for who suffer from it most.

Jocelyn never speaks of it directly but you can imagine how her life has changed. Not many months ago she had a retirement with her husband to look forward to. She had Charlotte graduating, getting a job, moving out, starting her life. Within months a horrible, violent, undignified death for her daughter and a husband with vascular dementia. The doctors say descent will be rapid.

I remember writing to her soon after she had told me about her husband's diagnosis, is there anything I can do? I explained David had so much money we could pay for any help at all. Regretted sending it the minute I had pressed send, just sounded vulgar. Wrong.

But got a lovely email back within the hour.

It is clear that you are one of life's angels with so much love to give Clara.

You will understand I married Trevor for better or worse. It will be a pleasure now to nurse him through the worse on my own. I have my faith, my memories of Charlotte and I have Trevor and this will keep me going every day

What is there to say?

Keep thinking of the day of the funeral. I was sat in the benches for our division at the Cathedral when press office Carol came up to me. She wanted me outside in a guard of honour as the coffin came in. You just do as you are told in these situations. I found myself next to Gabriel and that cold fish Kenyon right next to the door of the Cathedral.

Anyway right on the path blocking the entry on his haunches was a photographer. Scruffy, old fashioned raincoat, unshaven, not designer stubble, unshaven. All he was missing was a pork pie hat. I could swear he was chewing.

All these police officers around and no-one saying anything. He took some pictures and then disappeared down the path. I would have said 'is it me or.....?' but was not the time to speak.

Within a minute it started raining. Drops to heavy rain turning to proper downpour with heavy thunder. We had to stay there in our tunics, rain dripping off our hats as the coffin went by. When I say we were wet through I mean it literally, through to the underwear and skin. Had to stay like that through the entire ceremony.

There was tea afterwards in the town hall. It was not crowded. Not many had braved the rain from the Cathedral to the Town Hall. All the police had gone apart from senior ranks, I hardly knew anyone. I had managed to get back to my flat and change into a dark trouser suit quickly and put a comb through my hair.

Poor Kenyon toughed it out in his sodden clothes, stood on his own in the middle of the hall with his cup and saucer all alone. Always has a slight hunch as if embarrassed to be so tall.

"I would say you will catch a death of cold. You must be so uncomfortable."

"Yes well I do not understand the precise biology of all this. I think bacteria thrive more in colder conditions. Yet people tell you to take a cold shower to prevent getting colds. "

"But so uncomfortable. I have changed completely, underwear and all that."

He looked at me disdainfully, the mention of underwear.

"Yes well I suppose I felt that it all really does not matter, does it?"

He would have been happy to stand there in silence. Thought of something to say.

"What on earth was that press man doing there? I had no idea we would allow the press that kind of access at a funeral. I suppose in my life to date funerals have always been private events. It's one of the things where the police is so different."

"No that was not the press."

Kenyon was now looking over my shoulder but with an air of distant absent mindedness.

"That was the Force photographer. It was Gabriel's idea to get an upward shot our dark uniforms against a thundery sky. Reminded him of the funeral scene in Evita, the movie. The darkness of it all. He wanted you there as you had been the human face of these slaughters."

He sniffed. I could not tell if it was with derision for me or Gabriel. Or both of us.

Or the start of a cold.

PAUL

It was Johnny who persuaded me that TV bitch could still be lying. Perhaps I am too soft, perhaps she did still have the pen-drive. Johnny took a couple of brown rats and a plant pot round to her flat. She still did not fold. Looking back on it she never was going to, Johnny just wanted an excuse to do it.

Time to consult my consiglieri. I had not seen her for a while. I decided we would not meet at the usual place, instead we would make a night of it in Windermere. About time I treated myself, and her for that matter.

Sheila Moran she calls herself, bright girl, barrister, ruthless, I love her. She is one the real few pleasures in life. I had been seeing her for many years now. More years than I would care to admit. She put her finger on the real problem straightaway. She always does.

"The pen-drive is just a mystery but not one that needs solving. I can't think of who would have the wherewithal and the sheer balls to steal from a Chief Constable other than someone seizing an opportunity.

If you are asking me, it was the girl, it was an impulse and now she has destroyed it. If it is not her, then you are right, he probably mislaid it. After all he is hardly behaving sensibly in seeing you. Whilst he still off guard you should tell Mason you have the pen-drive, see what his pain threshold is.

I can't see how the papers could use it anyway but, even if they did publish, may actually do you some good. Bit of a profile at the moment may not actually harm you. I mean Paul, think of it, trying to represent that footballer was not a 'dumb move' to use your expression. You say it was but you don't make dumb moves. It was not a sudden irrational act. It was a punt by you, which does rather demonstrate your fundamental weakness. You would rather portray it as an aberration rather than admit it was a necessary move."

"Go on tell me about my fundamental weakness."

God, I do love this girl.

"Well as I can see it's not erectile dysfunction. You obviously just need those pills for Janice. No the walls are closing in on you. Thing is, Paul, you have never quite decided what you are. Are you a gangster or a businessman?

Look at Jamal, he is now establishing himself very nicely as a legitimate businessman, diversifying all the time. Hey he may even be an MP. On the other hand you have someone like Bungay in Bolton, just one of nature's criminals. He still goes round shooting people himself for kicks. What was that story you were telling me? He settled a drugs dispute on one of his estates by having the two protagonists fellate each other in front of him? Yes he is into all that shithead respect. It will be his downfall, trust me.

But you Paul, darling, are neither a near- legitimate businessman nor a natural recidivist criminal. You are just the brains behind Johnny. You have traded on this family man Manchester image which has served you well in the past, the mystique of it, but it now holds you back. You just have neither spent your money nor invested it in tangible things. It just sits there, difficult now to do something with it."

I had far less money than she thought.

"Johnny is getting old and you will never be able to replace him. You have no adult sons to take the business or to protect you. In fact if you tried to get anyone to replace Johnny they would realise you were ripe for the taking. You have already showed your weakness when you let the *MEN* take the piss out of you.

You don't want a pile in Spain or in the country to retire too. Even if you did buy one you would have everyone going through the finances. You actually still now want to live in your detached in Chadderton with Janice snoring next to you. Yes you would get out tomorrow if you could if you knew you would survive and could provide for the Janice and the girls, still see your grandkids and obviously......."

"Yes obviously."

"Yes well I will come onto that. Bear with me...where was I? But none of that can happen because you cannot just quit. In any walk of life you would have now sold your business and retired, but in this game you don't sell your business, you keep it or have it taken from you. You are struggling to prevent it being taken over, by force."

"Don't tell me, let me guess. Oh this is so hard, what are you referring to? The Bruen family?"

"Yes the Bruen family, Ma, Pop, Francis, Fred, Fraser and Foster, the Bruen family. You know it, come on Paul how many times have you told me? Your words, the old Ma and Pop routine is an act. Him in his sheepskin coat and flat cap, her with her big skirts and pikey earrings. He is a vicious greedy bastard and his sons are in his image, but there is just enough ambition and nous to always want more."

"He is a small time shithead."

"Oh Paul that old reflex, it's so sexy. He was a small time shithead but has acquired some knowledge along the way. He now has seriously feral but loyal sons who will do his bidding. He is wiping out all the opposition and has very carefully arranged for the twins to get sent down. He will then make his move. It's coming any minute now. "

"What? He's going to kill me? Best he could ever do was firebomb my door."

It wasn't Bruen, it was Jamal. He wanted more money. I wasn't going to admit that.

"Yes and you should have taken care of Bruen then. No first things first. The twins getting sent down means he can take over Moston and Harpurhey. The Keane family first and then he will come after you."

"He can't."

"Paul, he can and he will. And that is why you took the Dacic work."

I needed the money.

"You just could not afford for it to have gone elsewhere could you? To be passed over."

Only she could say this to me.

"So what's the move, darling?"

"Someone's got to kill Pop Bruen. It's as simple as that.

And soon."

JENNY

I had been looking forward to meeting Clara. Almost giddy with anticipation like on a boy/girl date. It has not disappointed, what time is it now, eight? Now I have a boy/girl date anyway.

We had been in since two. Clara had booked us in at the Italian place where the footballers go. Not a place I would even consider going, Pizza Express girl. She had texted me that she liked eating early afternoon and staying there into the evening rush. Did that suit? Yes it did.

I knew this was going to be fun so had decided to take the whole day off. I had got myself a new short green dress and a taxi to the place from round the corner. Worried all the time that perhaps I had overdressed.

When I arrived she was sat at the bar, bottle of white with two glasses already set out talking to a barman. She had on a pink suit, with a white blouse. Sounds naff but I can tell you it was not. It was smart, classy but just a bit different. She barely acknowledged me save to push me a glass of wine while she listened to the waiter. His mum was ill in Italy and he did not know whether to go back now or to wait for the holidays.

Well she had me right there. Loved that she never took her attention off the barman until he had someone else to serve but she had already got me a glass. Waiters had brought some antipasti to the spot where we were sat on high stools. She explained she had ordered for the two of us.

"It's a strange thing I have but I always want everyone to eat the same at a table. I mean that is what families do at meal times, that's the whole idea of sharing a meal isn't it? You don't bring separate dishes out at family meal times do you?

If I opened a restaurant there would only be one meal on the menu for that day. David thinks I am quite mad but he goes along with it. Poor fellow when I really want something he has to have it too. Anyway hope that is ok with you? Is it? You have any things you don't like?"

Happy to go along with it. We moved to a table, bench booth thing so we were sat next to each other. Crab and pasta, followed by veal in cream and mushrooms. Two bottles of Portuguese Vinho Verde 2005 consumed in no time, cold, almost sparkling. I am going to buy crates of that stuff when I get home. Drink the £5 stuff from supermarkets usually.

I found I was talking about myself and my career more than I ever had. After all it's not like Tim was ever interested. Alcohol helped obviously. Told her the story of Martha Maitland and her mum. She wanted to meet them privately, asked me to send some contact details.

I was telling her about the problems I had with Sarah and the Hooker article when I suddenly realised she had not been fielding calls or fidgeting with her phone as all cops do.

"The more you answer the more they will call. The Chief has a long drive to and from work and uses it to ring people to check up on them. He likes to lord it over us new joiners. He used to call occasionally about 6-6.30 on the way home. What I learnt to do was to ignore the call but call him a lot later at night when he was at home as if it may have been urgent. That stopped him pretty quickly. If he ever calls now he tries to call me with his number showing 'unknown', as if I would not be able to work this out."

I told her about how Hooker calls me regularly too when he is driving and is free with information. I knew I was going to tell her that today. I would not have done previously because that would involve breaking the rules of journalism, protecting your sources. Perhaps it is 'soppy' to comply with them. After all who made these rules? Are they written down?

Clara went silent, lost in contemplation. I wondered whether this had been a bad move. I had shown myself to be indiscreet, perhaps she may not trust me anymore. She spoke as if still contemplating.

"Yes I can imagine that's exactly how he would be."

Emphasis on word 'exactly'.

"Shall we do the 'isn't Hooker weird?' conversation? Tell you something Jenny, he works hard at pretending to be weird. I think he really thinks he is having everyone over. What about the ridiculous way he speaks? Affecting that estuary voice, honestly, when he is from Coventry. And all that stuff about compassion, tell me does he appear a compassionate, warm person to you?

He thinks he is a director rather than an actor. He is laughing, thinking he is having us all over. He will see the relationship as him controlling what he gives you and it will not really occur to him that you could have a part in this, that you could be controlling or influencing him. Just won't even occur to him. Do not think he realises how people can see through him, like withholding his number. So once you know all this you can use his indiscretion back against him."

"Don't see I can do this, Clara. I am just a reporter. He has the power and the information. He can stop that flow at any time. It's a game we are playing and I just have to go along with it. "

"Probably Jenny, but you compromise a person by degrees not in one go. You lead them to a place slowly so they barely realise they have crossed the line. You then get them to think they cannot now go back. If you wanted you could easily get Hooker to a point where he thinks you think you and him have some kind of a relationship. Then you would need to get him to think everything he told you you believed was in pursuance of the relationship. Love to see how he dealt with that. The smart move would be to cut you off, but I reckon someone as arrogant as him would do somersaults to try to regain control.

Not saying you should or could do that but I would like to be in your shoes and see how far I could make him twist."

She did a kind of shudder.

"Listen to me, fantasising, plotting, scheming, that's what damaged people do. People who are not like Jocelyn Purvis, Charlotte's mum."

"See what you mean. In fact did something similar recently with a guy in IPCC but that was different, I think. It's odd you should mention this. I sort of decided recently, after that argument with Sarah, I should take more risks as a journalist and make things happen rather than report what comes to me. The minute I did my luck turned without me seemingly doing anything much different."

"And part of that luck was the story about me knowing nothing about custody?"

"Honestly yes. It came from someone I barely knew."

"Oh I can guess who it came from. Someone who hates for me for what he thinks I am."

"Sorry it's…."

"….your job I know. I do understand. More interestingly so what you told me about Hooker you may have previously kept to yourself but now you are going to take more risks? Yes, can see that are growing into yourself."

She hesitated for a second.

"Jenny if you don't mind there is something I have to ask you. Every time I look at you I wonder whether you realise how sexy you are?"

She laughed.

"Don't worry that not a lesbian advance, I'm not, but it is the really striking thing about you. I cannot work out whether you know that and have decided to hide it because of the positions it puts you in or that you don't really realise it. Sorry if I embarrass you."

"Well Tim, my boyfriend, once said something like that but that was early on in our relationship….."

I trailed away.

"Don't worry I think you have answered. Every man sat in this restaurant has glanced over here at some point. And trust me it's not me they are looking at."

I thought they were. Weren't they?

"I'm sorry it's just when you are talking about Hooker you did not seem to be aware at all of the effect you could be having on him. I know he seems a cold fish but……."

Her turn to trail away.

It occurred to me I still did not know whether he was married or not or had kids, must check later.

"Right Jenny. Who shall we do next? Oh I know, scrawny Carol from press."

I was about to say I don't like her but she was in full flow.

"Met with madams like that before Jenny. Her game is easy to work out. Crisis, perpetual crisis. She bigs up everything that comes in and, when it does not turn out as bad as she has predicted, claims credit for heading off the danger. Yes spends her day laying down elephant repellent powder round Chester House and, hey, no elephants. Convinces the bosses the world is against them and only she can protect them. Oh yes I have seen this before and can see it now, got your number lady."

"Neil, previous crime reporter said he used to get himself to sleep thinking of devising the perfect way of killing her and not getting caught. When Roger Mason went missing she actually went hoarse from all the shouting down the phone she did with us."

She started to talk about Roger Mason. This is what I wanted. She was going to do it.

"It's funny all the problems and personal abuse that came my way, well our way the direct recruits when Roger appointed us, no-one ever noticed that I really did not need to take this job. There was some talk of how much I earned working in PR but the press can be lazy in many respects. No one seems to have noticed I am married to a man who is worth millions. Even the PR firm is his really. He founded it just for me."

"Not sure I even really knew you were married."

She saw me look at her hand which had an outsize diamond ring.

"Well you would not have seen this at work. David Henderson? No? You haven't heard of him? No reason why you should. He calls himself a commercial property developer."

She laughed.

"Do you know I honestly do not know what he really does? I suppose that's a stupid thing to say, he is a property developer. He just buys things and sells them and has a lot of money and he spends a lot of time on the phone talking to people about spending his money to make money.

He is just opening a restaurant to rival this somewhere round here. Well he is going to get a footballer to come in with him to make it look trendy. His name escapes me. David does own a couple of places in town. We had been going to one for a couple of years before I realised he was actually the owner. That's how clever I am.

Until I married David and that was what, eight years ago, I did not really know how many rich people there are in places like Alderley Edge, Hale Barns, Macclesfield. Ordinary people, not judges or surgeons, rich ordinary people who have gone out made money and their money makes money. You are not ever quite sure what they are doing or how much money they have. I could honestly tell you I don't know if David is worth five million or fifty million.

So why am I a superintendent in GMP working for under £70k? You will want to ask me but dare not. Oh my days, I really do not know. I would like you to tell me. I can only tell the story and see if it makes sense to you."

She had been drinking quicker than me, but she had wanted to tell me the story, you could tell.

"Well you know I had my own PR agency. I was doing some pro bono work for a new charity for children who were carers for their adult parents or siblings, trying to raise some money and up their profile. So I arranged a gala dinner launch at the Hilton, it had just opened, your colleague Steph covered it. David underwrote it all and I got some actors from *Hollyoaks, Emmerdale*, couple of boy bands to attend, all very C listy. David's friends came too.

As a punt I invited local dignitaries and sent one to Roger, who I had never met. I remember he did not reply so he was not on the guest list. Anyway he turned up. I did not know him but I remember it was black tie do but he was in his full tunic uniform. We quickly had to find a place for him so I sat him squashed next to me.

So we got talking about the difficulties he was having in recruiting to superintendent level. He had had a lot of criticism about what he was trying to do in recruiting in outsiders but he had ploughed on. However the candidates he had got were not remotely of the calibre he had wanted or expected but to abandon the enterprise would be humiliating for him after all the controversy. He told me was going to cut his losses appoint one or two dull, safe candidates who would not let him down and not do any publicity about it.

I asked him why he had done it in the first place? I can remember distinctly what he had said. The problem with policing was that it attracted the wrong people. It offered secure and well paid advancement for the mediocre and assiduously determined. It was full of limited, semi-competent 'non-events'. He had always vowed as Chief he would change that.

So I told him it sounded like he had lost his nerve and would be appointing some other 'non-events' and that was disappointing to hear. He had probably been hamstrung by an unimaginative advert no-one had seen. Indeed the very kind of people he wanted would either not have heard of the vacancies or would not think they could apply. He needed to be ballsier, less conventional, if he wanted to be successful. I was flirting with him, double daring him I know, but I think I believed it too. Did I? Oh I don't know, this wine."

We had now finished three bottles.

"So he asked about how to handle the PR of the matter. I told him who cares? You are into it now. You have already been criticised you may as well go through with it. I had had a few like now and it was hardly considered advice. Anyway he offered me a job there and then. I laughed it off but suspected with him this would not be the end of the matter.

It was not, he rang on the Monday and asked me to lunch. I thought it would be the start of a seduction but that I could see that it would be useful for me to get him interested in some of the charitable stuff I do. Instead it was the job offer again. This time really determined, did not seem part of a seduction at all. He had thought it through after we had talked and he did need to be bolder. He rehashed all the arguments he had made on the night. He really needed someone who was completely different who would break the mould, not an army officer or someone from a local authority.

So told him I did not need the work, the money or the hassle. Do you know what he said? 'So why did you accept my invitation to lunch?' Great comeback. Not sure what I said, anyway whatever it was it did not stop him. He just carried on, he could not guarantee the job but he would have a great deal of influence with the interview panel but, ultimately, if I was not good enough then so be it.

He did not promise me the world. In fact he would give me a difficult posting to make the point. He said he would obviously not appoint me to let me fail, he had an interest in it working. He would guess I would either not like it or would be a great success. He would make sure I had 'a semi-competent non-event' to hold my hand early on, then it was up to me.

Why did I go for it? Why did I? Oh I don't know. A very long story. I married David so I would never have to be under the control of any man. Yes I married a man with money to avoid being dependant. I have just realised how that sounds. I am sure you sort of understand."

She squeezed my arm.

"I really liked Roger, not quite in that way, but in the sense that he knew what he was. There was little pretence with him. I cannot exactly explain it but at the same time it also annoyed me the way he felt he could offer me a job over lunch. Hark at me 'oh you are awful but I like you.'"

She was giggling.

"Never seen Dick Emery? No you are too young. Sorry. Where was I? Ah yes Roger. I suppose that I had to acknowledge he was right about why I had accepted the lunch. If I was not going to take the job then I was looking to start a relationship with him around charities and was opening the door to a man with his reputation. I suppose I applied out of a mixture of irritation, intrigue and coquetry. Is that a word?"

She pulled a face at herself and laughed, falling onto my shoulder.

Fourth bottle ordered.

"Anyway I kept telling myself that I can back out of this at any point. Then I found I was putting my heart and soul into the process and 'Ta Da' got the job. To be honest I do not think, even then, even then, I would take it. It was more about proving to myself that I could get the job than actually doing it.

So Mason arranges a celebratory meal for his candidates. Looking back at it, a meal out for superintendents, really? Come on, it was more of his seduction routine for me. I guessed then this would the time he would make a move. I dressed as glamorous as I could to play the game, to piss him off, you know 'look what you could have won?' Got the old push up bra and my boobs out. I had not done that for the longest time, David does not like it.

And, hey, one thing you would not need is a push up for those bad girls."

She nearly grabbed my boobs.

"Oh Jenny I bet there's some heft there girlfriend."

She giggled, gulped some wine, straight back to the story.

"Anyway Roger is charm personified and can see quite deliberately tries to pays no more attention to me than to any of the others. But it was all too deliberate. I started to flirt with the army recruit Peter Jones. Pathetic I know but I was enjoying myself. I resolved I wasn't going to let it happen but I suppose I just had to know what Roger was going to do. I had decided it would be destiny. If he made a move I would not take the job. If he did not, well, one last think about the job.

So he invited us all back to his flat. The other two cried off at this point but Peter Jones the army guy, quite pissed, accepted. Roger seemed completely unperturbed. I would have loved to have said 'no' and left Roger with pissed Peter but by now I had to know.

Anyway guess how we got to his flat? Driven by his police driver who had presumably been parked nearby all night waiting for us. I think I got a bit uneasy even at that point, something wrong about that. Then I remember that Inspector Evans rang. I could see her name on the front of the phone as it lit up. He grabbed the phone as quickly as possible and had the phone pressed into his ear desperately trying to sound casual but you could hear she was shouting. I was sure I could hear my name.

I was getting the wobbles by then, but when we got to his flat….have you seen his flat?"

"Well I may have, in the course of journalist enquiries of course…… of course, I haven't. "

"No sorry I did not mean to suggest. It's just that I would want to meet someone else who had. The second I walked in I can remember the feeling that came over me. I just knew I was in the wrong place. It was soulless, practically unfurnished but he had a picture of himself in Chief Constable's uniform on the wall. By picture I mean a painting, a painting of himself on the wall of his lounge. Seriously, of himself.

He had gone out to his kitchen because someone rang again on the mobile. I am sure it was her again. Anyway I had a quick nosy. I had a look in his bedroom. He had a camcorder on a tripod pointing straight at the bed……"

A long pause as she waited for me to grasp the significance.

"No. You mean he was filming himself?"

"Well what do you think? It just all clicked for me. I had seen enough."

"Could be putting two and two together?"

"Yes and the answer is four. Anyway it was mind made up for me. I made my excuses and left. Took a very pissed Peter Jones with me, who tried to kiss me in the lift."

She laughed.

"What a night. Men are just ridiculous, well both dark and ridiculous. Anyway I was lucky, close shave, went to bed glad of a near escape and woke up the next day resolved. I decided I was going to take the job out of sheer anger. I mean how dare he?

Funny enough I still liked Roger no matter how angry I was. There was something about him that I knew that he would now leave me alone and not hassle me. Which is exactly what happened. He was true to his word and gave me a difficult posting and Brian Ashton. Four months later he disappears and leaves me now with Hooker who thinks I am some high flying tart.

I am sort of stuck. If I left then I feel everyone would say I only got the job because of a relationship with Roger."

"Bizarre story."

"I know, Jenny, I know. Thing is with a guy like Roger God knows how many other bizarre stories there may be. God alone knows the reason for him going missing."

"Sorry Clara I have to ask. Why have you told me this?"

"I just had to confide, hope you don't mind. Other than doctors and priests, journalists are the only people who have to keep a secret. If I told my friends they would just gossip."

"How do you feel now? Did you say 'stuck'?"

"I did feel like that, I absolutely did, Jenny. I was sure I was going to get moved before the shooting then after Charlotte was killed, I cried on TV and I started to get rave reviews for my press conferences. I suddenly realised this was something I could do. Perhaps I had wanted the job after all. It wasn't all Roger. But then talking to Jocelyn Purvis I also realise I want a baby. She told me Charlotte was the greatest 'joy' in her life. Charlotte. Joy.

Joy. If I had a girl, and I want a girl, I would call her Joy. I want to stay in the police and I want to have a child. David will think I have gone mad. God knows how he puts up with me. Oh what to do?"

Clara grabbed my arm put her head on my shoulder other arm across me, and held it there for some time. She then jumped up.

"I nearly forgot the reason anyway I got you here. Young girls going missing....."

She got out a file of her Chanel bag.

"Look have a read of this in your own time. What's going on is just, well it's unspeakable. I thought we could do something about it. When you have a view about it we will meet up for coffee?"

Think we had stayed as long as we possibly could, place was filling up with evening diners.

Back out on the pavement it's suddenly 8 o'clock. Dark. Clara whisked off by her driver in a black Merc. I refused a lift, I would walk. I wanted a gap between this world and Tim ball-scratching on the couch.

This is the real world of adulthood, walking home from an expensive lunch, secrets shared, passed files. Leaving school, joining the *MEN*, living with Tim was taxiing to the runway. This is take off. I feel confident, free. Definitely not soppy. I know it's the drink but who cares?

Soppy? Watch this. Here goes. Yes still got the number. Here goes. I'll show you soppy.

"Hi it's Jenny from the *MEN*. Hi. Hi.

You remember you asked me to dinner couple of months back in relation to that missing pen-drive? Yes Jenny. No I am fine. Well I have been thinking. It may have been bad timing or nerves or whatever but I keep thinking about the fact you did not have the decency to even try to fuck me on that date.

I was just wondering whether you did not fancy me or whether you would like to try to redeem yourself? "

SHARON

Friday's meeting was a disaster. To be honest some of the lads let themselves down. Perhaps I did as well.

We had been at it solidly though for nearly three weeks, twelve hour days with one day off a week. I had promised all the guys we would go home a bit early this weekend and had persuaded Kenny to stay at home (not hard) so I could cancel the meeting. Then Callaghan decides he wants to come to the meet and we all have to go to Chester House. We were all fraying at the edges, still, no excuse. It has been on my mind all weekend.

Good news is that this will be a Kenny free week. He is on a course on Tuesday and Wednesday at Bramshill so he will be taking this day off as a travel day. I don't know anyone else who does this, but he gets away with it. He will ring on Thursday saying one of the kids is sick and he has to work from home, and then probably put a day's leave in on Friday. I'm not going to see him this week, I know it.

The bad news is that Callaghan told me and Kenny that the Tweedledum and Tweedledee sergeants who were in the meeting on Friday are being seconded to the team for a few days.

They are, according to Callaghan, "a couple of bright things going to go on the Accelerated Promotion Course in a few months. I thought you may benefit from a completely different perspective on the investigation and have asked them to knock together a quick and dirty report. I have told them to be imaginative. It can't do any harm can it? "

I wish I had told him the truth; they are going to be as welcome as a fart in a spacesuit. Something else to manage. I won't tell the staff what else Callaghan said to Kenny and me later.

"...the meeting only confirmed my view. I've only been in the Force for a month or so but there seems to be a 'big job' mentality in everything you, we, do. Gabriel is very keen we start directing resourcing to community policing and away from these big jobs. So unless the dynamic changes by Friday then you should be planning to see a 75% cut in your resourcing. "

He did the inverted commas thing for big jobs.

So I have got an AWOL boss, a demoralised team, a couple of Chester House spies watching everything I do and the small matter of a triple murder to solve with a quarter of the resources I should have.

Callaghan told those sergeants to be imaginative. I will show him imaginative.

JENNY

11 a.m. in the Malmaison near Piccadilly for coffee she said.

I was five minutes late and in a rush so I did not see her when I walked in, I was looking for someone on her own. I could see a guy small, beautifully dressed, grey suit, white shirt, polished brown shoes, healthy looking, sat on the arm of an otherwise empty chair. He was smiling broadly, at me.

"Now this absolutely must be the very beautiful Jenny. Yes, looking slightly flustered for being late and probably all the more gorgeous for it."

Clara had been sat facing the window in a high backed armchair. She peered round.

"Now David is just going and, in fact, has overstayed his welcome. He is being nosy, wanted to see you in the flesh."

".......and very much worth the wait."

He stood up, suddenly went all play- business- like with Clara, buttoning up his suit.

"So you will be coming back to Cheshire tonight even though you will only finish work about eleven and the reason for this is.......help me?"

"The reason is the roads will be clear to go home and I get to see you darling."

"So I now have to stay awake so Madam can tell me about being a Football Commander."

This was addressed to me.

"And of course she will be up early and taking the train into Manchester because she won't want to drive in congested traffic. Wonders never cease. Love a woman's logic. Flat in Manchester which she uses regularly, but a night when it would really be handy she decides to drive home. Good job I love you. Nice to see you Jenny, heard so many good things about you. Saved this chair for you."

He strode off with confidence, insouciance, one hand in pocket.

"You really commanding a football match tonight?"

"God no. It's part of my assassination or assimilation plan or action plan or whatever, I have to shadow someone doing it, which is posh for watch them do it. Been putting it off for ages."

"David seems…"

"…nice, sweet, charming, small but perfectly formed? I know Jenny, don't join his female fan club, it's nauseating. He is nice to all the girls. Smartened himself up especially for you today."

"No I was going to say seems to, well, love you, he is proud of you."

She smiled.

"I hope so yes. He is getting used to me being in the police now, not been easy for him."

"It's something I want, somebody who cares for you."

"You have not got that with Tim?"

I hesitated.

"No well then," she jerked her thumb, "out he goes Jenny, show him the door before you think he is all you have got. And don't chase it, you will know when it comes, and it will. Here's hoping for you that when it does he is not gay."

That laugh.

"Anyway I will get us some fresh coffee but you said you had something you had to show me? All very mysterious."

I showed Clara the fax we had received in the news desk. Print out of a very long email from Sergeant Matt Donnelly to her couple of hours before he was shot. It outlines the ongoing feud between the two families. He states that not enough resources have been dedicated to this and that it is likely someone will be seriously injured or killed soon. Clara did not seem as worried or angry as I thought she may be.

"Yes, yes all true. I asked Matt to send this to me as a summary of what was going on some days before he was shot. I myself was worried."

"But it does not read like that Clara. It reads that he is warning you out of exasperation that nothing is being done. The person who faxed the printed email is trying to blame you."

I handed her the front sheet. It said she had 'blood on her hands'.

"Sorry if this is upsetting but I thought, on balance, you should see this. Whoever sent it rang the news desk yesterday asking why nothing had been printed yet. You can imagine the Editor now wants a story before someone beats us to it. I am sorry Clara. Look you said you actually asked for this, I can sort of spin it that you too were concerned that this was going to happen."

"No that would look like I gave you the story because I must have something to hide."

She really is switched on. She went to her Blackberry, head down not speaking.

"Yes thought so, I sent it on to old Gabriel himself straightaway as an example of how complex things are and that just concentrating on getting performance figures up could distort things."

Bloody hell.

"Did he answer?"

"Sure he did. To the effect of just get on with it."

"What those words?"

"No, can't recall what it was. I remember he must have sent it just before he heard of the shooting because he tried to recall it. I won't have the email now though. I delete my inbox as I go along for a clear screen. Never delete my sends."

I am not a person who gets easily flustered but could feel my head getting hot. Fog had descended on me. I just knew I would not do anything to upset Clara but wasn't sure what to do next.

"Oh dear how did I ever get into this? Come on Jenny cheer up. It's quite simple. You do the article as if you hardly know me. You obviously cannot use what I told you about sending it on to Hooker and you can put in a quote from me to effect of what I have told you about trying to understand the situation. Do me a favour don't go through the press office, they will just make it all worse."

"I'm sorry."

"Why are you sorry? There is nothing else to be done."

"Do you want me to do the quote for you? I will let you look first obviously."

She was almost exasperated, voice up a notch.

"Jenny it is fine. Yes do the quote please I trust you. I would rather you did not show it to me actually. I hate all this machination stuff and would prefer not to read it or have anything to do with it. You are doing your job. It's my daft fault for getting into this situation in the first place.

Come on give me some good news. I like good news. You getting anywhere with the missing girls piece?"

"Well I have written it and just waiting for the right time to send it up."

I was lying. I had done nothing. I was sure they would not run it. There is no way Sarah would do it if she knew it came from me anyway.

"You think the paper might not run it?"

"No, I don't think so. I have a contact in the *Mail* who might be interested."

"No I want it to be a local thing, but you are right to hang back if you think it would get rejected out of hand."

She put her hand on mine.

"Look Jenny, no need for the long face, if it doesn't work out then it's not the end of the world, but things can change quickly anyway. I am sure there will be an opportunity to get it published. Cheer up, you said you are on a roll at the moment, something will turn up."

JENNY

It came in the post, not even recorded delivery. I got it when I came home from work the day after.

Package with bubble wrap, typed label on front addressed to me at my home address. Inside two envelopes with two numbered discs DVD1 and DVD2 in small plastic wallets. No note.

Tim was lying on the sofa, (where else?)

DVD/CD player did not work on my lap top and we did not have a DVD player. Marvellous.

Tim had put the post on the table but he never asked what it was. I just had to wait until tomorrow when the coast was clear. Don't think I even bothered hiding the discs from him.

I was tied up in court that morning, bail hearing for an asylum seeker who had run over and killed a child. He got bail (go figure) which made it a headline story which I then had to file. I don't like to phone my copy in, not very good at doing it in my head, I have to type it out. So I had to head back to the office to file.

So it was only later I got a DVD player in town, only £35, huge thing though. Headed back to the flat. As I put key in door I thought about how great it would be to finding Tim, home early, on the sofa with someone else's hands down his trousers for a change. Would I be angry? Would I even pretend to be outraged? Or would I laugh and tell him that I was in the Premier Inn two nights ago with my high heels in another bloke's ears?

Anyway he was not in and he had left his porridge bowl on the side without rinsing it. He would have to go.

It took a bit of time to plug the DVD player in to the TV working out what lead went in where. When I got it to work it felt like it was by accident.

Then had to clear up all the packaging.

Then I then made myself a cheese and pickle on a white barm, bag of Monster Munch and a coffee. I had not had lunch.

This better be good after I have spent 35 quid on a DVD player.

Showtime.

SHARON

I have done something way out of character. Way out of character.

Normally I am quite careful in life. You have to be, if you are in the police. Well I think women have to be careful, you don't have the boys' club to protect you.

I know I tell it as it is because I don't know any other way, but I am a far simpler soul that people would believe. So I can't believe what I have now done. I had a major panic last night and nearly rang Kenny to tell him. Soon realised I cannot undo it, and if I cannot undo it, I have to go through with it.

Well it has got Kenny back on work on Thursday anyway. He's due in any minute now, our meeting with Hooker and Callaghan is at 10.30. Kenny is dropping the kids off at nursery (obv.).

And here he is, Kenneth Poole Esq, waddling in to the office as we speak. Bless him, well bless him and fuck him at the same time.

It's hard to know where to begin with Kenny. When he came over from Lincolnshire he was this obese, scruffy, policy wonk with massive specs and bad body odour. He takes up with Varna Barnes and she gets him eye surgery, proper hair-cut, slims him down and gets him buying expensive gear. He was nearly handsome at this point. 'Nearly' being the operative word.

But he has piled the weight on again and all his bespoke stuff doesn't fit anymore. He always wears three piece so you are treated to his substantial midriff popping out early on in the day. What seemed classy clothes now seem gaudy. Nothing ever quite matches too. Always has shirts with a white collar but has all manner of colours beneath.

Thing is about Kenny is it's his style and he sticks to it. It's odd, other blokes take the piss out of him but he does not seem to notice or let it bother him. Come to quite admire Kenny for this. For a bloke with fuck all confidence, he has a lot of confidence.

Thing is I never really have a final verdict on Kenny. Loads of people ask me what's it like to work with him? Instead of telling them he is a gormless fuckwit, which people expect, I say things like 'could do worse', 'he is harmless', 'lets you get on with it'. All true statements but not the full truth.

Full truth? He is a fuckwit who got where he is because Mason wanted to break up Kershaw's CID Mafia. For this he just about gets my vote, just, today.

And then there is Varna. Varna Barnes, now Varna Poole who, in her probation, blew all of 'C' Group at North Manchester. Claimed she could make any man come within 90 seconds. Varna, lazy bitch who got into the Major Incident Unit doing admin after taking two of her first five years in the police off sick with colds, bad backs, stress, falls and women's issues. Then in walks recently separated Kenny Poole.

Next thing she's engaged to Kenny, then pregnant, which was nine months sickness, then back at work falls through a dodgy chair and leaves with a £55k settlement. Varna and Kenny went on holiday with the money. Brought back pictures of them jet-skiing, her back just about held up it seems.

Varna made him move house from Rochdale to Knutsford because there are 'better schools there' (in other words to avoid her kids going to school with Asians), had him join the local Methodist church (he wears the alpha tie pin everyday now) and has him ferrying the kids everywhere. Her latest is she has decided she wants to be a local councillor, Tory of course.

She rings him incessantly especially if it is later than 5.30 and he is not home.

Kenny does need to grow a pair with Varna but you have to hand it to him I have never heard him bad mouth her, never. He is not embarrassed by her at all. I think he loves her. I would not mind having a bloke who loves me and just does everything I say; well I wouldn't mind having it for a while anyway.

As I said bless him and fuck him at the same time.

I actually thought we would go over to Chester House in Kenny's car. No, he is letting me drive him in my scruffy Astra while his BMW sits in the car park. He has lost his ACC's car and has decided not to insure his personal car for business use. By his calculations the 40p per mile does not cover the cost of using his car and depreciation.

He is humming to himself as if to appear casual. Don't think it is an actual tune or if it is a tune it is shit or he has got it wrong.

"How was Bramshill? Good course?"

"Usual s- h- one-t Sharon. You know the madrassa for the Guardianistas."

That's not Kenny, he got that from Mason. Mason hated the place. He never let anyone go there unless it was a compulsory course.

"Not gone down well with the team Kenny. You being away."

He doesn't answer he just stares out of the window. Humming. I can't resist.

"How was the accommodation?"

Before Varna had the first kid Kenny was on a compulsory fortnight's course there. She insisted on coming with him. Kenny had booked a hotel for the pair of them at the job's expense. Don Regan told me the *MEN* got the story but somehow Mason prevented them from publishing. Kenny's story was that he had IBS and didn't want the embarrassment of sharing an accommodation block with colleagues.

"Adequate."

He continues to stare out of the window. He isn't biting.

"Sharon, can I ask you something in confidence?"

"Shoot."

Christ he has worked out what I have done. Was it that obvious? Fuck if Kenny can work it out, then everyone else will.

"Thinking of taking out an employment tribunal against the Force, what do you think? Do you know how much the reverting two ranks has cost me?"

"Fuck me not this old pension chestnut again, two questions in one there Kenny. Er give me the pension one first."

"I reckon my pension lump sum will be massively less. Could have been £305k but now will only be £215k. And the pension itself will now be only £28k instead of £40k. Shocking."

"Truly shocking Kenny how will you possibly survive on the breadline with kids? Shall we have a whip round in the office? Where did all this come from?"

Trying to keep my temper.

"Well the calculation is easy enough. It's just that well Sharon you know me I never wanted to be an ACC, more of an operational cop."

I nod straight-faced pretending to be concentrating on the road.

"But I did it step up after Bally keeled over and I became ACC. So it's a bit thin when they post in outsiders to replace us after all we have done."

"Well you weren't qualified to be ACC in that you hadn't been on the course, you had best part of eighteen months of it with car and all that stuff, free petrol and health. You could have joined a gym for free. As a wild guess I would say you did not. There's a big argument to say everything you had was just gravy. People replacing you are qualified, and, anyway, you were an outsider not very long ago. Anyway what would be your grievance at the tribunal? Sexual discrimination? Fucks sake Kenny."

"No I was thinking whistleblowing. I did join a gym by the way. The kids go for their swimming lessons there."

His voice was wavering already and I had actually reined back on what I thought. It was this type of thing that made people dislike Kenny. No, people disliked him for many reasons. It was this type of thing that made me dislike Kenny.

"Whistleblowing? What's that?"

"Well if you make a protected disclosure and suffer a detriment as a result then you can sue for unlimited damages. Unlike the protected characteristics which are limited in the amount of damages you can receive"

Kenny will have researched this stuff. He is good at reading stuff that doesn't matter. Don't know how he can concentrate when he has this investigation. Correction, I do, he leaves it all to me.

"I know what whistleblowing is for fucks sake I meant what was the issue?"

"Did you know Roger was having an affair with Inspector Evans? You know the DCC's staff officer."

"Kenny I have heard they recently found a tribe in the Amazon who didn't know."

"Well yes sorry what I meant is that I actually know it to be true and that he cheated on her as well."

"Not sure you can cheat on your mistress. I am not going to stop driving because I am in deep shock but go on and do NOT do that coy-_I-know-things-you-don't shit you do when talking about your time with Mason."

"Well got a call from the Duty Officer one night. There had been a domestic at Inspector Evans' house. Her partner had got locked up for hitting her but she had minor injuries and it looked like she had actually attacked him and he had worse injuries. You know the usual."

I knew what he meant, but also noted he had not really heard himself, as usual.

"So the DC investigating the case had asked to speak to an ACC directly about a very sensitive matter. Had to actually turn out that weekend and go to the station to sort it out."

Bet you needed Varna's permission.

"Go on."

"Well the guy being interviewed was alleging that the domestic had started when he had found her on the phone to Mason."

"How come?"

"Well he suspected something was going on for some time. That night she had been texting furiously and he could see something was going on. So he made an excuse that he was going out to the pub and then came in through the back door. She was on phone ranting at Mason. Apparently she thought he was carrying on with some reporter."

"Which one."

"Can't remember."

"Oh fuck off Kenny."

"No I cannot remember, she has had a mental breakdown now, really bad apparently, hospitalised. If you gave me a list of names I would show you. Anyway he had told the detective he would go not guilty and invite the press to the court. He would not accept a caution and wanted his day in court.

Anyway I sorted it. She had not actually complained so it was a pro-active arrest. So got the detective to get a retraction from her and had a quiet word with CPS, at highest levels, to effect there wasn't enough evidence."

"Did not sound like there was enough evidence. Don't get it Kenny, sounds like it will have all gone away anyway. One word against another, she would never have pursued it."

We were parked up at Chester House now in the car park. Had to compose myself before I got out of the car.

"Kenny, why didn't you ring me? You always do when you get anything difficult."

The word 'difficult' was not really needed at the end of the sentence.

"Well high level political stuff Sharon, did not want you involved. Anyway I told PK about all this stuff some time ago. Then I suddenly get demoted."

"Did PK get back to you?"

"No sent a flunky from the NPIA. He told me the CPS made decision on basis of facts alone. The BBC reporter refused to speak, anyway she was in no fit state on loads of medication. He had the nerve to say that it would be in my interests to keep quiet about the whole thing."

I bet he did.

"Yes I think so too. Kenny you should not be let out on your own. You did not need to do anything. It would all have gone away anyway if you think about it. You really could fuck up a cup of coffee."

"Yes but all those leaks to the press. Remember all that business, the failed trial with the detective and Neil Sidebottom getting sacked. Mason cracking down on contacts with reporters. And there is Mason having an affair with a reporter."

"You mean your friend Roger who promoted you twice Kenny, albeit temporarily. You want to put his family through all that because you may have lost out on some money that you were not really entitled to anyway."

"Suppose."

"And aren't there time limits on these things anyway I seem to recall? Three months since the last act."

"Well they put me on this murder with the Incident Room in Chadderton and they know I live in Knutsford. It's a punishment."

"You chose to live out of the Force area, or rather Varna did."

We got in the lift. I was angry. He had gone all puppy dog. He would try to be conciliatory.

"Sharon, sorry, not thinking properly. You are right. You always give it to me straight and I appreciate that in you. It's what I like about you. I will tell Varna tonight I am not taking a tribunal. Bloody hell."

He will tell Varna tonight that he has changed his mind.

Then he will have to change his mind again.

JENNY.

GOD LOVES HIS CHILDREN

No sound. Just this message against a wobbly black card.

Then a big smiley face up straight up against the camera. Curly flicked blonde her, 30ish running to fat. Yes know her, TV reporter on the Beeb.

"Chief Constable, come over my big milky tits."

Nearly choked on my Monster Munch. Anyway she turns in her back bra and pants back to the sofa. Good quality picture, could see her cellulite. As she turned the song *Paranoid Android* by Radiohead starts up. To be honest I did not know the title of the song, had to look it up. Tim loves Radiohead, just depresses the life out of me when I hear it. Music should cheer you up, shouldn't it?

There seem to be three different videos and the film kept cutting in between them. It took some working out but there were three locations with three different women. One, I presume, was his flat, one looks like a hotel room, the last was definitely his office.

Madame Cellulite was in the flat. In the hotel room was someone I recognised, one of his superintendents, married woman. Remember she had been on *Woman's Hour* recently talking about balancing work and children in the job. We covered it in the paper.

In his office was..... well when I saw who was in his office I was, well I have no idea how I was. If I wrote I was shocked it would be way off the mark. God, she has been playing me.

Well as the song reaches that bit, the only bit of Radiohead I (used to) like, the choral bit. Well he does and in the office video he is actually stood on his desk. Would imagine takes some doing, him stood on his desk, her knelt on it. How do you balance?

Yes stood on his desk on the 11th floor of Chester House, big window behind him, blinds only half closed. Seemed to be dark outside but bloody hell; good job they clean the windows during the day.

I have not mentioned the third person, I know. Her knelt on the desk. I would never ever have believed it, never ever, ever. She had had me over alright. I was the more deceived.

The two- faced lying bitch.

SHARON

Now I did expect Hooker to be disconcerted by the death threat but I really didn't expect the reaction we got. To be honest I am also disappointed and, yes, disappointed in myself that this still disappoints me.

We were straight into see Callaghan that morning.

"Ok folks unless you tell me something new then it's going to be a massive scale back in resourcing."

"Sir, with respect I don't understand why we don't lobby the Home Office for extra funds, after all this has national attention."

Good point Kenny. I hadn't thought of that.

"Gabriel's view is that we have tried their patience with the bill for the party conferences. Look Kenny you can't just casually overspend because you have a big job anymore. The GMP overtime gravy train is finally pulling into the station. You will have to show me by how much spending more money is going to lead to the likelihood of capturing Keane as spending the money so far has got us precisely nowhere.

Gabriel wants us to police in the community and that's a lot of bodies out on the streets. The reason you haven't been able to do that in Manchester is you have been spending all your money on big jobs. I mean the amount you are spending on the Labour Party Conference is ridiculous and football is over policed. The economy is crashing round us which is going to have big implications.

And who knows, perhaps if we are more community focused we might pick these disputes up earlier before they escalate?"

"I see, so this is a political decision in essence and not an operational one. You are just making a point."

Nice one Kenny, and I have officially made my mind up about Callaghan. Cock, big time.

"And quite a brave one both politically and operationally. I mean when the Federation find out we are not dedicating all we can to this and obviously with the threat to Mr. Hooker's life."

I have to say Kenny played it very smoothly. Yes we get a number of these threats but this one had some details in it only the killer could have known. It used the term 'pre-emptive', it named the village Hooker lived in, it talked about how much he enjoyed killing the Bruens and leaving her with her skirt up showing her big red pikey knickers. It named the make of gun he had used to kill the Bruens.

"...it's highly likely, in conclusion, that the threat is from Keane himself."

"Or an inside job done by a malcontent to keep the funding, or shall we say double-time overtime, going."

Kenny was seamless.

"Yes Sir that is perfectly possible, but unlikely someone would do something so outlandish. There is nothing to be said further. There it is. It's your call. You are the ACC after all."

"Well before I take this to Gabriel I want the provenance of this double checking and verified."

"Sir, of course, we have done this already. Sharon has been over this and checked everything. We can't be 100% certain, you never can, but it appears genuine. If it has been done by a malcontent in the team they are hardly going to admit it. They will have covered their tracks. It remains, as I said, your call."

I have to say Kenny was impressive, animated by his resentment at demotion and the money he lost, but impressive nevertheless. Think I have said before he is at his best when he is down.

And yes we got the money for another four weeks. Kenny rung me late that night to tell me this (and that he was taking tomorrow off) and, by the way, Hooker had decided to have full close protection and an armed uniform police car outside his house at night.

"Fuck me Kenny it's all a bit of an overreaction. I mean some sensible precautions but it all seems over the top. Not sure any civvy would get all that. Don't know why, but bit disappointed in him. Expected a bit more bottle from a Chief."

"Well he's only human like us all."

The wise old Kenny routine. Perhaps he has a point. Go on, I will go there.

"I mean do you think it could have been made up by one of the team anyway?"

"Seriously doubt it Sharon, I mean who would put their job and pension on the line by doing that?"

Indeed. Who would?

"The only thing is, though, all that detail, the gun, red knickers, 'pre-emptive' spelt wrongly again, it did seem a bit contrived."

JENNY

It was her. Those boobs were as floppy and scuzzy as I imagined they would be. Disgusting.

The Radiohead song trailed away and the DVD ended the black card comes up again. And then this bit, which gave me the creeps.

FORGIVE ME

Did I sit there mouth aghast asking myself questions? Who had sent it? How had they got hold of it? What did they want me to do with it? Why my home address and not the office? How did Mason get an erection with her?

No, I went and made another cheese and pickle sandwich, I was still starving, but I was thinking all this as I made the sandwich.

Ok the second DVD. Could it top this? Surely not. Ripped the envelope. Bloody hell, not sure what this would be. I held the DVD in my hand quite self dramatically as if I was debating whether to put it in. Of course I was going to put it in. Suppose I was mentally steadying myself.

No idea what was coming. In retrospect it does seem obvious but at the time I really could not guess what it was going to be. For a horrible moment I thought it may be me in the Premier Inn two nights ago. Well, would you think straight in such a moment?

It was Mason and Sarah sat in his office, I presume before. It took me a while to work out he must set up his video long before the show started. Also took a long time to fully work out what was being said. Quite a few replays.

Forgive me if I omit the kissing and the playful touches across the couch. Yuk. I just can't bring myself to do it. The text gets the message across well enough.

Sarah. Well we have a job to do…..
(Inaudible)

Mason. Yes next bit you will tell me you were a reporter too, a long time ago

Sarah. Hey you! Less of the long time.

Mason. Yes and we know what a great source Kevin Kershaw was to the Manchester Evening News in those halcyon days.

Sarah. He could not resist me…..
(Inaudible)…..Neil still does a good job. Not as dedicated to his profession as I have been, though.

Mason. Well I hope you show that to me later. He is on his way isn't he? You told me last time you would get him moved.

Sarah. Yes I know, not as easy as that.

Mason. Well I am going to make it easy for you. Well we have been listening to a certain detective's phone for a while and he has been having some interesting calls with Neil. (Laughs)

Sarah (mock tones) I am shocked Chief Constable. Spying on legitimate journalistic enquiries in a free democracy.

Mason No spying on a constable who was leaking confidential information. Big difference. Yes well transpires there is a case coming up where he has pushed it a

bit too far. Still planning to give me
that Judy as a replacement

Sarah. It's Jenny. Yes she will be a
challenge for you. A proper challenge. She
is so fucking soppy I bet she has dolls on
her bed, practices dance routines in the
mirror and wears pyjamas with 'Sweet
Dreams' written on them.Hmm not sure you
would be able to crack that one Mr Chief
Constable.

Mason. Well we shall see. Madame Editor. I
will probably try the accidental text
routine I did with you. Anyway more
importantly she won't be as inquisitive as
the soon- to- be- departed Neil

Sarah (laughing) Oh no nothing like,
nothing like. Trust me (inaudible)
useless.

CLARA

"Some white wine Mrs Henderson?"

"No thanks, I'm fine."

"Yes you are Mrs Henderson. Yes you absolutely are. Hello I'm Don, Don Regan".

At the Chief Constable's Inaugural Award ceremony, basement room of the Midland Hotel. Black tie.

Don has been placed next to me. We've sat down first at our table, no 41.

"So I finally get to meet the gorgeous Mrs Henderson. And of course you get to meet Don Regan."

"Yes I do but I have never heard of you, Mr Regan. Are you a film or TV star or something? Specialise in overly forward ageing men?"

"I know, I know. Do you think I should dye my hair? What do you think, Clara?"

He turned his head to both sides. Greying. He looked quite good. Boyish face which meant could not guess his age.

"Hmm. Think that boat has sailed, Donald, may I call you Donald?"

"Yes my mum called me Donald when I was naughty boy.....oh go on, I set you up there. You are supposed to ask does she still call you Donald?"

I could not work out how much he had been drinking or whether he was naturally this exuberant?

"Well then Donald. I don't seem to have had the pleasure yet. What do you do in GMP?"

He laughed loudly as if this was so hilarious.

"Retired Clara. Coming up to four years now. Yes finished as head of Internal Affairs, called it Complaints and Discipline then. Yes don't try to hide your surprise I know look so young. Here because of NARPO, retired police officers. I thought you might recognise me from the media about the shootings I did?"

Yes. I knew I knew him from somewhere.

"Anyway enough of me let's talk about you. Far more interesting. Are the rumours true?"

I felt a wave of the disappointment. I thought he may have been a bit better than that.

"Oh you let yourself down there Donald. What a shame. What would you have said if I had answered 'what rumours?'"

"That Mason was trying to get through you to your husband's money for political backing. Then he found himself falling in love with you. Finally found something he could not get. Couldn't comprehend why a woman with a gay husband would not have an affair with him. One of the things that tipped him over the edge, possibly."

What as my old mum would say 'I'll go the foot of our stairs'? I had never heard anything like that.

"All true Donald. I can honestly say you the first person I have met who seems to know or has acknowledged my husband's money, in the police that is, or to do with the police. Well, well, aren't you Mr. Intriguing?

You need to know I am pretending to be composed but deep down Donald, deep down I am seriously impressed."

I was just about to say can you keep this level of performance up all night? But no, it would just invite a double entendre. And how did he know David was gay?

"Ok. Tell me something else I don't know?"

I found myself buttering the bread on the side plate next to me before everyone was seated. Rude but if I did not I would be giving Don my full attention. I did not want him to see that.

"Ok. I will Clara. Answer the first question."

"Honestly?"

"How else?"

"Roger, I think, recognised I had all kinds of hidden talents."

"Really, go on"

"Like pretending not to be offended when someone suggests I did not get my job on merit."

He went all fake dramatic, just a touch camp with it as well.

"Oh Clara. I have upset you. I need to redeem myself, instantly. What can I do?"

"As I said you need to tell me things I do not know. Who is he?"

I was whispering now.

A haunted looking man had slumped down opposite me on the circular table without introducing himself or his, well, frumpy wife. Grey hair longer than it should be on his collar, dusty jacket too big on his shoulders. She also looked like a proper lemon sucker, perhaps it was spending years with him?

They both gazed in opposite directions not speaking. He had picked up his fork off the table and was examining it. You knew instantly it was not that they were not talking. It was that they had run out of things to say to each other a long time ago.

Don stared straight ahead.

"That is Kevin Kershaw. Bet you have heard of him?"

BRIAN

Heard of 'Twitter'? No me neither.

Apparently lots of people use it to give their opinions of things. I am at a loss as to why anyone would be interested or would do such a thing. It's a kind of idiotic name 'Twitter' isn't it? Just don't see how it could catch on.

Well Acting Sergeant Julian Rose is at it again on Twitter. The man is just infuriating. I told Mrs H it would be a mistake to give that man an acting promotion. Does she listen to her chief inspector? I have only been doing this job for twenty years after all.

Only last month I had to have Mr 'Two Brains' in when our PR department pointed out to me he had a Twitter account. He had published five photographs of PCs all stood together with variants of the same uniform; fluorescent and black fleeces, jackets, caps and helmets, all under the heading #uniform policy?

You would think after doing something as asinine as that he would apologise and that would be the end of the matter. No, he asked me on what authority I was advising him as he was a private citizen as well as a police officer. I enquired later what I could do to close his Twitter account but apparently there is nothing I can do. Ridiculous, police should have that power.

People misunderstand him, some say he has some form of Asperger's but they are wrong. He is just one of these snide, underhand people who always has to get one up on you. Makes him feel good about himself.

When he does do something, he does not do what he is supposed to. When I had him in last time about Twitter I asked him what he was doing to get crime down on his patch and he started talking about trafficking of women into brothels in the City Centre, which does not get recorded as crime, or one or two crimes at best.

I told him that trying to stop trafficking was impossible and stop acting like Canute. He answered that this was to misunderstand Canute's actions who was demonstrating the limits of authority. He carried on that the modern psychological equivalent is called 'the fundamental attribution error'. Humans have a belief that that can achieve more than they can.

Then the cheeky bastard added that, "your belief that you can get crime down is a classic of this distorted thinking. An exaggerated belief in human agency over environment. It may be, though, on an evolutionary basis, advantageous."

So tell me this, does that sound like Asperger's?

Some people feel sorry for him but look at him now, acting sergeant, not so daft is he? He has worked Mrs H over. She is ok but does not have the necessary cynicism to be a police boss. Thing is, in the police, most people are trying to have you over in one way or another.

You know I can't help comparing him to Danny, Claudia's son. He's on a spectrum too like Acting Sergeant Rose, but with Downs. I have been with Claudia 13 years now, which makes Danny 15. He has never settled at any school and she is home teaching him at the moment. It means she cannot work or do much at all. It means we don't have proper holidays or even much time to relax.

I am going off the point. There is something wrong with Danny. There is nothing wrong with Acting Sergeant Rose.

You see, I am getting emotional, if Claudia heard me say there was something wrong with Danny well she would go berserk. No, Danny is fantastic, lovely guy, but he has challenges in his life. You can see Acting Sergeant Rose is middle class, educated, with all the advantages in life but still conspires to be a piss-taking twat.

So now Acting Sergeant Rose has persuaded Mrs H to have an official Twitter account which he can twit or tweet or whatever about missing girls. Madness. PR are telling me it is becoming quite popular. They can tell how many people look at it every day.

He has twitted.

Watch out exploiters of vulnerable girls #dayofactioncoming

When I was first told I really just could not believe it, even for him, but yes it really is true. Well he has pushed this too far this time. I know Mrs H likes his work but does she understand the operational implications of announcing in advance an operation? 'Oh by the way everyone, we will be raiding your house next week'. Like the Fire Brigade asking you to keep the fire going until they get there.

Things have not been going well last few weeks and could be doing without this, but putting him in his place may make a pleasant change.

There has been a big burglary spike over Autumn half term and I found out that idiot Brazier, who I put in roll call out of the way, had been authorising leave that week willy- nilly. I was furious with him. He told me he was trying to act with compassion as instructed by the Chief. He thinks he is being clever but he is heading for a mighty fall.

Then HQ wanted, with two days' notice, all our plans for Bonfire Night and staffing levels for Christmas. So I found out no-one in roll-call had cancelled those on rest days on New Year's Eve. So it was left to me to do it, the Bad Guy, but it has to be done. It's the busiest day of the year by far. Federation are complaining, suppose they have a job to do but staff know this rest day always gets cancelled. This is why people are paid so well to be cops. You cannot have it both ways.

Anyway Mrs H brought me in a bottle of wine yesterday to say thank you for sorting all this out. She did waver a bit when Federation first complained about this but came round to my way of thinking when I explained. I think the wine actually said 'sorry' as much as 'thanks'. I think she knows I have been left to dangle about the whole 'B' Group Parker thing also. I just can't even talk about that stuff at the moment.

So all in all I am ready to put Acting Sergeant Rose in his place.

Actually he is late.

"Sorry Mr Ashton."

Why doesn't he call me 'Sir' like everyone else?

"Just been on the phone to the *Manchester Evening News* about an article announcing our day of action."

Incredible.

"Well Sergeant it is precisely that I wanted to speak to you about. Indeed not sure you should be speaking to the *MEN* directly, that is what we have a press office for. More to the point, I don't recall ever announcing that we will be having a day of action in advance. It's like tipping off the offenders. Have you thought of that, Sergeant?"

"Yes Mr Ashton, thought the very same myself. But Mrs Henderson brought me round to her way of thinking. She told me how in PR, which she worked in for years, you have to change people's perceptions before you can act. If we just launched a Day of Action we could be criticised on the grounds of racial discrimination and we would not be able to defend ourselves because of the sub-judice rule. This prepares the ground, gets public opinion on our side first."

Before I can make my point, he carries on.

"I would take your point about losing potential evidence but Mrs Henderson reckons it is a price we have to pay for getting public opinion alongside. To date we have not mentioned race but anyway the Asian population is not as plugged into mainstream media as we are. Not many of them read the *MEN* and the offenders who we are talking about are so arrogant they probably would not change their behaviour anyway. You can see her logic on this. It's quite impressive.

Has she not discussed any of this with you? By the way, she told me I could speak to the *MEN* direct gave me the name of the journalist Jenny..."

What a complete twat. No Mrs H has not spoken to me, obviously, but he knows that. Just did not know what to say next. Suppose just should throw him out of the office, but that would feel like defeat. There must have been a long silence.

"You were a couple of years above me at school Mr Ashton."

What?

"Don't think so. Trafford Grammar. How old are you? I am 38."

"Yes Trafford Grammar. I am 35. I know I look younger. You were captain of Chess Club, do you not remember me? "

"Have to say I don't. Go on you are going to tell me you used to kick my arse at chess although three years younger. Another savant facet of your Asperger's, no doubt."

"No, not sure we ever played. I was no good. I hear you were solid. And for information I do not believe I am on the autistic spectrum or have Asperger's. To be honest it irritates when people say that. I was just trying to well be friendly as I do seem to annoy you a lot."

Christ what had I said? This lad had my career in his hands, if he complained. Jesus Christ. This could be really serious. I would not be able to deny this. No one would think he is capable of lying.

"I am, I am so dreadfully sorry. It just...."

I could not get any words out. This could be the end of my career, mocking the afflicted. Not sure who would ever employ me again, we have massive mortgage commitments, Claudia can't work. I could not read him at all, not sure if he even heard my apology.

"No. I have heard it in everything I have done. It does annoy me to hear it more and more as time goes on. I think people are deflecting away from what I am saying by labelling me. I actually hear it less in the police than anywhere else I have worked. In fact I enjoy working in the police more than anywhere. I am just reflecting Mr Ashton this is the happiest I have ever been."

"I thought you would have enjoyed school?"

"Hmm I did to a degree but found it……"

He was searching for the word.

"Boorish?"

"Yes precisely, boorish, Mr Ashton."

"Yes so did I. Julian. So did I."

BRODY

I can't wait for my police career to be over.

I've got that tattooed shithead Karl Parker sat opposite me now, watching me read his report, malevolently eager.

You would really think that a death on duty is what brings the police together. You would be wrong.

All started before the funeral. The shift, led by Parker, demanded that they be sat close to the front on the opposite row from the family where the plans had been to put the dignitaries. Someone contacted the *MEN* about that, so they got what they wanted.

Then Ashton refused to count attendance at the funeral as a tour of duty for people on other shifts on the division who were otherwise on a rest day. He had to cave in when pressurised. Everyone who attended on the division on their rest day was given a full day on their card. Loads of people turned up just to get the rest of the day off and went on the piss, in celebration of Charlotte's life obviously.

Federation also pressed for everyone on the shift to an agreed two weeks added leave which they can take at any time to help them 'grieve'. Think Federation beginning to regret what they have done though. It has got out of hand.

Two of them who arrived at the scene and are close to their pensions are trying to retire early with a sickness pension. 'Post traumatic' are the magic two words. Parker then wanted to do a sponsored walk from Harpurhey to Devon. Place where Charlotte died to where she was born. Note not a bike ride mind you, but a walk. He wants everyone on the shift who wants to do it to be paid each day as a tour of duty and expenses paid. Ashton again naturally refused and was overruled at HQ.

Now here's is the thing. Charlotte's mum has made it quite clear she does not wish any special fundraising and that all the money which was donated at first to go to the Benevolent Fund. So why? Why is he doing all this? Well why do dogs lick their dicks? Because they can. Parker is the sort who likes taking the piss for the sake of it. It entertains him. Parker then decided to put in a group grievance about Ashton. No-one from the shift will speak to Ashton, poor fucker. If he wants to speak to any of them somebody else has to be present.

So let us not speak falsely before the history is written. She was not made welcome on the shift. She told me she felt a 'bit of an outsider'. Now they all refer to her as if she was their favourite little sister 'Charlotte'.

To help them now get over the shock of their little sister "Charlotte" they all now want a weekend with partners at a hotel paid for by the Federation. They have found a counsellor who will facilitate some sessions to make it look kosher. Arranged for a weekend when they are on night duty, of course. Parker made me take this to Ma'am Henderson who is, of course, useless. To protect Ashton she has taken him out of the decision process. In other words she has hung him out to dry. Federation know it's a piss take but will fund it if Ma'am allows the time off. She will allow the time off if Federation have agreed to fund it. Not sure where this ends, if it ever does.

So now Parker is here with the latest. He has just presented me with a letter for the Chief and the IPCC.

You know I liked Parker at first. Thought he was a kindred spirit. Not above cocking up a story to get a conviction. Used to go on patrol with him, until he confided in me his story. Girl he was seeing (not his wife obviously) had been brought in for drink driving after her inspector had breathalysed her when she paraded for duty on mornings worse for wear.

He had been the custody sergeant. He poured coffee down the intoxilyser machine so it did not work. He then lied that he had told the new clerk to call a doctor to take blood. After an hour he staged a conversation on the CCTV in which he pretended to be appalled that a doctor was not on the way. He then put her in a van to go from North Manchester to Bury to go on the intoxilyser there. This at 8.45 a.m. in rush hour. It took 55 minutes. By the time she had gone on the machine at Bury she was well under the limit.

All told to me as if I obviously will admire him, not sure what club it is he thinks we are both a member of. I should have told him then what I thought of him.

So here he is now with a letter to Chief and IPCC stating he hopes there will be a full and wide investigation into the death of their 'much missed colleague, Charlotte Purvis'. It basically implies whilst they on shift they worked tirelessly whilst Matt Donnelly and his community team spent their time drinking tea with old ladies, bumming free lunches, regularly going out without body armour, not booking on properly, not being contactable by radio. And all with just a hint of the rumour that Matt and Charlotte were unofficially following Keane.

"Karl are you sure? Matt Donnelly was, is, an ok guy."

"Sir, there is a very strong feeling on the shift, very strong. We feel that we on the group are just at the bottom of the pile all the time and we are taking a stand. Come on Sir, if I had taken a probationer out, who was not signed up for independent patrol, when off duty in plain clothes with no armour or radio you know I would have been suspended by now."

"You would have been with your track record."

"Well as you know Sir I had a poor custody clerk nearly got me sacked. Civvies eh? To be honest Sir, I think I owe it to you to tell you this. The boys and girls on the shift have always liked you. You have always cheered everyone up, been funny about management. You have always stood up for us but there is now a real feeling that you have, well, gone native with the bosses……"

Shit-eating grin on his face.

"………. you don't seem to be supporting us. It's a difficult time after we lost Lottie."

"'Lottie'? Where does that come from?"

He lowers his voice.

"Sir, I was, perhaps, well, shall we say closer to her than perhaps people know. You can appreciate that I can't really speak about it, I am trying to do the right thing. It is really difficult."

The younger me would have hit him there and then.

"Bollocks. You bullied her because you could see, once she got a bit of confidence, she would stand up to you. You made sure she had a torrid time for the short time she was with us. She asked to work on another shift."

"Sir, as you well know, she wanted a shift system more compatible with her partner."

"Well, as you should well know, he was a solicitor and worked days not shifts so it made no difference. She just wanted away from you lot. That's what got her in the position she was. You and 'Lottie' an item, yeah right, bet you have told your counsellor that. Bet you have been hinting that to some of the girls on the shift for a sympathy shag. Life's just a playground for you and your fantasy world."

He looks worried for once. Good, I will carry on turning my hand into a fist, make sure he gets the message. I stand up. I am not entirely convinced I am not going to hit him.

"You need to get out of my office. And you have been told to cover the tattoos on your left arm."

"Just had another one done Sir, says 'Lottie', here look. It hurts at the moment when I wear a long sleeved shirt. I can get a Doctor's note if you wish?"

"And if I insisted you would turn that into a soap opera. You can only be the big man, can't you, if you are convincing everyone it's us against the world?"

He turns, composure regained, sure now he was not going to be hit.

"Yes I was taught by the master in that, wasn't I?

Take it's a no then re the letter?"

JULIAN

"Yes so did I Julian. So did I."

I could see Mr Ashton was not going to talk. I had already started rambling about my jobs just to fill the gap and carried on telling him about how I was the only child of older academics. My father a psychology lecturer and mother English. My mother had died of cancer when I was nine and had been brought up by my father. It had been quite a serious household, I was always disappointed at school with the level of discourse.

Mr Ashton looked like he was going to cry. Then he did. I do not mean a small tear rolling down his face which could go unnoticed, I mean proper crying. I suppose there was something sad in my story but this was an overreaction.

Mr Ashton just kept shaking his head with his hands over his eyes. I worked out it would be important for him that no-one see him like this so I shut his door. I thought I better stay with him to make sure no one else came into the office. I am not sure how long he just cried, head in hands. I did not say anything. I guessed he knew I was still there.

"It's just this 'B' Group business. It's not easy you know. I have started to become sensitive to everything that happens."

"Sorry Mr Ashton. I do not know what you are talking about."

He raised his hands out of his head.

"The grievance against me. A whole group who refuse now to even acknowledge me. It's as if I don't have feelings. You must know? Everyone …."

I don't listen to gossip.

"…..but you don't listen to gossip. You pride yourself on your logic. Tell me what do you think of this logically, Julian?"

So he told me the story but swore me to secrecy. Apparently if you are subject of a grievance, even one which everyone may know about, you still have to maintain confidentiality about it to protect the people who are accusing you. I think that is what he said. That makes no sense at all, not sure if he had got it right. But I did promise not to tell anyone, so I cannot say what he said. I think though I can say what I said to him after he had told me the story though.

"Well it's obvious you are right. Unfortunately being right does not equate with success. In fact it usually doesn't."

I was, obviously, talking from personal experience. I then remembered this.

"I once had a discussion with my father about how incredible it was that Nazis who committed genocide loved their animals and used to burst into tears when hearing Schubert. He replied that it was not a contradiction. He said it made perfect sense. Sentimentality is the flip side of the coin of fascism."

It had just come into my head. I was neither sure that fitted the issue Mr Ashton had told me about nor that, even if it did, he would understand. I reflected later it was a good example.

It also made Mr Ashton smile, just. I think he understood.

CLARA

"You live Macclesfield way don't you? Share a cab back?"

We are in the foyer of the Midland hotel. It's nearly midnight and the ceremony only ended half an hour ago. The whole thing went on far, far too long.

"Donald you have suddenly come back to life. Where were you all night? If ever there was man who peaked too soon."

I regretted saying even that. Would he come back with something smutty? No instead he looked a bit forlorn.

"I know, I know. I am sorry."

"And people say us girls are moody. No, but thank you I am staying here."

"What in the hotel?"

Well, somebody has perked up.

"Oh Clara, if only you had mentioned that earlier, given me your key. I could have switched the lights on, made you a hot chocolate, tucked you in."

"Yes that's a shame. A real shame. And here's me thinking that you were some high flying detective. I have my coat on, Donald, my coat. I am not staying here. I am staying in my flat over in the Quarter."

"Oh well even better. I will walk you home and you can decide when, on the journey, to tell me your husband is back in Macclesfield."

"He is at the flat actually."

"Oh Clara I am sure he is. Look it's a jungle out there. Anything could happen to a beautiful girl like you. You need me to walk you home."

"Donald, I feel that I am trapped in some bad *Carry on* film with you. So what's my line now? Yes, got it. The line is 'I am not sure if I am safer with or without you'. Hmm I will risk it. Give me a minute."

I went to the toilets to phone the driver to cancel him. Told him I would walk. I know, in these shoes. Don was intriguing though, have to admit. I wanted to know what he had to say for himself.

He took me to this tiny pub on the way. They clearly knew him there as they let him in even though doors had been shut. If nothing else glad of the pit stop in these heels which I was determined not to tell him about. Him in black tie, me in posh frock and coat, everyone glanced at least once.

"You see Clara, I know how to treat a girl."

"You certainly do Donald cheers."

Clink of glasses.

"Well what did you think of that?"

"Suppose I am a bit jaded from such things Donald. Did a lot in my previous job, role. But yes a lot of people seemed to enjoy themselves."

"It was disgusting."

"Well Donald you were a bit of a diva flouncing out when it came to Kevin Kershaw's award at the end. Lost you after that. I am guessing some history there?"

"I would not describe it as history, because it isn't over....."

"Is that hesitation a cue for me to ask for more? Or is that the end of the conversation?"

"Best the end re Kershaw. Anyway I was not thinking of him. I was thinking of the whole shebang. Oscars for the police. I found it just cringeworthy from start to finish."

"Oh Donald. Why so miserable? It is harmless, people enjoyed themselves all paid for by sponsors, did not cost the public anything. To be honest I think I put the idea of having something like this to Roger when I applied for the job. The wonder boy just seems to have followed through on it. You one of these people who have to criticise everything Donald? Were you not breastfed as a child or something?"

Breastfed! There was something about Don that made you say such things. Or is it that when you are with such a person that everything sounds like a double entendre. He did not pick up. He was gathering steam.

"Yes sponsors pay for it all. Some boring arse from KPMG, or EY or PWC, I don't know, next to me all night. Yes how does that work? They pay a lousy grand for the table and Hooker gives them millions to balls up re-engineering the Force or whatever they call it.

Notice how Hooker was on the Man United table? Don't know why we have to be in the pocket of the clubs. Hooker was dead against all this when Mason raised it you know? You know he's not really called Gabriel Hooker by the way?"

"I had heard something."

"No he's called Simon Jones. Brummy, like PK, had some kind of midlife crisis and decided to reinvent himself as Nigel Kennedy to make himself interesting.

Poor old Ralph Pollard old Lord Lieutenant, lovely guy, he stumps up for any good cause and wants nothing out of it. See where they put him? On the table practically in the toilets were with the also rans.

And another thing, hosted by Karl Parker, that bent bastard, Hooker's new mate. Trying to be a comedy host when he is only there because one of his shift died. Disgusting, absolutely disgusting. Did you hear that 'I told the gaffer I would do the jokes you hand out the gongs'?"

Not sure I have included all Donald's complaints. He moves from sunshine to thunder so quickly. He is now so animated, brow furrowed, rapid delivery.

"Oh no forgot."

He clicked his fingers in triumph at remembering.

"No I forgot the really classy bit by Parker was introducing the video message from the Home Secretary 'or as the lads on the shift call her, Jackie Big Tits'.

Oh yes and did you hear her father shouted something at him when he was doing the speech re Charlotte? "

"Yes he has dementia. Hardly got the chance to speak to Jocelyn she was so preoccupied with Trevor. He is so disorientated by the hotel she is going to drive back down to Torquay tonight. Poor thing. I offered her my driver but she insisted on going on her own, this late."

"Is that the driver who wasn't available to drive you back to the flat? Go on, you don't have to answer that. What did he shout out I did not get it?"

"He said, 'her name is Charlotte not Lottie'.

Yes there's something about him that's unsavoury that Parker character. I had to see him a couple of days about a confidential complaint issue. "

"Oh you mean the letter complaining about Donnelly? Yes Hooker put him up to that."

"No. I mean. What? How do you know such things? Seriously how do you know? How did it happen?"

"Well they meet all the time at every charity fundraiser, memorial event or what have you. Best mates now. Hooker ain't daft. He keeps Parker close to make sure the kind of criticisms I have been levelling on Sky don't get traction with the ground floor. I would guess Parker had been chunnering on at him and Hooker told him to write all his complaints formally in a letter."

"Why would he do that?"

"Well he knows Parker is the sort of snake who would say he told the Chief Constable and he did nothing so he's covering his back. Possibly he thinks it's some form of clever distraction, heap all the blame about the murders on Donnelly."

What blame? Never mind, do not like talking like this.

"So how do you know Parker? How do you know all this, Donald?"

"Parker? I was Head of Complaints when we tried to get Parker sacked for obstructing justice over a drink drive for some bird of his when he was a custody sergeant. Could not get it home. The rest, well if I told you how I knew then I would not know as much as I do."

"Oh Donald and there was I thinking I was getting special treatment. You build a girl up and then let her down. By the way 'bird' has not gone unnoticed. One minute you are Mr Morality and then you sound like Butler in *On the Buses*."

"I know, I know. Let me take you to dinner some time, make it up to you."

"Well Donald the thunder and sunshine experience is something else I have to admit. Hmm suppose depends on two things. Firstly this coyness has to stop. I want to hear everything you know and how you know it. Secondly, whether you are married?"

"Deal. Excellent. I know this place….. "

"Donald, did you just say 'I know this place'? What's the next line 'quiet, discrete, out of the way but good food'? I haven't agreed yet. I repeat the second question, are you married Donald?"

He did that I- find- myself- hilarious laugh.

"Well that just depends."

JENNY

Neil lived to be a crime reporter. He was in early fifties when the *MEN* let him go and had blubbed like an infant on his way out of the building. It wasn't good to see a grown man do that.

We had never really had a proper relationship as such whilst working at the *MEN* together. He was always ok with me but always seemed preoccupied, tense, busy. He never relaxed. If truth be known you sensed he thought he was a cut above like he was an investigative journalist and we were mere reporters. Perhaps that was unfair, but that was the way I felt.

Never really thought of him much after he had gone or what he would be up to. Did not even know his personal circumstances. I had this idea that leaving would have broken him and I imagined he would now be living on a house boat or in some smelly flat surrounded by empty bottles sleeping in until noon, that kind of thing.

However he had sounded full of life on the phone and eager to meet, giddy almost.

"Ah Jenny. I wish I could say I was expecting this call. But after Mason has been gone for six months and no contact. Well I have to say I thought it would never come. Need help with something?"

"Sort of Neil. I have found something out which, well, I will tell you when I meet you. It will make sense then. It's big and complicated."

"So big and complicated you can't tell me on the phone? Fantastic. Excellent. I won't do the 'Jenny don't drag me back in to this' speech. I want to know. Bloody hell you bet I am interested. You say where and when Jenny and I am there. Don't even start to tell me over the phone. No, let me guess. No don't, don't, I want to look forward to it."

So there he was sat at the table, most definitely not a broken man. He looked so much better, as if his face had been ironed since he left the *MEN*. Instead of just being unshaven he now had properly trimmed stubble. He had stopped dying his hair and looked better for it. Velvet jacket, pale blue shirt and mustard trousers so unlike the stained black suit and three day white shirt he used to wear as his uniform at the *MEN*.

"Well look at you."

He was talking to me.

"No look at you, Neil."

"Jenny Aaronovitch all grown up. Love the hair darling".

I had had it cropped expensively in town. Yes, it was like Clara's.

"And this restaurant."

Yes, it was the one Clara had taken me too.

"Look at you now Jenny. Look at you now. "

So he was now lecturing at Lancaster University in journalism. He did some freelance magazine article stuff for trade journals and was writing a biography of Cyril Richards, ex- Chief Constable. Neil liked him, man of real integrity he said. I thought he was a nutter, wasn't he?

"Funny Neil I had an idea that being sacked would have broken you."

"Suppose it has in a way. I was re-married with a second wife who did not work and young kids. Had to keep going, had no alternative, especially after the stroke."

"You've had a stroke?"

"Yes bad do. Could not walk properly for about a month. Haven't you noticed one side of my face is stiff?"

"No."

I really had not. I could tell now.

"No, no really. You look so much better than you ever did as if leaving was the best thing that ever happened to you."

"Not at all. I earn more now, a lot more, but it's work for money. Time in exchange for cash, dull. Don't hate it but just sort of contemptuous of it. I used to love what I was doing. Now it's put the time in, get cash out.

I do look better but I have to look after myself after the health scare especially with small brats. Don't start talking about what the issue is, not yet. Let's wait until the food arrives. What about you?"

I told him about my argument with Sarah and that from that moment onwards everything had picked up. I could not work out whether I had changed or just my fortunes had. I expected him to comment, to pass judgement, but he just nodded.

"And how are you finding Gabriel? Does he still drive that mobile hairdryer at work? Yaris? Corsa?"

"He did. He has stopped now, told me he had received death threats from Keane, obviously can't print that. He feels safer in a faster Audi."

"He's always had that Audi. He used to soft soap everyone that he did not subscribe to having a paid for police car as an ACC. What he omits to tell everyone is that there was another option of taking the money to purchase your own car. He took the money and bought a big fuck off A6. He drives it round Derbyshire and comes to work in a Yaris or whatever, Mason told me. God he hated him thought he was a total phony. You know it's not even his real name?"

"Yes, Simon Jones, a friend told me."

"Did they tell you the story that Hooker and PK used to live together? No?"

Most definitely, no.

"Well story goes that Hooker, Jones that is, is on his arse as an inspector and PK, his chief superintendent, puts him up while he sorts himself out. I spoke to my counterpart down in Birmingham and she reckons it was for a few days at best and that there is no more to it than that, but the cops down there turned it into an urban myth. Don Regan reckons otherwise, but then again Don thinks everyone is gay, apart from himself. Hey if we got talking about Hooker we would be here all night. Saw him on TV he seems to have lost the stupid glottal stop he used to affect."

"Yes, and the spiky hair. Told me he is having laser eye surgery next week. He is trying to re-invent himself."

Neil laughed.

"He can't change his name back to Simon Jones can he? You know like Prince, to squiggle, then back to Prince. That's would be priceless. You know Roger Mason once told me a joke about Hooker along lines of what the difference between Prince and Hooker? 'Well one's a little weirdo who hasn't done anything memorable for as long as anyone can remember...and the other one is Prince.'"

Hilarious, must tell Clara that one. She will hoot.

"Mason loathed him. He made his life as difficult as he could. You know that Judy Evans, well she was a staff officer to the Chief Super at Salford. Mason took a shine to her and, on a visit down there simply offered her a job working for Hooker."

"Yes Clara Henderson told me he made Hooker her mentor as a kind of joke she thought."

"Mentoring his mistress?"

"I am positive she wasn't his mistress."

"Really? Must have been losing his touch, Hooker wouldn't know that though. Hooker used to retaliate in the most petty ways that wound Mason up. Mason actually smashed his Labour party mug he had, but Hooker just got another one. Nothing much Mason could do about it with the Police Authority and Des Lyons....anyway talking of loathing people, how is hysterical Carol, not dead yet unfortunately?"

"Permanently angry."

"Do you know I did a bit of research on her working on my book about Cyril Richards. She was the future once. She was recruited to run the press office when its boss had been a police officer and its staff one clerk. It seemed modern and progressive to have a journalist running the press office. I think the Police Authority's idea was to get someone who could tell Richards to be a bit more media savvy i.e. stop him talking about God.

Soon transpired her press credential was nine months on features for the *Express* weekend magazine. She was fucking hopeless, but no-one ever got sacked by a Labour Police Authority in those days so they built the press office beneath her and now she is sat on a small empire of dimwit graduates. The only good thing she ever did was have a fling with Kevin Kershaw. Legend has it came to a hair pulling fight in the Old Grapes with our sainted editor. How is the old witch by the way?"

So the story I had to tell him did not take long. I can recall starting as we got our soup and he looked at me excitedly as I started and then put his spoon in the bowl as I came to the bit about tapping the detective's phone. He was lost, frozen in thought. The spoon sinking into the soup slowly until it fell in totally.

Silly of me really to blurt it out. After the way he had been on the phone and tonight I imagined he would be confident, fill the gaps in for me, tell me what to do next. He just crumpled, soup spoon submerged in bowl, eyebrows furrowed, it was as if it actually physically hurt him. I just wittered to fill the time on how I got the package and had had to buy a DVD player, cheese and pickle sandwich etc.

"Suppose it added a dramatic touch unfolding on a 42inch TV screen and not a blurry screen on a lap top."

It was a good point, had not really thought about it, but he was right. All the more disgusting though.

He got a second wind when the main course arrived.

"Jenny, this is so big you need to plot this through so very carefully. There are so many options and permutations of what could be happening and how you could react. No way could we, you, just do this at dinner.

I suppose, most importantly, Kenyon is due to release the public part of his report into Mason soon. All my instincts are that you should keep a close hold of this until he publishes. You know what Napoleon says 'never interrupt your enemy when he is making a mistake', make a great scoop after he publishes. If he knew about this you would have heard by know. Or, more to the point, if he knew and was planning to even allude to it you would have known by now."

The last sentence was not lost on me. Validation by Neil as a crime reporter. I would be lying if I said it did not mean something to me.

"I know. Neil, I have to ask. What was it that you were working on or knew that was so important they wanted rid of you?"

"I dunno. Never wanted to appear like a mad conspiracy theorist and never really laid it out in such terms but here goes.....there is no doubt Mason was good when he came to

Manchester but it all just seemed to go to his head. Power corrupts, just always seems to. Now the rumour I heard was that he saw himself as having political ambitions after office and was angling to be the Mayor when he retired."

"Mayor? Don't you have to be a councillor first? Anyway who wants to be a mayor?"

"No, a proper political mayor, like London, powers over all the agencies. Tory MP told me that was their ultimate plan for northern cities like ours. Problem is they are reluctant to give northern cities additional powers as Labour mayors will just spunk all the money up against the wall. Remember him saying what they needed was someone credible who could stand as a kind of independent as Tories could never win in Manchester."

"And Tories had tapped him up to do that?"

"So the story goes. You can see it though can't you? Number of things happened which make you think. He never applied for the Met job. I am sure he told me he wanted it when he first came to Manchester. Rumour is Met had told him he was seen as a security risk because of his lifestyle so he changed his ambition towards local politics. He started on the gang stuff to make a name for himself. He went to any charity function that would get him photographed. He appointed that Clara Whatshername who he met at a function because of her husband."

"Henderson. How would that help?"

"His money and other contacts who had money. I mean he was pushing it in appointing her, come on. I would have run the story about who she was."

I could see he regretted saying that, needed to move it on.

"Neil, I'll be honest, I did not even know her husband was minted, when she was appointed. Do now obviously. What else?"

"Well politically he had City believing he was a City fan and United believing he supported them. Divisional Commanders on both divisions were pulling their hair out with him interfering. Remember just before I left they both wanted to play on the same night. Cup replay and a midweek Premier game. He folded straight away. Never been done before, recipe for trouble, transport problems etc. and cops had to pay shed load of overtime but it happened against all advice.

Point being for all the 'coppers' copper' stuff, he courted all the institutions when it was in his interests. And of course..."

"What?"

"Well found out the obvious now. He would need *MEN*'s backing for a serious candidacy. So he was prepared to pay the ultimate price. Christ how did he do it? I refuse to believe anyone would shag Sarah Parker of free will."

"All makes sense Neil."

"That's the problem with conspiracy theories, though. They make sense. They make better sense than the truth. You want to believe them, especially when it's personal. Truth is the *MEN* did not have to get rid of me based on what had happened. I was only doing my job. I reckon he put her up to it because he was worried I may start figuring some things out. When you are corrupt you need diminished, vulnerable or incompetent people around you."

He tried to correct himself.

"Clearly that's what she thought of you by what she said on the DVD, but the DVD is now with you darling, isn't it? What does the sender want from you, do you think?"

"No idea. I mean there are so many things I could do. I just also cannot understand why she hounded me with such anger about finding out why Mason had really gone missing. Like she was goading me to find out the truth."

"Jealousy, as she mentions in the tape, I would guess would lie behind it. Trying to throw everyone off the scent? I don't know, she always had an unstable crazy side to her, it probably gave her a sense of superiority that she was setting you a task she believed you could not succeed at. Crazy, crazy manipulative bitch."

"Do you know Neil I thought you would ask to look at the tapes?"

"Never occurred to me. Not sure I would want to see Sarah. I am not sure. Anyway this will finish her off if you decide to play the card. Yes those red shoes will finally be poking out from under the house."

Neil suddenly brightened, animated at the thought of the demise of Sarah Parker.

"But I tell you what, Sarah Parker is going down, she is going down to..."

Oh baby yes, she was wasn't she? The bitch.

"Funkytown."

I made to high five Neil. He held his hand up limply.

"I was going to say Chinatown."

It just killed the moment, for a moment.

JULIAN

This is turning out into a terrible, disastrous night. Mrs Henderson is now lost in Manchester. There is a name for the weather outside, the pathetic fallacy. Its pouring down, wipers at full speed.

I am in the car with Mrs Henderson and she is trying to find where I live, which is just off Great Marlborough Street. I obviously know where it is, it's just that I do not drive, so have never got there by car.

I think what has gone wrong is that we have missed the turning off the Mancunian Way so we are trying to find a way back, Hilton Hotel, Bridgewater Hall and now we have gone past the Palace Theatre but in the wrong direction. The idea was we were to talk in the car to review how the night has gone but that is hard to do because she is concentrating on trying to find my flat and the weather doesn't help. Manchester rain.

I would be far happier now if she just let me get out of the car and walk, but she won't because of the rain. So I am sat in the passenger seat in silence.

People were against her taking me to the meeting in the first place. Sheila, on my team, sent her an email telling her not to do so. It was Mr Ashton who told me Sheila had gone behind my back to Mrs Henderson to warn her that what did happen would happen if I was allowed to speak.

Yes Mr Ashton, I have sort of befriended him, perhaps he has befriended me. He sent me an email after he had last had me in the office to apologise again for what he had said about me being Asperger's, which I am not.

A couple of days later he sent me an email asking me to come round to his house sometime. His wife Claudia was trying to home-school her son in maths and was struggling, could I give her some advice?

I had no idea why they thought I would be qualified to do this. It transpired they had looked up a paper I had done on education whilst at the policy institute. My first instinct was to tell them I was not qualified to give such advice but my father said I should accept but warn them that, whilst I would do my best, they should not to expect too much.

Mrs Ashton, Claudia, she was very nice, steatopygic, very noticeable. She just wanted some help with basic arithmetic. I cannot say I gave her any insights that an ordinary person could not give. I talked to her about behaviourism which I recommended as a teaching style for her son. Learn something by rote first, comprehension can come later, if at all, that's what my father advocated in teaching. He always used to point out that's how babies are taught by their mothers. You have what is hard wired, then you drill in skills, understanding comes last. It's very simple.

She was quite taken with this, gushing. She wrote down what I had said when, in fact, it is basic. She kept saying that this is where she had been going wrong with Daniel, trying to get him to understand things.

As we finished was surprised to find Mr Ashton making dinner. He had an apron on. 'Cuddle the Cook', it said. I tried to make my excuses but I seemed to have little choice but to stay for dinner. Moussaka, which I had never eaten before, salad, and garlic bread which I had also never had.

Daniel came in for dinner from watching cartoons on TV. He had smiley faces and fish fingers which to be honest I would have preferred. He got very excited when Mr Ashton told him how we used to play chess together at school. He wanted to play chess. He went on about it incessantly at dinner.

It was already well past the time I had scheduled to be home. So it mattered less to me staying on. I had this idea Daniel may take to chess but it soon became clear he just could not understand it. So he played on my side by moving the pieces against Mr Ashton.

Well Daniel and I lost the first two games quite quickly but the third was a marathon. I think I had mentally switched on back to playing. We had one of those games where you get down to a few pieces each. It was past ten. My indigestion from the moussaka and garlic bread had settled, my anxiety at getting home so late had gone, I was absorbed. Mrs Ashton had made us tea and sandwiches and put the fire on. She was listening to the radio low through the television, cardigan on shoulder but then she started watching the match next to her husband.

At five to eleven Mr Ashton held out his hand for a draw. Daniel shook it. He had never stayed up so late on a school night before he told me. I would now have less than eight hours sleep before work also which I do not like. Mrs Ashton would not let me go without a picture of the three of us next to the chess board.

She kissed me on the way out.

"Julian thank you for a wonderful, wonderful night."

Not really sure what was so wonderful about it. The three of them stayed at the door to wave me off. So, yes, Mr Ashton is like a friend of sorts and he told me that Sheila had gone to Mrs Henderson to complain about my presentation.

I was going to ask Mrs Henderson about this, whether she still wanted me to do the presentation. My father reckoned that would be the wrong thing to do.

"Firstly Mr Ashton has confided in you, as a friend. You would be breaking his confidence if you told him you knew that this had happened."

"Yes I see. I want to show Mrs Henderson the presentation then. To check she is happy with it. I do not want to let her down"

"Has she asked to see it?"

"No."

"Then she trusts you, just do it."

Perhaps I should have shown it to her, perhaps Sheila was right. There was an uproar after I had given the presentation. I noticed two men starting arguing in what I think was Urdu even when I was giving it. Afterwards there was a discussion which I really struggled to follow. Lots of people were talking in Urdu and some shouting at Mrs Henderson. To be honest I completely lost my concentration and could not listen. I never spoke at all after that to support her. I know I have let her down.

And I have done it again with the directions, let her down. I have just given up, left it in her hands. She has gone down the wrong street twice and has had to turn round. It is a massive car. The console looks like you could launch a nuclear strike from it there are so many illuminated buttons. Mrs Henderson doesn't look entirely comfortable driving it especially when she is manoeuvring in spaces.

Thirty minutes precisely after we left the meeting in Collyhurst we are eventually outside my flat. I could have walked home quicker. She switches the ignition off, loud exhale to calm down.

"There is something that tells you how to get to locations in here but I never use it. If I tell David how lost I got he will go mad. So right, ok Julian how do you think that all went?"

"I am sorry. I just don't know how to get here by car."

"No, the presentation, the meeting."

"I did my best Mrs Henderson but it just all seemed to run out of control."

"Yes it did a bit, but that is to be expected. No, I am happy overall."

"You don't have to be nice with me."

"No I am not being. I knew it would get a bit messy but you put your points over well, clearly, in unambiguous terms. They reacted like that because they feel they have to in front of each other but I am sure this has done the trick, or it will do."

"Don't you think that, well, Mr Ashton is right? We can't keep talking about this. Now we have acknowledged there is a problem we have to do something rather than all these preparatory meetings. We could be criticised for doing nothing while the abuse continues."

"Well Julian I don't recall Mr Ashton being remotely bothered about all this two months ago so it's a bit rich for him to start......look all in good time. I just know I need to have some support outside of the organisation before we take action, and we will. These people tonight are good people, they just feel a bit threatened but they will come with us. Trust me Julian. Tonight was good, honestly Julian. You did well.....bloody hell Brian has some nerve saying that. He will have no idea about what those girls are going through, he has no fucking idea."

I had never heard her swear before.

"Sorry Julian. Getting too emotional and I know I shouldn't. I bet you don't approve."

"Not at all Mrs Henderson. The best decision making is a mixture of reason reinforced by emotion."

"You surprise me, as ever, Julian. I thought you would be well, I don't know, sort of disapproving of emotion. I mean....."

"No I understand. No, you have to recognise all decisions are charged with emotion. If we took decisions based on pure logic and utilitarian principles the world would be a very strange place."

There was a quote from David Hume that I just couldn't remember precisely.

"Julian, I never knew. Do you get emotional about this work?"

"Well yes and no. Certainly not about the people but perhaps about the issues, as issues in themselves. In fact I have tried to take a kind of utilitarian, dispassionate approach to what I focus my energies on. I try to work out how I can mitigate against the most harm. This work seems to me to be the most productive based on this criterion, and sex trafficking also. But taking this approach has annoyed Mr Ashton who wants to chase detection figures."

"So is it a good decision to do this work? You are confusing me."

"Well yes on a utilitarian basis, but I have to admit this has some emotion for me personally. I like to do the right thing especially when others are not doing so, that makes me feel good."

"You sound like my brother in law Rear Vice Admiral Michael, 'in order for evil to succeed it is simply necessary for good men to do nothing'."

"Burke, yes, you nearly got the quotation correct. I don't like thinking in terms of good and evil. My Dad always says that nearly everyone thinks they are on the side of the angels.

No I try to do the right thing because it makes me feel better about myself, not because I particularly care about other people but, as doing the right thing is to take a calculated approach to reducing harm rather than chasing worthless detection figures, then, I think, my work produces a good outcome.

I think your approach is different. You seem to care personally about what happens to the girls. Therefore it makes you feel good to do something to help them. Just caring isn't enough though, you need a calculated approach which is why you have promoted me, I think, and not continued with the Sexual Exploitation Unit. But we finish up in the same place though."

"Sat here in the car at 10 at night with the Manchester rain beating down. Julian my head hurts. Well you have given me something to think about. You always do."

"Did you read Mr Hooker's piece on the Intranet last week?"

"No Julian I really try not to."

"You should read his stuff, you know, it's very good. This one is about the way you act towards others. Compassion is recognising how other people are simply a different version of you, a human. We are all just different humans. Seeing people in this way makes you make better decisions when dealing with them. It's about having compassion as though someone else is just a version of who you could have been. Those girls could have been you, for example."

"That is very true, in fact Mr Hooker said something similar to me recently. God you are a funnyosity, Julian, you like Mr Hooker? I should have guessed. You are definitely the first person I have ever heard say something good about him."

"Yes it's perfectly rational to be compassionate. I think he describes what you do and what very few others in the organisation do. You seem to understand other people's feelings and have a desire to help them although...."

"Oh now Julian there is something you are not going to say, now you have to say it."

"Well if you understood me better you would have realised I would have preferred to walk in the rain to get home."

She laughed, but I was not trying to be funny.

KENNY

I was forking the lawn for winter when Sharon phoned.

"I have just got the report from the bright young things. Guess what the big idea is Kenny? Put an undercover in as a freelance journalist into the family and see if they get access to Keane. Like that's going to happen."

I couldn't see why not, but she seemed convinced it was a bad idea.

"Anyway Kenny, not the reason I have phoned. We want to look at the sister Mairead."

"Go on."

I knew we would be doing. We always finish up doing what Sharon wants but you have to put her through her paces. Remind her who the boss is.

"I have been thinking about you said about it all being a bit contrived? Pre-emtiv. Well it is isn't it? Totally. And for that matter 'dark angel'.

I mean we have Keane as a deranged halfwit who commits a murder in broad daylight yet we haven't got a sniff off him. That's very disciplined for a nutcase isn't it? Not really the behaviour of someone who is unhinged. We think he is unhinged because of the brutality of the killings. They were savage, brutal, but not the act of a complete madman. He did not go into a school or kill a stranger. And there was a logic to them. He was trying to protect his family after the twins had been sent down. Charlotte just got in the way."

"Not sure I agree Sharon. Why do it and identify yourself?"

"Yes why identify yourself? Dunno, but he still escaped and now is trying not to be caught. He could have tried to put a balaclava on or something. He wanted to be recognised, to send a message. Again we think he is crackers because he did not organise a getaway driver properly. He did though manage both to get away and to stay away. Must have been some planning in managing to stay away. We only have the account of the cousin that he did not organise it properly.

Problem is this Kenny. We have bought this hook, line and sinker from the sister that he was behaving strangely. His sister, his sensible sister who gives us all the information, no one else. The family will just not talk, but she will. She has not moved away or distanced herself in any way from them. The family must know someone is briefing us from within. Yet we have not even heard a murmur of discontent. Yet there she is briefing us, and the press, under their noses. She is the one who has told us he is mad. She says he was a hypochondriac but he didn't visit the doctor much. It's got into all our heads because she is the sensible sister.

Yes she is sensible but she is his sister. A sister who we do not follow or listen to or watch her house. He has a cousin tell us he did not organise a proper getaway and a sister tell us he is mad. We are assuming he is crazy because they say so. I know she claims she has nothing to do with that side of the family and she has a regular job, whatever it is. But she lives near, she is still part of them, they don't disown her.

We should keep tabs on her and we should pull in the getaway lad for questioning again."

"No we should leave the lad alone, it may spook them. Let's just watch the sister first, see what it throws up. What do you think surveillance of her? Watch the house? Get a device in?"

"Take some time to get a device in, not even sure we have enough to do that, certainly not weeks after the event. Let's just follow her, have a look at her phone traffic see where it gets us….and you are right, pulling in the cousin would spook them. You should spend more time at home Kenny. "

I will let her take the piss, she's a good girl at heart.

I will remind her though, if this turns up trumps, who first spotted it was all contrived.

BOB

Ladies and Gentlemen I introduce to you.......drum roll......

... Maria! My girlfriend. Well a fuck buddy really. A fuck buddy involving the exchange of cash. So a prostitute. Sort of a prostitute but not really a fully paid up member of that esteemed profession. No nothing as honourable as that. More of a con-artist into the odd grift. She is a good friend though, if you remember she is a lying bitch who is always in it for herself.

Good sport, played the role of my girlfriend when I went missing. On notice to deny it all and say the cops misunderstood what she had been saying. She won't turn up at a civil hearing if it goes that far obviously, as she was acting under a false identity, or perhaps she would, she has the cojones.

Yes she got herself deliberately arrested on the night before I returned to work to extract a few extra quid from me. Well a couple of hundred. You have to admire the nerve of that; her in the cells when I come back to work.

Now Maria and I are trying an oldie but goody to get me off the hook. It could work, with Maria anything is possible. We agreed a small retainer with the success fee of a week's holiday in Majorca for her. I offered to come with her if she succeeds. She said she could not afford the distraction of sexy Big Bob with her all fortnight when she wanted to spend time with her kid.

That's a pro for you. She knocks you back for sex, turns a week's holiday into a fortnight, then adds the cost of a kid when I am sure she doesn't intend to take him. All in the best possible taste.

Hooker had broadcast to the world he goes to his local Alcoholics Anonymous so it was easy for her to find him there. Anyway she says Hooker is hilarious at AA but hard to get to know. A good attender he listens intently to others nodding furiously as they speak in encouragement. She has tried to catch his eye with the old cow eyes and tight tops showing her boobs but it hasn't worked because he is so wrapped up listening to others in the group. It's like he is the group leader.

Catching him before and after has not worked because he arrives on the last minute and leaves almost immediately. She has had to engineer sitting next to him and go for the arm on his arm, "I just love the way you commit to this meeting." Nothing at all.

"Fucking hell he is not a vagina decliner?"

"Honey, you know what I say. 'There are no truly gay men, just men who haven't met me.' No don't think he is gay, didn't get the vibe. Time for a direct approach."

So three nights ago she did, "look I know who you are. I have never met a man of power before and, I don't know how to put it, oh this is difficult but just call me anytime," and put a phone number in his hand.

"You are joking 'man of power'. Couldn't you think of anything better than that?"

"Bob, men are pathetic. All men. You should know, you are. He will have loved it."

"Did he?"

"Well he was the proverbial rabbit. Took the note and scarpered."

"Oh nice work, you have frightened him off."

"Bob. He took the note. Anyway got this text the other day, 'Sorry don't know your name you took me by surprise last night. I think we need to talk but not at the meeting.'"

"He wants to talk to you, not fuck you. Probably about that compassion shit he bangs on about."

"Bob he answered. He is interested. It's not a 'no'."

"We are running out of time. Hearing is in ten days. "

"Yes I know. I have texted him back. I will be in Chester on business and will be staying in a hotel in the town on Thursday night. No response yet so who knows?"

"It's a real long shot he may not be able to get away."

"Bob, he will come I am sure. In any case you got any better ideas?"

"One, a long shot, my insurance policy which may not work so I need you to do this for me. Do it for Uncle Bob, Maria. If not you won't have a fortnight in the sun with your boyfriend. You would have to make do with a bunk up weekend in a caravan with Uncle Bob in Shap.

And you won't have any warm gear will you, sugar tits?"

JENNY

It's all going to plan.

"Two full pages for a barely concealed racist article on the exploitation of young girls. Oh yes like you thought this is going to happen. We have spoken about this before. Is this some kind of resignation article? I am staggered, Jenny, fucking speechless, you seem to have completely lost the plot. Again. I am afraid this is going to have to get formal, a written warning."

Oh don't start blotching at the neck already Sarah. Not yet darling.

"Well I just thought. I don't know. It just seemed the right thing to do. A written warning is a bit harsh I need this job."

I was wearing a T-shirt which had 'Sweet Dreams' on it. It was under a cardigan but recognisable, couldn't work out whether she noticed it yet.

"I am so sympathetic to your article I can't shit but this is never going to see the light of day. I cannot even be arsed to give you the speech about what we are here for. This is so not going to happen. Capice? And yes, I do think you should start looking at Situations Vacant."

"I was more thinking of the right thing to do after spending £95 of the firm's money on dinner with Clara. Just felt I had to get the return for my money. Oh have the expense sheet here. You just sign there."

I put the dinner receipt in front of her. It was actually the meal I had with Neil. I clicked the biro I had with deliberation and handed it to her. She stared at the expense form. You could just see that something was stopping her from exploding in anger. An inkling that all was not right?

She spoke slowly and deliberately.

"OK Jenny what I am thinking is that I have overrated you and you are even more fucking stupid than I imagined. Say it ain't so."

"Well you see Sarah... may I sit down?"

I sat down anyway.

"Thanks. It was when you accused me of being a soppy journalist or words to that effect I forget. It got me to thinking......"

I decided to stop. We stared at each other.

"Go on lady, be very, very careful. You don't want to cross me."

"I hope you can see me shivering all over with trepidation."

I pulled the cardigan across me and shivered. Brrr.

"Well I was thinking this. Quite how soppy am I? I mean I never had any leads into Mason's disappearance did I?"

Sarah was now sat back in her chair, eyes burning into me but also impassive. She was not going to speak until I had finished.

This moment was going to happen. I have been rehearsing this for a week now. It was actually going to happen, right now. Here, now.

"But would I be so soppy as to let a Chief Constable fuck me on his desk and it be videoed."

Short pause.

"Which sort of breaks down into four constituent questions?

Soppy enough to be fucked by a Chief Constable who was fucking the entire world?

Soppy enough to let him do it in his office?

Soppy enough to let him video it?

Or, and here is the thing, so soppy as to perhaps not even realise he was videoing it?

Would I be that soppy? Who would be so soppy Sarah?"

Sarah's eyes had reddened and watered. A slight tremor. I did not know what was to come next. Would she break down or try to attack me across the desk? It was important that she did not attack me or that there was a scene. So I continued as planned.

"Well you must be in shock, Sarah, so I will carry on. Well the thing is I really do have the evidence. I can let you see it if you absolutely need to. And I think you may need to with what is coming up. Keep the pen that you have got to make notes of what I am about to say. Ready Sarah? Perhaps not? But let's get this over with eh? So you better start writing. Good.

That post as head of news desk is going to be given to me when I apply. Now you and me are also going to agree that I get it at a salary of £55k.

Also, Neil's compromise binding agreement...........Sarah you have stopped writing now concentrate."

"Sorry I was just….."

Sarah looked completely beaten then she suddenly rallied.

"You total bitch……"

I could see she was thinking about attacking me then restrained herself.

"I want to see the evidence. You are bluffing."

"That's no problem at all. You have a DVD player in this office and I will bring it in for you. It's mixed in with other stuff so I will have to get it just to the point of you knelt on his desk and, well, you know, it would be an internet sensation. So as I was saying continue writing please. Neil's compromise agreement needs to be altered so that on top of the sum he received he gets a full pension at 60 years."

"Can't do that, sorry love."

She had got all business like, sniffy.

"Not difficult it's your signature on it. Here it is re-written with Neil's signature. You just sign this and put it on his file. He will have the same copy. You retire in 4 months' time. Leave it with you as to how you wish to play it, ill health, you want to write your memoirs, perhaps a new job, write a novel. See I have given you time to do it. What a nice person I am.

And one last thing."

Sarah smiled, resigned, a 'go on surprise me look' on her face. She nodded her head to signal to continue.

"Do you see this T-shirt 'Sweet Dreams'? Soppy isn't it? Well I will give you tomorrow to think about my generous offer but will spare you the blushes of another conversation. I mean this is embarrassing for me so I have no idea what it must be like for you. Anyway, mine is a medium quite tight on my boobs. I got you an extra-large, won't be as tight for you will it?"

I tossed it across the desk.

"If I see you wearing it tomorrow it means you agree to my generous offer. Subject to me bringing in the evidence, obviously. But you have to wear the T-shirt to show good faith. I think we are done. Oh could you just sign up my expenses now. I will leave the article with you. It publishes next week please. Tuesday, middle spread."

Sarah started to cry silently.

"Kevin is dying and won't see me."

BOB

Maria has flu. I thought it was just a ploy to put the price up so offered her an extra five hundred notes but she still said not. So it's not a grift. She really would not be able to make Chester. She would have to cancel.

Shame. I fancied a bit of old fashioned honey trap blackmail. Large black and white pictures in a brown paper envelope, that kind of thing.

I told her not to cancel Hooker though. Plan B, told her to text him a reminder for tomorrow. I would go in her place.

"I think he will notice if you try the ladyboy thing Bob."

MARTHA

I love films. I hate James Bond films. Hate them. Detest them.

Phil Donnelly was my first love. Sixteen years old in two classes above me at school. His parents owned a bakery in Moston, which made him rich in my eyes. He was captain of school football team and wanted to go to Cambridge and read English. His parents were going to send him to Manchester Grammar for his 'A' levels to help him get there.

Yet even in a comprehensive in Moston he did not seem to get any grief about this. He just seemed to rise above it. 'Cool' is the word I suppose. I thought he was in his John Travolta capped black T-shirt.

I knew him because he had a younger sister in my year and I would occasionally be round at his house. I just knew he liked me. It was both no surprise and the biggest thing in my life when, outside the school gates, he asked me on a date to the cinema at half term. We went to see *The Living Daylights*.

He picked me up from this house and my mum came to the door to see him to give him a lecture on looking after me. I was mortified. He did not seem fazed and was, well, 'cool' about it. Bus ride into town. He paid for my ticket and bought me a coke and a chocolate bar to share without asking what I wanted. We held hands in the cinema and I spent the entire film ready for a kiss which did not come.

I could not see where he would be able to kiss me once we were outside as it would be daylight. In fact once we got out we did not hold hands. His easy conversation seemed to dry up. Something was wrong. What had I done?

We got off the bus and walked together in silence back to my house. Just before we turned for my street he stopped and said, "I'm sorry but I really wanted to kiss you in the cinema. Now I have missed my chance."

'Cool' Phil seemed distraught. Distraught because he had missed his opportunity to kiss a kid, a black girl from a council house, two years younger than him in the fourth form. I realised this was just a big a deal for him as it was for me.

Lord I can tell you that would be the most romantic moment in my life. I just kissed him there and then in full daylight, on the street. Do you know what he did? He buried his head in my shoulder kissed my neck and said, "you are hot chocolate."

Fucking marvellous. Hot chocolate.

Daydreaming, half asleep. He said it there, just outside this window I have my back to, what twenty five years ago? Be about ten yards away outside. What time is it? 4 o'clock. I have to drive home. My neck aches. Mum has fallen asleep on me and I have been day-dreaming. She's been fast asleep. It's been over an hour, not like her at all, not when I am here visiting that is. She would know I would want to get back to Coventry. She is fast asleep.

Loud knock on the door, far too loud. I can see through the window a guy is outside with flowers, huge bunch. Lumberjack shirt sleeves rolled right up to show oversized tattooed muscles, muscles you need steroids to get. Clearly wasn't expecting me to answer the door, sort of stops him in his tracks. He asks if Dolores is in and is through the door and past me before I invite him in, which I was not planning on doing.

"Hello Dolores just popped round to see how you are love? These are for you."

He holds out the flowers to her but she doesn't take them. She is dazed from the sleep. You can see she doesn't recognise him.

"Karl Parker, Dolores, Sergeant Parker. I was here, took poor Jesse away for you."

"I'm sorry I didn't recognise you…. "

"….with my clothes on, Dolores. No on my day off. How are you?"

He has a stupid cheesy smile on his face. I am not having this.

"I'm sorry Sergeant Parker but are you sure you should even be here? There is an investigation you know."

"Oh no, no, no. This is fine, s'all fine you see. The problem is all to do with the custody bit, well you would know, I can't say too much let's just say I understand how you must, you know. I am just here just to check on your mum. You must be the sister."

That's what I am is it 'the sister'? Thank you for the flowers. No you are not invited to sit down, Mum is very tired. Well thank you again. Goodbye Sergeant. All over, in/out, within 90 seconds.

It was all over and done so quickly I could not quite process it all but I had to get back home.

Well it all went round in my head all the way back to Coventry. I was still so angry but couldn't work it out in any logical format as had to concentrate on my driving. I talked it through a bit with Sebastian when I got home. He wasn't interested really, tried half- heartedly to offer me the sergeant's perspective but soon retired to bed.

I knew I needed to run this through again before I went upstairs.

Ok, I was tired and the loud bang kind of woke me up from a daydream, grouchy, stiff neck. I had been thinking of the Phil Donnelly 'hot chocolate' moment which depresses me to this day. I was annoyed that Mum had fallen asleep and it meant I would be home later than planned. I don't even like starting out driving when I feel a bit tired also. I was annoyed that it was me there again today and not my brothers who live closer but they only go to see Mum when it suits them, not when she needs it. I was also annoyed that I knew when I got home Sebastian would have looked after the kids, fed them, put them to bed and tidied up to the minimum standard but would want fussing over and praising for doing it.

Ok, so I was in a bad mood to start with. Then I get annoyed at his presumption but then again I was getting annoyed on Mum's behalf as she was tired and groggy. Perhaps I was judging him on a stereotype too, a cop with tattoos and oversized muscles.

That's me, hmm not good. Now him.

So he arrests my brother who is now seriously ill. It may not be his fault but he feels responsible. He may feel very bad about it. He may not have thought it was inappropriate to come round and this was something he could do to show he was sorry. He made the effort to do it. He did not have to do it certainly. You can see it as a nice thing to do. He may feel he has done something wrong is worried about his future. That is a normal human reaction after all, it doesn't make it a bad thing to do.

So he comes across bad tempered me answering the door. He is taken aback perhaps. He is the first cop I have seen in the flesh since Jesse died and I take my anger out on him. He blusters then because he is nervous and wants to change the atmosphere. He does something nice and I practically throw him out of the house.

And this all still bothers me because? Because? The sergeant's feelings? Not really. I cannot say I would be in a rush to apologise to him.

Ok what else? I had researched all these deaths and had noticed how involved the relatives get. It defines them, their anger. And here it is with me, less than a month. I had actually discussed it with Sebastian last weekend, the need to be dispassionate. Yes and the first time I see a cop, and this one is actually doing something nice, I lose my temper. Yes that's it, I lost my temper when I promised I would be dispassionate, remain dispassionate. That's it, I lost it within weeks. I am angry at myself. I need to be dispassionate in the future.

I can go to bed now.......

..... can't sleep.....

....I mean who does he think he is? In the house like he owns it, stood in the middle of the small room dominating it, calling my mother 'Dolores'. I have met a hundred cops like him in A& E, behaving in the same way, like they own the place. They park their vans and cars on yellow lines blocking ambulances, they breeze in demanding names and addresses, instant answers, wanting the prisoners they have brought for treatment at the front of the queue. They make themselves feel at home alright, just like he did. They go into the staff room uninvited and lounge around. I know the nurses hide the tea and coffee if they see them coming.

It's always about them, always. You know that poor girl who was killed, well run over? When you heard the Chief Constable on the TV it is like he thinks that was the only murder that really mattered, not the two grandparents shot in the head. The poor girl was lying on the floor when she was run over, the guy may not even have seen her. You don't know.

The same with the cop who goes missing. He doesn't feel bad about my brother, he wants it to be about him. And so there's that Parker stood in Mum's small lounge, grinning, lumberjack shirt, body warmer and stained jeans. He has not bothered to shave, his hair curling up over his collar. Pleased with himself, showing off his tattoos, his pathetic muscles. All self-regard. It's all about him. Look at me doing a nice thing. All with an air of scumbag entitlement.

That's it, 'an air of scumbag entitlement', heard that in a film recently. Perfect. That's him Parker, that's all of them. I've got it.

Now I can sleep.

Scumbag entitlement.

PART THREE

CHORUS

They did an experiment in America once where they made people sit in a room and then they pumped smoke into it. The more people who were in the room the less likely they all were to raise the alarm for a fire.

Reputations are like that. You can pump that smoke into that room but no-one will dare to shout 'fire' unless they can see it. They might think it but they won't say it.

There can be all that smoke but you keep your reputation as long as no one shouts 'fire'. People can privately think what they like. The more people who don't shout fire the less likely anyone else will.

Yes everyone has their private opinion of me but I am still the Chief Constable. I have kept my public reputation. There's no fire here folks.

Anyway people don't really know me, understand me. Do you think you do reader?

That's part of the game of reading fiction, trying to understand people.

Try to understand me.

MICHAEL

To be honest it was a balls up.

We had just not fully thought it through. Perhaps not enough people on the job but you could not spread your net too widely, staffing wise. These were the only guys with my full trust. In my defence also it is not every day I organise a burglary. Well the planning was Martin's work.

No, I am making excuses. It was bloody sloppy work on my part.

The whole thing did not go to plan from the start. We were working on the assumption he always went away for the weekend and we just needed to follow him to a place far enough away. Sure enough Jimbo picked him up outside Chester House driving his X5 on his own, no driver, which meant he would be going away. However, instead of turning right for the motorway to head south, he headed into town and threaded himself round Manchester. He wasn't going to his flat but to BBC Oxford Street. He picked up the girl from BBC news, a reporter called Rebecca Jobson. Jimbo recognised her.

Straight back to his flat for the obvious. Luckily he emerged from the garage alone in the X5 hour and half later, just as we were thinking of calling the whole thing off. Jimbo followed him straight down the A6 and onto the M56 to head south. Martin and Gibbo had eyes on the flat but we had not seen Jobson exit. All got quite tetchy as to whether we had missed her. Luckily, she came out about fifteen minutes later into a private hire cab.

We had confirmation from Jimbo that Mason was already past Sandbach services. He was having difficulty staying with him as he was doing 90 plus, so we were good to go. Told Jimbo to let him go, could not see circumstances in which he would turn round now.

Martin and Gibbo got themselves buzzed into the flats easily enough. Transpired she had just left the door on the Yale lock so we got in there no problem. We had an elaborate plan to disable the alarm but she had also not left it on, easy. Martin and Gibbo had cameras, lap tops and copying equipment and went to work.

They could not have been there more than fifteen minutes when I got a call from Martin. Jobson's purse was still on the bed, she could come back anytime. I was actually at my flat and, on reflection, should have been outside watching, but had not thought through this one. We had just been planning on whether Mason was there or not. Anyway we just had to get out with what we had.

Martin and Gibbo were back in my flat within minutes. I could see that Gibbo was pleased with what they had got while Martin was annoyed at what had gone wrong. Typical of both of them and why they worked so well together. Jimbo calls them Itchy and Scratchy.

They had copied some DVDs that was next to his bed and had downloaded the contents of the camcorder in the bedroom just as David described.

Gibbo was still hyper from the job.

"Hey his place is seriously weird. Hardly any furniture, stuff still in boxes but he has a painting of himself on the wall. Can you believe that, a painting, of himself? Crazy fuck."

"Well thanks lads. Good job, some piss poor planning on my part but it looks like a job well done."

"No I ballsed up, sorry Michael."

Martin was ruminating, annoyed. He always did this, went back over things that could not be mended. A real flaw, but that was the man.

"Oh fuck off it went fine in the end. He will not know there is anything missing will he Michael? You always do this, brood afterwards on a job Mart. Michael, by the way never mind 'thanks lads now fuck off' routine I want a proper look at this stuff."

We all stared at each other.

"Fuck me Michael, this is hardly the time to get discreet. We are into this now. Let's have a fucking look."

"Michael there is no need for me to look at this. Gibbo, be professional for once in your life there is no need. You don't need to know."

Martin's mood was worsening. I could not see the harm, boys were bound to confidentiality, and I was hardly on any high moral ground though was I? Gibbo was already trying to get a DVD into my computer.

So there we were two of us round my computer in my lounge watching the burgled sex tape of a Chief Constable. I bet that sentence has never been written before. Suddenly occurred to me that Gibbo would recognise Clara from the party if she was on there but I suppose he was right. The time for discretion had gone, long gone.

Clara was not there. I could not work out whether I was disappointed or not. It would have been a more complete job for David if we had found something. On the whole, I suppose, I was relieved.

Fair to say the sainted Chief Constable had mixed taste in his women judging by the recordings. The reporter was there. Martin stayed sat on the sofa with a beer I had got him staring into space, visibly irritated at Gibbo's excited commentary. He would come round.

The last DVD was different from the rest. It seemed to be a strange edited compilation with some modern depressing music. Nice sort of choral bit at the end but all a bit weird, disturbing.

"Hey the man's an artist, a fucking artist."

Gibbo's considered verdict did not lighten Martin's mood. I got us all a beer and we sat down with Martin to debrief.

"Well respect to the departed Chief Con doesn't make you a bad person I suppose. Not too choosy is he though? Who was that last bird? Minging, still a shag is a shag. Respect."

"No not really. You cannot admire that."

Martin was about to say more when Gibbo suddenly lifted himself from the sofa. For a second I thought a serious argument was about to occur. Instead he pulled something out of the front pocket of his jeans. It was a memory stick.

"Fuck, this was in the drawer next to his bed where the camcorder was. I was just going to have a look at it when you called."

"You mean it's not a copy?"

"Nope, sorry Michael"

"We better have a look then."

Martin came with us back to the computer, drawn face, really irritated now.

"You've changed you tune?"

"No I really do need to know what is on this now that we have stolen it from a Chief Constable, don't I Gibbo?"

We read it in silence. It was a report from the Head of CID, Kenny Poole.

"Nope, as I said, don't admire his style. The man is a liability and should not be a Chief Constable. He should have encrypted something as sensitive as this. We should not have been able to get this and we certainly should not be seeing it."

Martin now had a face like thunder.

"It's fucking funny though isn't it?"

Gibbo sometimes did not know when to leave it alone.

MARTHA

I have been outside this office for so long. I want to get Mum in to see him quickly. She will be tiring already. There she is sat upright staring ahead in her own world, can just hear her quietly tutting, talking to herself. I could have done this meeting myself but she insisted. There is another guy I have noticed waiting as well as us. Fat guy, scruffy, keeps sighing loudly looking at his watch. Hope he is not ahead of us.

I am ready for this. I am so ready. Just hope I don't thrown away my shot. Got everything in my head, just hope I can be clear. Mum said not to be hot-headed like I had been with the sergeant, just polite and clear. Oh Mum, she is here to protect me, her child, but I don't need saving from myself, I will behave.

Got the file on my lap.

Copy of letter Chief Constable Roger Mason sent out a letter to all staff that anyone who said or did anything racist or sexist or homophobic would be sacked. No ifs or buts, sacked.

Summary of excited delirium studies; it's where people get so excited they kind of boil over and die. The police and the Coroners courts love this now. For 'people', by the way, read 'niggers'. It's actually black people's fault for getting so excitable when they are held down by coppers.

Copy of the press reports about the staff still working in custody.

Copy of the IPCC transcript of the activity and phone calls in custody (got it from Jenny at the *MEN*. She can only have got it from the IPCC). I'll show it to you at the end.

Copy of press report that Hooker was bringing the disciplinary hearing forward ahead of any deliberations on a criminal case.

I had had him on the phone to me after the last bit of press. CPS had criticised his decision to hold a fast-tracked disciplinary hearing ahead of any criminal considerations, so he is trying to keep me sweet. He had rung me to assure me he will though personally oversee the discipline hearings and make sure there is a just outcome. He offered to meet me as well. Ok, why not? When? So here we are. This will be interesting.

Hooker's door swings open.

"Ah Mrs Brooks, Martha, sorry to keep you both waiting."

"Maitland, my mother's name is Maitland. Like mine."

He looked puzzled. I won't explain, he can work it out. Scruffy guy is coming in with us. He's a photographer. No I am not having this, but Mum has her coat off already and I can't afford an argument.

So there we are being snapped. I am trying to look as unhappy as possible. There is Mum and Hooker shaking hands and smiling, beginning to seriously regret this.

Sat in the corner are that Zoe and Phil from the IPCC. See neither of them have dressed for the occasion, jeans suffice apparently. They are in a little lounge area in the corner of the office and they are now moving to sit either side of Hooker at his desk. We could have fitted into that area. They have been talking about us for the last half hour while my mother has been sat out there in a trance.

So it's like that; we are talked about while we sit outside and then you move to put a barrier between us. Ok I get it, I get it. It's like that.

Hooker tries to start the meeting with his lowered voice of concern. He tells me that racism makes him feel physically ill.

"That's very interesting to hear Chief Constable but I want to discuss the facts of the case today which, whilst they may be underpinned by some underlying racist belief system, look to me to be more about incompetence."

If he had said that the case had nothing to do with race I would have argued the other way. I just want to set the tenor of the meeting, not him.

"So firstly can you explain to me why you have taken the unprecedented step of holding a disciplinary hearing ahead of any criminal deliberations?"

"Well I am glad you asked me that Martha and we spoke about this on the phone. You and I both know that there is an interminable delay while files are prepared, CPS consulted and invariably there is no criminal charge let alone conviction. I am talking years. Meanwhile the officers will be on full pay, some even reach their pensions and retire. I am determined to stop this. You may be surprised to know there has not been a single conviction of a custody officer in connection with a death in custody case."

"I am not surprised Chief Constable, I knew that."

"Yes, good, so, yes, so you know the chances of getting one are remote."

"In a case where a person is brought into custody seemingly unconscious but the officers say he is play acting, not searched properly, drinks a bottle of vodka unobserved in a cell, not visited properly and not afforded urgent medical assistance when required?"

"Yes I know I know, but I am advised that there would be a diffusion of blame."

"In other words GMP is so generally incompetent you can't just pick one person out?"

"Look you know Martha criminal convictions are difficult in these cases, very difficult. You know they will drag this out. And it is perfectly possible there could still be a conviction at a criminal court after the discipline hearing."

"I understand that holding the discipline case first is irregular and that it lessens the chance of a criminal conviction."

"I thought you wanted this to be dealt with swiftly Martha?"

"I do. I am merely asking you the question. You make the decisions."

"Well I have done. And I have decided to expedite the discipline matter and I ask for your support in this Martha, Mrs Brooks. We did expect the Federation to object legally but so far they have not. Soo... there will be a discipline procedure...for.... "

"Hayes and Brazier."

Phil saved Hooker.

"Just Hayes and Brazier?"

"Well there obviously can't be one for Charlotte Purvis."

"You must know I am not referring to her. What about Parker and the two PCs who brought him in? They did not search him properly. They tell Brazier Jesse was play acting which is clearly wrong. They all say he was fine when he was in the van and did this as he was being brought into the office. I can't understand how they could know for sure he was play acting?"

"Well I think it's important we concentrate on the people who most contributed to this tragedy."

"Tragedy? My brother isn't dead, Chief Constable."

"Yes of course, anyway, and we all pray for him. No they will receive a strong warning. I know Parker personally and he feels terrible about this. He brought you round some flowers Mrs Brooks?"

Mum does not acknowledge or object. She seems lost. I decide not to correct him again.

"So just Brazier and Hayes to take the rap? And everything will be ok. Things just carry on."

"No I have ordered a thorough review of processes."

"Lessons will be learnt, Chief Constable?"

"Well yes. I can give you my assurance that they will be."

"I was being ironic for the avoidance of doubt but, if lessons are to be learned, perhaps, I don't know, start with using the term 'mixed race' instead of 'half chat' which PC Brazier seemed to think was ok?"

Blood rising. I can now hear Mum tutting away, talking quietly to herself. She is getting impatient with me but I have to carry on.

"You won't let this shit happen again. But we all know it will. And how, how on God's earth did my brother get that bottle of vodka? Out of thin air? Have you worked out how that happened?"

"No. Well the CCTV shows the search was not thorough. He must have had the bottle on him all the time."

"That does not make any sense to me. Mum does not keep alcohol in the house. Did you ask that Sergeant Parker whether he gave it to him?"

All three groaned quietly, differently, but in unison. I promised myself I would not go there but just had to. I could see the IPCC guys giving each other a look behind Hooker's back.

Zoe, patronising.

"And why would he do that Martha?"

"I have no idea, but have you asked him whether he did?"

"Martha, you started by making the accusation that they held his face down in the van, without any evidence at all. Now this accusation. We have to be reasonable. We cannot just throw random accusations around."

"I am not making a random accusation. It is a possible explanation for my brother having a bottle of vodka in his cell. So I repeat, I am asking whether you asked him or the PCs with him."

Phil now takes the lead.

"Look, he did not give a bottle of vodka to your brother."

"Did you ask him that? Did you ask the PCs?"

They hadn't asked anybody. They were not going to ask him. The interviews had been completed and there was no need for more. Jesse must have had that bottle all the time.

"Look Martha. First time we spoke you accused them of holding his head down in the van. Then next time you asked us to ask him why he had taken flowers round to your mother when it did appear to be a nice gesture....."

"...or he was trying to soft soap an old lady because he knows he has done something wrong. He shouldn't have been there."

"He wasn't under investigation at the time. He said you were rude and practically threw him out of the house."

"So this is about me being rude is it? It's about me hurting the poor sergeant's feelings? You kept us out there for thirty minutes while you discussed how to manage me? The whole problem here is how you will manage 'the angry black sister' is it? I am the problem am I?"

Hooker was practically shushing me. He gestured with his hands to calm down.

"I think the issue is to focus on the objective and the obvious issue. It's the neglect in custody. The shameful neglect."

I have pushed it too far. Scumbag entitlement clouding my thoughts. I could hear my mum tutting away. I did promise her I wouldn't do this, not after the sergeant business.

"Now what I can assure I will do..."

Mum suddenly speaks up, not interrupting Hooker as such, just ignoring the fact he is speaking.

"Now I can't read any more Chief Constable, I can't concentrate, but I can listen still and I have been listening to the radio. Now then......."

Mum licked her lips. Everyone sat back. A wait before she starts again.

"Now then ...the thing is that everyone is losing trust today, the bankers have lost all that money, all that money, where's it gone, who knows? And no one trust dem politicians and lawyers and teachers and bankers and teachers..."

Mum. No. Don't save me from myself. Not today.

Hooker smiled, he was going to say something. My mum held her hand up to stop him.

"But I heard dis. With every group or what do you call it pro, pro...?"

"Profession, Mrs Brooks."

"I am called Maitland. I think my daughter told you. You don't listen enough, you should, you like talking but not listening. Yes profession that's the word. Where was I?

Yes people trust de police more than lawyers and solicitors and teachers and what have you. But when they meet people from these profess, when they meet people, their ting grows up, grows up, goes up. Now with the police it is, is not that. It is...excuse me Chief Constable, I am getting old."

It's not your age Mum.

"It's not that. Its de ting. You know."

So I have to save Mum? I was just about to speak when she starts up again. She has gone stagy Jamaican. Only really heard her like that when I was a child and she was fake angry. Why is she doing that? Think I know why.

"Yes. It's the more the people meet others the more they like them. The more they meet the police the less they like them. Dat's it. Different to everyone else. Goes the other way. The more people meet de police the less they trust dem, like dem. Now I see why. I can see it all now."

She pointed her hand at Hooker and then to the IPCC bods either side of him. This seemed a tremendous effort for her. Then another burst of energy.

"You see Chief Constable I know what you are going to do special for Jesse……. nuttin. That's what you is going to do. Nuttin. You just want to be the big man in the papers, big pictures of yourself. You talk to my daughter here, Marta, my daughter, and you think you are high, mighty, better than her. You, yes you do. You is the big man. The big high. Dat's what you really think, deep down. But you ain't. She is a doctor, an educated woman, she saves lives."

Pitch in her voice was rising.

"What do you do? Just fancy talk," she made a yapping gesture with both her hands, "fancy talk."

She held out an arm for me to help her up. I stood, I thought we were going. No, she hadn't finished. She tottered towards his desk, upright. Hooker edged back, ever so slightly intimidated. He was going to say something, then decided against.

"I tell you what you all is. You is all just all, just…..fuckers."

Spittle was forming on her mouth. And then she just stopped, slowly took her coat from the chair, and headed for the door without looking back at me.

"Come on Marta, get no sense here."

It must be the brain tumour, but I have never felt so proud of my mother.

Transcript of recorded events in Custody office in relation to Adverse Incident-Jesse Brooks.

Gleaned from i) CCTV at Front Desk with audio ii) CCTV in cell no audio iii) Police radio iv) Ambulance 999 communications

1909. PCs Bell and Sykes carry Jesse Brooks into the Custody area. Sgt Parker is behind them

PC Brazier is stood behind the Custody counter

Brazier. "Should you lads have gone home hours ago?"

Sykes. "Bit of overtime covering for those on the football. Anyway here is Jesse Brooks, Sgt, drunk and disorderly."

Brazier "Can he stand up?"

Parker "He's ok, Hong Kong. Had a skin full now just pissing about being a dick pretending to be unconscious."

Bell (inaudible) Laughter from all three.

Brazier "Ok well I'm not arsing about. Put the bell-end in cell 3. Bring us back his belt and stuff you know the score."

PC Sykes and Bell carry him to cell 3 with Sgt Parker. They lie him down, take his coat, shoes and belt off him. Sgt Parker leaves the cell and returns with a blanket which he places over the detainee. They all return these to the Custody desk where Pc Brazier goes through the pockets of the coat which are empty.

2013 Visited in cell by CDO Pendleton. Shakes detainee. (Custody record endorsed)

2050 Visited in cell by CDO Pendleton. Shakes detainee (Custody record endorsed)

2145 Visited in cell by CDO Pendleton. No contact with detainee (Custody record endorsed)

2211. Visited in cell by CDO Pendleton. No contact with detainee (Custody record endorsed)

2247 Visited in cell by CDO Pendleton. No contact with detainee (Custody record endorsed)

2316 PC Brazier can be seen on camera going up the cell block. No visit in the cell. (Custody record endorsed with visit at 2326)

0013 Custody record is endorsed with visit at 0013hrs by PC Brazier. No CCTV footage of him ether going up cell corridor or entering the cell

0045 Visit by PW Purvis. Shakes him and appears to have some conversation (Custody record endorsed)

0048 Upon PW Purvis leaving, detainee appears to take a small bottle of what appears to be vodka from under blanket and starts drinking. Drinks from bottle 0048-0112.

0135 Visit by PW Purvis. Shakes detainee and appears to have conversation with him (Custody record endorsed).

0215 Visit by CDO Pendleton. Shakes detainee. (Custody record endorsed)

0350 Another prisoner (Jenkins) charged at counter and released on bail by Sgt Hayes. PW Purvis, Brazier and Hall all can be seen going into back office. Sgt Hayes is at front.

There is a discussion in the back office which cannot be heard. Sgt Hayes can be heard. It is believed he is contributing to the conversation from the front office.

0401 Hayes "Yes heard this one. He sold Bowie bonds in 2002 for £50 million and they have just been wound up as now being worthless. Yes in a minute he will do the he owes it all to Tony Visconti and Mick Ronson speech............Ok will let you tell the story……. God forbid"

0415 Hayes "What about Andrew Ridgeley?"

0418 Hayes "I am sure the draw of your semi in New Moston would be too much for her Bob…….. Charlotte if can you drag yourself away from Stuart Maconie for a minute and do the visits. Remember those with a red star on the board have to be

woken and spoken to because they are
drunk"

0420 Visit by PW Purvis. Shakes detainee
and tries to speak with him. She pulls
back blanket and appears to slap his face.
She appears to turn to exit cell as Sgt
Hayes enters. He also slaps face of
detainee and claps at his ear.

Sgt Hayes thumps chest of detainee.
Appears to try to start to give mouth to
mouth. Then walks out of cell.

PW Purvis runs out of the cell through
front office into the back office. Returns
almost immediately with defibrillator
device and sees Sgt Hayes in front office.

Hayes "Where is Bob?"

Purvis "He (PC Hall) just said he had just
gone out for his nightly cigar. Doesn't
know where he is"

Hayes "For fucks sake, I need that device
to put over his mouth stop germs
(inaudible) in a drawer. Er ok.

0426 PW Purvis and Sgt Hayes go into cell.
Sgt Hayes puts defibrillator pads on
heart. Conversation between him and PW
Purvis. Pads are taken off by Sgt Hayes
then put on again. Conversation between
Sgt Hayes and PC Purvis. Both then appear
to read instructions on defibrillator.

0431 PC Purvis and Sgt Hayes both return
to front desk.

Hayes "Think it's in the drawer. How long will the ambulance be?"

Purvis "Forgot to call I was getting defibrillator and speaking to Glyn. Oh"

Hayes (shouts to back office PC Hall) "Jesus fucking H Christ get a fucking ambulance"

PC Brazier comes into Custody office from the side entrance.

Brazier "What's the rumpus"

Hayes "Cell 3. Not breathing. I am getting an ambulance"

Sgt Hayes goes to back office. PC Brazier walks up corridor to cell. PC Brazier puts what appears to be phone over mouth of detainee. Looks at phone and appears to start sending a text.

He picks up the empty bottle of vodka from next to detainee.

0431. Back office conversation reconstructed from recordings of BT 999, police and ambulance telephone and radio

Hall (via radio) "PC 3478 to comms I have been ringing you for two minutes now no answer. I need an ambulance in Custody."

Comms "PC 3478 why do you need an ambulance. Is it urgent?"

Hall (on radio) "Man is dead"

Operator 999 line. "Emergency which service do you require"

Hayes (heard on 999 line) "No he's not dead he just unresponsive, police, no sorry ambulance, ambulance. Tell them he's not fucking dead he is not breathing"

Operator 999 "I am sorry is that ambulance?"

Hayes "Yes but cancel no stay"

Hall "Apologies he's not dead but he's not breathing no cancel the Sgt. has got through"

Operator "Do you still want the ambulance?"

Hayes "Yes. Put me through now. Yes tell comms to standby operator is putting me through anyway"

Comms "Do you want an ambulance?"

Hall (heard on 999 line) "Sarge do we want an ambulance?"

Hayes (heard on 999 line) "No I am being put through"

Hall "Thank you no he is being put through"

Comms "3479. We have ambulance on the other end confirm you don't need one"

Hall "Yes. Sgt is on the other line"

Hayes (heard on ambulance line) "No they have not answered me yet yes we do need an ambulance urgent"

Hall (heard on ambulance line) "You sure?"

Hayes (heard on ambulance line) "Fucking yes"

Hall "3478 to Comms .Yes we do need an ambulance man not breathing."

Ambulance operator "Hello, hello, ambulance…."

Brazier (heard on ambulance line) "He is still breathing just. Got some evaporation on my mobile phone but he will shuttling off this mortal coil if (inaudible)"

Hall "3479. Correction. He is breathing"

Comms "Why do you need an ambulance if he is breathing"

Hayes (now on radio) "We need an ambulance. Man is unconscious and unresponsive. Can you get us one urgently?"

Comms "Yes Sgt no problem"

Ambulance line cut off.

0442 Hayes, Purvis and Brazier can be seen entering the front office.

Brazier "I will open the shutters for the ambulance. It's Kirsty who's coming, you know fit piece who came earlier for the mental job. I texted her. She has just texted me back two minutes away.

The defibrillator didn't work Chris because his heart has not stopped. I leave you alone for five minutes and you start trying to kill the prisoners.

Better he lives though Chris. He's a half chat. We will be fucked if he dies."

Hayes "CCTV, Bob, CCTV. Shut the fuck up."

The ambulance arrives at 0447 hrs (contd)……

PAUL

It wasn't actually easy contacting Mason. I hadn't got his private number. Did not want to be seen going to his flat. Had to guess his work's email.

```
Roger,

Hope you enjoyed Sunday lunch last week.
Yes got that item in the catalogue you
were talking about.

Anyway have lost my mobile and your no
with it. Could you send it me? Laters

P
```

Gave him a day. Now I know people like him don't miss emails. They claim they are busy but I could see him checking his Blackberry even when he was at my house. He had decided to ignore me. Foolish. OK up the ante.

```
Roger,

Need to discuss the catalogue item you
want in person. Shall I call round to your
flat tonight? Bout 8.30.Laters
```

Well that got me his mobile number within three minutes with a message to ring after 5.30 as now in a meeting. Time to show him who was boss.

```
Ringing you now. Kindly answer.
```

He did, he was in Police Authority and had stepped out of a meeting. A quiet hiss down the phone. I had clearly got the pen-drive back now so me and him were quits.

"No Mr Mason we are not quits. We are not quits at all."

"How come?"

"Well Mr Mason someone decided to firebomb my door after you practically allowed the *MEN* to publish my address, as a result I have the best CCTV system money can buy in my house including indoors. In my solicitor's safe is a recording of you coming to my house, coming in and asking me to kill a journalist."

"I didn't."

"Well I had to redact the tape. I learnt that word 'redact' when I was on my trumped up conspiracy to murder charge. The tape is now in the safe of my solicitor. You may eventually get off with it because of the redaction but who knows? It won't be good for you. So, in summation, no we are not quits and I would be ever so obliged if you answer my call promptly next time."

I clicked off.

There is CCTV outside my house but it is not even clear it is him as he has the coat over his head. I don't obviously have it in my house, but how would he know? He can't be certain I am bluffing.

I phone him back. He answered straight away.

"Well done cunt, answered in time. Some advice. Never dance with a stranger."

I am a proper gangster.

GINA

Do you know why I really ask for time off on nights? I say I have to have the grandkids and I need some sleep. It's not true actually. I do have the grandkids but I could get by with little sleep. No the reason is Tommy is unhappy when I am not there to make his breakfast in the morning and give him his packed lunch.

It's not easy to admit I still do this.

Tommy and I have had some terrible arguments about it all. I would prefer a day job but the extra pay for being on weekends and nights is 34% more. For me that's £7k more and Tommy won't let me give up that money. He wants his Oldham season ticket, his golf club fees, his Spain trip, his beer money. We are still in debt with cards, far more than he knows about. I used to keep swapping them over at 0% but my rating, or whatever that is, changed which meant I couldn't do this anymore. Now on payday loans. There is a day of reckoning coming. I ignore the letters from the pay day loans people and hide them from Tommy.

Tommy goes to bed about 8.45 to 9 when he is on earlies next day and insists there is silence in the house. He will not let me even have the TV on. Tammy bought me some headphones for Christmas couple of years ago. She knows what he is like. I am certain Tommy broke them deliberately. They worked for about three weeks, then they did not. I don't want to take them back to the shop to find out why they did not work. I lie there sometimes watching Tommy breathing in bed and just pray it will stop, a heart attack or something. I really hope he dies, soon.

I don't like the work in custody. It's not a job I even wanted. I was happy on the front desk at Milnrow. It was a lovely job, just round the corner, not too difficult, nice team spirit down there and got some right characters turning up at the front desk. Then came that incident of the man handing himself in on bank holiday and I had to be moved. Still don't think I did anything wrong. I did what CID told me to do.

Custody is just too much all going on at once. You can easily make a mistake there. I get flustered easily. I sort of knew we all were an accident waiting to happen but equally it was because Chris was so easy going that I wanted to stay on the shift. I could just about manage to do the shifts with flyers from Chris.

Other shifts were always complaining about the state of things when they took over from us when we had been on nights. It was because Bob is bone idle.

Did I lead Chris on? I did a bit, I knew he liked me. I tried to do nothing to encourage him but I didn't positively discourage him. I managed to keep him just thinking there may be a chance. I did not tell him I was coming round today to see how he is now he's on the sick. Truth is I suspected he may plan what did actually happen.

I suppose it was wrong of me to start washing up and hoovering but I just could not sit there in the mess. Embarrassing for us both I suppose but better on the whole. Someone had to do it, the place was a bomb site. He just sat there in his pyjamas watching me.

We could have left it there as one of those embarrassing things that had occurred when he was at a low point and ill. We are never at our best when we are ill. We could both have forgotten about it. Then seeing Chris crying on the couch I could not just leave him so I sat next to him. But no, he had to try to kiss me. He was unshaven and it scratched my face, not sure he had even cleaned his teeth, curtains open so anyone could see in.

Horrible, embarrassing moment but he could not even leave it there when I told him this was not sensible and he was not thinking straight. I had to push him off, eventually. He got the message but it took too long. Ugh, hate to think about it.

He had his head in his hands.

"Everything I do goes wrong. Everything."

He needed to pull himself together. No point in being overly sympathetic and indulging him, would not have helped.

"No Chris. This is just a bad time. We all have bad times. You have just got to get through this. It will pass."

"I am going to be sacked."

"I don't think so and anyway Chris, that is not the end of the world. It was only a couple of weeks ago you thought you were going to prison."

"If I lose my job I lose the pension and the finance for the girls for university."

Those girls and his wife, Sheila. Right, he needs telling.

"Christ alive Chris when are you ever going to learn? Sheila and the girls have taken you for everything and they will carry on until you grow a pair. Look at yourself, feeling sorry for yourself. Seriously. People have all kinds of difficulties in life, all kinds, you have no idea, no idea Chris. And you think a quick fumble with me will help things? That's all old Gina is good for, clean your house and a quicky to make you feel better."

I just walked straight out. I know I am not the best with words but there was no more to be said.

I hope that smartens him up. The shock to the system he needs.

Tough love.

KENNY

It's 6.20 p.m. long old day. It started with a good feeling about the sister but has faded fast. I wanted it to be right.

She took her child to school, got the bus into town and went straight to work. Came out for a sandwich and went back in. She got back on the bus, spent 40 minutes at her parents and has just got home with child. I just had visions of her delivering supplies to a safe house or something like that, disappointing. Just stood the surveillance team down, left the divisional lads watching the house.

So home again for me, can see three missed calls from Varna. Probably run ragged from dealing with the kids, one of them is poorly. Just on the M60 when Sharon calls to debrief the day as usual. She's worse than Varna. It's like having two wives.

"Another day in paradise Sharon."

"Cousin has just come to the house with takeaway."

"Nice, there is a connection. What do you think? They are shagging?"

"Who knows? I have got the teams visiting the local takeaways. Division could not tell where it was from other than it was brown paper bags."

"Seems like a wild goose chase to me."

"Perhaps. Think we should try to follow cousin when he leaves?"

"Have we got the staff?"

"Stupid suggestion really. Just getting giddy though. He may take us to a safe house."

"Think we should come back in?"

"I have already turned my car round."

"Ok well I'll let you get on with it, but let me know if any developments."

I hadn't taken my jacket off at home when it was Sharon, again.

"Fucking, magnificent, banquet for four. For four Kenny, for four. Not one or two or three. Four.

Murderous greedy bastard."

BOB

Check out the big brain on Robert Brazier.

The insurance policy has paid out. Big time.

To be honest I did not now need to meet him at Chester and I did not think he would turn up but I had booked the room anyway. It was definitely worth a punt, it would as good a place as any to meet him if he did appear. Decided to make a night of it, got the train there, pint in the first pub I see, a little Brazier tradition when I go away. Hotel was like, well, it was like every other hotel.

I had a hot bath, couple of the miniatures from the mini bar. I put on my red blazer, work white shirt (wasn't planning on taking the blazer off), grey trousers, the only tie I possessed, white socks, work shoes. Looked at myself in the mirror, couple of stains on the blazer which I damped down with a cloth, but all in all, not bad.

Went downstairs at just before seven, got reduced price if you ordered your food before then. Couple of pints for starters, soup and steak and chips, bottle of cheap red. Filled a little hole but would be hungry later. Ordered a third pint from the bar, needed to hold back and think clearly so no more until I was happy he wasn't turning up.

They had a Wednesday night game on, granny stabbers against Portsmouth. You could only see it in a little snug area which was walled off and had an open fire. Perfect, watch the game and, from there, could look out for him coming in. He probably won't show in which case I can get nicely pissed.

Now I don't know about you but have you noticed how anywhere you go when you just want to have a nice quiet drink there is always a fucking scouser nearby ruining your night? Yes in this case two of the twats turned up to watch the game sat in the corner. Man and wife or girlfriend or whatever and she seemed to have more to say than him. A scouse woman with views on football, Christ.

I am not listening to this shit all night. Time to make some polite conversation.

"Last won the league when Wham were No 1."

"What's that mate?"

"Wham were no 1 when you last won the league, that long ago. This seems to be your best chance. They will break up after this season. Torres, Alonso will go to proper big clubs. Gerrard and Carragher will stay for their Mickey Mouse legend status but win fuck all."

"Yeah nice one. Funny guy. Hey five times European Cup winners."

"Yeah well all the other teams managed to win it without killing anyone."

She now decides to join in.

"Nice tie porky"

"Nice tie porky? Seriously, is that the best you can do? Come on where is your legendary cheeky chappy scouse humour? You know Ken Dodd, Arthur Askey, Stan 'our chippy got bombed by the Germans' Boardman, the hilarious Jimmy Tarbuck, Freddie Starr."

"Yeah we get the message mate. If you don't mind we would like to watch the game."

God she had a horrible guttural screechy voice. But I think that did the job in shutting her the fuck up. Is there anything worse than a know all, scouse, female? Truly is there? Kill some time, think of ten things that are worse.

Supertramp, Noel Edmonds, Bryan Ferry, garden centres, Richard Madeley, golfers, Harry Secombe, John Motson,

Tommy Steele. Yes Tommy Steele, best one so far, half a fucking sixpence. How many is that? Nine.

I was stuck for the last one. I had given myself a self-imposed rule that I could not use a Holocaust example or another scouser in this list. By the way you know Hitler stayed in Liverpool don't you? Figures when you think about it.

I was lost in the reverie of trying to get my last one on the list. Had Jimmy Saville down, talentless Yorkshire weirdo but had to discount him, he does do a lot for charity, sort of redeems him.

When I looked up Hooker was just sat there against the wall on a bench seat. I mean it was a toughie that scouse poser I really had been struggling with it so you can see why I had been concentrating so hard that I did not notice him. And I have to say, did not immediately recognise him. Wasn't sure it was him, looked slightly different. Ah yes his hair wasn't spiked up like a puff.

He had a half of coke in front of him, jacket and tie. Sports jacket with a horrible striped shirt. He pulled out two leaflets from his pocket. They were similar, orange in colour showing a sunrise or sunset and some writing on the front.

Looking back I should have tried to see what they were before I made my move but was so excited I just could not help myself. Took my pint and plonked myself in front of him.

"Mind if I sit here Gabriel? Francesca sends her love but she can't come along. Shame really, you must have been looking forward to a bunk up, can see you put on your best jacket. And she is a pro trust me but hey ho! Suggest we go somewhere more discrete. You know a scouse free zone."

I nodded at the giro cheats. He stared me straight in the face through the pale blue specs.

"Well firstly you totally misunderstand my intention in being here and I can see absolutely no reason to move."

He quickly gathered up the leaflets and placed them back in his pocket as he spoke. He was quite cool about things, not quite as expected.

"Planning to recruit her into the Moonies or something? Or was it advising on STDs?"

He scratched his nose dismissively.

"I don't believe I have had the pleasure. You clearly know who I am."

He offered his hand out to shake.

"Oh don't know if my name my rings a bell. Bob Brazier?"

"But of course Mr Brazier. The workshy custody clerk who thought it was funny to go missing in the Lakes. Who could forget? Yes you cause the death, sorry near-death of a man, and then sue us for breach of confidence. Yes can remember from you from your picture in the *MEN*. What can I do for you? I suppose any warnings about what you think you are doing are otiose."

Yes I do know what 'otiose' means, twatty bollocks. He was too cool about everything. He must be rattled. He could not know what was coming next.

"What are you going to say next, 'come come Mr Bond you enjoy killing as much as I do'? Stop pretending to be cool you prick. It's not helping. In fact, it is fucking disconcerting like Cilla Black and Barry Grant over there."

Raised my voice at this point for them to just hear.

"Anyway piece of advice for you. You should lock your office. Seriously you are a Chief Constable for fuck sake. Anyone can get in there. By anyone I mean me."

"Ah well Mr Brazier I see by your Francesca reference you read the *MEN* spread on me when I joined, my attendance at AA and all that open office space stuff. I see absolutely no reason. I have a clear desk policy and think we should have a culture of general openness. There is nothing in my office that is secret. I have nothing to hide. But you clearly think otherwise. Go on amuse me."

"Well it's not what you left in the office it is what I put in......this. "

I produce Exhibit A. Exhibit B is in my pocket. He took a sip of his drink, nervous, but not as nervous as he should be.

"A recording device? Yes I think placing that in a Chief Constable's office is misconducting yourself in public office i.e. criminal conduct. Any product of that will be inadmissible as you do not seek the requisite permissions. To protect the Force I would get an injunction banning any publication. Anyway what have you found out? Me talking about some staff in mildly disparaging terms? Discussing some terrorism cases? None of it can go anywhere.

You see Mr Brazier I have learnt to live a careful life, a very careful life. I know my phone can be listened to by my secretary. I know that it's fairly easy to tape my calls as you cannot expect privacy on a work's phone. I try to be measured in what I say on that phone at all times. So whatever you have on that device cannot incriminate me. It doesn't does it? It really does not, does it? Anything else of a confidential operational nature you cannot use."

I drained my pint, have to say he was beginning to impress me.

"You got me there. I did not hear you say anything remotely interesting on that phone and that's the God's honest truth and the quality is pretty patchy. Bluff called eh? Want another one?"

"No thanks."

"Well I'm having another. Wasted journey but hope Portsmouth can keep them out for the second half."

KENNY

9p.m., chaos.

Utter chaos in MIT office room. Nearly everyone is on the telephone or doing something that seems urgent. I am finding it hard to work out what they are all doing. No one seems to be co-ordinating all this.

You are supposed to keep notes of your actions and considerations in incidents like this but it is impossible. Sharon has asked a young girl, forget her name, simply to write down what management decisions are being made, but she is spending all her time with Sharon who keeps disappearing out of the room. I hope this all just works itself out some way.

We are sure cousin is still in the house. Problem is we cannot get too close to the house. It is in a crowded cul- de- sac, some kids still hanging out on the street, must be freezing.

I am trying to turn out the surveillance team or I asked somebody to. No idea what has happened with that. We have Tactical Vehicle Crime Team (TVCU) on standby about a quarter of a mile away. They are not surveillance trained but nobody can get away from them if there is a pursuit.

Firearms teams are also on standby at the station. Don't know this firearms commander and his advisor sat over in the corner but they are not coming across as 'can do' types. He is a youngish superintendent off division, on- call, not a dedicated firearms leader. The advisor is doing all the talking not the commander, 'Where is Keane sleeping?' 'Where is child sleeping?' 'Could there be others in there?' 'Do we know if Keane is armed' 'Can we be sure he is there?'

It's the way he asks them he makes me feel it's my fault I don't know the answers. He wants a perfect scenario. He does not have one. It's a cul-de- sac so they can't drive down to look at the door and the approach, they would be clocked in Moston.

The divisional guys watching the house can only tell them so much.

Detective comes up to me, phone to ear.

"Sir, TVCU want to know what to do if cousin leaves with another, they are requesting they have firearms with them. ………"

The firearms advisor overhears, speaks up, confident, aggressive.

"We have no tactic for this kind of pursuit. We do not shoot out of windows when cars are moving. It's not America. They will have to stay with them until we catch up."

Yes that sums him up. He is great at the positive/negative decision. Yes we definitely cannot do this. I need 'can do' people. Where is Sharon, by the way?

Duty Officer rings from control room.

"Sir with respect this needs to be moved to a properly designated silver control with radio communications etc."

"Can you send someone over to sort this out with staff?"

"Not sure we have got the staff, Sir. "

"Well tell them no one can go home and it does not matter how much it costs."

"Sir, most of them are civilians and we cannot order them to stay. I will try."

"Well what do you expect me to do? Please just sort it out."

Detective is trying to get my attention. Phone to ear, radio in hand.

"Sir, cousin on the move as you can hear on radio. They want instructions."

"Is he on his own?"

He has to repeat it down the phone.

"Is he on his own?"

No reply. These people are not professional. For f**ks sake that is the obvious information I would have wanted to hear.

"Yes, they are certain, on his own."

I need to think this through. I can see Sharon coming across the room running, she grabs a radio.

"Chief Inspector Bentley to TVCU, do not stop the car or even try to follow it. You have been told that. No heroics, TVCU do you receive?"

Silence on the air.

"I tell you those fucking glory boy idiots want their piece of the action but if he is stopped and gets a message to Keane we are fucked. They are pretending not to hear."

She repeats down the radio.

"TVCU do you receive me, if you stop that car or follow it I will personally f**king ensure every one of you walks in uniform for the rest of your lives. Now do you receive me?"

Silence.

"Do you receive me?"

"Received Ma'am."

"Let the car go, do not even give him the chance to see you, w**kers."

The last word she said to herself, not down the radio. Just, I think.

Firearms commander and advisor have been talking in whispers in the corner of the room, a lot of frowning. They come up to me, they do not want to do the job. They cannot properly survey the house in the dark, the information is too imprecise, they do not know where Keane is or even if he is there, the child will be in the house. They have a specialist team for this kind of entry to deal with a man as violent as Keane and they are on in the morning. May be best if they wait until child has gone to school.

All the time the advisor is speaking Sharon is staring at him, she in his personal space. She has her tongue in the side of her mouth. This is getting out of hand. I get Sharon in my office.

"Well there is nothing we can do Sharon. Perhaps we should just stand the whole thing down? Yes we need to stand down before this all goes very wrong. Yes, do you think? "

"Don't know Kenny, don't see how we can walk away. Not sure about the child but it may be Keane would be less likely to start shooting if there is a child in the house. Look this is dynamic and this is North Manchester. People will be seeing the TVCU and the firearms teams arriving. Not sure we can wait.....but there is a lot we do not know."

Even Sharon is unsure. The firearms advisor is right, it's just too risky.

"He may not even be in the house Sharon."

"Oh he is in the house. He is in that fucking house."

My mobile goes.

"Insp Dodd here Sir TVCU Commander. I am off duty but just been rang by our sergeant the lads are all very unhappy about the way they were spoken to by Miss Bentley just then. They have already stayed on duty to be helpful. You need to know they had a TV crew in the back who were picking up all this. Now I suppose we can sort out whether they will submit a grievance another time...."

"Yes we can Inspector."

I cut him off, I really haven't the time.

TV crew? God knows what they may know or who they may have told. My mind is made up we have to go before the tom drums get round and this turns into a circus. Decision made, we have to go. I call the firearms commander and advisor into the room and explain the TV complication. We just have to go with all the confusion. Nothing is certain but we have to live with it.

It's knuckle head advisor speaking all the time. He point blank now refuses. There is a kid in the house and they have not had enough time to prepare. The young lad superintendent is just an irrelevance in proceedings now, no-one is even pretending he is in charge, not even him; he is cleaning his glasses while knuckle head talks. Sharon walks out half way through the exchange. That's unlike her, I thought she would have given him what for, but perhaps she feels she would have said something even she may have regretted.

Varna is ringing. Surely not now, better pick up though, she's already balled me out for missing calls today.

"Kenny, you know Charlie's sick, but you haven't called to ask how he is, have you? No you haven't. Too busy with your special enquiry again. I know what's going on don't I Kenny? No you are not concerned because that lezzer Sharon is noshing you right now isn't she? Bet she is on her knees right now with a mouthful of your dick right now .Yes I know how it works, get an enquiry and it an excuse to f**k about. Don't even try to tell me there has been a development or......."

Where is Sharon?

BOB

"So, Mr Brazier. Is this it? Is all this it? Tell me how and why did you come up with all this? It is quite extraordinary."

"Well, Gabriel, feel I can call you Gabriel?"

Now on fourth pint. No more, need a clear head still.

"I suppose the point is none of it is extraordinary. Quite the opposite, it is very ordinary, mundane. The trick I pulled with Francesca was not difficult. Knew you went to AA, just had to work out where. Luckily I knew someone as game as Francesca."

"Well she is not here now. I mean what were you going to do? Try to photograph or blackmail me. Seriously? I would say you watch too many films but I just don't understand what you really thought you were doing."

"Well what were you going to do with those leaflets? Or were they just your cover?"

"Go on, you first, amuse me re the device. Did you really plant it? You didn't, did you? Just a bluff?"

"Well you have me there. I suppose I could have got into Chester House on my warrant card past security easily enough during the night, but the doors onto the 11th floor are still locked aren't they? Unless the cleaner opens them. There is a rumour that there is CCTV on the floor so I would be recorded. I would have had to wear a balaclava. Would have looked stupid if caught wouldn't I?"

"You really considered it?"

"Yes suppose so and seeing as though you were super confident you would not have said anything incriminating in the office it was a good job I didn't even try this wasn't it? Still the bluff was worth a punt. You may have folded like a soggy kit-kat."

"I suppose what is most extraordinary about this whole thing is the pathetic half- hearted nature of it all Mr Brazier. You are sad really. You do know I am going to have to arrest you now for conspiracy to blackmail?"

"Won't this be just a tad embarrassing for you?"

"Perhaps and, I don't mean to be rude, but did you really think you could get away with this?"

"Be just your word against mine wouldn't it? You would have to explain what you were doing here."

"No I am not sure it would. I know she is not called Francesca and is Maria. I have actually never met her. She came to us when you mentioned your hare-brained scheme. To be fair she wanted some money but better than your holiday in Majorca I suppose?"

This is all going very, very wrong.

"You are making a big mistake, Gabriel, old boy. You see the thing is before you do this you ought to know I was just playing along then for a daft laugh I really did...."

"No you are the one making the mistake Manc. You are under arrest for conspiracy to blackmail."

Sonia and Derek Hatton were, of course, coppers.

SHARON

Men are fucking useless.

Just went out of the room to phone ACC Callaghan to get a decision, which I thought is what he is paid for. He has asked us to come to a consensus. Pointless telling him I would not have rung him had we been able to come to a consensus.

As for the two from firearms, just oxygen thieves. The advisor is a walking, talking stereotype; shaven headed, muscled, looks the part, talks the part but really thick as shit and clueless under pressure. They all spend their time on days in the gym and bullshitting on courses. No idea when they meet the real thing. Snowflake Brennan, the firearms commander no better; Graduate-Entry type spent his life getting promoted at headquarters and now to bolster his CV and credentials has volunteered to be a firearms commander which for the invertebrate just means doing as he is told by the advisors.

And another thing, while I am at it, trust me the TVCU boy racers would have got into a pursuit if I hadn't read them their fortune.

Poor Kenny has pools of sweat showing in his shirt under his armpits. He has the phone clamped to his ear and looks as if in physical pain, must be Varna. I do actually feel sorry for him. It is hard to think straight at the moment with all the GMP boys' clubs trying to fuck this up.

I needed to act quickly while Kenny has swung the other way so I went down to the canteen where all the firearms PCs were sat. Did not have to over egg the pudding, just explained the facts as they were.

"Right Kenny I have been to see the firearms lads in the canteen. Explained the situation to them, to wit their commander is so chicken shit scared he does not want to go in to get the man who murdered their colleague and wants to put it off until the morning. They will be known forever, throughout GMP, as the team that sat on their arses while a murderer of their colleague escaped out of the back door. They are, of course, 100% onside. They want to go in. Hopefully should be some upwards pressure from the team now. "

Callaghan back on phone. Apologies for a delay, apparently Mr Hooker could not be contacted at first as he was on an operational job in Cheshire. Did I hear that correctly? Chief Constable, on operational work out of the Force boundary? Anyway I tell him we cannot get a consensus. He suggests we ring Hooker on a conference call for something of this magnitude.

So here we are Kenny, Brennan and his sidekick and Julia in Kenny's office taking notes, all crowded round a speakerphone.

Mr Hooker is 'disappointed beyond words' that professionals cannot sort something out like this and he is being asked to referee. He mentioned it is typical of the Manchester mentality, everyone being part of big silos. He wants Kenny to get together with the firearms commander and thrash something out to get a consensus view.

Kenny was about to apologise. I jump in.

"Sir we need a decision. There is no falling out or animosity here. It's not a question of silos or personalities or power struggles. It's a judgement. One argument is that we need to strike quickly. This is because it is hard to hide the activity near the house, we know there is a TV crew with the TVCU who also know of our find, the takeaway people know of our interest. We have a degree of control and we need to seize the opportunity now. It will be very embarrassing if we lose him. We even could have the media here tomorrow. If I may speak for Superintendent Brennan......"

Well, everyone else does.

"…..he is concerned about going in without full planning. The full dynamic entry team was on duty today and need rest if they have to operate so the earliest we can get them is 8 a.m. tomorrow. This has the advantage of only staging the operation once the child is out of the house and at school. We believe Keane is there but we cannot be sure. To get devices into the house is more potential attention and delay and every second delay means the greater potential for Keane clocking what we are up to."

Hooker then went through everything again. Slightly more nuanced version of the weary questioning we have had from the firearms advisor. The banquet, the child, the TV crew, the lay out of the cul- de- sac, the firearms Keane may have, lay out of the house, what did the TV crew know? Could we ensure the TV crew did not pass on any information? What made us think the takeaway people may tell anyone? Why could we not be more discreet? Why did we suddenly come up with this after four weeks?

This was floundering not assessing the intelligence, questions we could not answer but which did not alter the position.

"I am really unhappy at being put in this position. It's just typical of the way…."

"Chief Constable, Sir, if I may?"

Firearms advisor spoke up.

"With respect Sir, Mr Hooker Sir, I think an important element has been left out, that is the safety of the firearms officers. I cannot recommend going in tonight. We do not know where he is sleeping, we do not know what ordinance he has and lastly, ultimately carrying a firearm is voluntary. You cannot order the staff in if they are not happy to do so. Simple as."

He was, of course, pleased with himself. You can see him now giving the lecture on the next course, 'so I said to the Chief Constable himself...'.

"Well Superintendent Poole, Superintendent Brennan, Chief Inspector Bentley, I think that sways it. We cannot do an operation which the staff do not want to do, it is voluntary to carry a gun. Ok, decision made. I would be happy to authorise this operation if the staff are willing. Until such time it will have to wait."

I repeat this back to him slowly, Julia is writing this down.

"Thank you Sir. Thank you very much for this clarity."

I click the phone off before anyone else can speak.

MAIREAD

I fell in love at twelve years old.

Dad had just been sent down for a year. I was so happy. It had all gone to Mum's plan.

I was sat in a dark lounge in my pyjamas with Mum, curtains closed against the evening sun watching *Eastenders*. As happy as anyone could ever possibly be.

A commotion at the door. Pat bursts to the room. He had his hand over his mouth which you could see was bleeding and one eye had an elephantine lump over it, completely closed. I remember him falling to his knees. When Mum tried to ask him what had happened, he could not speak. There was something very wrong with his mouth. He kept his hand over it as if he was holding it all together.

I expected Mum to panic but she did not. She told me to stay with my brother and she went to the phone. I can recall her tone on the phone. Flat, business like, measured, she was not ringing for an ambulance. Mum came back into the room eyes blazing, tears of anger. She seemed to know what had happened.

Pat was by now whimpering, like a dying animal. I had my arm round him.

"Mum, aren't you going to get an ambulance?"

"In a minute darling. In a minute. Someone is coming to help."

Within minutes there was a knock on the door. I ran to it. It was Paul talking on his mobile phone, a brick of a thing but I had not seen one actually used before. I had never seen Paul before.

He was crisply dressed in white shirt and pressed but faded jeans which cut a contrast with people out in the sunshine in our Moston street in deck chairs with shorts and vests. He did not even acknowledge me but walked straight into our lounge still talking on the phone.

Mum cried the moment she saw Paul. Pat had now collapsed to the floor.

"Irene there is a taxi outside. Straight to A & E."

He picked Pat up and started carrying him outside.

"Don't worry about......"

"Mairead."

"Mairead, I will look after her and get the twins in line. It's going to be alright. Ring here when you know anything".

I watched them go outside. There was a brief conversation between them. Mum did not seem to be as grateful as I would have thought. She shot him a look of what seemed to be contempt. It was an odd attitude to take to someone who had done all this for you.

He came back into the house, splatters of blood on his shirt.

"Sweetheart, your mum has asked you go straight to bed now while I find the twins. Could you do that for me?"

"Do you want a cup of tea? I will make you one before I go to bed."

I was determined to make some mark in the adult world. I was not going to be completely ignored. I was going to be a player.

He laughed.

"Yes I will have a cup of tea, but no sugar unlike your dad."

We stood in the kitchen while the kettle boiled. He asked me about Bluecoats school and I tried to be as casual and adult as possible, wished I wasn't in my pyjamas. I remember asking him his name and what he did for a living.

He laughed again.

"It's Paul, Paul Smith. I am an old friend, associate, of your dad's"

I noted he did not tell me what he did. I could guess. Just that minute the twins came through the door with Johnny Styles. Now everyone knew Johnny. I could see immediately that Paul was his boss or was senior to him in some way or certainly not frightened of him. Remember the twins knew who Paul was and called him 'Mr Smith'. He ordered them into the lounge in their own house. I knew that was the signal to go to bed.

Seemed there were endless comings and goings that night at the house. I wanted to go down to the bottom of the stairs but also wanted to do what Mr Smith had told me to do. I was determined to stay awake and watch people come and go from the bedroom window but must have drifted off.

I awoke in Mum's bed. I remember there was a package with a huge amount of cash next to the bed on my side. I lay there looking at it until Mum woke.

Mum explained. Pat would be alright. He had been attacked by the Bruen brothers, all older than him. He had been held down and beaten up for a long period of time. He had lost teeth and had bitten right through his tongue which was nearly in two parts. He had a broken cheekbone and had to stay in hospital for some days to be observed.

She had called Paul because he was an old friend of Dad's who Dad had arranged to look after us when he was in prison. He would be able to persuade the twins not to seek revenge on the Bruens. He had seen the Bruens' dad and had made sure this would not happen again.

I was looking at the money.

"He has given us this to help us but Dad will pay him back when he comes back from prison."

"I made Mr Smith a cup of tea. He was very nice."

Mum was very quiet for a while.

"Paul has been good to us but you must understand he is not really a nice man. Look at his friend Johnny. If you are nice man you don't have Johnny as a friend. I told you all this because I don't want you to be part of any of it. Any of it. And Mairead you are not part of it in any way. I need to go and see Pat at the hospital and then we will go out somewhere and I will tell you everything."

There was more?

So that afternoon we got a bus to Heaton Park and had a picnic. She said she would explain everything. She started by telling me what Dad did for a living, she said he collected debts people owed, she could not bring herself to say he controlled a drugs market. Hardly telling me 'everything'. She explained that the Bruens were in the same business as Dad but they were different. They were animals. Paul was the boss of all of this. He was more like Dad but his friend Johnny was an animal like the Bruens. She had not wanted to call him after Pat had been beaten up but she had no other choice to make sure the twins would be safe.

I knew all this.

She hated this life and would not have married Dad if she had not got pregnant with the twins but she had to see it through for the twins. She then told me that Dad was not my father.

"I see, Paul is my father that is why he is being so nice."

Mum laughed but got serious quickly.

"No Paul is not your father. I had you because I wanted some part of my life better than people like Paul and Johnny and the Bruens. Mairead you will be better than this. I know it. Your real father is well, a clever man. He is doing quite well now, a clever man. You are a clever girl that's why you are at the

Bluecoats school. I don't want you to be anything to do with this, anything. I hate that you are even called Keane.

One day I will tell you who your father is but you must understand this. The way we live, it is just not normal. Normal people don't have the police raid them at six in the morning, or get beaten up so badly they can't speak or have thousands of pounds in cash in the house. You are old enough to understand this now. It's not normal Mairead. It's not right and I do not want you to be any part of this, ever."

Poor Mum, as if I did not know this. I was her last hope for a better future. I think I had always known this somehow, but I now knew more things than everyone in this family. I knew my dad was a pervert. I knew I wasn't genetically the same as my brothers. I knew my mum had put my dad in prison. But I also knew my mum was deluded, having a child by a different father as a way of getting a better life was desperate, pathetic.

I was the only one in the family who knew everything. I was the only sensible grown up. I was the adult of the house. Me Mairead Keane, twelve years old.

I had already been planning my future, but this was the final piece of the jigsaw. I needed to team up with someone else who was a real grown up adult.

The man who I was now in love with.

BOB

I am Muhammed Ali on the bench after round one. I have given it all but Foreman is still standing.

I face ruin. I need to think. Seconds from ruin.

Derek and Sonia either side of me, hands on. Hooker is sat there like King Shit of Turd Mountain, arms spread out on the pub bench, smug as fuck.

I have two sides of folded A4 I need to get out of my blazer pocket and into Hooker's pocket or else I am finished.

"OK fair cop fair cop. I'll go quietly guv. Just let go of me, I'm not going anywhere."

I stand up.

"I know the drill. Empty my pockets. I know."

I put my wallet and room key on the bar table.

"And you want this the blank recorder just in case to check? Course you will, you will be milking this one. There nothing on it so fuck it."

I throw it into the fire. It has to go in. It does, check out Meadowlark Lemon. Both scouse cops dash to the fire. I quickly take the A4 sheets from my inside pocket and dive onto Hooker.

"Let's see those fucking leaflets then."

Top of my voice.

"Let's see those fucking leaflets. Do you love Jesus, Gabriel? Is he your personal saviour? Is that it?"

I just about managed to get the A4 sheets into his inside jacket pocket as if I was reaching for the leaflets. No idea whether I had been seen doing it or not, but I am out of options. Got as close to his ear as possible.

"Read them Gabriel, and don't let the fucking scousers see them."

By then I could feel them trying to pull me off him. My glasses had fallen off and I could hear them crack. In for a penny I thought. I hung onto Hooker making them pull at me. Seemed apt to start singing, why not? The scouse *Jerusalem*.

"When you walk through a storm, come on you scouse twats join in, you know this one."

In all the excitement I felt a Brazier fart brewing up nicely. Time to let it go. Oh yes, baby, silent but expressive and ripe. Fruity, that's the good stuff, real. You could taste it. Carry on singing.

"Walk on through my wind."

Hooker screwed up his eyes as the fart penetrated.

"What's with your stupid John Lennon specs Gabriel? You know why they call it John Lennon Airport don't you, you twats? Because when he made his money he left his wife and kid and flew out of the shithole. Boom, boom."

I lie on top clinging to him for dear life. His glasses have now come off too. The scousers are trying to pull my arms behind my back. I want to urinate in the excitement. So why am I holding back? Because it will stain my light grey keks? Old stain there anyway. If not now, then when? When would you get the chance to piss on a Chief Constable? Do it. Let it go, let it go.

Ah yes beautiful, soothing, sweet, warm release.

This is, indeed, my finest hour. Hooker's face as he realises he is now being pissed on. My one moment in time. Onto the chorus at top of my voice. Walk on, walk on.

It's never ever going to get better than this.

YNWA.

KENNY

Hooker is ringing me.

I hold the phone up to Sharon. She does the w**ker gesture. I would love not to answer. I know she would not. I just can't do that sort of thing. I should not have answered Varna earlier, cutting her off will cause problems later.

"We've done it. We've done it. Superb, superb work. Bill Callaghan tells me he just surrendered himself as the firearms officers arrived. Tremendous work. Just shows he must have known we were coming. I made the right call in the end. Well done to all the team."

"Yes Sir, we have the sister in custody too. She says he appeared a couple of days ago and she has been frightened out of her mind but with the kid in the house what could she do? We will interview her in the morning. There doesn't seem to be anything in the house apart from a false Irish passport with his picture, no firearms. Picked the cousin up at his house. He is saying nothing."

"Wasn't there a child in the house?"

"Yes Sir, Oisin, yes took him to the grandparents. All we could do in the circumstances. They were apparently as friendly as ever."

"I was thinking we need to do a big press thing, reassure people. Would you want me to host?"

"Well Sir Sharon was saying that was one of the Ripper mistakes. Appearing to have him tried and convicted before he is even interviewed. I know he has been named in the media but we need to avoid any suggestions of prejudicing a trial."

"Of course, yes of course. Charlotte's parents?"

"Yes Sharon has just briefed the FLO."

"Bruens?"

"Oh that can wait. No point getting them excited. They will know anyway on the jungle drums."

"Yes sure they will. They should be contacted though. We have to be seen to be being, you know, impartial. Anyway well done to all. Great work."

I could see some bald guy in jeans and sweat shirt out of the corner of my eye hovering to speak. Had to shout to Sharon.

"Young Mr Grace says we've all done very well. He wants us to make sure we tell the Bruens we have made the arrest."

"That's his contribution? They will know. They don't speak to the FLO anyway. She has to text them. I will get her to do it, might wake them up now anyway, fuck 'em. What time is it? 1.15."

Baldy wasn't going away, clearly wanted to speak.

"Sorry to bother you Mr Poole, Insp Dodd, TVCU. It's about a grievance I am trying to head off. The lads are upset about the way they were treated by Ma'am Bentley tonight. Appreciate this is a delicate issue I would like to get it boxed off. Can we talk in your office?"

I was about to tell him I was tired, it was late, I was in for the bollocking of my life when I did eventually get home, I would only get a few hours sleep before the kids wake and whether he had considered I may be a tad busy at this time?

In fact Varna is ringing now, but you know what? She can wait, I am in a good mood. No I am in a great mood. This will be funny.

Traffic w**k.

BOB

23 hours and 40 minutes in custody. Nice people in Chester Police station though. They answer the buzzer when you call and shit like that. You should see their cells. No graffiti or swastikas carved into the wall. They must just have had the decorators in.

I hate to admit it but the scousers, who were from the Regional Crime Squad, were ok as scousers go.

Both not fans of the Heysel deniers. She is an Everton supporter and he was from the Wirral and not interested in football so they had some redeeming features. They thought I was funny. It just so happened Liverpool were on Sky that night in the snug I had chosen. There you go.

I got a solicitor sent by the Federation, Rebecca, nice kid, quite fit, didn't do it for me (fat ankles) but she did for DC Francis which was a real help. He 'confided' in her to show off so got quite a bit of the story from her.

Maria, two faced unreliable bitch, had gone to the police straight away demanding huge sums. She never even attended one AA or had even met Hooker. Made it all up, the lying bitch. Anyway, long and short of it was that after a lot of messing about whether to pay her, she gave up on them.

Hooker had insisted on going to Chester. It was against their advice but he fancied being a real cop for ten minutes of fame. Scousers thought he was a tosser; he had ballsed everything up from the get go.

They had assumed it would still be a honey trap and I would have got someone else in. They were not banking on me being there. Presumably the leaflets were something about turning away from prostitution (Hooker would not even tell the scousers what they were about). Took me ages to realise he dared not reach inside his pocket to produce anything to them afterwards. Hooker couldn't think on his feet and had not asked anything about Maria which would have incriminated me. Instead he got stuck on talking about the tape. Anyway it was going so wrong they decided to intervene before he did any more damage.

Lucky old me then. CPS had insisted they needed a statement from Maria before they would even consider the matter. Maria could not be found for a statement and, in any case, the issue of her asking for money cast real doubt on her reliability. And that would be fixable, money talks. On reflection I reckon this was just her way of putting the price up for me. Crafty bitch, you can always rely on a prostitute to sell you down the river.

Bottom line there was no tape, so no case. So the best they would have was me trying to blackmail the Chief Constable with a blank recorder and that was not going to fly, I never actually made any demands anyway. I am an idiot, after all, with an unbalanced mind who goes missing.

There had been some talk about charging me with a minor offence. Obstruct police by throwing the recording? But there was nothing on it. Causing the burn on her hand? Not really my fault, not in law anyway. Drunk and Disorderly? Did they really want to have to explain all that to a court with a Chief Constable as witness? Good luck with that. Anyway I wasn't drunk.

I was never going to answer any questions but that was Rebecca's advice, I just went 'no comment' to everything. So with fifteen minutes to spare before I had to be charged I was released.

If I had been caught with those papers I would have been dead in the water.

But then again so would Hooker.

MAIREAD

You can see me as hopelessly romantic; devoted to the man I met in my pyjamas when I was twelve. Faithful to him, having his child and letting him keep his marriage and family life.

No, I can assure you, though, the bottom line for me was always business. I thought Paul saw it in the same way. I used to think he would never leave Janice and disrupt his family life but recently there has been a change. He wants to meet in hotels, he dresses up for our meets, buys me underwear, talks about love. But I am now not sure I would want him now in my plans. He just seems like an old man and a bit desperate. I know he pops pills before we meet, it's hardly a turn on. He may be better now in the background.

We used to meet for years in a flat Paul owns in Whitefield. All suited me perfectly. I was, and am, not unhappy bringing up Oisin on my own. It gets a bit lonely sometimes, but it will all be worth it in the end. It is going to be better once this is all over. Better to arrive than travel, in my case.

And I've learnt to enjoy the deception. I have got two voices, two lots of vocabulary, two attitudes, two names, Mairead Keane and Sheila Moran. It is, of course, my second name and Mum's maiden name. Work gets Sheila Moran, everyone else gets Mairead Keane.

I suppose Mum, Paul and Oisin get a kind of mixture. Only my mum in the family knows that I am not on the switchboard at work. I am a paralegal and qualified as a barrister i.e. passed the exams. Paul likes to think of me as a real practising barrister, I play up to it, try to sound posher. He has a real ego, he pretends he doesn't, but he does, he's a man. So I overdo the consiglieri bit and massage his ego, pretend he really is Gangster No 1 worth millions.

This bit was always going to be the most difficult and necessitated I played up to it all. Making sure the twins got sent down was a doddle, and blaming the Bruens for it simple. I knew I really needed to work on Paul to convince him he was under threat so needed some time. He was more than happy to actually spend a night away in the Lakes.

It transpired he was more bothered about some pen-drive that had been stolen, or just gone missing. I had to engineer the conversation round to what I wanted. I convinced him the Bruens were after him, that they had got the twins sent down. It's a lot easier, of course, to get a bloke to believe something wearing only a chain round your neck and with an erect cock in your hand.

"So what's the move, darling?"

"Someone's got to kill Pop Bruen. It's as simple as that.

And soon."

"You know I can't"

"Why not"

"Well think about it Mairead. The Bruens will just think it's the Keanes anyway. If he gets killed they will come after you anyway. And I, well, I just can't protect you from people as mad as the Bruens."

"So this is it? The moment we have never talked about. The moment the Keanes have to pay you back for your help?"

"Mairead this is not like you."

"I know it's just it's hard to have to put Pat through this. I know that there is nothing down for him in life but this."

I made my voice crack.

"Tears? Really Mairead? I bet you have thought this through more than I have. Don't be melodramatic."

Paul portrays himself as this family man swept up in world of drugs and violence but he can be nearly as calculating and ruthless as me, if I have already put the idea in his head.

It wasn't hard to get Paul to work through my logic. Pat had to do it but he had to remain a threat to the Bruens. It meant he had to be seen but then to disappear. This would give Paul some time to negotiate with them. The brothers were psychos and they were not organised. All the brains came from Pop. Paul would be able to present as a man who offered them a plan. He would tell them to stay calm, not do anything that would get them arrested. Pat would be picked up by the police in due course. Then they could make their move. He could offer them a partnership in the future. It would all make sense. He would be their new dad. Well, it would make a sense he could sell to the Bruens.

What of the Bruens then? There does not need to be a big plan. One may disappear, couple may suddenly find the police have a wealth of evidence against them.

Pat? Well we did not speak much. We could not speak much. Paul could not afford to be too involved with him in case he got caught. He could organise a false passport, a gun to fall into Pat's lap and a boat to Ireland, that's it. All at arm's length, of course.

The promise of more basque and suspenders trips to Windermere clarified Paul's thinking, he was in. I knew Pat would not take much persuading. This would be a perfect story for him. He hated Pop Bruen. He loved his parents. He wanted to be a saviour, having been in the shadow of his brothers. The romance of a secret life in Ireland would appeal to him, for a while at least.

We knew when and where the Bruens did their big shop. Billy was parked round the corner when the shooting happened just in case Pat could not hijack a car. Pat had not done a great job of appearing to be losing his mind in the run up so I had to elaborate for the press. I put the draft texts into his phone and told him when to send them.

I know……. 'pre-emtiv'. What was I thinking? Trying to be too clever. Sometimes Sheila Moran appears. How did I make such a mistake? Did it give me away?

The policewoman? I don't want to think about that, just tell myself innocents die in war.

Did I think Pat would come back? When I saw his face at the door I have to say I was annoyed with Paul. In my mind I thought I would never see Pat again.

Pat had been in contact with Billy. Billy had told him there was to be a big memorial party for the Bruens. Pop had always had one Friday before Christmas. His plan was to attack the brothers there. Paul thought this ruined all the plans, I reckoned not. Let Pat attack the Bruens, no harm could come of it. We would meet on Saturday to see what to do next in the aftermath.

So all to plan. Well mainly. These last few weeks have been the butchery of war. The thing that you have to go through if you are to finally succeed. This part could never go exactly to plan.

What time is it now? 6.30, arrested for 'harbouring an offender'. I have to wait to be interviewed in the morning. Apparently I need the rest. As if I am going to sleep. Hope Oisin is ok, Mum will know what to do.

I should be out of here within the day. Hope to pick Oisin up later from school as if everything is normal. Perhaps not, perhaps I am being optimistic, cops may want to drag this out. They usually do. A big job. It should be quite simple though. I can answer the questions as an innocent person would. Pat will just go no comment. He just will.

Most of what I will say will be true anyway. I will tell them Pat showed up a day or two days ago. What else could I do? I had a little one and did not want the cops coming in with guns. He was my brother after all. I had co-operated with the cops until now but sure you could see I just could not afford to have them raiding my house.

All true.

I will also have to tell them I had no idea of Pat's plans to murder. The cops will believe me. I have no criminal record. I have a decent job. A big advantage is that they will not be interested. They have caught Pat. The job is done as far as they are concerned.

Hope they don't involve Oisin though. Wonder whether he gave the game away at school? He was told never to talk about Uncle Pat to anybody, even the police if they ask questions. Just occurred to me he could not be in a better place than with his grandfather who will be drumming this into him first thing. Ironic, I suppose, after everything I have ever done is to get him away his influence. Anyway it's all moot now. Pat won't talk. Paul will protect me and Mum. It's all going to be ok. I can move to the next phase.

Paul will be able to rein in the Bruens, then dispose of them. Mum safe, me free. I am going to move to somewhere in South Lancashire. Oisin is going to go to Stonyhurst as a boarder, perhaps day boy. Paul can pay for it all. He can afford that at least. I am going to qualify properly as a barrister, join chambers, Sheila Moran QC, one day. One day, just you see. I am going to prosecute gangsters, and family paedophiles.

Family paedophiles. Yes the last thing, I forgot, Dad. My Daddy. It did not take me long to work out aged 11 years, he knew I wasn't his. That digitally penetrating me and doing other disgusting stuff was his revenge on Mum and me for me being me.

Well, I am going to wait until he is ill and dying. Then I am going to tell him I got his three sons sent away for life. And that his own wife got him sent down for ten years and that she had cheated on him all her life.

Then I am going to kill him with my bare hands. These hands here, so that he knows it is me draining the life out of him with a big smile on my face. The last thing he ever sees will be me, the bastard kid taking the last of his miserable, shitty life, and enjoying it too. And when he is dead I am going to gob on him.

All as I imagined.

All as I planned.

"Mairead, Mairead are you awake?"

It's that bossy female sergeant. She has even put her cravat on.

"Mairead, love, I need you to come with me."

'Love?' Change of tune there.

"Bit early to be interviewed isn't it. Haven't seen a solicitor yet."

"No. It's not that, love. Something's happened."

PART FOUR

CHORUS

I have finished the course.

All that smoke.

No fire.

PAUL

Someone's knocking on the door. Someone's ringing the bell.

Midnight. Janice changes from deep snoring to rabbit fear in a second. She actually lets out a kind of high pitched animal squeal.

She need not worry. If it was Jamal's boys they would not be knocking.

It was Roger Mason, of course, again. Drunk, wanted to confront me in my house about blowing him out re the pen-drive. Why had I done that? I had ruined him.

He is going to pay a price for this.

I phone my buddy. I will need some help with this one.

MARTHA

My mother went into hospital that night. She had had some kind of seizure and was found by the visiting nurse in the morning.

I had just got back into work when I found out. Had to drive back up to Manchester again.

The minute I saw her I knew there was no coming back. I know brain tumours can do this at any time but, well, you know what I was thinking. It was Hooker and the IPCC who did this to her. The cops did this to Jesse, now to her, one floor separating them in hospital.

I just sat there holding her hand, thinking of her and Dad in the 70s and 80s. House full of kids, making ends meet, sending their kids out to meet everyday racism. I wished we lived in Moss Side then or at least Cheetham Hill, would not have felt so isolated.

They would not have it for a minute. Racism was just ignorant people. We were better than that.

Things would get better.

BOB

I bugged the Chief's office. It was a piece of piss.

It was mainly as I described in Chester to Gabriel. I had to wait for cleaners to open up the doors to the top floor at 5 a.m. and then just went in and put this device just under his desk. I did actually take a balaclava to avoid CCTV. There is a rumour they have it on the 11th floor. When I got there I thought, if stopped, it would look suspicious, well bloody suspicious. I had my uniform on as was at work at seven so just tried to act nonchalant. The cleaner did not say anything. The door to his office was not even shut let alone locked.

I had been planning to get it back on another morning before I went to work but Maria's no show meant I had to bring that plan forward and get up early on a rest day which was a bummer. Same script for getting it back, it could not have been easier.

You don't even get sacked for it you know, seriously. DI Benson from South Manchester did it recently when he was trying to prove his gay partner, another DI, was having an affair. He just got a written warning. More people should do it. Great sport.

Hooker does chat some boring shit though. I did not lie, he never said anything remotely interesting. He calls his wife (presume he's married?) 'rabbit', and sings *If you tolerate this* under his breath when typing. He actually calls Pakis 'Asians', even when he is on a private call. I know, what a wanker.

You can tell he is two-faced from the different things he says to people but that probably goes with the territory. It's true I never heard him say anything interesting so I suppose it was a stroke of luck that what did occur actually occurred.

You can work it out from the transcript I did for him that night and put in his pocket.

Hello Gabriel.

Just finished with the Chair of Authority re the report into Mason. Yes yes.

No totally onside.

Yes well not difficult is it (laughs).

Came to your office on the off chance but you must have gone home. Thought I would catch you on your mobile. Publish? 4 weeks if ok with you.

No nothing. No criticisms at all. Just need to think through media.

Well careful wording and also as you know very careful crafting of the terms of reference in the first place.

Well only you and I know that.

No still have no idea.

Look Gabriel even if it appears one day I cannot think of a way someone can connect it to us. We decided never to mention what happened.

Look we have been through this. It only upsets everyone involved. There is a real bottom line to this if we even wanted now to admit we had those DVDs we would have a hell of a job explaining what we have been doing for the last nine months.

Elvis and Jesus

No we are not responsible. Don't worry we are in the clear. We've done the right

thing. You just have to do things like
this sometimes, in everyone's interest.

I have left it as long as I can.

Knighthood? No told you refused it a long
time ago.

And, yes, as you can see now Hooker never does say anything
interesting when he is on his own work phone.

There is other stuff there in the conversation about Callaghan
the new ACC from what I can gather but that's about it. Now I
don't entirely know what all the above is about but I don't
need to. It's some proper dodgy shit, dodgy enough for my
purposes.

Quite fortunate really that I never made a copy of the tape to
take to the meet. I decided it would to too difficult to play
aloud while in a hotel bar so simply transcribed it for the
meeting at Chester. It's on a file on my works computer but I
guess they would not be looking for any transcription. I kept
the original tape inside an empty carton of orange juice in my
fridge. They don't seem to have found it when they searched
my house.

If the scousers had found the transcript on my work computer
or searched my house properly I would have been royally
fucked, royally. But, being scousers, they probably all downed
tools after a long day of three hours hard graft to go home.

I cannot touch the transcript just in case they are monitoring
what I do on my works computer, but I think I am in the clear.

I had a little speech prepared for Gabriel that all I wanted was
for me and Chris not to be fired and our pensions not to be
affected. The panel could blame it all on the failure to
supervise us. From what I can gather he would not blink to
throw Golden Knickers under the bus. Quite easy after all that
about her not even knowing she was in charge. So that's all I

wanted. If you look at what that conversation appears to be, well, it's quite a modest proposal isn't it? I am a reasonable guy, just get off my case.

I cannot make direct contact with him now. Too much attention on me, just have to hope he gets it. I think he does, after all I have not been suspended from working yet. He is having a hell of a week though. The Keane thing is an epic goatfuck. I mean you arrest the main man which leaves the family exposed. You then send a text to the aggrieved victims to tell them in the middle of the night? Why?

You put an eight year old child in the house they are most likely to attack. Within two hours the parents are shot dead in the bed and the house burnt to the ground. Did the Bruens know a kid was there? Who knows? Fucks sake.

You have to admire him though he is a ruthless bastard. Putting some water between him and it all. Top two detectives suspended, IPCC investigation, story in the *MEN* today of arrogant, out of control detective culture inherited from Mason, bullying of traffic officers on the night, raid on the house against the advice of the firearms advisor and, it is suggested, our Gabriel.

Well here's hoping he really is as devious as he appears to be.

To be honest the real worry is Chris. His swede has gone so I cannot confide in him. His lawyers have built up a good case about managerial neglect which is a gift to Hooker. They have shown how there are no checks in custody, that missed visits are rife, that he has not been on a training course for ten years, that being on twelve hour shifts impairs your judgement. In normal circumstances I would say this would get you nowhere. Bottom line is we did not do our jobs, but it's all useful stuff for management to hang their hat on not sacking us.

Problem is organisation now want an adjournment. Just been rung by solicitors now. Callaghan, who is hearing the case, has been busy with events of last two days and cannot afford to take two days out of work to do a contested hearing. Chris's solicitors had been asking for an adjournment on grounds of his mental state which had been refused. It seems this may be looked on more favourably now.

"Plan to agree Bob unless you have a view."

Well I cannot tell my solicitor everything I know, can I?

"Yes I do, a strong one. We do not want an adjournment. There is no need for one. All we want is an indication we will not be sacked, we will stick our hands up tomorrow and it all can be weighed off in an hour."

You can see their reasoning. They would be looking for time to inoculate themselves against what it is on that DVD whatever it is. Perhaps quickly re-write the report, new information come to light. Find some way of silencing me or explaining what the DVD is. No it has to be now.

"No get back onto them. Insistent. It has to be tomorrow. We will be there come what may. Don't ring Chris's solicitor. I will speak to Chris personally and square him up."

CHRIS

I will be sacked tomorrow. 26 years loyal service for fuck all. Four years shy of about £150k lump sum and £25k salary for the rest of my life. Instead nothing. Nothing. Nada. Zip. Thanks Chris for 26 years, now fuck off.

Bob has been on the phone wants hearing to go ahead. I could not be even arsed to argue with him. Fuck it, why not? Makes no difference. He thinks that we have a chance of keeping our jobs but he is in a fantasy world, he always has been. Those dark hints have added up to nothing, of course.

"Chris, it's the right thing to trust Uncle Bob. It's going to be ok tomorrow. It really is. Hey, for the record Chris, you are a good guy."

"Bob, it isn't, it really isn't going to be ok. And hey, for the record Uncle Bob, you are a dick"

But there's not just Bob. Everyone has let me down, everyone. Sheila promised to stay with me until death parted us, until her lecturer parted her legs. Kids, well I can't speak. I know Sheila hasn't made it easy for them but they have let me down. Gina, well she showed her true colours. Nice to me when she wanted something, thought a bit of vacuuming would put everything straight. No, she is welcome to her shitty life with Peter Sutcliffe.

But you know who let me down most? The job. It shit all over me, dropped its trousers and curled a big steaming dump on Sergeant Hayes.

Ashton, the Nazi twat, never comes into the office and but wants me to book prisoners in faster. He never checks or shows any interest at all in anything in the charge office. Visits are missed all the time by everyone. Why am I singled out? Punishment by consequence? Is that how it works?

No one cares about custody until it goes wrong, and then they don't really care. Nothing will change, me sacked, job done. That black bitch sister will spout off in the media. She will probably become a campaigner, get an MBE for not giving a shit about her brother when he was alive. But people will still die in custody and people like me will be blamed for it. It will all carry on.

It shows how seriously they take it all that they give me Bob and Gina to work with. Bob and Gina.

Bob should have gone years ago when they caught him with that under-age prostitute in Chinatown. Now it's all just a joke, Hong Kong Bob. Fuck knows how he got away with that. What do they do? Put him to work inside in custody where he can do no harm. The white-socked time bomb.

Gina? Well there's civilianisation for you in a nutshell. No good at any job she has ever done, any of them. Gina, the Traffic Warden who did not like confrontation. Nine months off with post- traumatic stress when someone just pushed her over after she had given a ticket. Then they put her on front desk at Milnrow. What could be cushier? She still managed to balls that up. Told a wanted rapist, who was handing himself in, that as it was bank holiday there would be no-one available to deal with him and come back tomorrow. Think she thought she was doing the lads in CID a favour. She's frightened of her own shadow but likes the money. Nobody else would employ a 53 year old on such good money. Bob and I have kept her going out of sympathy.

Nobody wants to be a custody sergeant. Everyone complains about us but no-one actually wants to do it. There's hardly a queue of people wanting to risk their careers whilst working full shifts. What thanks do we get for it? Fuck all. Dumb insolence from kid cops, bollockings from Ashton.

Fuck them all. Seriously, fuck them.

I know now the press release will already have been done.

GMP is committed to the highest standards…we regret that……our hearts go out to…..

Federation have told me the press office will give out enough clues to the media to find out where I live. If they think they are going to doorstep me after the hearing, no chance.

Tell you this as a final truth, Bob is full of shit. He never had a plan, just too up himself to admit he was out of his depth. He is one of lives armchair critics mouthing off about people who actually do things. Well I am going to show you Bob. Unlike you Uncle Bob, Hong Kong Bob, I am actually going to do something.

Something positive.

KENNY

I think it speak volumes that he was staring at his computer screen with his back to me when I walked in. I nearly turned round and walked out. Why should I even waste my breath? But I had told Varna I would say what I had to say, so I stood my ground. He didn't turn to speak.

"You wanted to speak before you go? You know I really shouldn't be talking to you now you have been put on restricted duties, gardening leave as such. I am a witness to the events. We certainly cannot talk about events."

"Should I be grateful to you?"

He swivelled in his chair and just stared at me. Resignedly, big sigh. No offer of a seat.

Bloody hell, that threw me off guard. He had huge black glasses on.

"What do you want Kenny? Oh and I am sure you won't be offended if I ask you whether you are recording this?"

I was offended, best not to answer.

"There is just one thing I want to say. And it is this. You are a complete c**t who has sold me down the river. If I ever get the chance to bury you believe you me I will."

He did that blinky thing he does behind those outsize specs. Glad I had said that. Felt a bit odd doing it and I had to steel myself but I felt like, well, this is the kind of conversation real people at the top of organisations have. I could tell anyone who asked I had done it. Not many call a Chief Constable that word. I had, and he is.

"Hmm. If you prick us do we not bleed?"

Not sure what that meant or whether he wanted me to answer. He got some keys and went to his safe in the corner.

"Well yes actually. You know and I know that I was doing a good job when I was ACC Crime. But you had this thing in your mind that you wanted a clear out of Mason's people because you felt insecure."

He was reaching into the safe.

"Really? What a fool believes, Kenny. Feel better for all this? Never actually heard you swear before."

"Well yes I do. Other people can see you for what you are. Just needed saying by someone. You need to know that."

He returned to his desk with a file. He placed it firmly down on the desk, drew in a long breath.

"Kenny I am not popular, got it. I used to be popular in another life and it got me nowhere. In fact it made me very ill. Kenny sit down. Does Milan Dacic ring a bell with you? Must do Kenny. Dacic produces a gun a Walther .22 in the middle of the day in the Lowry? Paul Smith? You know who Paul Smith is? Takes it from him and walks out with it. Ringing any bells now Kenny? Something you would remember?"

"Yes, did a job for Roger on that. He wanted confidentiality."

"I bet he did. Man produces a gun to threaten citizens. Gangster walks out with said gun. Car chase ensues. We get all this gratuitous information from a gangster's moll, which you see fit to include in an official report. Your contribution is? Is what Kenny? Is what? That's right. You did absolutely nothing. Zero."

"Chappell and Warnock were not pressing charges. Nothing could realistically be done."

"Really Kenny? That's not quite accurate is it? What they said is they would be guided by the police. If we had pursued the matter they would have had little option but to support us. And you seemed curiously uninterested in what material they had."

"They wouldn't say. Dacic would just have said it was a replica. We would never had found the gun would we? It would have been just a load of grief and heartache and got us nowhere. These are the kind of things you have to do when you are a detective. It's like being a janitor, clearing up other people's mess."

"Clearing up whose mess? Ex-cops? Wealthy businessmen? Football clubs? Gangsters? Oh I know about clearing up the mess people leave behind. I know all about that. For example Kenny, Walther 22? Walther 22?"

He did the shrug of amazement. Not sure what he was driving at.

"You intrigued by how I know all this?"

"Amaze me, Chief Constable."

"I have your report here. In fact got the whole Friday afternoon email exchange. Mason, as you both agreed, deleted the email and transferred it onto a pen-drive. For reasons we do not fully understand he did not put it in a safe but managed to, well let's just say I now have a copy of it. Remember your exchange? I quote

Cheers Kenny,

Hell of a read. Yes you are right NFA this would unravel before our eyes. Still, the gangster who can't get it up lost in Salford without his pills…LOL…..I am away next week so the great blinky non-event is in charge. You can call me if anything important happens.

You Kenny reply.

'LOL? Anyway yes, will do, I will try and stay awake during his morning management

yawnathon. I reckon he will mention
compassion three times. Are you buying or
selling at three?

It goes on ending with him reminding you to delete email trail
also before secretaries see it on Monday morning."

"So all this, all this, was about a bit of banter? Doesn't surprise
me you are being vindictive over something like that. It just
disappoints me, Chief Constable, it disappoints and saddens
me. I really thought a Chief could, should, rise about
something like this. "

"No Kenny. No. It's not about banter. I know Mason used to
joke about me. I know people do generally. Do you know why I
had that spiky hair, the glasses, why I behaved as I did?
Because Mason hated it, but it was the only stand I could take.
To offer to people in the organisation you can be different, you
can go down the road less travelled. You would even
comprehend that would you? Or know what I am talking
about?

You choose the other road Kenny, but he still joked about you
behind your back. Kenny, you rang the CPS trying to persuade
them to drop a domestic case against the Chief that was not
even a case. Christ, Kenny don't you see?

After PK told me about this we had to decide what to do with
you. You have to understand the debate was whether to bring
disciplinary proceedings or to try to put you somewhere where
you could do least harm.

PK argued disciplining you would all bring a lot a lot of upset
for Mason's family. Personally I would have done it but PK did
not want to see the family upset. He has gone out of his way to
make sure Mason's family were not upset. Not sure I would
have done, perhaps I am not as nice a guy as him. Plus there is
always the reputation of the service. It was he who persuaded

me from not hanging you out to dry. I did you a favour, a massive favour against my better judgement.

I put you in charge of the enquiry on grounds that there was no real detective work to be done and Keane would be found soon enough. Anyway Sharon Bentley was always there to watch your back, but you still managed to balls that up."

He stopped and stared at me and spoke so quietly it was nearly whispering.

"Walther 22. You really have not clicked have you? It's a Walther 22 that Keane used to kill PW Purvis."

"With all respect that may be due, she was run over, not shot. And, just for info, we don't use the term PW it's PC so as not to discriminate Sir."

"Correct Kenny, my fault. The gun?"

"You don't know it's the same one that killed the Bruens."

"Well Paul Smith and the Keanes are connected. You know Keane is saying it was a hit ordered by Smith who sorted out the gun for him. How many of this type are there in circulation in the Manchester area Kenny? I would ask you to tell me that but you would not have a clue would you?"

"Well one could speculate but Mr Hooker I am here to tell you I have recorded this conversation. What do you think of that, Mr Hooker?"

He took off his massive specs and started to clean them. He held them up to the light.

"Everyone seems to be at that game at the moment, recording me. Do you think I had not worked that out?"

He put his specs back on and stared at me.

"Tell me, what would you seriously propose to do with the recording Kenny?"

MICHAEL

Should we have put the pen-drive back?

Our thinking was that enough had already gone wrong and we had secured our objective. We agreed not to go back on the basis that Mason would always think it would be the reporter who took it. It's not as if he would ever think someone went to the efforts we did only to take a lousy pen-drive.

I suppose it would be a salutary lesson for them both in the internal contradiction of trusting someone who is prepared to be unfaithful.

I feel bad now after reading she got arrested on a trumped up anti-terrorist offence. Still she was released no charge. No real harm done.

David got a bit choked when I phoned him to tell him he was right about Mason using video cameras, but wrong about Clara. Normally I would ask the client what they wanted to do with the material but this was different. I could tell he was about to cry down the phone. He was in no fit state to decide, agreed to discuss further at Mere Golf Club on Sunday.

Unfortunately that fat prick Chappell had put himself down to play with us in his clown trousers. Not with his usual partner Brian Warnock. Spent the round telling me about the spectacular fall out he had had with Warnock over some work which he had originally offered me. I would have loved to have told him I knew exactly what he was talking about. I just told him it sounded like a sound legal debt he would have to pay. Chappell said he just wanted to see Warnock's firm go under. Unpleasant man.

He wouldn't leave us alone in the clubhouse too, downing pint after pint telling us he was on medication for stress. Presumed he was planning to drive home too.

We had to make our excuses and talk in my car in the car park. I spelt it out to David. A man like Mason cannot be a Chief Constable. He would have to go. Clearly I could not go through any formal channels because of the provenance of the recordings. In any case there did not seem to be a need to make a fuss. Lots of people could get hurt, not least Clara, in all the speculation.

I simply needed to put the recordings in the hands of someone who could make Mason go. Ruled out the IPCC or the Police Authority. They may do something more formal with it, could get very messy. Left me with the HMI or someone within the force. A toss up what to do.

What I didn't tell him was that I had been in contact with Box. However, it was clear to me they wouldn't be asking too many questions or shed too many tears if Roger Mason had a sudden demise.

The pen-drive? I was going to send it back to its author, an ACC Poole, then I noticed that the report also had an email at the end showing Mason's deliberations and marking it NFA. Reading through all that made up my mind where to send the report and, indeed, the DVDs.

Jimbo was tasked to hand over the other material. He found the recipient at his home address and handed them over personally to make sure absolutely no-one else saw what was contained. A short note was inside.

Mason retires from Force within the month and no more will ever be heard of this matter

Five days later he went missing. That's it.

But there's always a postscript to everything.

There was a reporter named in some desultory conversations at the end of one of the DVDs. I had decided, if all did not go to plan, I would send a couple of copies of the DVDs to her as she is named in a conversation in one of them, but there had been no need, it had all gone to plan.

After that poor police girl had died I resolved to get a personal assistant, I don't know in a strange way it was sort of in her memory. It didn't work out at all. The PA always tried to anticipate what I would want or need and often got it wrong. She even posted the package I had for the reporter which I had left next to my desk, which is the kind of carelessness on my part which necessitated a PA in the first place. Ironic, I suppose.

Seems to be no harm done anyway.

CLARA

I had never noticed before but Old Trafford doesn't look right. One stand is a lot bigger than the rest. David says that the money is to be made at the other side of town now.

Hooker has been keeping me waiting now on the 11th floor for thirty minutes.

He rang me before seven o' clock just to tell me he wanted to see me. He explained that he did not want me to set off for work then have to turn round to be in his office for 9.30.

So he did it out of concern for me, not because he is already driving from Derbyshire. Decided to wear a trouser suit and not uniform. That would annoy him, he has this thing about everyone being in uniform. I will say I had my uniform at work and had no notice.

Brian answered the phone at his desk. Good God what time does he get up? He has been looking tired recently. Does he have any idea what it will be about? He tells me he had a torrid time at a Force performance meeting yesterday from Callaghan. Everything is up that should be down and vice versa. He was giving me all the figures and why the Force's stats were misleading or were just plain wrong, something about detections in the pipeline and ethical standards of reporting. I stayed on the line because he wanted to talk, but wasn't listening.

I am not even going to pretend to play that game with Hooker so was not bothered trying to comprehend. I could feel Brian talking slowly enough for me to be taking notes of percentages up and down and all sorts of other stuff, not sure how long Brian would have continued if I had not told him I had to go.

Could it be the leak of the email he wants to see me about? That was a strange one, it all just never really took off. Jenny did her best and underplayed it. Naughty really, she picked up on one reference in the email to Brian and made the email seem like it was a complaint about him. She accompanied it with separate pictures of him and Charlotte.

Could see how upset he was on top of everything else. He shed a tear or too and had to go home early. He is a delicate soul really, takes things to heart. Gives everything to the organisation. It will break his heart eventually.

I did have a strained conversation with Bill Callaghan two days later. He rang to mildly rebuke me about the missing girls article in the *MEN*. Then the real reason, did I have any idea who may have leaked the email?

"No not really."

"It's just, Clara, Donnelly's email account has not been touched since the day of the shooting so it doesn't seem to have come from him, unless he printed it off, and there is no sign of that."

So they had thought it was him and had checked. They would now think it was me. Have they been through my email account? Was I going to be accused? That's easy to answer. The truth. I absolutely did not do it.

Does Hooker want to see me about the missing girl initiative? Left it a bit late. I mean it's been weeks since the article and he said nothing at the time. Scrawny Carol still won't talk to me as I did not go through her department, again. When the article was published she screamed like I never heard before on the phone, had to hang up on her. As I said she got Callaghan to call me.

Jenny played a blinder. She is a star. She told me she got to write the editorial and edit any critical letters so the coverage was all supportive. She even put in a nice quote from Hooker.

This is a really important issue and raises matters of deep concern. I congratulate Supt Clara Henderson and the Manchester Evening News for campaigning to

bring this this out into the open. I
pledge that the public can expect to see
action from GMP and its partners on this

"God it must have killed him to have to say that."

"He didn't. I made it up. He rang the editor to complain but, if you think about it, where could he go after it had been published?"

"I am not sure if I should say I am proud of you Jenny but big kiss anyway. Did you get in trouble with the editor?"

Jenny laughed.

"On no not at all. I drafted a letter from her to him. The letter told Hooker to stop being so soppy."

"Seriously?"

"Oh yes those exact words, Clara, those exact words."

"She sent it?"

"Sent it? Sent it Clara? She handwrote it. I insisted."

This was not the girl I had met in the restaurant. Well it was I suppose. You could see she had potential then but she has come on so quickly. I felt so proud of her. Don't care how limp it is to say it, 'girl power'. People can really change you know, they really can, Hooker is right about something

Poor old Kenny Poole walked past me about twenty minutes ago looking quite lost. Sure the pinstripe in his jacket did not match his trousers. He must be in a very difficult place though and have dressed himself in the dark. I would guess seeing Hooker would not have made his day any better.

Mr Smug knows I am here. I can just see he is on the phone, been a long call. I will check my make- up, I am in his eye line he should be able to see that, that will annoy him when he sees me through the glass.

The door opens.

"Clara come in, has Sheila not got you a coffee or tea? It's black coffee isn't it? Two coffees please Sonia."

He moved his head close to mine. I think he wanted to do the kissy, kissy thing. Seriously? What is going on? And what are those glasses?

All senses, full alert girl. Full alert.

"Sorry to keep you waiting. Just been on the phone to PK actually. He has been fantastic over last few days, cannot tell you how difficult it has been. Really."

"Sorry Gabriel, what's the deal with them Ronnie Corbett specs? Bit of a dramatic change."

"These are ancient from years back. My normal pair were broken few nights ago and I had not replaced my spares because having eye surgery. Supposed to be today, had to cancel. These are temporary."

"Oh I see, yes not been a picnic here on division too. Everyone is very upset. I did see poor Kenny coming out just then. He must be distraught."

"Well yes the fire was terrible but there are other things too. It's just like a game of three dimensional chess. Kenny, yes, I have decided to put him on gardening leave while we get to the bottom of this."

"Eight years old."

"Think his children are younger. Two and another on the way is it? He left it bit late didn't he?"

"No I mean Oisin Keane was eight years old."

"Oh yes eight, dreadful, and by the way, just for your piece of mind no one here is blaming the divisional staff and you. It's clear you were kept out of the loop on this."

"Yes well first thing I knew was when I got the call that there had been a fire. To be honest did not even know that this was even being considered."

"You're right, you're right. It's awful but some people are so quick to look for someone to blame when something terrible happens. Its human nature but...look Clara, between us, this is the kind of thing that is just so wrong with this place. Behaviour of Kenny and Sharon on the night was just simply unacceptable, reckless. Well I cannot say too much but it is clear I need to break the grip of CID on this force, well the old school generally."

Well this is not a different Gabriel after all. He should never play poker he is so transparent. He wants something from me.

"Anyway to business, I am moving Chief Superintendent Fenton across to head up CID, clean out the stables. So I need a new head of North Manchester as Chief Superintendent."

"Who?"

"I am looking at her."

OK. Unexpected, but I am not doing the shock performance in front of him. I am not going to make this easy for him. Need to know what the game is.

"Well it was not long ago I think you had me in remedial class as Mason's bit on the side."

"Come on you exaggerate Clara."

"Do I?"

I was close to being angry and not entirely sure why.

"Ok. First things first, I have never brought up your relationship with Mason."

"Whoa, back that bus right up. I did not have a relationship with Mason."

"No I am sure you are right."

"You are sure I am right? I AM right. I know I didn't. Did I have an affair with Mason? No I did not. Trust me I would know if I did and I did not. It's not a question of opinion, Gabriel."

"Look we are getting off track here. I am offering you a promotion."

"Yes, back on track, ok let's do back on track then. How come? So how come? I thought we were shit, I was shit, missing all our targets, doing the wrong things, didn't Brian get a hard time yesterday about all this?"

"Look they don't really matter in the long run. I am trying to take a broader view."

"They don't matter in the long run? Can I quote you?"

"Look, ok, we did tar you with the Mason brush, but that was wrong. You are that fresh approach we need. You are very popular in the media. You seem to get it to work to your advantage let's say that."

He smirked. I am trying to watch myself but I could happily kill him the little smug bastard.

"I did not leak that email."

"Of course you did not. But someone did, and one cannot help but wonder if they have the reply I sent and, if so, why they did not leak that? Let's not go there shall we?"

"Go there if you want to. Read my lips Joe 90, I did not leak that email. I know you checked. It was not me."

"Ok no matter, no biggy, no need to be like you are, Clara. Look, you have done a good job with the shootings and the fire, come to think of it. The missing girl initiative is a success."

"We have not achieved anything yet."

"Don't underestimate yourself, Clara. Bill Callaghan has been telling me the conference you have organised is sold out and that you have handled the ethnic issue really well. Look you can do this with the right support. I know it is daunting but we believe in you."

We? Him and Callaghan? Or the drenched monk?

"Oh that means so much."

What am I so angry about?

"I would like Brian Ashton as the Superintendent to help me. He deserves it."

To be honest I am not sure about Brian. I do owe him though.

"Sorry Clara no, no, no. He really let you down over the custody issue. Badly. I mean I think he is too much of a one trick pony. We have been lucky that lad, forget his name, did not die. We would have been flayed at a coroner's inquest, flayed alive. A lot of this is down to the fact that Ashton was so concentrated on figures, figures, figures he was just not doing his job. That's what your friend indicated anyway in the piece on the shootings. No he is damaged goods, seriously damaged."

Look bottom line is we've already appointed someone in your place. If you don't take the promotion we would have to think of somewhere to put you."

Bastard. Bastard.

I had sort of figured doing some work with the missing girls, getting it off the ground, resigning, having a baby and continuing the work in some campaigning charitable capacity. But that is not going to happen is it now Clara darling? Well not to my time frame, no it is not. Gabriel and his crony or cronies, whatever they are up to, are not going to let me do that are they?

The games people play. They spend so much time playing them it has never occurred to them that I did not leak the email to threaten him. Or that possibly, just possibly, stopping young girls from being passed around Asian men like dog meat may just be the right thing to do, rather than a tactic to get publicity and promotion.

They can think what they want. I am going to accept the promotion. Carry on with this work. Show him I do not need his support or development. Certainly not from him or any man. Too much has happened to walk away now, there is unfinished business. Don't know how I am going to tell David though. Have to put the baby back a year or two.

I could of course bring it forward. David would like that. Hooker would hate it. Two birds, one stone. Joy. Yes accept the promotion and then announce my pregnancy. Joy indeed. Or would that just play into Hooker's hands? Would the missing girl initiative just wither?

How on earth did I get myself in this position?

I've not been out of his office for more than ten minutes when it comes to mind. I still don't know enough about Hooker's personal life. Did Jenny tell me he lived with PK once when he was homeless after a break-up? Is he married now, kids? What about him makes me so angry? I don't see compassion. I don't know what I see but it's not that.

Just getting my thoughts in order when thunder and sunshine Don texts me.

Hear congrats are in order. Dinner to celebrate? Please say yes. An act of mercy. I will throw myself off Barton Bridge if you do not say yes

I reply straightaway.

It would be an act of mercy for your wife
Donald to let you

He rings.

"Take that as a yes then, Clara. Sorry Chief Superintendent
Henderson. Taken you just over one year to achieve a rank it
took me 28 years to get. That's something to celebrate."

"Donald, I won't even ask how you know before my husband
does. Hmm, I have just realised I know nothing about Hooker.
You can tell me about his personal circumstances and I will let
you buy me dinner."

"Right there is Kenyon, Hooker, Callaghan and a few other you
won't know. Now all of them at some....."

"Donald, I was asking about his family circumstances."

"Well Mrs Henderson I was actually explaining in a roundabout
way which would have started to make sense if you had not
been so impatient, but you can wait until dinner now for so
rudely interrupting me."

BRIAN

All four bars showing on my mobile, full strength signal. Reception is lousy in my office so moved up to the third floor and am sat in the meeting room waiting for the call.

Any minute now.

I have forwarded my works phone to my mobile and am doing emails on my Blackberry. It's now 11.10, should have heard by now.

It is moving day. Poole and Bentley out, Fenton over to CID to sort them out and Mrs H has had the curly finger to attend at Chester House for 9.30 today. It can only be one thing, she is finally on her way. These things work sequentially so they should be filling her vacancy any minute now.

Hang on here it comes......

......no, it's Claudia asking have I heard yet? Got a bit snappy with her, I told she would be the first to know.

No it's a certainty, Mrs H has to go after everything that has gone on. Crime stats are shocking. When I was acting Super we were running at 1.1 robberies a day, it is now 1.9, burglaries were 3.1 now they are 5.6 (seriously 5.6!), car crime was 5.3 a day and it has gone down admittedly, but not by much.

I was publicly worked over by ACC Callaghan yesterday at Force Performance but I managed to grab him as the meeting broke up. I showed him my calculations and also put him on the inside track as to how Tameside division are getting their reductions (by employing two detectives to investigate false reports). He said he was, and I quote, 'impressed'.

He now knows what to do if he wants to get the crime stats moving back in the right direction, restore me to acting Superintendent. Yes there is a tide in the affairs of man, and I was right to take it at the flood yesterday. Timing, it transpired, was perfect.

Wonder where Hooker will put her? It will surely have to be a non-job at HQ.

She was in 9.30 with Hooker, so she would have found out before 10, so what time is it now? 1115.

Any minute now.

BOB

I feel like a paedo.

Chris's house is near a primary school and have been sat outside for an hour and it's now their playtime. I can see a couple of neighbours wondering what I am doing just sat in my car, better knock on his door again, just to make the point I actually am not a nonce. I know he isn't in though, his car has gone.

I just don't want to leave here at the moment of triumph. I want to be the first to tell him. His phone is off so just keep hoping he will come back at any minute. I will take him on the piss, make him pay for it all, get him to proposition Mrs Pendleton.

Beginning to think he has gone for the old two pencils up the nostrils and underpants on head jobbie, turn up naked in a shopping centre in Weston Super Mare. That has its place as a tactic but you really have to know what you are doing.

Many have tried that old gag to get a pension. Old Benny Dewar I remember doused himself in petrol like a Vietnamese monk in front of Chester House once. Always think he must have shit himself sat there in the freezing cold in case someone came walking towards him with a cigarette. It got him the pension though. His wife walked out on him the day it was paid into his account. Suppose you have to admire both of them really.

Not sure Chris is made of the right stuff to pull this off. Once you are into this kind of caper it easily can go tits up on you. Happened to someone in Colditz the TV series didn't it? Some POW tried to pretend he was mad wetting himself on parade etc. Turned him crazy. No, if you are going to pull this kind of stunt off you need a clear head. I laid one down early as an insurance policy.

In fact just thinking about all this, I might change my plans. I was planning now to go sick and live it large for a few months as result of all the stress of being in the paper. Clearly would help the claim I have against the Force and IPCC. Perhaps I should just go back to work and grind it out for the sake of my liver and sanity. Something to think about. Definitely having a month or so off though, get some winter sun, see how sorry Maria is. I am feeling benevolent. Good old Bob. It all worked out very nicely thank you.

Yes. I got fined 14 days' pay. It's the maximum they can do to a constable without sacking you. Bit steep but the pension is intact and that was the goal.

With one bound old Hong Kong Bob was free.

It could not have been smoother really apart from Chris's no show which nearly derailed everything. They indicated to my solicitors as soon as we walked in we would not be sacked if we threw our hands in. Apparently Callaghan accepted that there were serious organisational failings in oversight and it would be wrong to single us out. Our solicitor seemed surprised. I suppose I was as well, but there was no need to be. Good old Gabriel. I will keep to my side of the unstruck bargain.

Found out that Chris's team were told his punishment was going to be to be reduced in rank. Solicitor told me that his brief had argued that that was draconian in terms of loss of pay etc. It was GMP's side who pointed out that, as all of his last three years were as a Sergeant, if he went with an ill-health pension at twenty six and a half years he would get an index linked full pension related to his Sergeant's pay. Bonus.

Result for old Chris then. Ill-heath pensions are like hen's teeth now but they seemed convinced the door was being opened to that. We insisted the hearing went ahead, which we thought was going to be a problem without Chris there, no it was not.

All done and dusted in two hours, driving out of Chester House at twelve o'clock.

Yes forgot to say. Guess who I saw before the hearing in the foyer of Chester House holding car keys, a screaming baby and seemingly ten months pregnant? Varna Barnes.

I was going to just walk past but then could see she was trying not to catch my eye so I thought fuck it.

"Varna Barnes, PW 270..."

I could not remember the last number. She looked past me as if this conversation was not happening. Mistake, for her. Last chance.

"Read about you becoming a councillor. Thought you would have enough on your hands with the sprogs and all that Varna."

No response. Is them the evil eyes? It is. Oh dear, she is going to have to have it then. I reached for my wallet.

"Here Varna never paid you the tenner I owed you. I know we called it quits but to be honest I knew it was 87 seconds, so you won by three seconds. If you ever want to give old Bob the chance to win his money back......"

She had turned her back on me, seemed to be getting a bit teary. When did she get so sensitive all of a sudden? Always was a funny girl though. You could do things to her you wouldn't do to a farmyard animal but she wouldn't let you fuck her. Said she was saving herself for the right person. Just then could see her chubby hubby coming out of the lift with some Chester House dolly propping him up. He looked shocking, red eyed, shambling.

Worked it out later that he was probably not in a fit state to drive. Varna had had to come in to pick him up. If I had thought it through I would have guessed things would not be good for her and family right now. Way I see it it's not fat boy's fault the kid got fried but nowadays everything seems to be the cops' fault.

I suppose should have been more sensitive but, hey, I had my own problems. I could have given Varna some tips to help Kenny put the wheel back on but that bridge is now burning.

Parents are starting to arrive in cars to pick their kids up. Time to go, getting thirsty anyway.

Just got a text from Chris. Hurrah, he's ok. Yes very funny. Reply to it before I set off.

Touché. Mon ami. Emperor Hiro Hito commands you to come out of the jungle. The war is over.

Haven't got time to phone him, I will ring later.

Start the car up before I get served with a sex offender notice.

MATT

Mags said she would wait with the kids until she came. She would have to stay anyway to be able to open the door to her as I was still not good moving about. She just wanted to see what she was like, which was as gorgeous as ever. Cardigan, blouse and jeans but still glam. So, so, fuckable.

She did not visit me in hospital when I was really ill. Sharon Bentley told me recently that was because when I was hallucinating from the anaesthetic I constantly shouted her name. Some sexual references also, Mags thought there must have been an affair going on. Sharon thought it was hilarious.

"What exactly did I say?"

"Trust me you don't want to know. Your wife is a forgiving woman even having her round now. Anyway, you were zonked out. I remember you went on about Ma Bruen's knickers."

No I remember that, that wasn't hallucinating, Charlotte's last words. That girl could have been anything but she dies in an ambulance in Harpurhey 22 years old, flattened by a car, talking about Ma Bruen's knickers.

It had been arranged for some time for Ma'am to come round. I did offer to cancel with the murder of Oisin Keane and all the shit that was flying around but she insisted. A date was a date. She said she would bring food round, could be anything at all she would have it taxied over. Spicy chicken pizza delivered from local Dominos was good enough for me. She would have exactly the same.

She had a bottle of white and a bottle of red, flowers for Mags, obviously, and chocolate for the kids.

"Matt's a lager man really, Mrs Henderson."

Did Mags really have to say that? I had to insist I was fine with wine.

Anyway it was all whispery, girly 'how's the patient? ' in the hallway for about five minutes, 'must have been hard for you with the kids', all that garbage. I had to go and sit back down in the lounge, my shoulder was aching. Some further hushed conversation in the hallway was luckily interrupted by the pizza delivery and with that Mags was gone with the kids to her mother's.

Mags had left out an army's supply amount of potato salad, tomatoes, lettuce, cold pasta shells, and coleslaw in the kitchen, far too much. She had even bought another of those cushion trays especially for Ma'am as I could not get comfortable sitting around a table on a chair. Tried it for a couple of days before she came but couldn't do it. She would have to eat on her lap.

It felt odd having food served to you in your own house by a superintendent. Her cutting up pizza on my worn out couch. Could see her looking at the wedding photo on the small table next to her. Mags with the bottle specs she had before the surgery.

She made herself at home alright though, stuck into that white wine straight away. Never said a word about the fact we did not have any wine glasses. She asked a lot about the injury and skirted round the shooting but happy to fill me in on everything that had gone on.

She told me that Pat Keane started talking on interview which was a big surprise. He would not talk about the actual shooting but said the whole thing had been arranged by his sister. It was her who had sent the messages he was supposed to have sent after the killing and her who had got him the gun.

Detectives were sceptical at first but there were beginning to be some indications that she was involved in some way. They had enough to remand her while they made enquiries. I never really knew the sister but I could not see that myself. The family must have dragged her into it in some way.

Ma'am then got onto the murders a few days ago. Both parents had been shot in the head, petrol pored over them and set on fire. The kid had died from smoke inhalation they reckoned. They hoped, more like. He was found not far from his grandparents. He must have got up and then gone into the burning bedroom.

They had arrested all the Bruen brothers but they really had no proper evidence. The brothers were, of course, not saying anything. There was a lot of phone traffic between them all in the early hours of the morning, but that was the night that Keane had been arrested so it's not surprising.

Forensics seemed to indicate it was not them. They had all been arrested soon after the fire but there was no residue or anything anywhere. Apparently Kenny Poole had done an excellent job in getting them all rounded up so quickly.

"It would have been Sharon Bentley, Ma'am, from what I have heard. Don't know Mr Poole but the lads that do reckon he is a complete knob. Never came to see me you know."

"Point is you were right, Matt, it was a powder keg and no-one was listening to you."

"Didn't imagine anything like this carnage. And you did listen Ma'am, you asked me for the email that finished up in the *MEN*. Tell me, and this is between us, why did you leak it? It could have damaged you."

"I didn't. I just assumed you had. You did, didn't you?"

"Absolutely not. How could I? Not set foot in the station since....."

"Oh that's funny. I met the Chief today and told him I was seeing you tonight. He has just phoned, sends his regards and said not to worry about that Parker letter.

You see I sent your email to Hooker. He answered it telling me to stop worrying about dispute and get crime down. He is now panicking with all the attention on him that he may be blamed and is trying to keep us both sweet. He doesn't realise I never kept his reply.

Anyway his message to you was that he had agreed with the IPCC for him to handle it and he would make sure it was all alright for you. "

"Well, logically I knew I had done nothing wrong, although that's not the way I feel. This secret surveillance stuff was just bollocks, Sharon Bentley said there was loads of CCTV to disprove it. Just don't know why he didn't sort this out earlier."

"Hmm, I picked up he was worried that the Force may be criticised at some point for not doing enough about gang crime. I think word had got back about what you were saying at the hospital and then there was Don Regan on Sky TV. You were to be offered up as the scapegoat. He now realises there is a trail to him and that if he backed you into a corner then you and I could embarrass him. Lordy Lord, probably thought the press leak was a warning shot."

A big gulp of wine.

"Do things work like that?"

"Well they seem to do in the police. Do you know what Matt? My friends ask me what the police is like. It occurred to me today. At my level it's like that TV series *House of Cards*, everyone scheming, plotting, looking for blame, except, except it's just that, well no-one seems to be any good at it."

"A shit *House of Cards,* like it. Talking of which see Brazier and Hayes have got away with it. What's that all about? "

"No idea but it does sound like what I was saying. For some reason ACC Callaghan thinks this is the smart move but from where I am standing they should just have been sacked."

"They are blaming you I take it? All that bit about you not knowing what was going on in custody."

She downed the last glass of white wine. Bottle gone.

"We haven't got any more white wine. Just lager in the fridge."

"Why didn't you say? I will get the lager if you let me move onto the red."

"Aren't you driving Ma'am?"

"No taxi staying at my flat in town tonight…. no they are not blaming me."

She brought me a lager and a fresh glass for her.

"No not at all. In fact get this. They are going to make me Chief Super on the division, promotion eh?"

She leant over from her chair to clink glasses, wine and lager. Nice view down her blouse. I just so would, she would only have to ask me nicely.

"Well that's a turn up. Fancy that. Who's to be the new Super?"

"Do you know Matt name escapes me?"

"Not Ashton then."

"No looks like Brian is getting the blame for quite a lot of things. Well you know the story in the *MEN* about the shooting was bad for him, also the custody thing also. He found out just before he was going home, he is to move sideways to work on a project for Callaghan on how we record crime. One of the things Callaghan said was that they felt there was some substance in Parker's grievance and he had been insensitive to the needs of staff at a traumatic time."

Well I never thought I would feel sorry for Brian Ashton but if he stood up to Parker then then makes him ok in my eyes. Poor guy, company man and they have shat on him. What did Brody say about the bosses 'if you collaborate with them they will sell you, if you oppose them they will buy you?'

"I was thinking Matt when you come back I want you as an inspector. Need some good people round me, people I trust."

"Doesn't work like that Ma'am I am afraid. I need to pass the inspectors' exam. Never been able to study with the kids."

"I am sure I can swing it."

"You can't swing this, with respect, Ma'am. You have to pass the exam to be an inspector. Remember this was all played out when Mr Mason promoted you in. You have to pass the sergeants' exam to be a sergeant. You have to pass the inspectors' exam to be an inspector but you do not need any qualification to be a superintendent."

She was well into that bottle of red as well.

"Well this is the ideal time Matt to study then, while you are recuperating. I will get you promoted to work for me one way or the other."

She's beginning to annoy me. It just doesn't work like that. It might have done for her but not in the real world I live in. She also has no idea about married life and kids. You cannot just pick up the books and life stops. Too much going on. Don't feel like doing much anyway at the moment, you know, I have a few issues like a broken shoulder, leg infections and Charlotte.

Charlotte. I can't see how I will ever go into a police station again. I will always be the one who got her killed, if I hadn't taken her for lunch, if I hadn't shouted at her and drawn his attention to her, if I had pulled her away from the car more quickly.

And her nibs is now getting promoted, moving up and getting pissed in my living room on the strength of it all. She expects me just to put all that behind me and get on with it? All because it suits her.

And Christ, poor old Ashton. He has been right royally shafted with his trousers still up. She drops in, runs round the shower without getting wet and gets a promotion. Ashton who, no matter what you think, has been grinding it out for years for years, gets a ticket to Palookaville.

She must have sensed my mood was changing.

"I can see you are tired Matt. I will be going. I meant what I said about being an inspector."

She got up and leant over me to kiss me on the cheek before she left. She stayed over me and said into my ear.

"Now is there anything I can do for you before I go?"

That's what she said. I will repeat it.

"Now is there anything I can do for you before I go?"

Think we all know what that means, and this time I am not hallucinating. I just had to say the word am she would have tugged me off, right there, right then. I know it. But at that very minute she had pissed me off, I was tired and on top of everything else had not entirely shrugged off that cold. In any case it just did not seem right in the lounge, next to the wedding photo.

So I just said, "no thanks, just glad you came round."

Pathetic wasn't it? I should have taken her up on the offer, shouldn't I? Course I should. You regret the things in your life you did not do, not the things you did do.

Or perhaps I was right to knock her back? No complications, clear conscience, did right by Mags. I did the right thing and anyway the moment is something I can think about for a long time though, isn't it?

You know what I mean.

BRODY

My first inspector told me this. Five simple rules of policing.

1. The Sgt is always right
2. When the Sgt is wrong, Rule 1 applies
3. Money and policewomen will get you in the shit
4. Never change your story, even if it is to the truth
5. If your mate dies, get to his locker before his wife

I knew nobody would be looking out for Matt Donnelly, not many of the old school left to do such a thing. So late, on the night he was run over, it fell to me and my trusty sword to watch Sergeant Matthew Donnelly's back. It was not clear whether he would live or not after all and there was work to be done.

Locker first. Good to see the sealed bag of a block of cannabis at the rear, a bit of the old school in the lad. It's an old trick. If found for any reason you can always say you had forgotten it was there and you had simply omitted to book back into the property store. Obviously would come in handy if you came across some shitbag who was really pissing you off. Good boy Matt, he will thank me for taking care of this.

Otherwise nothing of real personal interest. Pictures were all of his wife and kids on the inside of the door but that don't necessarily make him a family man. Everyone does that, but he definitely was not a shagger. The giveaway signs? Change of clothes, aftershave and deodorant. None of that there, all he had was uniform. Disappointing really, when you were a community officer years ago (it was called 'on the area' then) it was positively expected that you spread the love with the residents of the parish. It was the perk of the job. How else would you get information?

O tempora o mores.

In a drawer on his desk in his office though was a file of the Bruen/Keane saga, made for very interesting reading though.

Thought I would certainly keep hold of that, it may come in useful.

Well more than useful. I hereby produce one item; a printed email from Matt to Madame Ceausescu sent on the very day of the shooting, gold dust. Be a bit embarrassing for organisation and especially Polly Perfect if someone should, say, later decide to fax it over to the *Evening News*. More to the point it would be very good for Matt if it all came on top for him.

I was going to throw that cannabis away but finding the email made me lose my concentration. I took it home with me in a carrier bag. I think I can now put the cannabis to some good use too. No not that, you should know me better than that. Would never touch that shit, turns your brains to mush.

Planting drugs on someone is fair game if they deserve it isn't it? I mean it is when it serves justice.

I think it has become clear to those in the know that Brooks is just not clever enough to put a bottle of vodka down his trousers and not get caught. No that's Parker alright, thinking it would be funny. He gets a kick out of a cunt's trick like that, he always has. Parker thinks he is the master puppeteer; everyone being investigated, man on a life support machine, shafting Matt Donnelly and Ashton, taking flowers to the mum, pretending he shagged Charlotte, doing charity walks, befriending the Chief, hosting the award ceremony, being a cunt generally.

Well it is one of the oldest tricks in the book but it still works. This cannabis will come in useful thank you.

Come in Sergeant Parker your time is up. Your final lesson from the real master.

Happy Christmas.

PAUL

I heard Janice went to see a divorce lawyer the afternoon I was arrested.

Jamal will let me rot this time. Johnny's no good on his own. No options left. Probably will die inside. Should have stuck to pint pots.

Just read Dacic has now has fallen out with the new coach at Real and isn't playing. He will be gone at the end of the year. Someone will still sign him though. They will want to believe he can change, but people don't. They never do. The next club will have to sell him on also. He will get passed from pillar to post, his graph line going down and down until he ends up in prison like me.

Or playing for West Brom.

JENNY

6.30 a.m. Manchester Airport off to Tenerife. Just under a year since I was last doing this.

Ridiculous queue to book baggage in, everyone wanting to get away before Christmas. 165 people, Rob counted them. Two check in desks. I've gone for coffee and a panini while Rob slowly kicks the bags towards the front of the queue. He will text me if he gets there before I finish, which will not happen.

Rob is, of course, the inspector from the Counter Terrorism. Rob's idea the holiday too, obviously to avoid being on his own for Christmas. His wife, in retaliation for leaving her, has taken his child down to Worcester for Christmas to see her parents. Come to think of it's not retaliation, what else would she do when she is now on her own?

Anyway chance to see what Tim has texted me without Rob's prying eyes.

Have to say I have been more impressed with Tim since I turfed him out. He has shown a bit of the spirit he used to have in the early days. I thought he would go with a shrug but not at all. No there was a horrible scene in the flat.

"Tell you what, when you got the crime reporter position I was really proud of you, really proud. Told everyone at work. Do you know what one of the solicitors said? Do you know what he said? 'Won't be long before some hairy- arsed cop is hanging out of her mate.' Really didn't think but yeah well he was right, wasn't he?"

Indeed he was. Also become apparent over last couple of weeks that Rob was not as separated from his wife and two year old as he first had me believe. So he will do very nicely for now, some sun and a few treats on holiday then it's order of the boot time in the New Year.

Tim, in the meantime, has managed to get himself arrested last week when Manchester United were playing away. He asked for me to be informed when he was in custody in London and gave this flat at his address. Cops knocking on the door at midnight to check the address.

He also managed to get back into the flat complex last night. Well this morning, four hours ago to be precise. He kept banging on my door singing that Nilsson song, *Can't Live*. When he finished he wailed *All by Myself*, don't know who sung that originally. He had actually brought backing tracks with him, not the songs, proper karaoke tracks. He also knew the words. He may have had a few drinks after United were at home yesterday but he had obviously planned this when he was sober. Quite romantic when you think about it.

Rob was too chicken to confront him. Knees hunched up in bed saying he would, "fill the cunt in, but it's more than my job is worth". Yeah right, Rob. He never even made an effort to move out of the bed. Rob actually called the police without asking me. I did not want Tim being locked up twice in one week to be honest so I went to the door to tell him to go before cops arrived.

This made him start singing again but no backing track. Did a football song, tune of *Winter Wonderland.*

There's only one Jenny Aa-ron-o-vitch, one Jenny Aa-ron-o-vitch

With her massive tits, and her cheeky smile

But she's living with a fucking paedophile

Tim, how long had it taken you to think of that? Quite funny I suppose. He left after finishing the song. Rob cancelled the police.

"He's a lucky boy. I would have filleted him."

Yeah right. Just go to sleep Rob.

Open Tim's text, sent at 6 a.m..

Enjoy your hols with married lover boy, bitch. Ladbrokes offering 2/1 he will back with his wife by Easter. Evens that he texts his wife from the poolside 'I've made a terrible mistake. Boohoo. Please have me back. I miss the children'

I text back.

His cock is bigger than yours. A lot bigger. End of

Turn my phone off. All quite childish. Might go round the block with Tim when I get back from holiday. Yes would end it all on better terms that way. Make Tim feel better about himself. But not for long, Tim's not a long term bet.

A year since I was last away in Tenerife him. My life seemed to be in black and white then, now technicolour. Even last couple of weeks have been busy-busy as I finish up as crime reporter and move to heading the news desk.

Quite a shock to see Mairead Keane in the dock though charged with conspiracy to murder. Tried to catch her eye to smile at her at court but nothing there at all. Zonked out, blacked eyed. Callaghan told me off the record he is not sure whether they will ultimately have enough to convict her. She cut a pathetic figure at her son's funeral handcuffed to the prison officers. Lawyers would not let us run that picture.

So sad though, even Paul Smith was crying. New editor did not have the bottle to run with that picture. I would have run it; he should have done, Smith was arrested a couple of days later.

I did not get to see Dolores Maitland after the disciplinary was over. I went round after getting no response on the phone.

Neighbours said she was in hospital. Martha told me she hadn't long. I thought about seeing her, then decided I wanted to remember her from my visit. Martha sent me all sorts of information to use for my piece and a damning quote about Hooker. Some dozy sub took all the meaning out of her quote. No one was interested away, think the disciplinary made page 15, few columns.

Of course the discovery of Chris Hayes' body two days later became the big story. He left his house on the morning of the hearing but drove to the Lakes. He walked up Helvellyn and must have his uniform in his ruck sack. Just near Striding Edge he took off his walking gear, put on his uniform and jumped.

Some matey Cumbrian detective told me he sent a text to his wife.

```
This is a suicide, a definite suicide.
Just making sure the Coroners and insurers
see this in my sent box on the phone so
you don't get the pay out on the insurance
```

He had forgotten she had changed her mobile number and she never received the text. He also texted a final picture of himself in uniform to Bob Brazier, the PC who had gone missing.

```
4real Bob.4real
```

"It's always got to be about them hasn't it? Always."

Martha was strangely unmoved by the suicide. She said the way she felt I could publish what she had said, but I didn't obviously. I can understand she is bitter but it seemed a bit much.

PK's report into Mason is never going to be published. First they told me there was going to be a delay, then they rang me back day after to say it was now not going to be published at all. Confidential copy would be given to Police Authority. End of that. Again no one could care less.

See whether Tim has responded before go back to Rob. Turn my phone on.

Two texts already. It's Tim.

```
Ha, still love you loads……bitch. Don't
bring back an STD because you will be back
with me before long and you know it
```

And the other from Clara. Love her to bits, thinking of me at this unearthly hour.

```
Jenny, tried to phone but switched off.
Roger Mason has been found.
```

So Rob isn't going to get a takeaway coffee after all. Who knows whether he will get on the plane? He should go home, be a proper man. He has a two year old child for pity's sake.

I have some stuff in the joint bag but nothing in there worth making a scene for, not at this time. Would they let him on the plane with my stuff in the bag? Doubt it. Not my problem. Everything I need for now is in my hand luggage. Prefer Christmas at home, Mum's cooking, in my soppy single bed.

I am heading out of the Airport.

THE END

CHORUS

The obituaries were miles off the truth about the man. You could tell they guessed something was wrong but they did not know. So they played it straight. Only four non-committal columns in the *Telegraph*.

I would guess there will be no big funeral or remembrance service either.

Good.

From what I can see no-one went in front of the cameras. There was just a press statement issued by the clerk to the Police Authority….great servant of policing, no need now to complete the Kenyon report, confidential report will be circulated to members, hope no more speculation, time to draw a line.

It did the job, public had had enough, papers had also had enough. Hacks do not like being up north for too long especially during the Christmas break. It was only Manchester, not London, after all. A little local difficulty.

Death the greatest censor of them all. Don't rake up the ashes of the past and start a fire now.

Do I feel sorry for him? Dead. Plastic bag round his blue-bottled head, orange in mouth, basque and suspenders. Do I fuck.

It was less than a year ago I had Hooker and that charlatan in my office. An unexpected deputation. Pained expressions, sex tapes, reputation of service, resignation within days please, say it's domestic difficulties, more time with your family. No need to be difficult about this. Business not personal.

Of course they did it together because neither would have the balls to do it on their own. I could not work out who had actually got the tape and gone to the other. It would be PK pulling the strings though.

I think what angered me was those two non-events dealing with such a matter. Did they for one minute think where those tapes must have come from? I could tell they had no idea. They were blackmailing me with a product they had no control over.

Of course I thought then it must have been Smith behind the tapes. Who else could it have been? He must have got them from Jobson. I could not believe my stupidity in going to see him and actually sending him to Jobson. Sign of my illness though, I think, at that point.

It was the sheer naivety of the pair playing at man of the world big boy politics with me. Did they really think they could have covered up such stuff? Did they not think that Smith would simply come back for more?

The memory still rankles. Hooker spraying his pants thinking he was a player. PK pretending this was so, ever so, painful for him. He kept saying, 'it is what it is'. What does that fucking mean exactly?

So what would you do in such circumstances to save yourself? Well we have been here before, at the very beginning when I was flying out of Ireland. Of course you would have no idea, you would have just meekly gone along with it. You have to read books about people who would know what to do.

So here's a tip for free. What you do is you do is the thing your opponent least wants you to do. You should try this. It always works but you need bottle. It works. That why I appointed Poole, it's what Kershaw would not want to happen.

PK and Hooker would have preferred me to resign or tell them to send it for investigation. They would not have wanted to me to kill myself. They would not be able to explain what they had done so they would have to cover up, which they would be no good at, and they would balls it up.

So that was my plan when I went round to Smith to confront him. I just wanted to know why he had done what he had before I topped myself. Looking back on it he did a good job of not giving away that he didn't have the tapes. And his idea of just going missing was genius. He came up with it after spending a long time talking to someone on the phone, sounded like a female voice.

I had to cut a deal with him, I can't tell you about it, to get his help including an Irish passport. His speciality, apparently.

I had substantial amount of funds I was hiding from my wives. Kenny Poole made me quite a packet with his tips on bank stocks which I cashed in, just before the crash, luckily. Anyway it was enough to keep me going for long time. Wonder whether Kenny hung onto his bank stocks? He would have lost a packet if he has.

I left Dublin Airport on foot walked about quarter of a mile out of CCTV range and changed behind a petrol station, shaved my head and put on some glasses. Walked back in and caught a plane to the States paid for by Smith. Off I went, the new me. On the plane I celebrated with a few miniatures, and realised no-one would yet know I was missing.

I was there on the plane, still the Chief Constable of Greater Manchester, high above you all. I had got away with it. As I told you then right at the beginning it was star-bitingly good. The rest is history. Well the history you know about.

All I could do was laugh about what PK and Hooker would do with the tapes now. Admit what they had done? Or hang on see if I turned up quickly? They must have gone to bed every night wondering what to do.

Do Baha'is pray? 'Dear God, please let Roger Mason be dead and there be no note. I know you created me as one of your unfunnier jokes, so I think you owe me. Please, please, do this for me. PS Remember the knighthood we talked about?'

Any decent investigator would have, at least, found my accounts. Sharon Bentley would have found them. I was lucky it was PK and his NPIA buffoons.

So I walked the Pacific Crest Trail, and grew a big beard. It ate up some time.

Clever, getting out of this like that? Yes obviously but not so bright getting in the mess in the first place. I will admit it, I was unwell, but here's the thing. I would never have achieved so much if I had been well. Would not have been so driven, would not have taken such risks, would not have been the success I was.

I was planning to walk into a police station few weeks after the Kenyon report had been published claiming to not know who I was. I was so looking forward to it. It would have been titanic to have truly turned the tables on those twats.

It took the shine off it when I realised there was not going to be a public report, just a confidential one to the Police Authority. But it was still pretty good value. Flew back to Ireland, this time Knock Airport. Went up to Westport, Co. Mayo to do it, making it look as if I had been in Ireland all the time. I tried to find somewhere suitably remote so the news would just filter through.

Had a nineteen year old Garda on the front desk, like a spotty young Roy Keane. Did the old 'I don't know who I am and what I am doing here?' routine. He recognised me, instantaneously. Told me I was Roger Mason. Can you believe that shit? Turns out they are all news mad over there. Everyone in the station seemed to know about the case. Can you imagine if the head of Cork police went missing in Manchester? No one in England would have given a shit.

Anyway did the whole nine yards. Saw a dishevelled psychiatrist in Galway called, wait for it, Michael Patrick McGinty. Looked more like Paddy McGinty than a doctor too.

Talked so fast took me a while to understand what he was saying. Think it took me longer to understand him than he understand me. Wily fucker, like a lot of the Irish.

No that's not right. He was like a lot of the Irish, they do the old 'I'm just a simple man, like the craic, get me a Guinness, you're a good man' thick, bluff routine but think they are wily fuckers, when the truth is they are more right first time than they realise.

"Some form of narcissistic personality disorder with bi-polar impressively held together."

What about my amnesia?

"You've made that up, d'ye think I'm an eejit? You think you are a clever fecker who has been having everyone over. Which you probably have, fair play to you. You think you are having me over now, so you do. Put a lot of money on you having been on medication and then for some reason stopped taking it."

Yes, Lithium. In fact not a bad summary for couple of hours with him. Wasn't going to tell old Paddy that.

"Tell me this Paddy. We have been here what, just over an hour, nearly two? What makes you so sure of all this?"

"Well you call me Paddy and not doctor, that's too cocksure. You have not cracked up under the pressure. You are too well dressed and all that. You have been looking after yourself haven't you? This amnesia carry on I am not sure you even think I believe that old bollocks. I think want me to know it's bollocks.

You are a narcissist. You want me to know you are having people over. You are telling me that being a Chief Constable was a piece of piss, that you had everyone dancing to your tune and that everyone around you was fecking barmy. Yet you are here in the wild west of Ireland talking to old Paddy here instead of being High Commissioner of London. You think you are not mad and doing something fecking clever. You think you are the sanest person on this planet, pretending to be ill. Truth is if you were well you would realise the shit you are in. All you will be doing now is thinking how to use me and this situation rather than think on how you got yourself into this mess."

Yes well you can fuck off now Paddy right back to your goat. Sorry, feck off.

"I'm impressed but you don't know the truth."

"I know the truth alright, Mr Mason. I don't know the facts, but I know the truth. I have been doing this for a long time. Tell me, I am right, you have had periods of depression haven't you?"

Well he can piss right off. Anyway thought he would have to let me go but he has had me compulsorily admitted. Mainly on the basis I was claiming not to remember anything when he knew I was lying about that. Twat. Started to feel worse minute they gave me the medication.

So Christmas on my own in this in this shithole. The dark, damp windy weather all the time. Place smells of cabbage, too hot. I thought I would never be in places like this ever again.

I wasn't allowed papers but got a good old boy of a cleaner to bring me yesterday's English papers. What do I read in the papers? PK had topped himself over Christmas. Perhaps there is a benevolent deity or is it just karma. Both, perhaps, I should become a Ba'hai.

He tied a plastic bag round his neck. Typical of him neat, sensible, dull. Bet he laid out his will and private papers, paid the paper bill, 'Crito we owe a cock to Asclepius', that kind of shit. I made that bit up about him wearing suspenders, basque and an orange though. Just made me feel better putting the thought in your head.

Why did he do it?

Well he will want people to think he was so upright he could not bear the thought of being caught out lying. He clearly had not told people what he and Hooker had done. He was never going to mention what he did with the tapes and had retained control of the investigation and report to cover his tracks.

Yes he would want you to think he was like his Baha'i mate, old David Kelly. So honourable suicide was the only option. He could not bear the thought of losing the sainted philosopher king image. That's what he wanted you to think, probably even convinced himself.

Odd thing about it all was tribute to him was by Bill Kennedy, bluff Chief of Merseyside, who the article said was acting Chief of GMP? What had happened to Hooker?

Managed to persuade the good old boy I knew here, on the promise of a bung when I got out, to get me to a telephone. Managed to get through to Judith, policy officer on the Police Authority, good friend. Apparently on day I re-emerged they held a closed door meet at the Police Authority. Des was in his place in Portugal so it was Lady de Brunner the deputy Chair, Hooker and Kenyon, no note taker.

She emerged with a face like thunder, walked straight out of the building to her car and her phone has been off ever since. It was left to Kenyon to sort out the announcement that Hooker had, for personal reasons, asked to step down from his role and would take up a place at the National Improvement Agency heading up a team looking at strategic alliances between forces. The post of GMP chief would be advertised but in the meantime Bill Kennedy would head. Kenyon instructed it to go out at 1pm on Christmas Eve, so no-one would pick it up. Crafty cunt to the last.

They took me out for the first time on New Year's Day. Brilliant, sunny cold beech on Achill Island, Keel Beach. Sun and the wind off the waves and cliffs made you dizzy. Some mad bastard surfing though, bringing in the New Year. Dick.

A sudden rise in my spirits, being out in the sun and the medication kicking in. It suddenly hit me. I haven't got away with it, I have won. One year ago they thought they had finished me off. Now Kenyon is dead and Hooker will forever carry round the suicide vest he thought he had put on me.

They will have to let me out of this place some point, I am not mad. When they do I am going to have some serious sport. I am still officially the Chief Constable so will tell them I am coming back to work in a week or two. That will be good, have not ruled up actually turning up at Chester House. Tell the press I will be there.

I know what to settle for. All my back pay, ill health pension (index linked obviously) and a little bit extra for my troubles. I think an extra £500k, for signing a confidentiality agreement. Sure they can lose that in the accounts. Yes only £500k, I know, no need to be greedy, the lump sum should be close to that anyway, make a nice million in total. So will make it quite easy for them. Win win, when you think about it.

Yes will email them as soon as I get out of here. Tell them I am feeling better, got a doctor's note to show I am sane, phased return to work, 'thanks for holding the fort while I have been away guys, got some big plans'.

In the meantime start doing a bit of media. Start with selling my story of going missing. Get a few quid for that. Build it up with some articles on the neglect of mental health at the top of organisations, some comment pieces on policing. Build it up again slowly but surely.

Everyone will want the story, so they will ignore the smoke in the room. There's no fire.

Victory.

Total victory.

28906819R00265

Printed in Great Britain
by Amazon